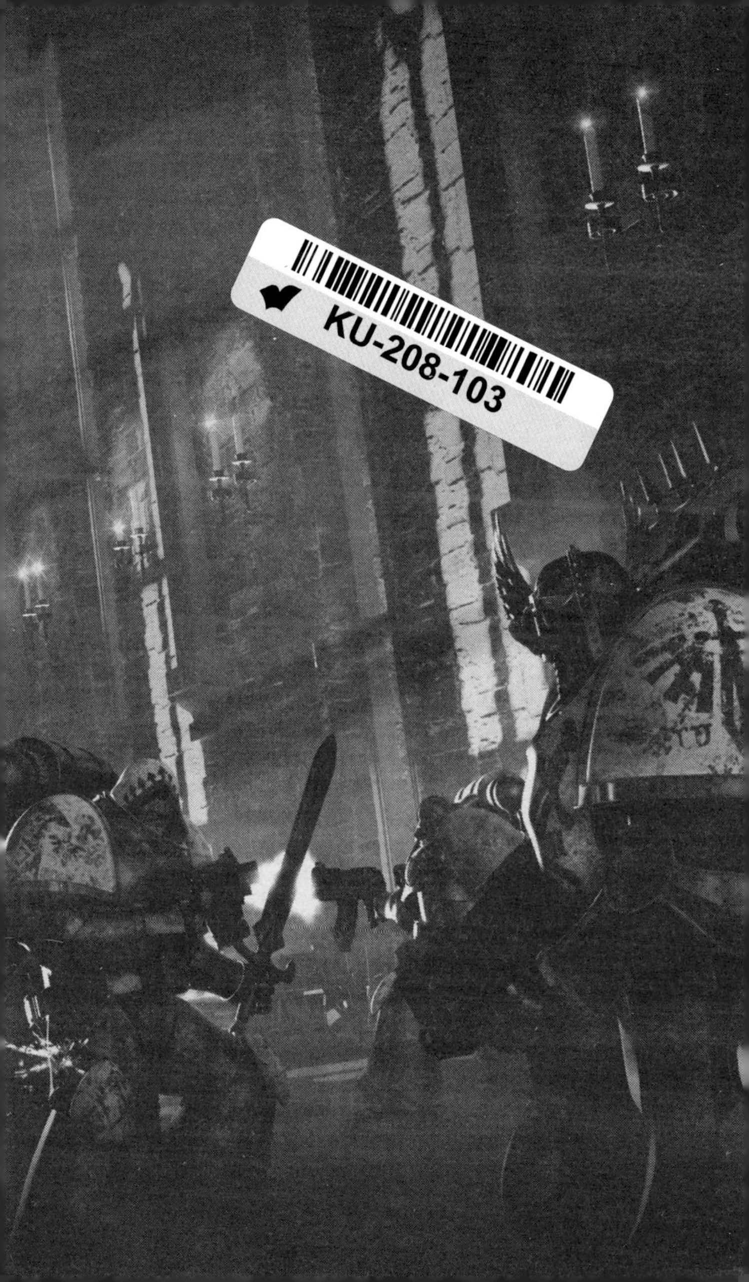

THE HORUS HERESY

Mitchel Scanlon

DESCENT OF ANGELS

Loyalty and honour

Special thanks to Graham McNeill.

A BLACK LIBRARY PUBLICATION

First published in Great Britain in 2007 by
BL Publishing,
Games Workshop Ltd.,
Willow Road, Nottingham,
NG7 2WS, UK.

10 9 8 7 6 5 4 3 2 1

Cover illustration by Neil Roberts.
First page illustration by Neil Roberts.

A CIP record for this book is available from the British Library.

ISBN 13: 978 1 84416 508 7
ISBN 10: 1 84416 508 6

Distributed in the US by Simon & Schuster
1230 Avenue of the Americas, New York, NY 10020, US.

See the Black Library on the Internet at
www.blacklibrary.com

Find out more about Games Workshop
and the world of Warhammer 40,000 at
www.games-workshop.com

THE HORUS HERESY

It is a time of legend.

Mighty heroes battle for the right to rule the galaxy.
The vast armies of the Emperor of Earth have conquered
the galaxy in a Great Crusade – the myriad alien races have
been smashed by the Emperor's elite warriors and wiped
from the face of history.

The dawn of a new age of supremacy for humanity
beckons.

Gleaming citadels of marble and gold celebrate the many
victories of the Emperor. Triumphs are raised on a million
worlds to record the epic deeds of his most powerful and
deadly warriors.

First and foremost amongst these are the primarchs,
superheroic beings who have led the Emperor's armies of
Space Marines in victory after victory. They are unstoppable
and magnificent, the pinnacle of the Emperor's genetic
experimentation. The Space Marines are the mightiest
human warriors the galaxy has ever known, each capable of
besting a hundred normal men or more in combat.

Organised into vast armies of tens of thousands called
Legions, the Space Marines and their primarch leaders
conquer the galaxy in the name of the Emperor.

Chief amongst the primarchs is Horus, called the Glorious, the Brightest Star, favourite of the Emperor, and like a
son unto him. He is the Warmaster, the commander-in-
chief of the Emperor's military might, subjugator of a
thousand thousand worlds and conqueror of the galaxy. He
is a warrior without peer, a diplomat supreme.

As the flames of war spread through the Imperium,
mankind's champions will all be put to the ultimate test.

~ DRAMATIS PERSONAE ~

The Order

Lion El'Jonson	Commander of the Order
Luther	Second in command of the Order
Zahariel	Knight Supplicant of the Order
Nemiel	Knight Supplicant of the Order
Master Ramiel	Training Master of the Order
Lord Cypher	Guardian of the Order's traditions
Brother Amadis	The Hero of Maponis, Battle Knight of the Order
Sar Hadariel	Battle Knight of the Order
Attias	Knight Supplicant of the Order
Eliath	Knight Supplicant of the Order

The Knights of Lupus

Lord Sartana	Master of the Knights of Lupus

The Dark Angels

Brother Librarian Israfael	Chief Librarian of the Dark Angels

The White Scars

SHANG KHAN	Leader of White Scars Expeditionary Force Bearers
KURGIS	Astartes battle-brother of the 7th Chapter

The Saroshi

LORD HIGH EXALTER	Leader of the Saroshi Bureaucracy
DUSAN	Saroshi exegetist

Non-Imperials

RHIANNA SOREL	Composer and Harmonist
LORD GOVERNOR ELECT HARLAD FURT	
	Overseer of the Sarosh territories
CAPTAIN STENIUS	Captain of the *Invincible Reason*
MISTRESS ARGENTA	Fleet Astropath, *Invincible Reason*

PRELUDE

It begins on *Caliban*.

It begins back before the Emperor came to our planet, before there was even the first talk of angels. Caliban was different then. We knew nothing of the Imperium and the Great Crusade. Terra was a myth; no, not even that. Terra was a myth of a ghost of a memory brought to us by our long-dead forefathers. It was an ephemeral and half-forgotten thing with no bearing on our lives.

It was the time of Old Night. Warp storms had made it impossible to travel between the stars and each human world was left to fend for itself. We had passed more than five thousand years in isolation from the rest of humanity: five thousand years. Can you imagine how long that is? Time enough for the people of Caliban to develop our own culture, our own ways, drawing from the patterns of the past, but separate from what had gone before. Free from the influence of Terra, our society had developed in a manner more in keeping with the world in which we lived.

We had our own beliefs and customs, aye, even our own religions.

There's precious little of it left now, of course. It was all swept away by the coming of the Emperor. It is amazing to me, but there are children born of Caliban today who have never even heard of the Watchers or ridden a mighty warhorse. They have never known what it is to hunt the great beasts. This is the sorrow of our lives. Over time, the old ways are forgotten. Naturally, those who came in the Emperor's wake claimed this was all to the good. *We are making a new world, a better world: a world fit for the future.*

We are making a better world.

It is always the way with conquerors. They don't say they have come to destroy your traditions. They don't talk about banishing the wisdoms of your grandfathers, turning the world upside-down, or replacing your ancient beliefs with a strange new creed of their devising. No one willingly admits they want to undermine your society's foundations and kill its dreams. Instead, they talk about saving you from your ignorance. I suppose they think it sounds kinder that way.

But the truth of it remains the same, regardless.

I am getting ahead of myself though, for at this moment in Caliban's history, all these things were unknown to us. In time, the Emperor would descend from the heavens with his angels, and everything would change. The Great Crusade had not yet reached us. We were innocent of the wider galaxy. Caliban was the sum total of our experience, and we were content in our ignorance, unaware of the forces heading towards us and how much they would transform our lives.

In those days, Caliban was a world of forests. Except for a few places given over to settlement or agriculture, the entire planet was covered in primordial, shadow haunted woodland. The forest defined our lives. Unless a man made his home in the mountains or lived near the coast, he could spend his entire life without once seeing an open horizon.

Our planet was also the domain of monsters.

The forests teemed with predators, not to mention all manner of other hazards. To use a word we didn't know then, a word taken from the lexicon of Imperial Cartography, Caliban is a death world. There isn't much here that is not capable of killing a man, one way or another. Carnivorous animals, poisonous flowers, venomous insects: the creatures of this world only know one law and that is 'kill or be killed'.

Of all the dangers to human life, there was one class of creatures that was always viewed as being set apart from the rest. They were more fearsome and brutal than any other animal we knew.

I am talking about the creatures we called the great beasts.

Each great beast of Caliban was as different from its fellows as a sword is different from a lance. Each creature represented the only example of its kind, a species of one. Their diversity was extraordinary. An individual beast might appear to be modelled after a reptile, or a mammal, or an insect, or else combine the features of all of them taken together in chaotic collaboration.

One might attack with tooth and claw, another with beak and tentacle, another using horns and hooves, while yet another might spit corrosive poison or bleed acid in place of blood. If they had one dominant feature, it was that every one of them appeared to be crafted directly from the stuff of nightmares. Allied to that, they each possessed qualities of size, strength, ferocity and cunning that made them the match of any ordinary human hunter, no matter how well-armed he might be.

It would not be overstating the case to say that the great beasts ruled the forests. Many of the customs we developed on Caliban owed their origins to the beasts' presence. For humanity to survive we had to be able to hold the beasts at bay. Accordingly, knightly orders were formed among the nobility to create warriors of exemplary skill and ability, armed to the highest standards, and trained to protect human society against the worst predations of these monsters.

They were aided in this by the persistence of certain traditions in the making of weapons and armour. Most of the technology our distant ancestors brought with them to Caliban had been forgotten in our isolation, but the knowledge of how to repair and maintain pistols and explosive bolts, swords with motorised blades, and armour that boosted a warrior's strength and power had been preserved. Granted, they were relatively primitive versions and they lacked the reliability of the more powerful models later brought to Caliban by the Imperials, but they were effective all the same. We had no motor vehicles, so the knights of Caliban rode to war on the backs of destriers – enormous warhorses selectively bred over thousands of years from the equine bloodstock brought to our world by its first settlers.

In due course, the knightly orders went on to build the great fortress monasteries that still serve as many of the major places of settlement in modern Caliban. Whenever one of the beasts began to prey on a settlement, the leader of the local nobility would declare a hunting quest against the creature. In response, knights and knights-supplicant would come to the area from every land, seeking to prove themselves by killing the beast and completing the quest.

This, then, was the pattern of life on Caliban for countless generations. We expected it to continue indefinitely. We thought our lives would follow the same well-trodden path as the lives of our fathers and grandfathers.

We were wrong, of course. The universe had other plans for us.

The Emperor was coming, but the first currents of change in our society were already at work long before his arrival. Some time before the Emperor came to Caliban, a new knightly order had been founded among our people. It called itself simply 'the Order', and its members put forward the startling proposition that all men were created equal.

Previously, it had been traditional for knights to be recruited strictly and solely from among the nobility, but the Order broke with accepted practice to recruit from all layers of society. So long as an individual could prove by his deeds and his character that he was worthy of knighthood, the Order did not care whether he was a noble or a commoner.

It may seem a minor matter now, but the issue sparked no small amount of turmoil and controversy at the time. Traditionalist diehards among the more established orders regarded it as the thin end of a wedge that they thought would inevitably bring the whole edifice of our culture crashing down, and leave us as easy prey for the great beasts. In one case, this issue even led to open warfare.

A group calling itself the Knights of the Crimson Chalice attacked the Order's mountain fortress at Aldurukh and laid siege to it. In what would later be seen as one of the defining moments of Caliban's pre-Imperial history, the knights of the Order sallied forth and counter-attacked before the enemy had completed their siege lines.

The resulting battle was decisive. The Knights of the Crimson Chalice were routed, and the survivors hunted down to the last man. With this victory, the future progress of the Order was guaranteed. Supplicants flocked to them from all walks of life and, within the space of barely a few decades, the Order had become one of the most powerful and well-regarded knightly groups on Caliban.

This was only the beginning, however. Whatever subtle changes were brought to our society by the rise to prominence of the Order were as nothing compared to what would happen when the Lion came to Caliban.

With the benefit of hindsight, we now know that Lion El'Jonson is one of the primarchs, wrought in gene-labs by the Emperor to lead the armies of his angels, but at the time he was far more extraordinary to us.

We were not an unsophisticated people, nor were we primitives. Imagine the effect, though, as word spread across our planet that a man had been found living wild, like an animal, in the deep forests of the Great Northwilds, his features handsome and beautiful beneath the matted hair and the mud caked to his body.

No one knew who he was, and he spoke not a word of human language. He had survived for years, naked and unarmed, in the wilderness of the most dangerous region on Caliban – a place where even fully armoured knights hesitated to venture unless as part of a larger group. Nor was it the end of the wonders associated with this strange figure.

In light of the details of his discovery, the wild man came to be called Lion El'Jonson, meaning 'The Lion, the Son of the Forest' in the old tongue of Caliban. Having been brought to human society, Jonson soon demonstrated a prodigious talent for learning.

He quickly assimilated human ways, learning the habit of speech within a matter of days. From there, his rate of progress increased exponentially. Within a few short months, he was the equal in mind of our finest savants. A month later, he had exceeded their greatest achievements and left them trailing in his wake.

He never spoke of his days in the forest, nor could he account for how he had come to be living there or where he had come from, but his powers of reason and intelligence seemed unaffected by his time in the wilderness.

His intellectual capacity was matched only by his physical power. None could match his strength or prowess in combat, and he swiftly mastered the skills of knighthood to be accepted into the Order.

As might be expected, given his abilities, Jonson rapidly ascended through the Order's ranks. His achievements were legendary, and coupled with a natural talent to inspire intense devotion in others, his presence soon led to a marked upsurge in recruitment. As the number of knights within the Order increased, and new fortress monasteries were built to accommodate them, Jonson and his supporters started to *press for a crusade to be mounted against the great beasts. Their proposal called for a systematic campaign to clear the beasts from the forests, region by region, until Caliban was finally free from their scourge.*

Objections were raised to the proposal, of course. The Order was the dominant military power on Caliban, but it was still only first among equals in the eyes of the other knightly orders. Given the size of the scheme Jonson had put forward, it would require the actions of every knightly order working in unison to a common plan to have any hope of succeeding. This was no small undertaking, considering that the knights of Caliban had always been inclined to feud and squabble amongst themselves. Combined with this, the plan would also need the support of the wider nobility and the common population. In general, though, we are not the kind to easily follow after leaders on Caliban: each man has too high a regard for his own opinions.

Then, there were other problems. The faint-hearted said it would be impossible to truly clear the beasts from the forests. It was too grand a scheme, too much the product of hubris. Some viewed the great beasts with supernatural dread, believing that any plan of extermination would only awaken an apocalypse by uniting the beasts against humanity.

Finally, there were concerns, even among those who backed Jonson's aims. Some of them counselled caution. Jonson had envisioned a span of six years from the beginning of his war against the beasts to victory, but even his allies thought this was not enough time to achieve the plan's objectives. They feared he had failed to take full account of the human factor. He had forgotten that the plan would be carried out by individuals who did not share his own extraordinary mental and physical abilities. Jonson might be superhuman, but he was the only one of his kind on Caliban. His plan would not be carried out by supermen. The real, hard work would be done by mortal men.

In the end, Jonson carried the day. His supporters argued that the people of Caliban had skulked for too long behind the walls of their settlements. They had lived too much in fear of the beasts. Man was made to have dominion over the wilderness, they said, not vice versa. It was time to restore the world to balance, to end the reign of the beasts and give mankind dominion over the forests.

'This is our world,' he said. 'It is not the world of the beasts. It is time we took our stand.'

So, the decision was made and Jonson would have his campaign. One by one, the beasts were hunted down and killed. They were driven from the forests. They were tracked to their lairs and destroyed. In one thing at least, though, some of those who had opposed Jonson were proven right, for it took more than six years to finish the campaign.

It took ten years of constant campaigning, ten years of hardship, ten years of friends maimed and lost, but ultimately it was worth it. Our cause was just, and we achieved our ambitions. Ten years, and not one of the great beasts remained.

It occurs to me that I have been slapdash in one respect in telling this story, for I have made no mention of the one man who could hold forth knowledgeably on all the topics before us. I have talked of Caliban, of Lion El'Jonson and of the campaign against the great beasts, but I have neglected to mention the most important player in our drama.

I am talking about Luther.

He was the man who found Jonson in the forest and gave him his name, the man who brought him to civilisation and taught him the ways of human society. He was the one who, through all Jonson's exploits and honours, stood side-by-side with him and matched him. Luther had not Jonson's advantages in matters of war and strategy. He was born a man, after all, not created to be more than human. Yet, as Jonson's actions began to change the face of Caliban,

Luther kept stride with him, equalling the wild man's accomplishments with his own.

Too often, the Imperium portrays Luther as the devil. Some say he grew jealous of the Lion, for though the two of them had shared in many victories, it was always Jonson who was lauded for these triumphs. Others say Luther grew increasingly bitter at being so much in the Lion's shadow. They say a secret seed of anger was born in Luther's heart in those days, the seed of future hatreds.

But those who repeat such things are liars. Luther always loved Jonson like a brother.

I know Luther well, and you may be assured I am well-placed to comment on his secrets. Luther is the key to understanding so much of how our world came to be where it is today, but it is better if we do not speak too much of Luther now. It will only work to the detriment of my story. To begin a tale with too many secrets tends to cause confusion after all. In my experience, it is always better if you build towards these things more slowly.

Poor, poor Luther; we will get to him in time, you may be certain of that point. We will get to it all in time. I will account for everything in time.

For now, though, the stage of my story is set.

It is the tenth year of Jonson's campaign against the great beasts. Nearly all the beasts have been killed, and only a few stragglers remain in the less hospitable and more thinly populated regions of the planet.

Once the last of the great beasts are gone, we will all be able to build new lives. We can found new settlements. We can clear the trees for fuel and lumber, and plant new fields. For the first time, we will have control over our existence in ways we never had before.

A golden age beckons our people.

It is before the Emperor came to our planet, and before the time of angels, but the old ways are already dying. The world of our childhood will not be the world of our future. Many *are unhappy at the prospect, but it is entirely possible that the world we inhabit tomorrow will be like nothing we could have foreseen.*

Change can bring out the worst and best in us, or something of both qualities at the same time. Some look to the horizon and fear the future, while others look and see it shining in welcome.

It is the tenth year of Jonson's campaign and the world turns beneath our feet. Unknowing, we stand on the brink of a bright new age of progress. We stand on the brink of learning of the Emperor, of the Imperium. We stand on the brink of becoming angels, but, as yet, we know nothing of these things.

On Caliban it is a time of innocence, but already the storm clouds gather. It is said that a man should be wary of weeping angels, for wherever their teardrops fall, men drown.

This is the shape of our lives. These are the days that made us, that formed our conflicts and decided our future. This is a time of which much will be written, but little understood. The histories created by those who follow after us will be riddled with falsehoods and fabrications.

They will not know why we turned from the Lion.

They will know nothing of our motives, but you can know them. You can know it all. Come listen, and you will hear my secrets. Come listen, and we will talk of Luther and Lion El'Jonson. We will talk of schism and civil war.

We will give voices to the dead.

Come, listen, hear my secrets.

Let us talk of the Dark Angels and the beginnings of their fall.

BOOK ONE
CALIBAN

ONE

It began in darkness. Zahariel's eyes snapped open an instant before Lord Cypher's men came for him. He awoke to find a hand descending to clamp across his mouth. They dragged him from his bed, put a hood over his head and tied his arms behind him. With that, he was hauled blindly down a series of corridors. When at last they came to a halt, he heard one of his captors knock three times on a door.

The door opened and he was pushed inside.

'Who is brought before us?' asked a voice in the darkness.

'A stranger,' Lord Cypher said beside him. 'He has been brought here bound and blinded. He comes seeking entrance.'

'Bring him closer,' said the first voice.

Zahariel felt hands at his arms and shoulders. He was propelled roughly forward and forced to kneel. A shock ran through him as his bare knees met the cold stone floor. Unwilling to let his captors think he was afraid, he tried to suppress a shiver.

'What is your name?' he heard the first voice again, louder this time. Its tone was rich and deep, a voice accustomed to command. 'Who are your people?'

'I am Zahariel El'Zurias,' he replied. In keeping with ancient custom, Zahariel recited his full lineage, wondering if it would be the last time he ever spoke the words. 'I am the only living son of Zurias El'Kaleal, who in turn was the son of Kaleal El'Gibrael. My people are descended from the line of Sahiel.'

'A nobleman,' said a third voice. In some ways this voice was more arresting than the others, its tone even more magnetic and compelling than the first. 'He thinks he should be allowed among us because his father was important. I say he isn't good enough. He isn't worthy. We should throw him from the tower and be done with it.'

'We will see,' said the first voice. Zahariel heard the telltale rasp of a knife being slid from its sheath. He felt the uncomfortable sensation of cold metal against his skin as a blade was pressed to his throat.

'First, we will test him,' said the voice in the darkness. 'You feel the blade at your throat?'

'Yes,' replied Zahariel.

'Know this, then, a lie is a betrayal of our vows. Here, we deal only in truth. If you lie, I will know it. If I hear a lie, I will cut your throat. Do you accept these terms?'

'Yes, I accept them.'

'Do you? Understand, I am asking for an oath. Even when I take the knife away from your throat, even when I am dead, even when this knife is rusted and dull and useless, the oath you make by its edge will still be binding. Are you prepared to make an oath?'

'I am prepared,' said Zahariel. 'I will make the oath.'

'First, tell me by what right you have come here? Who are you to claim entrance to our gathering? By what right do you claim to be worthy to stand among us?'

'I have completed the first portion of my training and I have been judged worthy by my masters,' said Zahariel.

'That is a start. But it takes more than that to be welcomed among us. That is why you must be tested.'

ZAHARIEL HAD KNOWN they would be coming for him. Master Ramiel had told him as much the previous day, though, as usual, the old man's words were cloaked in shadows, concealing as much as they revealed.

'You understand I cannot tell you much,' Master Ramiel had said. 'It is not the way we do these things. The initiation ritual is ancient. It pre-dates the Order's foundation by thousands of years. Some even say our ancestors may have brought it with them from Terra.'

'I understand,' said Zahariel.

'Do you?' his master asked.

He turned to stare at Zahariel with quick, hooded eyes. In the past, Zahariel might have felt the need to look away under the intensity of his gaze, but now he met the old man's eyes directly.

'Yes, I think you do,' said Master Ramiel, after a short pause. A smile creased his weathered face. 'You are different, Zahariel. I noticed it in your face when you first joined our order.'

They were sitting in one of the many practice halls inside Aldurukh, where knights and supplicants spent their days honing the skills they needed to survive on Caliban. The practice hall was empty, the hour so early that even the supplicants were not yet awake. Ordinarily, Zahariel would also have been abed, but a message from Master Ramiel had brought him to the practice hall an hour before daybreak.

'In the course of the next night, you will attend your initiation ceremony into the Order,' said Master Ramiel. 'During the ceremony, you will swear your oath of loyalty and will begin your journey to becoming a knight of the Order.'

'Do you wish to take me through the procedures for the ceremony?' asked Zahariel. 'So I know what to expect?'

Ramiel shook his head, and Zahariel knew the old man had other things on his mind.

'Despite the claims of some of our rivals, the knights of the Order are not entirely immune to the lure of tradition. We understand the vital role it can play in our lives. Human beings crave ritual; it gives meaning to everyday life and adds gravity to our deeds. More than that, it can even help us to understand our place in the world. Granted, we disagree with those who hold a religious view of such things. We see no supernatural significance in tradition, whether our own, or anyone else's. In our view, the most important function of ritual and tradition is not to achieve any effect in the outer world, but to create stability and balance in the inner world of the mind. If tradition has any outer function at all, it is to create a sense of social cohesion. It might almost be described as the glue holding our society together.'

The old man paused again. 'You are looking at me strangely, Zahariel. Have I touched a nerve?'

'No,' said Zahariel. 'I'm just tired, master. I hadn't expected a lecture on tradition at this hour in the morning.'

'Fair enough; you're right, I didn't bring you here to discuss the social aspects of tradition. I am more concerned with the symbolism of some of the Order's rituals. I want to make sure you understood their significance before they come for you.'

Master Ramiel rose to his feet and walked into the middle of the room. In accordance with the Order's traditions, there was a spiral design inscribed into the floor of the practice hall, stretching from one end of the room to the other.

'You know why this is here, Zahariel? The spiral?'

'I do, master,' said Zahariel, rising to join Ramiel. 'The spiral is the foundation of all the Order's sword work, as much a part of its physical doctrines as the *Verbatim* is the cornerstone to our mental disciplines.'

'Indeed so, Zahariel, but it is so much more than that. From your first day, you have been made to walk the spiral on the practice hall floor, launching pre-set routines of attack and defence at different stages of your journey. Do you know why?'

Zahariel hesitated before answering. 'I assumed it was an ancient sword ritual of Terra. Is that not so?'

'Possibly,' admitted Ramiel, 'but by rigorously practising the spiral, endlessly repeating its patterns day after day for years until the movements become second nature, you will master an unbeatable system of self-defence.'

Master Ramiel began walking the spiral, his staff moving as though in an elaborate ballet of ritual combat. 'The knights of the Order regularly defeat representatives from the other knightly orders in tourneys and mock duels. The spiral is the reason.'

At last, Ramiel reached the centre of the spiral and indicated the lines encircling him with a wide sweep of his staff. 'Look at the pattern laid out before us. This room has been here ever since the monastery at Aldurukh was founded. You see how smooth the edges of the spiral are in places, worn down by the feet of the thousands of warriors who have walked its path since it was put here. But what is the spiral, Zahariel? What do you see here?'

'I see attack and defence,' Zahariel replied. 'It is the path to excellence, and to the defeat of my enemies.'

'Attack and defence?' Master Ramiel slowly nodded his head as he spoke the words, as though considering them. 'It is a good answer, as far as it goes. Spoken like a true warrior. But a knight must be more than just a warrior. He must be the guardian and guide of our people. He must protect them from all their enemies, not just the human and bestial ones. It is not enough to protect our people from the beasts, or from predatory warlords and bandits. The path to excellence is a far harder and rockier road than that. No, we must try to shield the population of Caliban from every threat that assails them. We must do our best to protect them from hunger and want, from disease and malnutrition, from suffering and hardship. Ultimately, I grant you, it is an impossible task. There will always be suffering. There will always be hardship, but for so long as the Order exists, we must strive to defeat these evils. The measure of our success in this case is not so much that we win the battle, but that we are willing to fight it at all. Do you understand?'

'I think so, master,' Zahariel answered, 'but I do not see how it relates to the spiral.'

'The spiral is an ancient symbol,' Master Ramiel said. 'They say it was found carved on some of mankind's oldest tombs. It represents the journey we take in life. You are young, Zahariel, and so your experience of these things is limited, but I will tell you of a mystery of life that is revealed to a man as he gets older. Our lives repeat themselves. Time and time again, we face the same conflicts. We take the same actions. We make the same mistakes. It is as though our lives circle the same fixed point, repeating similar patterns endlessly from birth to death. Some call this "the eternal return". That which is true for individuals is also true for the mass of humanity as a whole. One need only look at history to see that repeating the same mistakes is hardly the folly of individuals alone. Entire cultures and nations do exactly the same thing. We should know better, but somehow we never do.'

'If this is true, if the spiral represents our lives, where does it lead?' asked Zahariel, looking at the design on the floor beneath them. 'The spiral never comes to an end. Every place where its lines should end, they turn back on themselves, creating a repeating pattern.'

'What does it remind you of?' asked Ramiel.

Zahariel cocked his head to one side and said, 'It's like a serpent swallowing its tail.'

'An ancient symbol indeed,' nodded Ramiel, 'one of the oldest.'

'What does it mean?'

'It is a symbol or rebirth and renewal,' said Ramiel. 'A symbol of new beginnings and immortality.'

Zahariel nodded, though the sense of much of what Ramiel was saying was lost upon him. 'If you are saying that our lives repeat themselves, isn't that the same as the teachings of the religious diehards? They say after death our spirits are reborn in new bodies. They talk of their own spiral as well. They say it exists in the underworld, and that by walking it we choose the path of our rebirth. Is that true?'

'I don't know,' said Master Ramiel.

Seeing the expression of Zahariel's face, Ramiel smiled again. 'Don't look so shocked, Zahariel. I know it is commonplace among supplicants to view their masters as the font of all wisdom and knowledge, but there are limits even to my insights. I can only comment on the paths we walk in life. As to what happens after death, who can say? By its very nature, death is an insoluble mystery to us. No one has ever returned from its lands, at least not to my knowledge, so how can anyone define its nature? Are we simply a collection of physical processes that begins with birth and ends with

death, or is there more to us than that? Show me the
man who claims to have the answer to that question,
and I will show you a liar.'

Without waiting for him to comment, Master Ramiel
continued 'We are digressing, however. I called you here
because I wanted to emphasise the symbolism underlying some of our traditions. I told you earlier that I
couldn't reveal too much about your forthcoming initiation ceremony. It would not be seemly for me to do so.
It is better you experience the ceremony without precon-
ceptions. I simply wanted to ensure you had some
inkling that the outer circumstances of the ceremony, the
ritual and its accoutrements, have a significance that
extends beyond their mere physical aspect. All these
things are symbolic. Remember, this is not just an initiation, but a ceremony of rebirth. Symbolically, you will
be reborn from one state into another. You will make the
transition from supplicant to knight, and from boy to
man.'

'Tomorrow, the old Zahariel will be dead,' Master
Ramiel said finally. 'I wish my best to the new Zahariel.
May he live a long and worthy life.'

IT WAS MORE an interrogation than a test.

Zahariel knelt on the stone floor, his head hooded, his
hands bound, and the knife still at his throat. He knelt,
while his unseen captors hurled rapid-fire questions at
him one after the other. At first, they questioned him at
length about the *Verbatim*. They insisted he recite entire
passages from memory. They made him explain each
passage's meaning. They asked him about his sword
work, whether it was better to respond to a two-handed
descending strike by evading the blow or by meeting it
with a parry.

'What kind of parry?' the first voice asked after they
had heard his answer. 'Your opponent is right-handed

and his blow comes at you on a high diagonal line. Do you deflect to your left or right? Do you follow with a riposte, a counter-slash, or a punch with your free hand? Should that hand even be free? Where is your pistol? Answer quickly.'

So it went on. They asked questions about warhorses, about hunting beasts, about pistols, swords, lances, strategy and wilderness survival. They asked him about the dangers of sweetroot flowers, the most secure places to seek shelter in the forest during an unexpected storm and how to recognise the difference between the tracks of a mellei bird and a raptor. They asked him to explain the decisions that needed to be made in setting up an ambush, what warning signs a commander should look out for when adopting a defensive perimeter, and what was the best way to attack an enemy who had the advantages of both higher ground and a fixed position.

'What are the accepted grounds for challenging a knight from another order to a duel?' the second voice, the one he knew was Lord Cypher's, asked him. 'What form should the challenge take? How do you choose your seconds? What about weapons? Where should the duel take place? Is honour the only consideration, or should there be others? Answer quickly.'

There were more men in the room, he was sure of it, but only three of his captors contributed to the interrogation. They handled it smoothly, as though each was well practiced in these situations, swiftly following every one of his answers with yet another question.

At times, attempting to confuse him, two of them would ask different questions in tandem, sometimes all three at the same time. Zahariel refused to be flustered or intimidated, he refused to let his confidence be undermined by the off-putting conditions. It did not matter that he could not see or that his hands were tied. It did not matter that there was a knife against his throat.

He would not fail this test. He had come too far. He would not fall at this latest hurdle.

'This is a waste of time,' the third voice said. 'You hear me? We are wasting our time. This whelp will never be a knight. It doesn't matter what his masters say. He doesn't have what it takes. I have a sense for these things. I say let's cut his throat and be done with it. We can always find another candidate for the path to knighthood, one that's more worthy of the honour.'

The questions of the third man were always the hardest. Most of the time, he did not ask questions at all. Instead, he verbally abused Zahariel as though trying to denigrate him in the eyes of the others. Where the other two did not react when Zahariel answered a question correctly, the third man always responded with bile and sarcasm. More than once, he accused Zahariel of being 'book-learned' rather than a man of action.

He accused him of lacking staying power and fibre. He said Zahariel did not have the true inner resolve that was necessary to become a knight. Again and again, he tried to persuade his confederates that Zahariel was not what they were looking for.

'He will bring shame to our order,' the third voice said, during one particularly heated exchange with the others. 'He will be an embarrassment to us. He is useless. We must be harsh in these things. One weak stone in a wall is enough to bring the whole structure crashing down. It is better to kill him, here and now, than take the risk that he may one day destroy us. He should have been drowned at birth like a tainted child.'

'Too far,' said the first voice, the one that held the knife against Zahariel's throat. 'You play your part, brother, but this is too far. The young man before us has done nothing to earn such disdain. You treat him too harshly. He has proved he is worthy to train further among us.'

'He is worthy,' Lord Cypher's voice agreed. 'He has passed the test. He has answered every question. I vote in his favour.'

'As do I,' said the first voice. 'What of you, brother? Has he convinced you? Will you make it unanimous?'

'I will,' the third voice said, after what seemed like an eternity's hesitation. 'I have played my part, but I had no doubt about him from the outset. He is worthy. I vote in his favour.'

'It is agreed,' Lord Cypher said. 'We will administer the oath. But first, he has been in darkness too long. Bring him into the light.'

'Close your eyes,' said the first voice as the knife was taken away from his throat.

Zahariel felt hands at the hood over his head, pulling it away. 'Then wait a moment before you open them. After being in the dark, you may find the light blinding.'

The hood was lifted from his head and, finally, he saw his interrogators.

At first, all Zahariel could see were blurred shapes and outlines as the brightness of the room stabbed at his eyes.

Slowly, his vision was restored. The blurs coalesced into discrete bodies and faces. He could see a circle of knights in hooded robes surrounding him. A number of them held torches, and as the ropes were cut from his wrists, he looked up and saw the faces of his three interrogators gazing down at him.

As he expected, one of them was Lord Cypher, an old man that many of the younger supplicants felt was long past his prime.

Lord Cypher blinked and squinted at him through eyes that were already well on the way to succumbing to cataracts. The two other faces he saw belonged to far more impressive individuals. On one side stood Sar

Luther, a hearty and robust figure who favoured Zahariel with a friendly smile, as though trying to encourage him not to be too intimidated by the solemnity of the occasion.

On the other was a man who was already a legend, who, rumour had it, would eventually become the Order's next Grand Master: Lion El'Jonson.

In his first years with the Order, it was the closest Zahariel had ever come to Jonson, and he felt his senses and reason desert him at the incredible presence of the warrior. He towered over Zahariel, and the young man found himself staring intently at the magnificent, leonine specimen of physical perfection in unabashed awe.

Luther laughed and said, 'Careful, boy, your jaw's in danger of dropping off.'

Zahariel snapped his mouth shut, fighting to throw off his adoration of the Lion, with only moderate success. The Lion spent most of his time in the forests, leading his campaign against the great beasts, and only rarely returned to Aldurukh for any extended period. As such, it was an honour of unprecedented worth to be accorded the attention of such a senior figure, and to be inducted into the Order by such a mighty legend.

'We should bring matters to a close,' said Sar Luther. 'I am sure our friend would like to get up off his knees sooner rather than later.'

As he spoke, Zahariel was struck by the resonance of Luther's voice, knowing that its power would make men follow him into the depths of hell if he ordered them to march beside him.

He had been so astounded to see Lion El'Jonson standing before him that he had almost ignored Luther entirely. Belatedly, it occurred to him that he had been doubly blessed. His initiation ceremony had been officiated over by two of the greatest men of his era, Jonson and Luther. While it was true that Luther could in no way match Jonson's extraordinary physical stature and musculature, he was every bit as exemplary and heroic a figure. In their own ways, they were both giants.

'Your tone is inappropriate,' said Lord Cypher, fixing his half-blinded eyes on Luther. 'The initiation of a new member of the Order is not a time for levity. It is a sombre and serious matter. One might almost describe it as sacred.'

'You must forgive my brother, Lord Cypher,' Jonson said, placing one of his enormous hands on the old man's shoulder in a placatory gesture. 'He means no harm. He is simply mindful that we all have other pressing matters that demand our attention.'

'There is no more important matter than the initiation of a new supplicant,' remarked Lord Cypher. 'The young man before us is still on the threshold. He has come forward into the light, but he has yet to take his oath. Until then, he is not one of us.'

The old man stretched out a hand for the knife in Lion El'Jonson's grasp, the knife they had earlier pressed against Zahariel's throat. Once Jonson had passed it to him, the Lord Cypher put his thumb to the edge to test it.

'Now is the time for the shedding of blood.'

He turned to Zahariel and brought the blade down upon his palm.

The cut went diagonally across his left palm, causing a moment of pain, but it was shallow and only intended to shed his blood for the purposes of the ceremony.

It was symbolic, just as Master Ramiel told him.

At the climax of the ceremony there was a taking of oaths.

'Do you, Zahariel, swear by your blood that you will protect the people of Caliban?'

'I do,' he said.

'Will you swear to abide by the rules and strictures of the Order and never reveal its secrets?'

'I will.'

'From hereon in, you will regard every one of our Order's knights as your brothers, and never raise a hand against them unless it be in the form of a judicial duel or a sanctioned matter of honour. This you will swear against the pain of your own future death.'

'Against my death, I swear it,' he answered.

There was a particularly chilling moment in the oath-taking, for Lord Cypher held the knife up before Zahariel to enable him to see his face reflected in its surface beside the red smear of his blood on the edge of the blade.

'You have sworn a blood oath,' said Lord Cypher. 'These things are binding. But now, you must go further.'

Lord Cypher turned the blade so that it was balanced in the flat of his palm. 'Put your hand on the knife and swear to the most bloody and binding undertaking. This blade has already taken your blood. It has cut your palm. Let the knife be the guardian of your oaths. If by any future deed you prove that the words you have spoken here are lies, let the blade that has cut your palm return to slash your throat. Swear to it.'

'I swear it,' said Zahariel, placing his hand over the knife. 'If my words here today are lies, let this knife return to slash my throat.'

'It is done, then,' the Lord Cypher nodded, satisfied. 'Your old life is dead. You are no longer the boy named Zahariel El'Zurias, the son of Zurias El'Kaleal. From this day forward there will be no more talk of lineage and the antecedents of your fathers. You are neither nobleman nor commoner. These things are behind you. From this moment on, you are a knight of the

Order. You are reborn into a new life. Do you understand?'

'I understand,' Zahariel said, and his heart swelled with pride.

'Arise, then,' said Lord Cypher. 'There is no more need to kneel. You are among brothers. We are all your brothers here. Arise, Zahariel of the Order.'

TWO

THE WOUND TO his palm would not leave a scar. It would heal in time, and within a few months there would be no physical sign that his hand had ever been cut. Strangely, to Zahariel, it was as if the wound was always there. It did not in any way pain or disable him. Afterwards, when he grasped the butt of his pistol his grip would be as strong as it had ever been.

Despite this, Zahariel felt the presence of the wound even after it had healed.

He had heard that sometimes men experienced a phantom itch when they had lost a limb, a curious malfunction of the nervous system that the apothecaries were at a loss to explain. It was like that for Zahariel. He felt a vague and insubstantial sensation in his hand, at times, as though some part of his mind was reminding him of his oaths.

It was always with him, like a line in his palm, invisible to the eye, but present all the same, as though it was etched into his very soul. If he had wanted to give it a name, he supposed he would have called it 'conscience'.

Whatever the cause, the sensation of the phantom wound in his palm would stay with him for the rest of his life.

In time, he would almost become used to it.

ZAHARIEL AND NEMIEL had grown up together.

Barely a few weeks separated them in age, and they were related by blood. Though distant cousins, born to different branches of the same extended family of the nobility, their features were so alike they could be mistaken for brothers. They shared the characteristically lean faces and aquiline profile of their ancestors, but the bond they shared went far deeper than any accidental similarity of their features.

According to the monastic traditions of the Order, all the knights of the fellowship were counted as brothers to each other. For Zahariel and Nemiel though, the fact of their brotherhood went beyond any such simple platitudes. They had each thought of the other as a brother long before they had joined the Order as supplicants. In the years since, the bond between them had been tested countless times and proven true. They had come to rely on each other in a thousand small ways, even as their friendly rivalry spurred them on to greater heights.

It was natural that there was an element of competitiveness, of sibling rivalry, in the relationship between them. From the earliest days of their childhood, they had tried to outdo the other in every way possible. In any contest, they had each striven to be the victor. They each wanted to be the fastest runner, the strongest swimmer, the most accurate shot, the best rider, the most skilled swordsman; the exact nature of the test did not matter so long as one of them could beat the other.

Their masters in the Order had recognised the competition between them early on and had actively encouraged it. Separately, they might have been counted as average candidates for knighthood. Together, driven on by their mutual rivalry, they had become more impressive prospects.

Their masters said it quietly, for it was not the way on Caliban to give unnecessary praise, but Zahariel and Nemiel were both expected to do well and to rise far in the Order.

As the elder of the two, even if it was only by a matter of weeks, their competition was perhaps harder on Nemiel than it was on Zahariel. Sometimes, their rivalry felt like a race he could not win. Every time Nemiel thought he had finally beaten his rival, Zahariel would quickly prove him wrong by equalling and exceeding his achievements.

At some level, Zahariel recognised the important role his brother played in his triumphs. Without Nemiel to measure himself against, to strive to overcome, he might never have been granted entrance into the Order. He might never have become a knight. Accordingly, he could never begrudge his brother's triumphs. If anything, he celebrated them as loudly as he did his own.

For Nemiel, however, it was different. In time, despairing of ever outdistancing his brother, he began to harbour secret reservations about Zahariel's achievements. Despite his best efforts to control his thoughts, Nemiel found there was a small voice within him that wished Zahariel would not be too successful.

Not that he ever wished harm or failure on his brother, but simply that Zahariel's triumphs would always be more limited in magnitude than his own. Perhaps it was childish, but the competition between them had defined their lives for so long that Nemiel found it difficult to outgrow it.

In many ways, his relationship with Zahariel would always be as much about rivalry as it was about brotherhood.

It was the nature of their lives.

In times to come, it would decide their fate.

'IF THAT'S THE best you've got,' taunted Nemiel, dancing away from Zahariel's sword thrust, 'you'd best give up now.'

Zahariel stepped in close, bringing his training blade close to his body and slamming his shoulder against his cousin's chest.

Nemiel was braced for the attack, but Zahariel's strength was greater, and the two boys tumbled to the stone floor of the training hall. Nemiel cried out at the impact, rolling and bringing his sword up, as Zahariel stabbed the ground where he had been lying.

'Not even close to the best I've got,' said Zahariel, panting with exertion. 'I'm just toying with you.'

The bout had been underway for nearly fifteen minutes: fifteen solid minutes of sparring back and forth, lunge and feint, dodge and block, parry and riposte. Sweat drenched both boys. Their muscles burned and their limbs felt leaden.

A circle of their fellow supplicants surrounded them, each cheering on their favourite, and Master Ramiel watched over the fight with a mixture of paternal pride and exasperation.

'Finish it, one of you, for the love of Caliban!' said Ramiel. 'You have other lessons to attend today. Finish it, or I will call it a draw.'

His last comment gave Zahariel fresh strength and purpose, though he saw it had the same effect on his cousin, no doubt as Master Ramiel had intended. Neither boy would settle for a draw, only victory would be enough to satisfy either of them.

He saw Nemiel's muscles bunch in preparation for an attack, and lunged forward.

His sword stabbed out towards Nemiel's stomach. The blade was dulled and the tip flat, but the weapon was still a solid lump of heavy metal in Zahariel's hands that was capable of wreaking great harm upon an opponent. Nemiel's weapon swept down and pushed the blow to the side, but Zahariel's attack had never been about his sword.

With Nemiel's blade pushed to the side, he carried on his lunge and hammered his fist against the side of his cousin's head. The blow was poorly delivered, but it had the effect Zahariel was looking for.

Nemiel cried out and dropped his sword, as his hands flew to his face.

It was all the opening Zahariel needed.

He finished the bout by driving his knee up into Nemiel's stomach, doubling him up and sending him crashing to the floor in a winded, head-ringing heap.

Zahariel stepped away from his cousin and looked towards Master Ramiel, who nodded and said, 'Winner, Zahariel.'

He let out a great, shuddering breath and dropped his sword to the floor. It landed with a ringing clang, and he looked over to where Nemiel was picking himself up from his pain. Ramiel turned from the bout and marched resolutely towards the arched exit, leading his students towards their next gruelling lesson.

Zahariel held out this hand to Nemiel and said, 'Are you alright?'

His cousin still had his hands clutched to the side of his head, his lips pursed together as he tried to hide how much his head hurt. For a brief second, Zahariel was sorry for the hurt he had done to Nemiel, but he forced the feeling down. It had been his duty to win the bout, for giving anything less than his best would have been contrary to the teachings of the Order.

It had been two years since his induction into the Order, and the ninth anniversary of his birth had passed less than a month ago. Not that there had been any special reason for marking the day, but the instructor knights of the Order were very particular about marking the passage of time and keeping the census of ages and merits of its members.

Nemiel had turned nine a few days before him, and though they were alike in features and age, their temperaments could not have been more different. Zahariel could see that Nemiel had already forgotten the outcome of the bout, having learned how he had been defeated.

'I'm fine, cousin,' said Nemiel. 'That wasn't bad. I see what you did, but you won't get me that way again.'

That was true, thought Zahariel. Every time he fought his cousin and employed a method he had used previously, he was roundly beaten.

You could beat Nemiel, but you could not beat him the same way twice.

'Try not to be too disappointed,' said Zahariel. 'I may have won, but it wasn't a pretty victory.'

'Who cares about its prettiness,' snapped Nemiel. 'You won, didn't you?'

Zahariel's hand was still extended towards his cousin, who finally accepted it and hauled himself to his feet. He dusted his robes down and said, 'Ah, don't mind me, I'm just sore about getting beaten again, in front of Ramiel as well. I suppose I should think of all the times I've put you on your back, eh?'

'You're right,' said Zahariel. 'I think there's something in human nature that makes us concentrate too much on our disappointments at times. We should remember how lucky we are.'

'Lucky? What are you talking about?' said Nemiel, as they followed the other students from the training halls. 'You just beat me in the head, and we live on a world infested by killer monsters. How is that lucky?'

Zahariel looked at Nemiel, afraid he was being mocked. 'Think about it; of all the eras of Caliban's history, we have been fortunate enough to be born in the same period as men like the Lion and Luther. We are to take part in the campaign against the great beasts.'

'Oh, well I can see how that would be considered lucky, getting to march into the forests and face a horde of monsters that could swallow us whole, or tear us apart with one sweep of their claws.'

Now Zahariel knew he was being teased, for Nemiel could always be relied upon to boast of how fearsome a creature he would slay when he was finally allowed to declare a quest, venture into the forest and prove his mettle against one of the great beasts.

Instead of backing down in the face of Nemiel's teasing, he continued.

'We're here, supplicants of the Order, and one day we will be knights.'

Zahariel gestured to their surroundings: the high stone walls, the racks of weapons, the spiral on the floor and the giant mosaic on the wall depicting the Order's symbol, the downward pointed sword. 'Look around you, we train to become knights and eradicate the threat of the beasts from our world. The moment when the last beast is slain will be written into the annals of the Order and Caliban, and will be preserved for thousands of years. History is unfolding, and if we are lucky, we will be there when it happens.'

'True enough, cousin,' said Nemiel. 'People will say that we lived in interesting times, eh?'

'Interesting times?'

'It was something Master Ramiel said once, you remember, when we were outside in the dark petitioning to join the Order as novices?'

'I remember,' said Zahariel, though in truth he remembered little of the night they had spent in the darkness beyond the safety of the gates of the Order's fortress monastery, save for the terror of the great beasts, and of the night.

'He told me it was a phrase from ancient Terra,' continued Nemiel. 'When people lived through periods of change, the kind of days when history is made, they referred to them as "interesting times". They even had an expression: "May you live in interesting times". That's what they used to say.'

'May you live in interesting times,' echoed Zahariel. 'I like it. The expression, I mean. It sounds right, somehow. I know knights aren't supposed to believe in such things, but it sounds almost like a prayer.'

'A prayer, yes, but not a good one, "May you live in interesting times" was something they said to their worst enemies. It was intended as a curse.'

'A curse? I don't understand.'

'I suppose they wanted a quiet life. They didn't want to have to live through times of blood and upheaval. They didn't want change. They were happy. They all wanted to live for a long time and die in their beds. I suppose they thought their lives were perfect. The last thing they wanted was for history to come along and mess it all up.'

'It's hard to imagine,' Zahariel said, picking up the sword he had dropped and returning it to the weapons' rack. 'Imagine anyone being that contented with their lot and not wanting to change it. Maybe the difference is that we grew up on Caliban. Life is so hard here that everyone grows used to blood and upheaval.'

'Maybe things were different on Terra?' suggested Nemiel.

'Maybe, but maybe it's because we take it for granted that our lives on Caliban are always about struggle. In comparison, Terra must be like a paradise.'

'If it even exists,' said Nemiel. 'There are people who say it's only a myth, made up by our ancestors. Caliban is where our culture was born, and Caliban is where it will die. There are no starships, or lost brothers on other planets. It's all a lie. A well-meant one, created to give us comfort when times are bad, but a lie, nonetheless.'

'Do you believe that?' asked Zahariel. 'Do you really think Terra is a lie?'

'Yes, maybe… I don't know,' said Nemiel with a shrug. 'We can look up at the stars in the sky, but it's hard to believe anybody lives there. Just like it's hard to believe a world could be so perfect that you'd never want it to change. You were right, cousin. Our lives are struggle. It's all we can ever expect of things, on Caliban, anyway.'

Further discussions were prevented by Master Ramiel's booming voice coming from the archway at the far end of the chamber.

'Get a move on, you two!' bellowed their tutor. 'It's an extra turn on the sentry towers for you two tonight. Don't you know you've kept Brother Amadis waiting?'

Both boys shared an excited glance, but it was Nemiel who recovered his wits first.

'Brother Amadis has returned?'

'Aye,' nodded Ramiel. 'By rights, I should send you to the kitchens for your tardiness, but it will reflect badly on your fellows if you do not hear him speak.'

Zahariel sprinted alongside Nemiel as he ran for the archway, excitement flooding his young body with fresh vigour and anticipation.

Brother Amadis, the Hero of Maponis... *His* hero.

THE CIRCLE CHAMBER of Aldurukh was well named, thought Zahariel as he and Nemiel skidded through its arched entrance. Flickering torches hung at the entrance, sending a fragrant aroma of scented smoke into the enormous chamber. The hall was already packed, hundreds of novices, knights and supplicants filling the many stone benches that rose in tiers from the raised marble plinth at the chamber's centre.

Mighty pillars rose at the chamber's cardinal points, curving inwards in great, gothic arches to form the mighty roof of the dome, a green and gold ceiling from which hung a wide, circular candle holder filled with winking points of light.

The walls of the chamber were composed almost entirely of tall lengths of stained glass, each one telling of the heroic actions of one of the Order's knights. Many of these glorious panels depicted the actions of the Lion and Luther, but many more pre-dated them joining the order, and several of these depicted the warrior known as the Hero of Maponis, Brother Amadis.

One of the most senior knights of the Order who still participated in the Lion's great quest to rid the forests of Caliban, Brother Amadis was known throughout the world as a dashing and heroic warrior, who embodied everything it meant to be a knight: not just a knight of the Order, but a knight of Caliban.

His deeds were epic tales of heroism and nobility, adventures every child on Caliban grew up hearing from the mouths of their fathers.

Amadis had personally slain the Great Beast of Kulkos and had led the knights in battle against the predations of the Blood Knights of the Endriago Vaults. Before the coming of Jonson, it had been assumed by many that Brother Amadis would eventually rise to become the Grand Master of the Order.

Such had not been the case, however. Though all believed that the position would be Jonson's upon the successful conclusion of the beast hunt, Amadis had borne the Lion no ill-will, and had simply returned to the great forests to slay monsters and bear the honour of the Order to places near and far.

The number of youngsters presenting themselves before the mighty gates of Aldurukh had as much to do with his renown as it did the presence of the Lion. Zahariel remembered hearing the tales of him vanquishing the Blood Knights at the hearthfire on many a stormy evening. His father would always choose the darkest, most haunted nights to tell the tale, weaving a grisly tapestry of the horrors and debauched blood feasts of the knights to terrify his sons, before bringing the story to its heroic conclusion when Amadis defeated their leader in single combat.

'It looks like everyone who's anyone is here,' said Nemiel, as they jostled for position among the stragglers in the topmost tier of the Circle Chamber. They elbowed past newly accepted novices and supplicants who had not served as long as they had. Grumbles followed them, but none dared gainsay a boy who had been part of the Order for longer. An unspoken, but wholly understood hierarchy operated within the Order, and its structure could not, ever, be broken.

At last they found their proper place, further forward than the inferior supplicants and behind or beside those of a similar rank and stature. Though the centre of the Circle Chamber was some distance away, the view afforded from the upper tiers was second to none in terms of its panorama.

The centre was empty, with a single throne-like chair set in the middle of the floor.

'It looks like we made it in time,' Zahariel noted, and Nemiel nodded.

Banners hung from the chamber's roof, and Zahariel felt a familiar wonder envelop him as he stared at them, reading the history of the Order in their pictorial representations of honour, valour and battle. Gold stitching crossed ceremonial standards of green and blue, and red-edged war banners outnumbered the ceremonial ones by quite some margin. The entire roof was hung with banners; so many that it seemed as though a great blanket had been spread across it, and then slashed into hanging squares.

A hush fell upon the assembled novices, supplicants and knights at some unspoken signal, and Zahariel heard the creak of a wooden door opening, the metallic walk of a man in armour and the harsh rapping footsteps of metal on marble.

He strained for a better look, finally seeing the man who had made him want to become a knight. One man marched to the centre of the chamber in the burnished plate armour of the Order.

Zahariel tried not to feel disappointed at the warrior before him, but where he had expected a towering hero of legend, the equal of the Lion, he now saw that Brother Amadis was simply a man.

He knew he should have expected no more, but to see the warrior who had lived in his heroic dreams for as long as he could remember as just a man of flesh and blood, who did not tower over them like some mighty leviathan of legend, was somehow less than he had hoped for.

Yet, even as he tried to come to terms with the reality of seeing that his hero was after all, just a man, he saw there was something indefinable to him. There was something in the way Amadis walked to the centre of the chamber, as though he owned it, the confidence he wore like a cloak, as though he understood that this gathering was just for him, and that it was his right and due.

Despite what might have been perceived as monstrous arrogance, Zahariel could see a wry cast to Amadis's features, as though he expected such a gathering, but found it faintly absurd that he should be held in such high regard.

The more Zahariel looked at the figure in the centre of the chamber, the more he saw the easy confidence, the surety of purpose and the quiet courage in his every movement. Amadis held tight to the hilt of his sword as he walked, every inch a warrior, and Zahariel began to feel his admiration for this heroic knight grow with every passing second.

Surrounded by knights of such stature and courage that it was an honour simply to be in the same room as them, Zahariel had assumed that such warriors knew no fear, but looking at the weathered, handsome face of Brother Amadis, he realised that such an idea was preposterous.

As a boy in the forests of Caliban, he had certainly felt fear often enough, but he had assumed that once he became a knight the emotion would be utterly unknown to him. Brother Amadis had faced terrible foes and triumphed *despite* fear. To know fear, real fear, and to gain a great victory in spite of it seemed a more noble achievement than any triumph where fear was absent.

Brother Amadis looked around, and nodded in quiet satisfaction, apparently satisfied at the quality of the men and boys around him.

'If you're expecting a long and inspiring speech, then I'm afraid I've none to give you.'

Amadis's voice easily projected to the far reaches of the Circle Chamber, and Zahariel felt a thrill of excitement course through him at every word. Only the Lion and Luther had voices of such power and resonance.

'I'm a simple man,' continued Amadis, 'a warrior and a knight. I don't give speeches, and I'm not one for grand shows, but the Lion asked me to talk to you here today, though I'm no public speaker, that's for sure. I have returned to Aldurukh and I will be working alongside the instructor knights for a spell, so I expect I'll be seeing you all over the next few weeks and months before I return to the forests.'

Zahariel felt his pulse quicken at the idea of learning from a warrior such as Amadis, and felt wild, uncontrollable elation flood him.

'As I said before, I'm not usually one for theatrics, but I do understand their value, to you and to me,' said Amadis. 'Seeing me here will drive you on to become the best knights you can be, because I give you something to aspire to, a reason to want to better yourselves. Looking out at your faces reminds me of where I came from, what I used to be. Many tales are told of me and some of them are even true…'

Polite laughter rippled around the chamber as Amadis continued.

'As it happens, most of them *are* true, but that's not the point. The point is that when a man hears the same things said of him often enough, he begins to believe them. Tell a child often enough that it is worthless and beneath contempt and it will start to believe that such a vile sentiment is true. Tell a man he is a hero, a giant amongst men, and he will start to believe that too, thinking himself above all others. If enough praise and honour is heaped upon a man, he will start to believe that such is his due, and that all others must bow to his will.

'Seeing you all here is a grand reminder that I am not such a man. I was once a would-be novice, standing out in the cold night before the gates of this monastery. I too walked the spiral under the rods of instructor knights, and I too undertook a beast quest to prove my mettle to the Order. You are where I was, and I am where any one of you can be.'

Amadis's speech seemed to reach out to Zahariel, and he knew that he would remember this moment for as long as he lived. He would remember these words and he would live by them.

The words of this heroic knight had power beyond the simple hearing of them. They seemed to be aimed directly at every warrior gathered in the chamber. Looking around, Zahariel knew that every knight, novice and suppliant felt that every word was for him and for him alone.

Thunderous applause and spontaneous cheering erupted in the Circle Chamber, the knights and supplicants rising to their feet. Such displays were almost unheard of within the walls of Aldurukh, and Zahariel was swept up in the infectious enthusiasm of his brethren.

He looked over at Nemiel, his cousin similarly caught up in the wave of pride.

Such was the power, strength and conviction in his words and delivery that Zahariel vowed, there and then, that he would be the greatest knight the Order had ever seen, the most heroic warrior ever to sally forth from the great Memorial Gate to do battle with the enemies of Caliban.

Despite the pride and hubris inherent in such vows, he made a silent oath that he would never lose sight of what it meant to be a knight, the humility that must accompany all great deeds and the unspoken satisfaction in knowing that doing the right thing was reason enough to do it.

Eventually, the applause died down, as Amadis lifted his arms and waved away the clapping and cheering.

'Enough, brothers, enough!' he shouted with a smile on his face. 'This isn't what I came here for. Despite my earlier words, I do seem to have given a bit of a speech, but hopefully it wasn't too boring, eh?'

THREE

THE NIGHTMARE ALWAYS began the same way. It was two years ago and he was seven years of age, one of nearly two hundred would-be aspirants who had come to the fortress monastery at Aldurukh seeking to be accepted as knights-supplicant by the Order. From whatever pleasant fantasy was drifting around inside his skull, the darkness would always come to wrench him back to his first day with the Order.

It had been mid-winter, the only time of year at which the Order recruited, and hundreds of children would arrive at the fortress, desperately hoping they would be among the handful chosen to start on the pathway to becoming a knight.

The rite of selection was the same for every one of them.

The guards manning the gates would tell the waiting aspirants there was only one way to be accepted for training within the Order. They must survive a single night beyond the gates of the fortress until dawn the next morning. During that time, they had to remain standing in the same spot. They could not eat, or sleep, or sit down, or take rest in any way. What was more, they were told they each had to surrender their coats and boots.

It had been snowing the day Zahariel took the test, and the snow lying in wide drifts against the walls of the fortress and upon the branches of the trees at the forest's edge gave the scene a curiously festive appearance.

Nemiel had been beside him; the two of them had each decided they would become knights, assuming they managed to pass the test and were found to be worthy.

The snow was thick on the ground by the time the test started, and throughout the day, the snowfall continued until it had risen as high as their knees. Though the forest was several hundred metres from the walls of the fortress, the darkness beyond the tree line seemed to reach out from the haunted depths like a living thing, enveloping them in its silky embrace like an unwelcome lover.

As he dreamed, Zahariel turned in his sleep, the phantasmal cold making him shiver in his cot bed. He recognised the dream for what it was, but such knowledge did not allow him to break from its inevitable course. His extremities had grown so numb, he felt sure he would lose his fingers and toes to frostbite, and knew that in the morning after the darkness, he would wake and check to make sure his nightmare had not translated into the real world.

Throughout the test, the guards had done everything in their power to make the ordeal more difficult. They had wandered among the ranks of miserable, barefoot children, alternating between cruelty and kindness in their attempts to break them.

One guard had called Nemiel a pus-brained simpleton for even thinking he was worthy to join the Order. Another had tried to tempt Zahariel by offering a blanket and a hot meal, but only if he would first give up on his ambitions and leave the test.

Once again, Zahariel could see the guard's face leering down at him as he said, 'Come inside, boy. There's no reason for you to be standing out here, freezing. It's not as if you'd ever make it into the Order. Everybody knows you haven't got what it takes. You know it, too. I can see right through you. Come inside. You don't want to be outside once night comes. Raptors, bears and lions, there're a lot of different predators come around the walls of the fortress at night. And there's nothing they like more than to see a boy standing in open ground. You'd make a tasty morsel for the likes of them.'

So far, the nightmare had followed a familiar course, treading the paths of memory, but at some point, never the same one twice, it would deviate into madness and things of which he had no memory, things he wished he could erase from his mind as easily as his pleasant dreams were wont to vanish.

In this variation, Zahariel stood beside a fair-haired boy he had never seen before, in his nightmares or in reality. The boy was a youth of wondrous perfection and pride, who stood with ramrod straight shoulders and the bearing of someone who would grow into the mightiest of warriors.

A guard with a gnarled face and cruel orange eyes leant down towards the boy.

'You don't need to finish the test,' said the guard. 'Your pride and fortitude under pressure has attracted the attention of the Order's Grand Master. Your fate has already been decided. Any fool with eyes can see you've got what it takes to be the chosen one.'

Zahariel wanted to cry out, to tell the boy not to believe the falsehoods he was hearing, but it was what the boy wanted to hear. It promised him everything he had ever desired.

The boy's face lit up at the news of his acceptance, his eyes shining with the promise of achieving all that he had ever wanted.

Thinking the test was over, the boy sank, exhausted, to his knees and leaned forward to kiss the snow covered ground.

The cruel laughter of the guards brought the boy's head up with a start, and Zahariel could see the dawning comprehension of his foolishness slide across his face like a slick.

'Foolish boy!' cried the guard. 'You think because someone tells you that you are special that it must be true? You are nothing but a pawn for our amusement!'

The boy let out a heart-rending howl of anguish, and Zahariel fought to keep his eyes fixed straight ahead as the boy was dragged to the edge of the forest, red-eyed and crying, his face pale with shock and disbelief.

The boy's cries were muffled as he was hurled into the dark forest, the tangled webs of roots and creepers dragging him deeper and deeper into the choking vegetation. Though the boy's pained cries grew weaker and weaker, Zahariel could still hear them, echoing in unimaginable anguish long after he had been taken by the darkness.

Zahariel tried to shut out the boy's pain as the weather grew colder and the number of aspirants standing outside Aldurukh dwindled as other boys decided it was better to bear the stigma of failure than to face the ordeal for a moment longer.

Some went pleading to the guards, begging for shelter within the fortress and the return of their coats and boots. Others simply collapsed, worn down by cold and hunger, to be carried away to fates unknown.

By sunset, only two-thirds of the boys remained. Then, as darkness fell, the guards retreated to their sentry points inside the fortress, leaving the boys to endure the long hours of the night alone.

The night was the worst time. Zahariel twisted as his dream-self shivered in the dismal darkness, his teeth chattering so violently he thought they might shatter. The silence was absolute, the boy's cries from the forest stilled and the guards jibes and taunts ended.

With the coming of night, the silence and the power of imagination did a better job of terrorising the boys than the guards ever could. The seeds of fear had been sown with talk of predators prowling around outside the fortress, and in the still of the night, those seeds took root and sprouted in each boy's mind.

The night had a quality that was eternal, thought Zahariel.

It had always existed and always would exist. The feeble efforts of men to bring illumination to the galaxy were futile and doomed to failure. He dimly perceived the strangeness of the concept as it formed in his mind, expressing ideas and words that he had no knowledge of, but which he knew were crushingly true.

Afterwards, it was the sounds that Zahariel feared the most.

The ordinary sounds of the forest at night, noises that he had heard more than a thousand times in the past, were louder and more threatening than any sounds he had heard before. At times, he heard sounds he swore were the work of raptors, bears or even the much-feared Calibanite lion.

The crack of every twig, every rustle of the leaves, every call and scream of the night: all these things sounded heavy with menace. Death lurked just behind him or at his elbow, and he wanted to run, to give up the ordeal. He wanted to go back to the settlement where he was born, to his friends and family, to his mother's soothing words, to the warm place by the hearth. He wanted to give up on the Order. He wanted to forgo his knightly pretensions.

He was seven years of age and he wanted to go home.

As horrible and unearthly as the noises had been, it was the voices that were the worst part of the ordeal, the most loathsome invention of his nightmare.

Between the roars and the snap of branches, a million susurrations emerged from the forest like a cabal of whispering voices. Whether anyone else could hear them, Zahariel did not know, for no one else reacted to the sounds that invaded his skull with promises of power, of flesh, of immortality.

All could be his, if he would step from the snow-covered esplanade before the fortress and walk into the forest. Without the presence of the guards, Zahariel felt able to turn his head and look towards the tangled, vine choked edge of the forest.

Though forests carpeted much of the surface of Caliban and his entire existence had been spent within sight of tall trees and swaying green canopies, this forest was unlike anything he had seen before. The trunks of the trees were leprous and green, their bark rotten and diseased. Darkness that was blacker than the deepest night lurked between them, and though the voices promised him that all would be well if he stepped into the forest, he knew that terrors undreamt of and nightmares beyond reckoning dwelt beneath its haunted arbours.

As ridiculous as it seemed to Zahariel, he knew that this dream-shaped forest was no natural phenomenon, a region so unnatural that it existed beyond the mortal world, shaped by its dreams and nightmares, stirred by its desires and fears.

What lurked within its depths was beyond fear and reason, madness and elemental power that seethed and roared in concert with the heaving tides of men and their dreadful lives.

And yet…

For all its dark, twisting, horrid power, there was an undeniable attraction.

Power, no matter its source, could always be mastered, couldn't it? Elemental energies could be harnessed and made to serve the will of one with the strength of purpose to master its complexities.

The things that could be achieved with such power were limitless. The great beasts could be hunted to extinction and the other knightly brotherhoods brought to heel. All of Caliban would become the domain of the Order, and all would obey its masters or die by the swords of its terrible black angels of death.

The thought made him smile as he thought of the glories to be won on the fields of battle. He pictured the slaughter and the debaucheries that would follow, the carrion birds and worms feasting, and the capering madmen that made merry in the ruin of a world.

Zahariel cried out, the vision faded from his mind and he heard the voices for what they were: the whisper in the gloom, the hinting tone, the haunting laugh and the jealous vipers that cracked the panels of tombs and composed the platitudes of his epitaph.

Even unmasked, the tempters of the dark realm of the wood would not leave him, and their blandishments continued to plague him throughout the night, until his feet were ready to carry him to willing damnation in the darkness.

In the end, as it always was, it was Nemiel that stopped him, not through any word or deed, but purely because he was there.

Nemiel stood at his shoulder throughout the night-mare, as he had on that cold, fearful night. Unbending and unbroken, his best friend stood by his side, never wavering and never afraid.

Taking heart from his cousin's example, Zahariel found new strength fill him and knew that, but for the strength of his brotherhood with Nemiel, he would have faltered in his inner struggle. With the strength he drew from his presence, he refused to bow down to his fears. He refused to give in.

He had seen out the night with Nemiel beside him.

As the relentless logic of the nightmare gave way to memory, the sun rose over the treetops of the forest, and the dark whisperers withdrew. Only a dozen boys remained standing before the gates of Aldurukh, and Zahariel relaxed in his bed as the familiar pattern of reality reasserted itself.

Many of the other hopefuls had failed the test during the night and had gone to the gates to beg the guards to let them in. Whether any had heard the same voices as he had and ventured into the forest, he never knew, and as the first rays of sunlight reached their freezing bodies, Zahariel saw a gruff, solidly built figure emerge from the fortress and march towards them.

The figure had worn a hooded white surplice over burnished black armour, and carried a gnarled wooden staff at his side.

'I am Master Ramiel,' the figure had said, standing before the aspirants. He had pulled back the hood of his surplice, revealing the weathered face of a man well into his middle fifties. 'It is my honour to be one of the Order's masters of instruction.'

He raised the staff and swung it in a wide arc, indicating the dozen shivering boys before him.

'You will be my students. You have passed the test set for you, and that is good. But you should know it was more than just a test. It was also your first lesson. In a minute, we will go inside Aldurukh, where you will be given a hot meal and warm, dry clothes. Before we do, I want you to consider something for a moment. You have stood in the snow outside the fortress for more than twenty hours. You have endured cold, hunger and hardship, not to mention other privations. Yet, you are still here. You passed the test and you endured these things where others failed. The question I would ask you is simple. Why? There were almost two hundred boys here. Why did you twelve pass this test and not the others?'

Master Ramiel had looked from one boy to another, waiting to see if any of them would answer the question. At length, once he had seen that none of the boys would, he had answered it for them.

'It is because your minds were stronger,' Master Ramiel had told them. 'A man can be trained in the skills of killing, he can learn to use a knife or other weapons, but these things are nothing if his mind is not strong. It takes strength of mind for a man to hunt the great beasts. It takes strength for a man to know cold and hunger, to feel fear and yet refuse to break in the face of it. Always remember, the mind and will of a knight are as much weapons in his armoury as his sword and pistol. I will teach you how to develop these things, but it is up to you whether these lessons take root. Ultimately, the question of whether you will succeed or fail will be decided in the recesses of your own hearts. It takes mental strength and great fortitude of mind and will to become a knight.

'There, you have heard your first lesson,' Master Ramiel had said grimly, his eyes sweeping sternly over his new charges as though he was capable of seeing into their very souls. 'Now, go and eat.'

The command given, Zahariel's mind floated up from the depths of his subconscious towards waking as he heard a distant bell ringing and felt rough hands shaking him awake.

His eyes flickered open, gummed by sleep, his vision blurred.

A face swam into focus above him and it took a moment for him to recognise his cousin from the callow youth he had stood next to in his dream.

'Nemiel?' he said with a sleep drowsy voice.

'Who else would it be?'

'What are you doing? What time is it?'

'It's early,' said Nemiel. 'Get up, quickly now!'

'Why?' protested Zahariel. 'What's going on?'

Nemiel sighed and Zahariel looked around their austere barracks as suppliants dressed hurriedly, with grins of excitement and not a little fear upon their faces.

'What's going on?' parroted Nemiel. 'We're going on a hunt is what's going on!'

'A hunt?'

'Aye!' cried Nemiel. 'Brother Amadis is leading our phratry on a hunt!'

ZAHARIEL FELT THE familiar mix of excitement and fear as he rode the black steed between the trees in the shadowy depths of the forest. He shivered as fragments of his dream returned to him, and he strained to hear any hint of the screaming or whispering that had dogged his latest episode of dreaming.

There was nothing, but then the excited jabbering of his comrades would have blotted out all but the most strident calls from the forest. Zahariel rode alongside Nemiel, his cousin's open face and dark hair partially concealed by his helmet, but his excitement infectious.

Zahariel had been selected to lead this group, and nine suppliants rode behind him, each one also mounted on one of the black horses of Caliban. The root strands of any other colour of riding beast had long since died out, and only horses of a dark hue could be bred by the Order's horse masters.

Like their riders, each horse was young and had much to learn, on their way to becoming the famed mounts of the Ravenwing cavalry. The knights of the Ravenwing rode like daring heroes of old, leading exponents of lightning warfare and hit and run charges, they were masters of the wilderness.

They could survive for months alone in the deadly forests of Caliban, heroic figures in matt black armour and winged helms that concealed the identity of each warrior.

To be one of the Ravenwing was to live a lonely life, but one of heart-stopping adventure and glory.

Five other groups of ten riders made up the hunt, spread throughout the forest in a staggered 'V' formation, with Brother Amadis roaming between them as an observer and mentor. They were many kilometres from the Order's fortress monastery, and the thrill of riding through the forest so far from home almost outweighed the cold lump of dread that had settled in Zahariel's stomach.

'You think we'll actually find a beast?' asked Attias from Zahariel's right. 'I mean, this part of the forest is supposed to be clear isn't it?'

'We won't find anything with you prattling on!' snapped Nemiel. 'I swear they can hear you back at Aldurukh.'

Attias flinched at Nemiel's harsh tone, and Zahariel shot his cousin a curt glance. Nemiel shrugged, unapologetic, and rode onwards.

'Pay no attention to him, Attias,' said Zahariel. 'He's missing his bed, that's all.'

Attias nodded and smiled, his natural optimism glossing over the incident with good grace. The boy was younger than Zahariel, and he had known him ever since Attias was seven and had joined the Order.

Zahariel wasn't sure why he had taken the younger boy under his wing, but he had helped Attias adapt to the disciplined and demanding life of a supplicant, perhaps because he had seen something of himself in the boy.

His early years with the Order had been hard and if it hadn't been for Zahariel's guidance, Attias would undoubtedly have failed in his first weeks and been sent home in ignominy. As it was, the boy had persevered and become a more than creditable supplicant.

Nemiel had never warmed to the boy and made him the frequent subject of his often cruel jibes and scornful ridicule. It had become an unspoken source of antagonism between the cousins, for Nemiel had held that each supplicant should stand or fall by his own merits, not by who helped him; where Zahariel contended that it was the duty of each and every supplicant to help his brothers.

'It's a great honour for Brother Amadis to lead us on this hunt, isn't it?'

'Indeed it is, Attias,' said Zahariel. 'It's not often we get to learn from such a senior knight. If he speaks, you must listen to what he says.'

'I will,' promised Attias.

Another of their group rode alongside Zahariel and pushed up the visor of his helm to speak. The helmets the supplicants wore were the hand-me-downs of the Order and only those issued to team leaders boasted an inter-suit communications system.

Zahariel's helmet allowed him to communicate with the leaders of the other groups of riders and Brother Amadis, but his fellow supplicants had to open their helmets to be heard.

The rider next to him was Eliath, a friend of Nemiel and companion in his mocking games. Eliath was taller and broader than any of the other suppliants, his bulk barely able to fit within a suit of armour. Though his flesh was youthfully doughy, his strength was prodigious and his stamina enormous. Though what he possessed in power, he lacked in speed.

Eliath and Zahariel had never seen eye to eye, the boy too often taking Nemiel's lead when shaping his behaviour towards his fellow suppliants.

'Did you bring your notebook with you, Attias?' asked Eliath.

'Yes,' said Attias. 'It's in my pack, why?'

'Well if we do find a beast, you'll want to take notes on how I gut it. They might stand you in good stead if you ever face one without us.'

A tightening of the jawline was the only outward sign of Attias's displeasure, but Zahariel knew it was a jibe that was somewhat deserved. The younger boy would carry his notebooks with him at all times and write down every word the senior knights and suppliants said, whether appropriate or not. The footlocker at the end of Attias's bed was filled with dozens of such notebooks crammed with his tight script, and every night before lights out he would memorise entire tracts of offhand comments and remarks as though they were passages from the *Verbatim*.

'Maybe I'll write your epitaph,' said Attias. 'If we do meet a beast, it's sure to go for the fattest one first.'

'I'm not fat,' protested Eliath. 'I'm just big boned.'

'Enough, the pair of you!' said Zahariel, though he took pleasure in seeing Attias sticking up for himself and Eliath taken down a peg. 'We're training for a hunt, and I'm sure Brother Amadis doesn't consider baiting each other as part of that training.'

'True enough, Zahariel,' said a sanguine voice in his helmet, 'but it does no harm to foster a little rivalry within a group.'

None of the other supplicants heard the voice, but Zahariel smiled at the sound of Brother Amadis's voice, knowing he must have heard the exchange between the supplicants.

'Healthy rivalry drives us to excel in all things, but it cannot be allowed to get out of hand,' continued Amadis. 'You handled that well, Zahariel. Allow rivalry to exist, but prevent it from becoming destructive.'

Over the closed communications, Zahariel said, 'Thank you, brother.'

'No thanks are necessary, now take the lead and assume scouting discipline.'

He smiled, feeling a warm glow envelop him at his hero's praise. To think that a warrior as great as Amadis knew his name was an honour, and he spurred his mount onwards as he felt the responsibility of his command settle upon him.

'Close up,' he ordered, riding to the front of the group of supplicants and taking his place at the point of their arrow formation. 'Scouting discipline from now on. Consider this enemy territory.'

His voice carried the strength of conviction that came from the approval of his peers, and without a murmur of dissent, his squad-mates smoothly moved into position. Nemiel took up position behind him and to the left, while a supplicant named Pallian assumed the same position on the opposite side.

Eliath and Attias took up position on either side of the formation, and Zahariel turned in the saddle to make sure his squad was lined up in position.

Satisfied that all was as it should be, he returned his attention to the terrain ahead, the thick trunks and heavy foliage rendering the forest a canvas of shadows and slanted spars of light. Leaf mould covered the ground, and the smell of decaying matter in the darkness gave the air a musty scent that was reminiscent of spoiled meat.

The ground was rocky, but the horses of the Ravenwing picked a clear path between the boulders and fallen tree trunks.

Strange noises drifted between the trees, but Zahariel had grown up in the forest, and he let the rhythm of the undergrowth drift over him, sorting the various calls of the wildlife of Caliban into those that were dangerous and those that were not.

Most of the great beasts had been hunted to extinction by the Lion's great crusade, but several enclaves of lethal predators still existed, though they were far from any such places. Less dangerous monsters still lurked, unseen and unknown in almost every part of the world's forests, but such creatures rarely attacked groups of warriors, relying on stealth and surprise to attack lone victims as they moved between the safe havens of the walled cities.

Amid the hooting, cawing cries of birds, Zahariel could hear the clicking, creaking noise of the forest, the wind through the high branches and the crunch of hooves over broken branches. Moving silently through the forest was virtually impossible for any but the Ravenwing, but still, Zahariel wished they could be riding in silence.

Even though the worst of Caliban's predators were mostly dead, there was no such thing as a beast that could be easily overcome, even with such numbers.

They rode on for what seemed like a few hours, though without any sign of the sun above, it was difficult to judge the passage of time. Only the changing angles of the beams of light that penetrated the forest canopy gave any hint to how long they had been travelling.

Zahariel longed to communicate with the other groups of riders, but did not want to appear nervous or unsure of the course he was leading. This was supposed to be training them for going on a hunt of their own one day, and the idea that he did not know where he was going was not one he wanted to cultivate.

The paths through the forest were well-worn through countless training exercises, but so many existed that it was next to impossible to know which ones led to their destination. He and Nemiel had consulted the map before setting out, and their route had seemed simple enough in the walled confines of the fortress monastery. Out in the forest, however, it was quite a different proposition.

He was fairly sure he knew where he was and where their path should lead them, but it would be impossible to know if they had succeeded until they arrived. Zahariel hoped that Brother Amadis was nearby and would take note of how he was leading his fellows.

His thoughts were interrupted as they rode beneath low hanging branches into a shadowed clearing, the sound of the leaves brushing against his helmet startlingly loud in the silence of the forest.

Even as the thought struck him that the forest was silent, it was already too late.

Something dark and winged dropped from the trees, its body scaled and reptilian.

Claws like swords flashed, and one of his squad was dead, both he and his mount shorn in two by the ferocity of the blow.

Blood sprayed and horrified cries echoed from the clearing. Zahariel drew his pistol as the beast struck again. Another supplicant died, his armour torn open and his innards hooked from his belly. The horses were screaming, the scent of blood maddening them, and the supplicants fought to control their crazed mounts.

Cries of horror and anger resounded, but there was no sense to them. Zahariel turned his mount towards the beast. Its large body was easily the size of one of their horses, undulating as though a million serpents writhed beneath its glistening flesh. Its spiny head snapped and bit at the end of a long, snake-like neck, its jaws long and narrow, filled with razored fangs like the teeth of a woodsman's saw. Its wings were filmy and translucent, edged in ridges of horny carapace and ending in long, barbed claws.

Zahariel had never seen its like before, and his momentary horror at its awful appearance almost cost him his life.

The beast's wings slashed as though it were about to take flight, and one of the barbed hooks scored a deep groove across his breastplate, pitching him from the back of his screaming horse.

Zahariel hit the ground hard as he heard another anguished scream of agony. He struggled to rise, his movements awkward in his armour. He reached for his fallen pistol as a wide shadow engulfed him, and he twisted his head as the screeching, reptilian bird towered above him, its jaws wide and ready to snap him in two.

FOUR

ZAHARIEL ROLLED AS the beast's beak stabbed down-wards. He slithered onto his back and brought his pistol around. Three shots boomed from the barrel in a blaze of light and Zahariel was momentarily blinded by the brightness. The noise was deafening, his helmet only slightly muffling the sounds. He scrambled away from the beast on his backside, fully expecting every second to be his last.

He heard more shots, and as his vision cleared he saw Nemiel crouching behind a tree and pumping shots from his pistol at the beast as it clawed at the remains of Zahariel's horse.

Blood like molten wax oozed from three neat holes in the beast's chest, but if they had discomfited it, Zahariel could not tell, for it fought and roared as fiercely as it had when first attacking.

The beast's wing shot out and clove through the trunk of the tree Nemiel was using for shelter and slammed into his cousin's chest. Nemiel dropped to the ground, his breastplate cracked, but still whole, for the impact with the tree had blunted much of the force of the beast's blow.

Zahariel scrambled to his feet as he saw the scattered remnants of his squad panic in the face of the monster. Eliath was pinned beneath his mount, the horse's flank opened from neck to rump, and Attias sat petrified at the edge of the clearing. The young boy's mount stood stock still, its ears pressed flat against its skull and its eyes wide with terror, rooting them both to the spot.

The beast turned towards Attias and let out an ululating roar, spreading its wings and bunching its muscles as it prepared to attack

'Hey!' screamed Zahariel, stepping from the cover of the trees and waving his arms above his head. 'Over here!'

The beast's head turned on its sinuous neck, its blood-frothed jaws opening wide and its black, soulless eyes fixing upon him. Zahariel drew his sword and aimed his pistol at the drooling monster.

'Ho, ugly!' he shouted. 'If you want him, you have to take me first!'

He had no idea whether or not the beast understood the words he was saying, but there was little doubt that it understood the challenge of his actions on a primal, animal scale.

Without waiting for a response, Zahariel opened fire, the pistol bucking in his hand, and wet blooms of filmy blood burst from the beast's chest. It screeched and lunged towards him, its head shooting forward like the thrust of a sword.

Zahariel leapt to the side, the blade of its beak slashing past him, barely a hand's span from skewering him. Faster than he would have believed possible, the beast's head twisted in the air to catch him a glancing blow just below his hip.

He flew through the air and slammed into a tree, the breath exploding from his lungs and his weapons tumbling from his hands as he fell to the ground.

Shouts and cries of terror sounded around Zahariel and he shook his head as he tried to get his bearings once again. He heard his squad crying out in fear and he spat blood as he pushed against the stinking ground and lifted his head.

Though his vision swam crazily, he saw Eliath finally drag himself from beneath his dead mount and Nemiel pick himself up from the beast's blow to drag himself behind another tree. Attias had snapped from his horrified paralysis and had ridden his horse into the trees, the beast lumbering back towards the tasty morsel of boy and horse.

Zahariel used the tree next to him to haul himself to his feet, feeling a screaming pain in his twisted leg. He searched the ground for his fallen weapons, eventually spying the gleam of sunlight on the steel of his sword. He couldn't see his pistol, and had no time to look for it.

He grimaced in pain as he swept up his sword and limped towards the clearing, as the beast's jaws snapped out and bit Attias's horse in two. The boy flung himself from the saddle just as the monster struck, and landed with a thud on a fallen log, rolling over it, and flopping to the ground in a heap.

Zahariel's armour hissed as breaches in its structure caused it to fail, the mechanisms of its protective systems grinding and seizing. The full mass of the plate began to weigh heavily on him, and he grimaced in pain as the plates at his hip settled on his hurt leg.

'Spread out!' shouted Zahariel. 'Get to the trees and spread out! Don't bunch up!'

More pistol shots boomed, and Zahariel saw Pallian run forward to drag Attias back to the trees. The beast leapt over the dead horse and its beak shot out, catching Pallian by the shoulder and wrenching him from his feet.

The boy screamed as he was lifted high into the air, but his screams were cut short as his arm and most of his shoulder was bitten through. He fell, trailing a drizzling arc of blood from the ruin of his body, the curve of his arm moving down the beast's throat with a horrid peristaltic motion.

Blood geysered from Pallian, and his screams filled the clearing, as the agony overcame the shock of the wound. The beast turned its head back to the fallen boy, its wing-claws slashing twice. Pallian screamed no more.

Zahariel cried out as Pallian was dismembered by the beast, and stepped into the clearing, his vision blurred with tears of pain and terror. He raised his sword and held it unsteadily before him as he faced the monster that he knew would kill him.

He knew that fact with cold certainty, but he could not allow others to suffer and die without at least trying to save them.

'Get away from them, you bastard,' he snarled. 'These are my friends and they're not for the likes of you!'

The beast looked up, and though its eyes were empty and cold, Zahariel could sense its monstrous hunger to kill. Beyond even what it needed to feed and survive, this creature needed to inflict pain, and took some primitive enjoyment from the act of slaughter.

The beast turned from Pallian's body and let loose a tremendous roar as it saw Zahariel advancing towards it, his sword aimed at its heart. The beast's wings rippled, and Zahariel knew what was coming. He brought his sword up as the creature's right wing slashed towards him.

He swayed aside and swung his sword around in a downward arc that chopped into the wing where the claw began. Milky blood sprayed, and the claw was shorn from the beast, as Zahariel's leg finally gave out beneath him and he dropped to one knee.

The beast howled in pain and drew back its injured wing, its jaws opening wide as it prepared to end his life. A shadow moved beside Zahariel as the beast lunged forward. The sight of its thousands of teeth filled his vision.

Even as he smelt the rankness of its gullet and saw the scraps of flesh stuck between its teeth, a silver steel blur slashed over his head, as an armoured figure rode past him with a thunder of hooves and a mighty war shout.

A long, heavy-bladed sword stuck edge on into the beast's mouth, the wielder's strength and the beast's momentum driving the blade through its jawbone and into the middle of its skull.

The sword juddered to a halt and the rider released the blade as he rode onwards, expertly wheeling his horse as the beast fell, its lunging body collapsing to the ground before Zahariel.

The rider rode alongside the beast's skull. He drew a magnificent, rotary barrelled pistol and aimed it at a point between the monster's eyes. Zahariel watched the hammer draw back and flinched at the percussive bang as the explosive bolt detonated with a hollow boom inside its skull.

Viscous fluids leaked from the monster's skull and the dark, predatory hunger in its black orbs of eyes was finally extinguished. A last, foetid exhalation gusted from the beast's mouth, and Zahariel recoiled from the rotten stench.

He looked up as his saviour holstered his pistol. The man wore the dark armour and hooded white surplice of the Order, the front of which was embroidered with the symbol of the downward pointing sword.

'You are lucky to be alive, my boy,' said the knight, and Zahariel instantly recognised the commanding tone.

'Brother Amadis,' he said. 'Thank you. You saved my life.'

'Aye,' said Amadis, 'and by the look of it you saved the lives of your friends, Zahariel.'

'I was… protecting my squad…' said Zahariel, the last of his strength beginning to fade now that the battle was over.

Amadis swung down from his saddle and caught him as he fell to the grass.

'Rest, Zahariel,' said Amadis.

'No,' whispered Zahariel. 'I have to get them home.'

'Let me do that for you, lad. You've done enough for one day.'

'You were lucky,' Nemiel would say to him later, 'but luck can't be relied upon. It's a finite resource. One day, it always runs out.'

For years afterwards, whenever Zahariel told the tale of their confrontation with the winged beast, his cousin would always make the same remark. He would say it privately, out of earshot of their brothers, in the arming chamber or beside the practice cages, as though he did not want to embarrass Zahariel in front of others, yet equally he was incapable of letting the matter rest.

Something about the whole affair seemed to have worked its way under Nemiel's skin, as though the battle had become a source of subdued annoyance to him, even irritation. He never showed it in his face, nor let it invade his tone, but at times it felt as if he were chiding Zahariel in some way, as though he felt compelled to subtly make the point that all of his cousin's later successes, all of his glories, had been built on a lie.

Zahariel would find this behaviour curious, but he would never raise the issue with his friend. He would do what Nemiel could not; he would let the matter rest. He would never question Nemiel's words. He would listen to them, ignore the hidden bitterness, and accept they were well meant. For him to do differently might have endangered their friendship.

'You were lucky,' Nemiel would say. 'If it wasn't for luck and Brother Amadis, the beast would've killed us all.'

Zahariel could not disagree.

A WEEK LATER, Zahariel was made to tell the tale of the fight to his fellow supplicants in the training chambers. Each time he told of how he had stood before the monster, it would always seem a far more thrilling affair than it had been in reality.

It would seem a story of high ideals and grand adventure to his listeners. It was not that he lied about the specifics of it in any way, but he would learn that repetition had a way of softening the edges of human experience. Each telling sounded like a fairy tale or fable.

During the mad, frenetic rush of battle, it had been a life or death struggle, a hard-won victory achieved through the action of blood, sweat and tears. It had been a close-run thing, and to the very end, Zahariel thought the winged beast would kill them all. He thought the last instants of his life were to be spent gazing in horror into the beast's widening mouth as the black void of its maw expanded to swallow him whole.

If he were to be left any headstone or grave marker, it would take the form of a regurgitated bolus created sometime later, incorporating only those parts of him that were indigestible to his killer.

This was the end he expected. The creature had seemed too strong, too formidable, and far too primal a force to ever be killed.

But for Brother Amadis, those thoughts would have been correct.

He would keep these thoughts from his fellows when he told the tale. He would be asked to tell the story often, but he realised no one wanted to hear of his private doubts. They wanted to hear something more stirring, full of heroic exploits and the expression of valour, something that spoke of the inevitable triumph of good over evil.

It was human nature, he supposed, but his listeners expected him to be the hero of his story. They wanted him to be confident, wise, debonair, unflappable, dashing, handsome, charismatic, even inspiring. The truth was that at the time he had fully expected to fail. He had not allowed that thought to undermine his resolve, but it was there all the same.

No one wanted to hear that truth.

No one wanted to know their heroes could have feet of clay.

Occasionally, in the brief quiet moments he would experience in the life ahead of him, he would wonder at the folly of human judgements.

To his mind, his victory had been more special precisely because he had been afraid.

His fellow supplicants, however, seemed to think it was improper to speak of the emotion at all. It was as if fear was a secret shame in every human heart, and his listeners wanted to be reassured that their heroes did not feel it, as though it meant they might one day be freed from their own fear.

It seemed to Zahariel that this was wrong.

The only way to overcome fear was to confront it.

To pretend it did not exist, or might somehow disappear one day, only made it worse.

BOOK TWO

BEAST

FIVE

Years passed, and Zahariel's standing within the Order grew. His fight with the winged monster of the woods had almost cost him his life, but it had been the making of him. The senior masters of the Order knew his name, and though the monster had been slain by Brother Amadis, the knight had ensured that every member of the Order knew of Zahariel's bravery in fighting it.

The dead boys were buried with full honours, and life went on as before, with the supplicants training and living within the walls of the fortress monastery on the road to becoming knights.

Zahariel spent more time than ever honing his skills with pistol and blade, more than ever determined that he would not be at the mercy of another beast in his lifetime. The next time he faced a monster of Caliban, he would be ready to kill it without a moment's pause.

As the latest lesson concluded, Master Ramiel said, 'Always remember, you are more than just killers. Any fool can take a knife and try to push it into his enemy's flesh. He may attempt to strike, feint and parry with the blade. Given some instruction, he may even become proficient. But you are more than that, or you will be. You are knights-supplicant of the Order, but in future, you will be the protectors of the people of Caliban.'

'Fine words, eh?' said Nemiel, moving to one of the rest benches and picking up a linen towel to mop his face.

'Fine indeed,' agreed Zahariel, 'just as fine as the first hundred times I heard them.'

The lesson had been spent mastering the principle of the inner circle sword defence, and both boys were lathered in sweat from the sparring session. Though honours were still more or less even between them, Nemiel had begun to claw ahead in their perpetual rivalry.

'Master Ramiel does love to quote the *Verbatim*.'

'True, but I think he thinks we're all like Attias, writing down every pithy quote we hear.'

'Well, so long as we master the fighting, I can live with hearing a few repetitions now and again,' said Nemiel.

'I suppose,' agreed Zahariel. 'Next time we fight a beast, we won't be so unprepared.'

A heavy silence fell between them. Zahariel cursed himself for bringing up the subject of the beasts, for it always served to remind Nemiel of how his cousin had won glory and plaudits for his role in protecting them long enough for Brother Amadis to kill it, when all Nemiel had won was time in the infirmary.

'Do you think the beast was sentient?' asked Nemiel.

'What beast?' replied Zahariel, though he knew fine well what his cousin meant.

'The winged beast that attacked us in the forest all those years ago.'

'Sentient?' asked Zahariel. 'I suppose that depends on what you think the term means. I think the beast was intelligent, yes. I really believe it. But was it truly sentient? I remember Brother Amadis saying that the true test of sentience was whether a creature was capable of planning towards the future, and using reason to solve its problems.'

'So what do you think then, cousin?' asked Nemiel. 'Do you think the creature was sentient or not?'

'I don't believe I know. I think it's too difficult for a human mind to understand the workings of an inhuman one, but I can only tell what it felt like to fight it.'

'And what did it feel like?' asked Nemiel.

'It felt like the beast was a spider and I was a fly.'

ZAHARIEL RAN THE oily rag through the barrel of his pistol, clearing it of the residue of repeated firing. The gun was starting to pull to the left, and it had let him down in the firing drills with the rest of the supplicants.

When he had pointed out the weapon's fault, the knight armourer had simply recommended that he clean the barrel thoroughly before trying again. The implicit insult in the armourer's comment had angered Zahariel, but he was still just a supplicant and had no recourse to answer back to a full knight.

Instead, he had politely thanked the knight armourer, and returned to the dormitories to break out his cleaning kit and meticulously clean every moving part of the weapon.

Not that he expected it to do any good. He suspected that the imperfection with the weapon was more to do with the weapon's age than any impurities lodged in the barrel, for he was as fastidious with his weapons as he was with his armour, more so, in fact.

'The armourer told you to clean your weapon more thoroughly, eh?' said Nemiel, watching as Zahariel angrily sat on his cot bed, lifted another component of his pistol and began cleaning it with vigorous strokes of the cloth.

'As if I don't keep it clean enough already!' said Zahariel.

'You never know,' said Nemiel, 'it might help.'

'I keep this weapon cleaner than anything else I own. You know that.'

'True, but the armourers know what they're talking about.'

'You're taking their side?'

'Side?' said Nemiel. 'Since when did this become about sides?'

'Never mind,' snapped Zahariel.

'No, come on, what did you mean?'

Zahariel sighed and put down the breech and the brush he had been cleaning it with.

'I mean that you seem to be relishing this.'

'Relishing what?'

'That you managed to beat me in the firing drills,' said Zahariel.

'Is that what you think, cousin? That I need your gun to fail for me to beat you?'

'That's not it, Nemiel,' said Zahariel. 'I just mean–'

'No, I understand,' said his cousin, rising from the cot bed and making his way down the central corridor of the dormitory chamber. 'You think you're better than me. I see that now.'

'No, that's not it all!' protested Zahariel, but his cousin was already walking away, his pride ruffled. Zahariel knew he should go after Nemiel, but part of him was glad he had finally given voice to the irritation that his cousin took such relish in watching him fail.

He put the disagreement from his mind and continued cleaning his weapon, head down, putting the background noise of the dormitory from his mind as he focused his efforts on making his pistol shine as good as new.

A shadow fell across him, and he sighed.

'Look, Nemiel,' he said, 'I'm sorry, but I need to get this done.'

'It can wait,' said a sonorous voice, and he looked up to see Brother Amadis standing at the foot of his cot bed, dressed in full armour and white surplice. Amadis carried his winged helm in the crook of his arm, and his black cloak was gathered at his left shoulder.

Zahariel dropped the magazine feed onto his blanket and sprang to his feet.

'Brother Amadis, my apologies, I thought...' he began.

Amadis waved away his apology and said, 'Leave the pistol and come with me.'

Without waiting, Amadis turned away and marched down the length of the room, each of the supplicants in the dormitory watching with awed faces as the heroic knight passed them.

Zahariel smoothed down his robe and quickly followed Brother Amadis towards the door. The knight was marching quickly, and Zahariel struggled to keep up.

'Where are we going?' he asked.

'It is time for you to move deeper within the Order,' said Brother Amadis. 'It is time for you to see the Lord Cypher.'

THE LORD CYPHER.

It was not a name: it was a title of office given to the man responsible for preserving the Order's traditions, and Zahariel felt nerve-wracking fear at the thought of being brought before the old man.

Might he offend the Lord Cypher through some inadvertent breach of the Order's protocols? Might he have forgotten some ancient formality when presented to him that would forever dash his chance of ever becoming a knight?

Brother Amadis led him deeper into the heart of the monastery. Their path took them down into the dark catacombs that riddled the rock the fortress was built upon. They passed darkened cellars, forgotten chambers and ancient cells as they journeyed ever downwards and ever deeper into the ground.

The air was cold, and Zahariel saw his breath feather the air before him as he followed Brother Amadis into the darkness. The knight carried a flaming brand, the leaping firelight reflecting from the glistening rock of the tunnel they travelled along. Intricate carvings decorated the walls, depicting scenes of war and heroism that reached back many thousands of years.

Who had carved them, Zahariel could not say, but each one was rendered as a masterpiece, though none now travelled to see them.

At last their path took them into a long, vaulted chamber of dripping echoes and orange light. The walls were fashioned from enamelled bricks that reflected the light of the torch and threw back hundreds of reflections from the many candles spread throughout the chamber in a wide, spiral pattern.

The Lord Cypher stood at the centre of the spiral, his hood pulled up, and his surplice dark, as tradition dictated. A golden hilted sword protruded from beneath his robes, and his gnarled fingers were curled around the weapon.

'Welcome, boy,' said Lord Cypher. 'It seems your peers judge you worthy to move upwards through our Order. Deep chasms lie beneath this rock, boy – deep chasms and deep places long forgotten by the world above. Mysteries lie entombed within this world and secret places that only the wise may know of. You know nothing of this, of course, but here you will take the first step on the road to knowledge.'

'I understand,' said Zahariel.

'You understand nothing!' snapped Lord Cypher. 'Only by understanding where you have come from can you understand what will be. Now begin to walk the spiral.'

Zahariel looked over to Brother Amadis.

'Don't look to him, boy,' said Lord Cypher. 'Do as you are told.'

Zahariel nodded and began following the path of the candles, walking purposefully, but carefully.

'Though our Order is nowhere near as ancient as many of the other knightly orders of Caliban, it has accumulated an impressive array of customs in the course of its history. I am the Lord Cypher of the Order. Do you understand what that means?'

'I do,' said Zahariel. 'The man appointed to the role of Lord Cypher is expected to police those customs. He ensures that the Order's rituals are preserved, and advises on matters of protocol as well as officiating at ceremonies.'

'And my name, boy? Do you know it?'

'No, my lord.'

'Why not?'

'It is forbidden to know your name.'

'Why?'

Zahariel paused. 'I… I am not sure. I know that no matter the identity of the man appointed to the position of Lord Cypher, it is forbidden to call him by his real name once he takes up its mantle. I do not know why.'

'Indeed. *Why* is often the most interesting question, but often the one not asked. Where when, how and what are mere window dressing. Why is always the most important question, would you not agree?'

Zahariel nodded as he continued walking the spiral. 'I agree.'

'I have a variety of arcane titles: Master of Mysteries, Keeper of the Truth, the Lord of the Keys, or else simply Lord Cypher. Do you know why this is so, boy?'

'No, my lord. It is simply the way things have always been with the Order.'

'Exactly,' said Lord Cypher. '*It is the way things have always been with the Order*. The value of tradition is that it guides us, no matter that the real reasons may have been forgotten. Beliefs and actions that have seen us prosper in the past shall serve us well in the present and the future. I have held this position for over twenty years, and though the role is usually given to one of the Order's more venerable knights, as a younger man, I was chosen with the hope of infusing new blood into the role. Above all else, it is my task to maintain the Order's customs as a living tradition, rather than allowing them to degenerate into ossified relics.'

Zahariel listened to the old man's voice, its hypnotic rhythms lulling him into slowing his walk around the spiral. Soon he would be standing before the old man, his steps carrying him in tighter and tighter circles around the candles.

'Yet my role is one of contradictions,' continued Lord Cypher. 'It is one of the most senior positions within the Order, and yet I hold very little real power. In many ways, my role as guardian of the Order's traditions is symbolic. If that be the case, then who really holds the power of our Order? Quickly boy, before you reach the centre.'

Zahariel forced himself to concentrate, working through the obvious answers as his steps carried him inexorably towards the centre of the spiral.

The Lion and Luther seemed obvious candidates, but then he remembered something Brother Amadis had once said, and the answer was clear to him.

'It is the masters of instruction, men like Master Ramiel, who keep the customs of the Order alive,' he said.

'Good,' said Lord Cypher. 'Where then does my power lie?'

'That you are close to the Order's senior masters?' suggested Zahariel, as he came to a halt before Lord Cypher. 'Your opinions can always find an ear among those in power.'

'Very good,' said Lord Cypher, his face hidden in the shadows of his hood. 'You kept your answers short and that is good. You'd be surprised how many candidates witter on incessantly during this walk of the spiral.'

'Nervousness, I suppose,' said Zahariel.

'Indeed,' agreed Lord Cypher, 'it makes men talk too much, when it would be more impressive if they knew the value of silence and demonstrated how to use it. Your terseness gave you an aura of confidence, even when I know you did not feel it.'

That was certainly true, for Zahariel had felt his heart drumming wildly in his chest all through the walk, terrified of making a mistake, terrified he might stumble and fail in this test. Either his terror had not shown or the Lord Cypher's poor eyesight had caused him to miss it. Whatever the truth, Zahariel accepted the old man's compliment in the spirit it was offered.

'I thank you, Lord Cypher,' he said, bowing slightly. 'If I was confident, though, it is because I have been well-trained by my master.'

'Yes, you are one of Master Ramiel's students. That explains it. Ramiel has always been known for his good work. Did you know he trained under Master Sarientus, the same man who trained both Lion El'Jonson and Luther?'

'No, my lord, I did not know that.'

'Tradition, boy, learn it. Know it and understand it. Without it we are nothing.'

'I will, my lord,' promised Zahariel.

'Maybe you will, but I see that you still have questions, eh?'

'I suppose,' admitted Zahariel, unsure as to whether he should voice such doubts. 'I don't quite understand what I have achieved by walking this spiral and answering your questions.'

'For yourself, nothing,' said Lord Cypher, 'but we know more of you now. At each stage of a supplicant's training we must decide whether or not to continue it and whether any such trainees have the mark of greatness that merits special attention.'

'Do I merit such attention?'

Lord Cypher laughed. 'That is not for me to say, boy. Another will decide that.'

'Who?' asked Zahariel, suddenly bold.

'Me,' said a rich, heavily toned voice of strength and power from the shadows.

Zahariel turned as a giant in a hooded white surplice stepped into the light of the candles, though he would have sworn that no figure had been standing there a moment ago.

The figure pulled back his hood, but Zahariel needed no further confirmation of the man's identity.

'My lord,' he said.

'Follow me,' said Lion El'Jonson.

LORD CYPHER RETREATED into the shadows as the Lion marched around the circumference of the chamber. Brother Amadis bowed his head as the mighty warrior passed him, and Zahariel was seized by sudden indecision.

After Lord Cypher's monologue on the value of tradition, should he walk the path of the spiral in reverse or should he simply follow the Lion?

The decision was made for him when Brother Amadis said, 'Best be quick, Zahariel. The Lion doesn't like to be kept waiting on nights like this.'

'Nights like what?' asked Zahariel as he made his way after the Lion.

'Nights where there are revelations to be made,' said Amadis.

Unsure of what that meant, Zahariel moved past Amadis and hurried to catch up with the Lion, who appeared to be retracing the steps they had taken to reach this place. The Lion did not speak, but followed an unerring path upwards, along smoothly chiselled passageways, rough caverns and winding stairs hacked into the rock. Each step took them higher and higher, and where Brother Amadis had led him into the depths, it seemed the Lion was leading him into the heavens.

Zahariel's breath heaved in his lungs, his legs tired after such climbing, though of course the Lion's stride never faltered or changed in pace, despite the length and speed of their climb.

Their climb led them into a narrow cylinder of curved bricks, within which was a tightly wound screw staircase that was barely wide enough for the Lion's shoulders.

After another ten minutes, Zahariel could feel a chill breeze from above, and scented the fragrant aroma of the deep forests. He knew they must be close to the top of the tower. Ghostly moonlight grew in luminosity, and at last, worn by the journey, Zahariel emerged onto the top of the tower, a wide space high above the fortress monastery, ringed with regular crenellations along the parapet.

The tower was quite useless for defence, too slender and tall to play a part in any siege the Order might find itself subject to, but ideal for an eagle-eyed watchman or stargazer.

It was a clear night. The sky above Zahariel was a black, perfect dome studded with a thousand points of light. Zahariel stared up at the constellations and felt a deep, abiding sensation of peace that quite overcame his exhaustion.

He supposed it was a feeling born of satisfaction. For many years he had exerted every ounce of his will and strained every sinew in the hope of becoming a knight. Tonight, he could be one step closer to achieving his ambition.

'It is good to look up at the stars,' said the Lion, finally breaking his long silence. 'At times like this, a man needs to take stock of his life. I find there is no better place to take stock than beneath the stars.'

The Lion smiled, and Zahariel found the smile dazzling.

It was clear that the Lion was trying to put him at his ease, but Zahariel found it almost impossible to talk to him as though he was any other man. Jonson was too big, his presence too imposing.

A man could no more ignore his extraordinary nature than he could ignore the wind and the rain, or the transition from day to night. There was something similarly elemental about the Lion.

Lion El'Jonson was the apotheosis of all humanity's dreams for itself. He was perfection given human form, like the first example of a new race of man.

'The cleansing of the forest is entering its final stage, Zahariel. Did you know that?'

'No, my lord, I had thought the campaign was likely to continue for some time.'

'No, not at all,' said the Lion, his brow furrowing slightly, though Zahariel could not be sure if it was in amusement or contemplation. 'According to our best estimates, there are perhaps a dozen or so great beasts left in total, certainly no more than twenty, and they are all in the Northwilds. We have scoured every other region of Caliban and cleared out the beasts that were hiding there. Only the Northwilds are left.'

'But that would mean the campaign is nearly over.'

'Nearly,' Jonson said. 'At most it should take another three months. Then Caliban will finally be clear of the great beasts. Incidentally, you realise Amadis has asked that you be recorded in the annals of the Order as having assisted in slaying one of the last of them? A fearsome creature as well, from all accounts. Though Amadis killed it, you should be proud of your actions in the fight. You saved the lives of many of your brothers.'

'Not all of them,' said Zahariel, remembering Pallian's screams as the beast tore him apart. 'I couldn't save them all.'

'That is something every warrior must get used to,' said the Lion. 'No matter how skilfully you lead your warriors, some of them will die.'

'It was only a matter of luck that I didn't die,' Zahariel said, 'the sheerest chance.'

'A good warrior will always take advantage of chance,' said Jonson, looking up at the sky. 'He should adapt to the changing circumstances of battle. War is all about opportunity, Zahariel. To be victorious, we must always be ready to take hold of opportunities as they arise. You showed initiative in fighting that beast. More than that, you demonstrated excellence, precisely as the *Verbatim* defines these things and sets them out as our ultimate aim. We cannot know what mysteries the universe holds, or what challenges we may face in the future. All we can do is live our lives to the fullest extent we can, and cultivate the virtue of trying to achieve excellence in all things. When we go to war, it should be as master warriors. When we make peace, we should be equally adept. It is not good for human beings to accept second best. Our lives are short. We should make merit of them while we can.'

Abruptly coming to silence, the Lion continued to stare up at the night sky, as Zahariel stood beside him.

'I wonder what is in the stars?' the Lion said. 'The old tales say there are thousands, perhaps millions of planets out there, just like Caliban. They say Terra is one of them. It is strange, don't you think, that every child born of Caliban knows the name Terra? We count it as the source and wellspring of our culture, but if the tales are true it has been thousands of years since we had contact with that source. But what if the tales are false? What if Terra is a myth, a fable invented by our forefathers to account for our place in the cosmos? What if our fathers' tales are lies?'

'It would be terrible,' Zahariel said. He felt a shiver and told himself the night was growing colder. 'People take the existence of Terra for granted. If it all turned out to be a myth, we might start to doubt everything. We would lose our moorings. We would not know what to believe.'

'True, but in other ways it would free us. We would no longer need to be responsible to the past. The present and the future would be our only boundaries. Take the current campaign against the great beasts as an example. You are young, Zahariel. You cannot be aware of the bitter arguments, the threats and the recriminations that were directed towards me when I first advanced the plans for my campaign. All too often, I found that the causes of these objections were rooted in some dated custom that had long ago worn out its welcome.

'Tradition is a fine ideal, but not when it serves as a shackle on our future endeavours. If it wasn't for Luther and his fine oratory, I doubt the plan would ever have been approved. It is the same with so many issues that confront us today. The diehards and the sticks-in-the-mud oppose us at every step, irrespective of the value of the plans I put forward. They always make reference to the past, to tradition, as though our past was so filled with shining glories that we might actually want to preserve it forever. But I am not interested in the past, Zahariel. I think only of the future.'

Again, the Lion paused. Standing beside him, Zahariel wondered what Lord Cypher would make of this speech decrying the value of tradition. Might this be another test, one designed to see whether he would simply acquiesce to what the Lion was saying or stand up for the values of tradition.

As he looked upon the Lion's countenance, he saw a strange intensity to the way he stared up at the sky, as if he loved and hated the stars at the same time.

'Sometimes, I wish it was in my power to wipe the past away,' the Lion said. 'I wish there was no myth of Terra. I wish Caliban had no past. Look at a man without a past, and you will see a free man. It is always easier to build when you build from scratch. Then again, I look at the stars and I think I am too hasty. I look to the stars and I wonder what is out there. How many undiscovered lands? How many new challenges? How bright and hopeful might our future be if we could make it to the stars?'

'Such a thing seems unlikely,' said Zahariel, 'for the moment, at least.'

'You are right,' said the Lion, 'but what if the stars were to come to us?'

'I don't understand,' said Zahariel.

'Truthfully? Nor do I,' said the Lion, 'but on nights when the stars are bright, I dream of a golden light, and of all the stars of the heavens coming down to Caliban and changing our world forever.'

'The stars come down to Caliban?' said Zahariel. 'Do you think it means anything?'

The Lion shrugged. 'Who knows? I feel I ought to know its relevance, but every time I think I sense a connection to the golden light, it fades and leaves me alone in the dark.'

Then, as though shaking off the last of such a dream the Lion said, 'In any case, the stars are denied to us, so we will build the future here on Caliban. Still, if we are to be limited in that way, then we will not allow it to limit our vision. If we are only able to build our lives on Caliban, without access to the stars, then we will make this world a paradise.'

The Lion extended an arm, sweeping it in a broad gesture across the night-time panorama of dark forest and treetops below the walls of Aldurukh.

'This will be our paradise, Zahariel,' the Lion told him. 'This is where we will build a bright new future. The campaign against the great beasts is only the first step. We will create a golden age. We will make the world anew. Does that sound a noble aim to you?'

'It does, my lord,' said Zahariel, the words coming out as a reverential whisper.

'An aim worth committing our lives to?' asked the Lion. 'I raise this question, here and now, because of your youth. It is the young who will build this future, Zahariel. You have shown promise. You have the potential to be a true son of Caliban, a crusader, not just against the beasts, but against every other evil that ails our people. Does that seem a worthy purpose?'

'It does,' Zahariel replied.

'Good. I am glad. I will look to see how you perform in the years ahead, Zahariel. As I say, I think you have potential. I will be interested to see you live up to it. Now, you have been kept from your duties long enough, I think.'

The Lion inclined his head, as though listening to the slight sounds drifting from the forest below. 'I should return also, it is not good form if I am away for too long. People notice. My place in the Order is as much about forging bonds of brotherhood among the knights as it is being wise and canny in matters of war.'

A moment later, the Lion was gone, disappearing into the tower like a banished shadow. There was nothing showy or contrived about this sudden disappearance, for the habits of stealth simply came easily to Lion El'Jonson in a way that only a man who had lived alone as a youth in the forests of Caliban could know.

With the Lion gone, Zahariel looked at the stars high overhead.

For a while, he thought of what the Lion had said. He thought about the stars, about Terra, about the necessity to build a better world on Caliban. He thought about the golden age that Jonson had promised.

Zahariel thought about these things, and knew that with men like Luther and Lion El'Jonson to guide them, the Order could not fail to achieve this utopian vision of the future.

Zahariel had faith in the Lion.

He had faith in Luther.

Together, these two men – these giants – could only change Caliban for the better.

He was sure of it.

It occurred to Zahariel that he had been blessed with good fortune of the kind few men were granted in their lives. No one could choose the era in which they would be born, and where the majority of men struggled through times not unlike the times their fathers had known, Zahariel had been lucky.

As he saw it, he had been born in an age of great and momentous change, a time in which a man could be part of something bigger than himself, a time when he could devote his efforts in line with his ideals and hope to make an achievement of real significance.

Zahariel could not see precisely what the future might hold, he could not see his destiny written in the stars, but he had no fear of what it might be.

The universe, it seemed to him, was a place of wonder.

He looked to the future and was unafraid.

SIX

THE CRUSADE AGAINST the great beasts was to continue for another year before the last bastion of monsters was ready to be assailed. The dense, tangled and lethal forests of the dark Northwilds remained to be purged of the monsters, yet this was the one place the warriors of the Order and its allies had not yet entered.

In part, this was due to the due to the difficulty of mounting any organised, systematic hunt within its depths. Much of the forest was so dense as to be virtually impenetrable to riders, and even the hardy warriors of the Ravenwing would not ride within such places unless called to do so by their masters.

Settlements existed within the Northwilds, heavily defended villages with high walls built upon great rock plains or within the depths of wide hills, but these were few and far between, and populated by resentful people who bemoaned their lot in life without ever daring to improve it.

In truth, the real reason the crusade had not yet ventured into the Northwilds was the antipathy of the Knights of Lupus.

A knightly brotherhood known for its scholars and great libraries, the Knights of Lupus had vehemently opposed the idea of any campaign against the beasts, and had spoken out against Luther and Lion El'Jonson many years earlier.

Alone of the other orders who had voted against Jonson's proposal to rid the forests of the great beasts, the Knights of Lupus had refused to go with the will of the majority once the matter had been decided. Instead, they had made warlike noises, threatening to launch their own counter-campaign of war against the Order and its allies.

In the end, Luther broached a compromise. The details of the agreement he made had never been revealed, but whatever terms had been offered, the Knights of Lupus had retreated to their mountain fastness in the Northwilds, and took no action against the Order.

For ten years, the Knights of Lupus had watched from their fortress as Jonson's campaign achieved victory after victory. Region by region, the great beasts were cleared from the forests of Caliban.

As the years went by and the campaign came closer to realising Jonson's ambitions, the minds of most people on Caliban turned to the beckoning of a golden age.

The Lion's campaign had progressed to the very border of the Northwilds, long a Knights of Lupus stronghold, and the only region of Caliban left where the great beasts still existed.

Almost inevitably, when the Order entered the Northwilds there would be conflict.

* * *

A GROUP OF armed suppliants gathered in the centre of the training halls in the pattern of an outward facing circle, their swords extended before them in a defensive posture. Zahariel stood in the centre of the circle, back to back with Nemiel, while another class of suppliants surrounded them and watched their sword drills.

Brother Amadis walked a slow circuit of the circle, his hands laced behind his back as he oversaw this latest training session of the Order's suppliants.

The suppliants gathered around the circle were a year or so younger than the students forming the circle and were all armed with wooden training swords. Though blunt, each had a lead bar at its core, which would make any impact painful in the extreme.

'You have trained in this manner for years,' said Amadis, addressing the younger suppliants, 'and you appreciate the defensive strength of the circle, but you do not appreciate its symbolic strength. Who within the circle can tell these students why we fight in this manner?'

As so often happened, Nemiel answered first.

'By standing in a circle, each warrior is able to protect the man to his left. It's a classic defensive formation to be used when heavily outnumbered.'

'Indeed so, Nemiel,' said Amadis, 'but why the inner circle?'

This time, Zahariel answered, saying, 'A circle is stronger with another circle inside it. It's an old battle doctrine of Caliban.'

'Correct,' said Amadis. 'The idea of concentric circles, each inside the other, has been the basis for the defences of all the great and abiding fortress monasteries of Caliban. By creating an inner circle to guard and watch over the wider grouping of warriors on the outer circle, the defence cannot be breached. Now attack!'

The younger supplicants threw themselves at the circle, their wooden blades stabbing and chopping towards the older boys. The boys in the outer circle fought well, deflecting the blows of their attackers with a skill borne of an extra year's training, but they were outnumbered three to one and inevitably some strikes hit home.

Zahariel watched the battle unfold with clinical precision, turning on the spot with Nemiel always at his back as they struck out at any potential breaches of the circle. Swords clashed and clattered for ten minutes, but not a single breach had been made in the outer circle.

Amadis shouted names as he declared boys 'dead', and those boys limped from the circle holding bruised and broken arms, and nursing their shame, as the outer circle drew closer to keep their line intact.

Zahariel stabbed and cut as the younger supplicants threatened to overwhelm them and Nemiel did likewise on his blind side. The bout continued for another fifteen minutes, with no sign of the circle formation breaking, and then Amadis called an end to the session.

Both Zahariel and Nemiel were drenched in sweat, the battle having taken its toll on their reserves of strength. Fighting at such intensity for any length of time was difficult, but fighting at the inner circle was particularly draining.

Brother Amadis walked amongst the exhausted supplicants as he said, 'Now you see the benefit of the inner circle and the strength we gain from its presence. Remember this when you go into battle and you cannot fail. It is a truism, but alone we are weak, together we are strong. Each of you will one day face battle and if you cannot look to your brother and know without thinking that you can trust him, then you are lost. Only when such bonds are ironclad do they mean anything, for the moment that trust is not instantly reciprocated the circle breaks and you are dead. Dismissed!'

The supplicants picked themselves up from the stone floor of the training hall, in ones and twos, wearing linen towels draped around their necks, and nursing tired and battered limbs.

Nemiel wiped the sweat from his face with his sleeve and said, 'That was a tough one and no mistake.'

Zahariel nodded, too tired to answer.

'He's working us hard, eh?' continued Nemiel. 'You'd think we were actually about to go into battle or something.'

'You never know,' said Zahariel at last, 'we might be. The representatives of the Knights of Lupus are due to arrive later today, and if what I hear is true, we might indeed be making war soon.'

'On the Knights of Lupus?' asked Attias, coming over with one of his notebooks tucked under his arm.

'It's what I hear,' said Zahariel.

'You got all that Brother Amadis said?' remarked Nemiel as Eliath joined them.

'I did,' said Attias, 'give or take a word or two.'

'Maybe if you practised more swordplay instead of scribbling in your books you wouldn't have left us open to attack,' said Eliath, though there was no malice in the words, only good-humoured banter.

'And maybe if you weren't so fat, you'd have been able to avoid their attacks.'

The boys smiled at the familiar jibes, though they were spoken in jest rather than with malice. In the year since the attack of the winged beast in the forest, the four of them had passed beyond the rancour that had divided them and had become fast friends, the shared near-death experience bringing them closer than anything else could.

Attias had filled out into a fine figure of a boy, with handsome features, broad shoulders and taut muscles corded around his limbs. Eliath was still the biggest of them, his muscles bulging and powerful, any hint of fat long since burned from his slab-like frame, though he was still the least agile of them.

'Seriously though, you think we might make war on the Knights of Lupus?' asked Attias.

'I don't know, maybe,' said Zahariel, wishing he had not brought the subject up. Brother Amadis had told him that Lord Sartana of the Knights of Lupus was travelling to Aldurukh to protest at the Order's knights venturing into the Northwilds, and though he had not been told to keep the information to himself, he still felt like he was betraying a confidence in sharing it with his brothers.

'Zahariel, Nemiel, get cleaned up and report to my chambers in fifteen minutes. Full dress surplice, weapons and ceremonial attire.'

Both boys looked up in puzzlement, surprised at the arrival of Brother Amadis.

'Sir?' said Nemiel. 'What's going on?'

'The Lion wants the best of our supplicants on display when Lord Sartana walks into the Circle Chamber, and you're it. Now hurry, he's already here and apparently in no mood to dally. Move!'

ZAHARIEL SHIFTED NERVOUSLY from foot to foot as he and Nemiel stood at the edge of the plinth at the centre of the Circle Chamber. They had marched in with Brother Amadis at their head a few minutes ago, thrilled and not a little honoured to have been allowed to follow him in through the western Cloister Gate.

The higher entrances to the chamber were for the lower ranked members of the Order, and only the senior knights were permitted to enter the chamber through the Cloister Gates.

Normally, supplicants and those lower in rank than a full knight were forced to enter and sit in the benches high above, but the senior members of the Order had granted special dispensation for this occasion.

The corridors and chambers of Aldurukh were fairly buzzing with activity, their little group passing knights, squires and supplicants rushing from place to place on no doubt vital errands in preparation for the arrival of Lord Sartana.

Ceremonial banners were being dusted off and hung from the roof of the chamber, the warlike banners of red and crimson replaced with those that recalled a legendary past, and conjured images of brotherhood and confraternity.

Robed and hooded members of the Order were filling the stone benches around the centre of the chamber, though no supplicants other than those accompanying senior brothers of the Order were present.

'Is this Sartana really that important?' whispered Nemiel, careful to keep his voice soft, for the Circle Chamber's acoustics were incredible.

Zahariel nodded. 'I think so. He's the most senior member of the Knights of Lupus.'

'I thought they had pretty much died out?'

'No,' said Zahariel, 'though they are much reduced from their former glory, it's true.'

'What happened to them?'

Zahariel thought back to what he'd heard the seneschals talking about below the halls and chambers of the noble knights in the years after he had first joined the Order.

'They were opposed to the Lion's campaign against the great beasts, and retreated to their mountain stronghold while the Order and its allies began cleansing the forests. I heard that a significant number of their knights and supplicants defected to join the Order when they saw how successful the campaign was.'

'They left their own brothers?' asked Nemiel in surprise.

'So they say,' agreed Zahariel. 'I imagine they must have been hard and joyless years for them, since the recruitment of new supplicants dwindled to barely more than a handful each season. Within a few years, perhaps another decade at most, the Knights of Lupus faced the real prospect that they would cease to be viable as a knightly order.'

'How sad,' said Nemiel, 'to be on the brink of oblivion, not through glorious heroic death or epic battle, but by obsolescence.'

'Don't write them off yet,' said Brother Amadis, appearing at their shoulders. 'There's never more life in a beast than when it thinks it's cornered.'

'Brother Amadis, I have a question,' said Nemiel.

'Yes? Go on, but hurry, Sartana will be here soon.'

'Zahariel tells me that the Knights of Lupus have almost no supplicants, that their numbers dwindle.'

'That's not a question,' pointed out Zahariel.

'I know, I'm getting there,' said Nemiel. 'What I mean to say is that is it not a little… well, brash to flaunt the Order's supplicants before Lord Sartana like this?'

Amadis smiled and said, 'Very perceptive of you, young Nemiel.'

'So why do it?'

'It is a good question, so I will indulge you,' said Amadis. 'In all likelihood, Lord Sartana does not come with conciliation in mind. I believe the Lion and Luther wish to make a tacit display that will speak of our strength in the years ahead.'

'And if Lord Sartana can be made to think that he cannot oppose us, he will more readily agree to our warriors campaigning in the Northwilds,' completed Zahariel.

'Something like that,' agreed Amadis. 'Now be quiet, we are about to begin.'

Zahariel turned his gaze to the eastern Cloister Gate as two lines of hooded banner bearers entered, their faces cloaked in shadow and their steps ponderous. They parted, with grim solemnity, as they reached the edge of the circle, and followed its circumference until they formed a ring of banners around the plinth.

Each banner was planted in a cup sunk into the floor, and the banner bearers knelt behind them, heads bowed as the masters of the Order entered.

The Lion and Luther marched into the chamber, resplendent in black plate and flowing white cloaks that hung from bronze pins at their shoulders. The Lion dwarfed Luther as always, but to Zahariel's eyes, both were cut from the same magnificent cloth. The Lion's expression was grim, while Luther's was open, but Zahariel could see the tension etched in the tight lines around his eyes and jaw.

The knights of the Order gathered in the benches stood and banged their fists on their breastplates at the sight of their most heroic brothers, the noise deafening as each knight displayed the proper respect for his betters.

The senior knights of the Order accompanied the Lion and Luther, including Lord Cypher and several of the highest ranked battle knights, the warriors skilled in leading armies and marshalling great numbers of troops. It seemed this was to be more than a tacit display of strength, but a very real show of martial might.

A warrior in gleaming bronze plate armour and a long wolfskin cloak stood alongside Luther. The skull and upper jaw of the lupine beast was fashioned into the peak of the warrior's helmet, its front paws draped over the pauldrons at his shoulders.

This then was Lord Sartana, a powerful man with age-weathered features and a drooping, silver moustache. His eyes were heavy lidded and grey, and his expression one of belligerence. He was clearly all too aware of the none-too-subtle display of the Order's strength. A trio of wolf-cloaked warriors accompanied him, each with a similarly bushy moustache and each older than many of the most senior knights of the Order.

The warriors reached the centre of the circle, and the Lion raised his hands for silence, which was duly delivered. Zahariel spared an excited glance at Nemiel at the sight of so many senior knights in such proximity.

The Lion turned to Lord Sartana and extended his hand, 'I welcome you to the Circle Chamber, where brother meets brother without rank or station, where all are equal. Welcome, brother.'

To Zahariel's ears the words sounded flat and devoid of meaning, as though the Lion had swallowed the bitterest ashes to speak them.

Lord Sartana clearly thought so too and disdained to accept the proffered hand. 'I asked for a private meeting, my Lord Jonson, not... this!'

'The Order is a place of honesty, Lord Sartana,' said Luther, his voice conciliatory and soothing. 'We have no secrets, and wish to be transparent in our dealings with you.'

'Then why these blatant theatrics?' snapped Sartana. 'You think I am some simpleton to be impressed by your parade of new recruits and senior knights?'

'These are no theatrics,' said the Lion, 'they are reminders of your brotherhood's status on Caliban.'

'Our status?' said Lord Sartana. 'So you agreed to this meeting simply to humiliate me, is that it?'

Luther stepped between the two warriors, eager to defuse the hostile atmosphere before things degenerated to a point where weapons might be drawn.

'My lords,' said Luther, again modulating his voice to sound entirely reasonable and placating. 'Such talk is beneath us. We are here so that all may witness the fairness and justice of our talk. It must be seen that there is no dishonesty between us.'

'Then let us speak of how your warriors have violated the treaty between us,' said Sartana.

'Violated the treaty?' snapped the Lion. 'What treaty? There was no treaty.'

'Assurances were given many years ago,' said Sartana, 'by you, Luther. When you journeyed to our fortress, you claimed that Jonson gave an iron assurance that he would keep his warriors away from the Northwilds. As we both know, that has not been the case.'

'No,' said the Lion, an edge of anger entering his voice, 'it has not.' Zahariel wondered that any man could stand before such a threat. 'Your men slaughtered a group of our hunters. Men with families were killed by fully armed knights, who sent a lone survivor back with the butchered bodies of his comrades.'

'Those men had come to map the valleys on the edge of the Northwilds.'

'The edges of your territories are home to beasts!' said the Lion. 'Beasts that still ravage our lands. The town of Endriago alone has suffered nearly two hundred dead at the hands of a beast! The time has come to finish the job and destroy the last of the great beasts.'

At the mention of Endriago, Zahariel felt Brother Amadis stiffen his stance, and saw that his hands had drawn into clenched fists.

'You might clear the great beasts from the rest of Caliban,' said Sartana, 'but the Northwilds, and the lands of the Knights of Lupus were to be sacrosanct. We were promised that our lands would be a haven, and that the beasts there would be left in peace. This agreement had the force of a treaty. By sending your warriors into our lands you are an oath breaker!'

'Talk sense, man,' said the Lion. 'There was never any assurance made about leaving the Northwilds alone. What kind of sense would it make for us to do so? What would be the virtue of slaying the beasts everywhere else on Caliban, only to leave a pocket of the creatures still remaining? No, if there was any violation, it was by the Knights of Lupus when they killed the Order's warriors. All the rest of it, these falsehoods and lies, are simply a flimsy pretext to justify your actions.'

'Then you set the stage for war, Lord Jonson,' said Sartana.

'If that is what it takes to free Caliban of the beasts, then I do, Lord Sartana,' said the Lion, and Zahariel could hear a fierce relish in his tone, as though goading Sartana into a war had been his intention all along.

'I will not stop in the pursuit of my goal of ridding Caliban of the beasts,' said the Lion, 'and if your warriors try to stop me, it will be the end of them. Your order has fewer warriors and most have not set foot from your libraries in years. Do you really think you can stop me?'

'Probably not,' admitted Sartana.

'Then why stand against me?'

'Because in your monomaniacal quest to destroy, you will not be satisfied until you have all Caliban under your heel,' said Lord Sartana. 'The Knights of Lupus do not wish to be subject to your decrees. Now if this farce of a "discussion" is at an end, I will take my leave and return to my brethren.'

Without waiting for any dismissal, Lord Sartana turned on his heel and marched from the Circle Chamber, his wolf-cloaked acolytes following him.

A thunderous silence fell on the assembled knights of the Order at such audacity, each warrior looking to his neighbour as if to confirm that they understood the import of the words that had passed between the Lion and Lord Sartana, that they were as good as at war with the Brotherhood of Lupus.

Brother Amadis broke the silence, stepping from his position at the edge of the circle and calling out to the Lion.

'My Lord Jonson!' cried Amadis. 'Is it true? Is Endriago attacked by a beast?'

At first, Zahariel wondered if the Lion had heard the question, for long moments passed before he turned to face Amadis. His face was set in stone, and Zahariel felt a shudder of fear pass along his spine at the look of warlike fury etched into his features.

Then, as though a ray of sunlight passed over his face, the vengeful anger was gone, and a look of deep concern took its place.

'Brother Amadis,' said the Lion, 'I'm afraid it is true. Word reached us only yesterday. A beast has slain a great many of Endriago's people, though no one knows yet what manner of creature stalks the dark forest.'

'Endriago is the place of my birth, Lord Jonson,' said Amadis. 'I must avenge the deaths it has caused to my people.'

The Lion nodded and listened to Luther's whispered comment, as Amadis dropped to one knee.

'My Lord Jonson,' said Amadis, 'I declare a quest against the Beast of Endriago.'

SIX

Afterwards, Zahariel would always think of it as his finest moment. It was not that the years that followed would be short on glories, far from it. He would win his share of battles. He would be acclaimed and lauded by his fellows.

He would be honoured by the Lion.

He would know all these things and more. Yet, somehow, the moment he cherished most occurred on his homeworld of Caliban in the days before the Emperor came to their planet.

It was in the time before angels, in a time when he had been a young man on the verge of adulthood. Perhaps his age would play a part in making the recollection of those days more vivid in his mind later.

At the time, he had been just two weeks shy of his fifteenth birthday. The fact of his youth would add an extra gloss of glamour to his reminiscences. It would make his achievement seem more worthy somehow, more memorable. With his first step over the threshold

of manhood, he had braved horrors and endured hardships that most men could never, nor would ever,
survive.

One element would certainly set this moment apart
from his later triumphs. He had not yet been made an
angel. He had not yet become Astartes. It would make
what happened all the more remarkable. It was one
thing for a superhuman to succeed in such circumstances, it was quite another for an ordinary human
being to do so, especially one who was only halfway
through his teens.

Perhaps it was something else.

Perhaps, in the end, he would treasure the moment
simply because it spoke well of his character. After his
transformation into an angel, most of his memories of
the days when he was still a man would become dull
and hazy.

There were thousands of moments, important ones,
he would forget altogether. He would have difficulty
remembering the faces of his parents, his sisters, the
friends of his childhood. The only matters fixed in his
mind would be those relating to his time among the
angels, as though in crossing the bridge from human to
superhuman he had said goodbye forever to many of
the things that had defined his earlier, human life.

Whatever the case, the memory would burn brightly
in his mind throughout his days. He would keep it with
him, through the centuries, as one of the few significant
remembrances left to him from the time of his youth.

It would alter the course of his years in subtle ways,
for it would help him remain true to his ideals. It would
sustain him when every other hope was gone. He would
always see it as one of the defining moments of his existence.

It was the beginning of his sense of himself, the
seed-story of his personal myth.

It said these things to him. Once, he had been a man. Once, he had been a knight. Once, he had fought the good fight and protected the innocent.

Once upon a time, he had hunted monsters.

ALMOST FIVE MONTHS had passed since Brother Amadis had set out on his quest to destroy the Beast of Endriago, and the time had dragged like a lead weight upon Zahariel. He missed the easy camaraderie of his hero and the sense that his worth and presence were valued and appreciated within the Order.

Though Master Ramiel was a teacher of great skill and wisdom, he treated Zahariel just like any other suppli-cant, which was how it should be, but after being singled out by Brother Amadis, he found it hard to adjust to being... ordinary.

Without the presence of Brother Amadis, the games of one-upmanship had resumed, with Zahariel, Nemiel, Attias and Eliath squabbling like young novices once more.

Zahariel had tried to keep Nemiel's desire to best him at everything from annoying him, but try as he might, his cousin's constant, niggling attempts to undermine him began to ossify into a core of resentment in his heart.

Since Lord Sartana's visit to Aldurukh, a significant proportion of the Order's strength had been diverted from the final stages of the campaign against the great beasts towards the conflict with this new enemy.

In a series of decisive engagements, the Knights of Lupus had been driven back to their fortress at Sangrula – Blood Mountain – which, according to wild rumours flying through the fortress monastery, was now under siege.

The boys had gathered over their afternoon meal to discuss the state of the war against the Knights of

Lupus, and to bemoan their status as supplicants and hence their exclusion from the fighting.

'I heard it said that they've started burning their own settlements so as not to let the Order's knights capture them,' said Eliath.

'That's true,' said Attias. 'I heard Master Ramiel say that to Sar Hadariel yesterday.'

'Why would they do something like that?' asked Nemiel. 'That's just stupid.'

'I don't know,' said Attias. 'It's just what I heard.'

'Perhaps because they've proved by their actions that they're no more than treacherous turncoats and every moment of their continued existence is a stain on Caliban's honour.'

'That's a bit of a harsh assessment, isn't it?' said Zahariel.

'Is it?' said Nemiel. 'Then how come the Order has taken up the task of ending their existence?'

'Has anyone stopped to think that maybe, just maybe, Lord Sartana was speaking the truth?' asked Zahariel. 'That maybe we did break our word to leave their lands alone?'

'It crossed my mind,' said Nemiel, 'but what does it really matter now?'

'What does it matter?' repeated Zahariel. 'It matters because we may be about to fight a war under false pretences, that we engineered this war to serve our own ends? Doesn't that concern any of you?'

Blank faces gave him his answer, and he shook his head at their acceptance.

Nemiel leaned over the table and said, 'History is written by the victors, Zahariel, and among the many bitter pills the losing side must swallow in any war is the fact that their sacrifices were all for nothing. Sartana's claims about the Lion may well have been scurrilous, even outright fantasy, but the Order's chroniclers were never likely to record them even if they were truth, were they?'

'And the chroniclers of the Knights of Lupus?'

'Are sure to die with their masters in the siege of their fortress.'

'How can you be so blasé about this, Nemiel?' asked Zahariel. 'We're talking about killing fellow knights.'

Nemiel shook his head. 'No, we're talking about killing our enemies. Whether they're fellow knights or not is immaterial. Whatever the rights and wrongs of it, in the heat and fire of war the initial cause of the dispute between us and the Knights of Lupus will soon be forgotten. Even the war won't linger long in memory.'

'That's tragic,' said Zahariel.

'Such is the tragedy of human existence,' said Nemiel, quoting from the *Verbatim*. 'The lives of individuals are fleeting ephemeral things, lost amid the unforgiving, bloody tides of history.'

Zahariel shook his head. 'Maybe so, but on Caliban, those tides flow more darkly than most.'

AFTER THE MIDDAY meal, the supplicants retired to the dormitories to gather up their weapons for afternoon practice under the remonstrative eye of Master Ramiel. Zahariel had been unsettled by the conversation over their meal, uneasy at the speed with which the knights of the Order had followed Jonson into war.

Surely it was every sentient being's wish to avoid war, to take all possible actions to avoid the loss of life? Though youthful, Zahariel was wise enough to know that sometimes war and killing were unavoidable, but this war with the Knights of Lupus seemed to have begun with undue and unseemly haste.

As he lifted his serrated sword and buckled on his pistol belt, he heard a distant skirling trumpet call, a lilting refrain of three high notes that repeated over and over again. He looked over to where Nemiel and the others were readying their weapons, knowing that he knew the meaning of these sounds, but unable to connect that knowledge with his senses.

'Brother Amadis,' said Eliath, and suddenly sense and meaning was imparted to the trumpet blasts.

'The Returning Knight,' said Attias.

Zahariel smiled, recognising the infrequently heard melody that announced the return of a knight from a beast quest. So many of the great beasts had been killed and the crusade was almost at an end, hence the joyous notes were heard all too rarely these days.

The four boys ran from the dormitories, heedless of the thought that Master Ramiel would punish them for missing his lessons in swordplay and pistol work. The thrill of seeing Brother Amadis once again within the walls of Aldurukh outweighed the petty concerns of a timetable.

Others had also heard the trumpeter, though how the sound had carried through the fortress when its origin was high on the towers of the fortress was a mystery to Zahariel. Fellow supplicants hurried with them, and even a few of the younger knights made their way to the great gateway at the heart of the fortress, eager to be the first to greet the return of Brother Amadis.

Zahariel found himself once again in competition with Nemiel, his cousin pulling slightly ahead with a grin of triumph. Attias was behind him, and Eliath ran solidly at the rear of their little group.

The corridors wound down around the great bastion towers of the gateway, stone spirals lined with murder holes that led to the ground level. A sizeable throng had gathered, but still they were able to force their way to the front, as a booming echo drifted down from the darkness above.

Mighty chains juddered and shook off dust as heavy winches, pulleys and counterweights moved in an intricate ballet that opened the colossal Memorial Gates of Aldurukh. Massive portals of dark timber and bronze swung open on greased runners, iron wheels and bearings guiding them as they opened.

Bright light from a lifeless sky poured in, pooling on the stone flagged esplanade and spreading in a widening fan to illuminate the gloomy interior of the fortress monastery. Motes of dust spun like glimmering diamonds, dancing in the air as the passage of the great doors disturbed them.

Zahariel strained to see Brother Amadis, but beyond the blinding rectangle of light that built at the doors, he could see nothing beyond the dark smudge of the distant forest. Fellow supplicants pressed in around him, equally eager for a view, but Zahariel and his brothers kept their position with a mixture of strength and sheer bloody-mindedness.

At last a cry went up, and Zahariel saw movement in the gateway, the swaying silhouette of a rider making slow progress into the fortress. As his eyes adjusted to the glare from the bright sky beyond, Zahariel's heart leapt as he recognised the distinct and unmistakable outline of Brother Amadis.

Even as he rejoiced in the return of his hero, he had a sudden presentiment that something was wrong.

Amadis held himself erect with the last reserves of his strength, for his surplice was drenched in sticky blood and his left arm hung loosely by his side, the bones clearly shattered.

His face was pallid and bloodless, and a growth of stubble that was practically a beard fringed his face in dark hair. Nor had his destrier escaped unscathed: several deep gouges had been carved in its chest and flanks, and whole chunks of its mane had been torn out. Its tail was missing, and a series of clotted gashes on its rump spoke of a desperate flight from something terrible.

Amadis's eyes spoke of unimaginable pain and determination, and his head turned as though he sought something lost.

Knights rushed forward to aid the stricken hero and help him from his saddle. Their movement broke the spell of his condition, and a clamour of voices arose at the sight of the terribly wounded warrior.

Zahariel was swept forward in the press of bodies, a willing passenger in the advance of the crowd.

'Get back!' shouted a powerful, aged voice. 'Give him some damn room!'

Zahariel saw Lord Cypher striding through the masses, parting them by force of personality and authority, and darted to one side to follow in the wake of his passing. Within a few moments, he had left his fellows behind and stood above Brother Amadis with Lord Cypher kneeling beside the wounded man.

Amadis fought to form words, but bloody froth built on his lips, bubbling up from pierced lungs.

'Don't speak,' said Lord Cypher. 'You'll only make it more painful.'

'No...' gurgled Amadis '...need to speak.'

'Very well, lad. Do you have a valediction?'

Amadis nodded, and though Zahariel was horrified by Lord Cypher's implicit assumption that Amadis was going to die, he had seen enough wounds to know that these ones were mortal.

Amadis nodded and Zahariel saw that the blood at the knight's stomach was wet and still flowing, the flesh torn open and ropes of intestine pushing at the hand that vainly attempted to keep them within his body.

With his free hand, Amadis reached for his rotary barrelled pistol and painfully slid it from its leather holster.

'Zahariel,' said Amadis.

Lord Cypher looked up and saw the boy, quickly beckoning him to kneel beside the dying knight. 'Hurry, boy, and listen well, not many get to hear the last words of a knight of the Order. Those who listen to a valediction have a duty to the dead. Tradition, you see.'

Zahariel nodded, intent on the dying Amadis as he lifted the pistol towards him.

'Take it, Zahariel,' said Amadis, the creased lines of pain on his face easing as death stole upon him. 'It's yours. I want you to have it.'

'I can't,' said Zahariel, tears gathering at the corners of his eyes.

'You must, it is my wish that you carry it with you,' gasped Amadis. 'It is my legacy to you. Remember me when you fire it. Remember what I taught you.'

'I will,' promised Zahariel, taking the blood-slick weapon from Amadis. Its weight felt heavy in his hand, heavier than a mere contraption of metal and wood ought to feel. It carried a weight of responsibility with it, a duty to the honourable warrior who had borne it before him.

'It's a good weapon... not failed me yet,' coughed Amadis. 'Don't suppose it ever will now, eh?'

'No,' said Zahariel, suddenly very aware of the silence that filled the gateway.

'Damn, but there's no pain now, that can't be good, eh?'

'It means the end is near, lad,' said Lord Cypher.

'Thought so,' nodded Amadis. 'Damn Beast of Endriago got its claws into me. Big bastard too... a Calibanite lion... thought there was only one of them.'

'A Calibanite lion?' said Zahariel. 'I thought Lord Jonson killed the only lion?'

'I wish he had...' said Amadis with a grimace. 'Might not be lying here... I just wish...'

Whatever Amadis's last wish had been, it would forever remain a mystery, for his eyes glazed over and a soft breath whispered from between his lips.

Zahariel's head bowed and tears flowed unashamedly down his cheeks at the passing of this great hero. He gripped the pistol Amadis had given him in both hands, hot anger filling him at the thought of the knight's killer still alive and roaming the dark forests.

Lord Cypher reached out and pressed his palm over the dead knight's face, gently closing his eyes.

'So passes Brother Amadis from the Order,' he intoned with grim solemnity.

Zahariel looked up, as Lord Cypher placed a gnarled hand on his shoulder and pointed at the gun Amadis had given him.

'That is more than just a weapon, boy,' said Lord Cypher. 'It is the weapon of a hero. It carries a weight of power and potency that your own pistol does not. You must do honour to the weapon and the memory of the man who gave it to you.'

'I *will* do honour to it, Lord Cypher,' said Zahariel. 'Have no doubt about that.'

Lord Cypher's eyes narrowed as he caught the vehemence in Zahariel's voice. He shook his head.

'No, lad,' he said. 'Anger and loss cloud your judgement. Do not say it, for it cannot be taken back once uttered.'

But Zahariel was not to be dissuaded, and he stood with the bloody pistol clasped tight to his breast.

'My Lord Cypher,' said Zahariel, 'I declare a quest against the Beast of Endriago.'

'YOU SHOULDN'T HAVE declared a quest,' said Nemiel.

It was three nights before Zahariel was due to set off on his quest. Knowing he would want to spend the next two days and nights in quiet meditation as he prepared for the journey, his fellow supplicants had chosen this as an opportune time to hold a feast in his honour.

There had been food and wine, and Master Ramiel had granted them special dispensation to hold the feast in the caverns below Aldurukh. The feast took place in torchlight, around a long table that they had carried down from the dormitory dining room.

The setting was in keeping with custom. According to Lord Cypher, if Zahariel succeeded in his quest, he would be reborn from one life into another, from a boy into a man.

'Strictly speaking,' Lord Cypher had said, 'as these things are counted, you are currently suspended between life and death, your soul sojourning in the underworld until the decision of your future status is made.'

Zahariel had thought it superstitious nonsense, of course, tradition based on old myths, but Lord Cypher still paid service to their world's ancient ways, and as a fellow witness to the passing of Brother Amadis, Zahariel had honoured his advice by seeking out an underground venue for the feast.

Despite the celebratory tone and surface cheer of the proceedings, Zahariel noticed a mournfulness underlying all that was said to him. His friends wished him well, but there was no hiding the edge of grief in their demeanour. It was an uncomfortable realisation, but eventually Zahariel understood that they were saying farewell with no expectation of ever seeing him alive again.

No one expected him to return from his quest except as a corpse.

'You could have waited, Zahariel.' Nemiel's voice was insistent beside him. 'You didn't have to declare a quest on the beast that killed Amadis.'

'Yes, Nemiel,' said Zahariel, 'I did. You didn't see the life pass from him. I did.'

'You know what the senior knights are saying?' asked Eliath.

'No,' said Zahariel, 'nor do I care. I have declared a quest, to no less a person than Lord Cypher. It cannot be taken back.'

'Well you should care,' said Nemiel, jerking his head towards the ceiling. 'The things the knights are saying... They think it's hubris. They don't know why Lord Cypher is allowing you to take up this quest. He should know better. It's a suicidal errand.'

'You'll have to be clearer, Nemiel,' said Zahariel, gesturing to his goblet. 'It could be I haven't taken enough water with my wine, but I'm having trouble following you.'

'I'm talking about the beast you'll be hunting,' said Nemiel, with a grimace of exasperation. 'Up at the knights' table they're saying it's a Calibanite lion, one of the worst predators of the woods. They say it's taken more than two hundred lives already, and this is up in the Northwilds where there are hardly any people.'

'A quest is supposed to be hard, Nemiel,' said Zahariel. 'It's how we prove ourselves. It's how we show we're ready for knighthood.'

'Hard, yes, but this goes way beyond that,' countered Nemiel. 'Everyone says this quest beast is worthy of the true heroes among us like the Lion or Sar Luther. No offence, cousin, but you're not one of them and you never will be. You don't have the skills or experience to take down this beast, any more than I do. Everyone upstairs is saying you're insane. I know you desperately want to be a knight, we all do, but if you ask me, you should have waited for a less dangerous beast. No one would have thought badly of you for it. There would have been no loss glory.'

Zahariel shook his head. 'It's not about the glory, and I don't care how people speak of me. You should know that about me by now.'

'Aye, I know, but you must be able to see that this is madness? I wasn't exaggerating when I said I thought it was suicide. You can see that, can't you? Why did you take it?'

'I've waited years for this,' said Zahariel, speaking slowly and measuring his reply. 'Ever since I was accepted as a supplicant by the Order I've dreamt about this moment. To be honest, it never occurred to me not to take up this quest. When Brother Amadis died, I could feel that it was right. I couldn't wait for another. Besides, remember what Master Ramiel says, "You don't choose your beast; the beast chooses you." You should know that lesson well enough.'

Trying to defuse the tension, Zahariel smiled at Nemiel to show he was only joking, but his cousin was unwilling to soften his stance. Still annoyed, Nemiel stared back at him in frustration. Attias and Eliath sat in silence, seeing that to intrude on the cousins' discussion would not be prudent.

'IT'S NO LAUGHING matter, Zahariel. This beast could kill you. Remember, I was there when the winged monster attacked us. It's easy to think you're immortal when you're wearing armour and armed with a fine pistol and motorised sword, but our weapons and our artifice mean nothing in the face of such creatures. This isn't something to be treated lightly. It's a serious business.'

'I know it is,' replied Zahariel. 'Don't misunderstand me. I realise the dangers of the quest ahead of me. I know the weight of it. But what you see as a terrible problem, I see as an advantage. You know the Order's teachings as well as I do. In all our lessons with our masters, in all the combat drills and practice sessions, in all the mock duels and tourneys we have experienced since we came here, we have been striving for one thing: excellence. It is the only quality that gives any meaning to a man's life. It is the only thing that makes us worthy of knighthood. It is the Order's founding ideal. You know the words, "The life of mankind should be devoted to the pursuit of excellence in all its forms, both as a species and as individuals".'

'You don't need to quote the *Verbatim* to me,' snapped Nemiel. 'Master Ramiel drummed it into both our heads. I know it by heart as well as you.'

'Then you'll remember something else that is written in it. "To help achieve and demonstrate this excellence, we will test ourselves to our limits. Only through the sternest challenges can we know the true shape of our character." That's what the Order's teachings say: to our limits, the sternest challenges. I'd hardly be following those lessons if I had refused this quest because I was afraid I might find it too hard.'

'Those are our ideals, yes,' agreed Nemiel, 'but we have to be realistic. If the stories about this beast are true, it's the kind of creature that only a party of experienced knights could bring down. Even Lord Jonson was badly wounded before he brought his Calibanite lion down. It's not a suitable challenge for a supplicant.'

'You may be right,' admitted Zahariel, 'but when Amadis gave me his pistol I had to accept the quest. If we start trying to choose our quests on the basis of how easy we'd like them to be, we will be on the slippery slope to ruin. Anyway, let's not argue. The decision is made, and it's too late to change it. I've committed myself to this quest. The most we can do is share a drink and hope we both live to see each other again.'

Zahariel stood and lifted the goblet in his hand.

'To the life tomorrow, cousin,' he said, raising the goblet in a toast.

In response, Nemiel smiled in resignation and raised his own goblet.

'To the life tomorrow,' replied Nemiel, his eyes glistening with tears.

SEVEN

'You TAKE THE trail eastwards,' said the woodsman.

He led the way on foot down the forest path while Zahariel followed behind him on his destrier. 'You keep going 'til you reach a piece of clearing just past an old tree that's hit by lightning. It's fire-black and split in two down the middle, you can't miss it. That's where the gathering party was heading. Course, it could be they never reached it. If they did, you should be able to pick up their tracks from there.'

The man's name was Narel. Lord Domiel of Endriago had introduced Zahariel to him as he prepared to leave the frightened town through the splintered and heavily barricaded main gates.

Narel was one of the woodsmen who lived in the castle and worked the lands surrounding its walls. Braver than his fellows, he had agreed to lead Zahariel into the forest in search of the beast. Specifically, he had promised to show Zahariel the trail taken by a party of men and women who had failed to return after daring to venture into the forest yesterday to gather much needed firewood and foodstuffs.

'People told them they was being foolhardy,' Narel said. 'They told them they'd likely run into the beast, but what was they to do? They all had youngsters, and plenty of mouths to feed back home. Winter's coming, and if you want to stay alive you've got to gather food and fuel. It's just the way things are out here. Besides, they was well-armed, and there was a dozen of them all together, so you'd think there'd be safety in numbers. There ain't no safety in these woods now though, I guess, not from the beast.'

Narel was nearly half the age of Lord Domiel of Endriago, but it had swiftly become clear that the woodsman was as garrulous as his lord and master. All the way along the trail, as he guided Zahariel through the forest, Narel had yattered on incessantly. He had a tendency to talk quietly while constantly casting anxious glances at the trees and the undergrowth around them. The woodsman was clearly nervous, as though he expected the beast to leap out at them at any moment.

'Course, those youngsters won't get no food now,' said Narel, checking for the twentieth time that there was a round in the breech of his bolt-action rifle and the trigger safety was off. 'Could be they'll starve, unless someone takes them in. Not me, though. I got sympathies, but me and the wife have got our own pack of hungry mouths. That's the real tragedy of it, you ask me. Every time the beast kills, it makes another band of orphans. Killed more than a hundred and eighty people all told. That's a lot of children having to go without mothers or fathers.'

Zahariel could understand the man's nervousness. From what Narel had told him, he had known most of the beast's victims, at least the ones that had come from Endriago. A number of them had even been his relatives. Given the size of the community and the extended kinship relationships that operated in Caliban's more isolated regions, such a situation was not unusual.

Everyone in Endriago had lost neighbours, friends and family members to the beast that stalked the forests. In his short time in the castle, it had been obvious to Zahariel that fear of the beast was a palpable force within its walls. He would have been hard pressed to find a man, woman or child who was not terrified of the creature.

The people of Endriago no longer ventured outside their settlement unless it was absolutely necessary, and having seen the fury and depth of the claw marks on the castle gate, Zahariel was inclined to feel that such fear was entirely justified.

The beast had turned them into virtual prisoners behind the castle's battlements, and this combined with Brother Amadis's death, made Zahariel more determined than ever to kill the foul monster.

The current situation could not last forever. As Narel had said, the seasons were changing. Winter was on its way. Soon, the inhabitants of Endriago would be given a hard choice. Their food stocks would need to be replenished if they were to get through the bitterly cold months ahead.

Either they faced a slow lingering death through starvation, or they would have to enter the forest and risk the wrath of the beast.

The party of men and women that had gone out yesterday had already made their decision. It had ended badly for them, but there was an entire settlement whose further existence hung in the balance.

If the beast was allowed to continue unchecked, if no one hunted it down and killed it, there would be more tragedies in the forests around Endriago.

There would be more grief. There would be more orphans.

Many lives had already been taken, and no community could afford to suffer such losses indefinitely.

The weight of responsibility on Zahariel's shoulders was enormous.

If he failed to kill the beast it was not just his own life at stake, it was the life of Endriago and all the families that dwelt within it.

'Anyway, this is it,' said Narel. He had halted partway along the trail, and looked at Zahariel with an expression of acute discomfort. 'You remember I said I couldn't take you the whole way. I mean, I would, but I got a wife and youngsters myself. You understand, right? I got people to look after.'

'I understand,' replied Zahariel. 'I should be able to find my way from here.'

'All right, then,' nodded Narel.

The woodsman turned to begin the journey back to Endriago, glancing briefly over his shoulder at Zahariel before he left. 'I wish you safe passage through the dark, Zahariel of the Order. May the Watchers guide you and comfort you. Be sure I will make an offering on your behalf tonight. It has been good to know you.'

With that, he walked away and did not turn back again.

ONCE THE WOODSMAN was gone and Zahariel had continued a little way ahead on the trail, he found his mind dwelling at length on the words Narel had said to him before he left.

It was obvious that Narel did not expect him to survive.

The woodsman had not used any of the standard expressions of farewell. There had been no mention of the 'life tomorrow' or similar phrases. In their place, he had made a curious decision in his choice of words. He had wished safe passage to Zahariel in the dark.

He had asked for the Watchers to guide and comfort him.

He had even gone so far as to promise to make an offering on his behalf. On Caliban, these were not the words that anyone would say to someone they expected see again. They were words of benediction, not of farewell.

According to one of the more commonly held beliefs about death on Caliban, once a person died his soul journeyed to the underworld where it would be made to walk a spiral path, which – depending on the deceased's actions in life – would lead him either to hell or to rebirth. This was the source of the words Narel had said to him. They were from a well-known funeral rite, where, in the context of the ceremony, they were intended as a plea, asking for the guardians of the spirit world to intervene on behalf of the dead.

Zahariel took no offence at Narel's words. He did not suspect they were anything but well intentioned. There were no great cities on Caliban, but even by those standards the settlements of the Northwilds were comparative backwaters.

The old ways held considerable sway in places like Endriago.

By his own beliefs, Narel had probably thought he was paying Zahariel a great honour in attempting to ease his journey through the underworld, a prospect he no doubt saw as inevitable once Zahariel came face-to-face with the beast.

To Zahariel's mind, though, the woodsman had been wasting his breath.

It was not a matter that was much discussed, at least not openly, but there were many interpretations of religion at the heart of Calibanite culture. On the one hand there was the planet's traditional religion, still popular with much of the common population as well as with a few diehards among the nobility, which incorporated elements of both ancestor worship and an animistic folk belief said to be derived from the ancient wisdoms of the planet's first human settlers. Its adherents believed that the forests of Caliban were alive with guardian spirits.

Of special significance to their beliefs were a class of shadowy unseen watchers who would sometimes choose to intervene in human affairs for their own mysterious and unknown purposes.

These 'Watchers in the Dark' were not said to be the only kind of supernatural creatures at large on Caliban. Among those of the traditionalist faith, it was claimed that the great beasts were evil spirits that had taken on physical form in order to create suffering and hardship among mankind.

With this in mind, it was not uncommon for individuals and families to make votive offerings to the Watchers in the Dark in the hope of persuading them to intercede in keeping the beasts away.

In contrast to such folk beliefs, however, the knightly orders of Caliban tended to follow a more agnostic creed. They rejected the influence of the supernatural altogether. If such entities as gods and spirits existed, it was argued they would be unlikely to intervene directly in human affairs.

It was said that such creatures would be so alien in their desires and perceptions they could never share mankind's understanding of the world, much less be able to recognise when their help might be needed.

Instead, the philosophy of the knightly orders held that the real impetus that shaped a man's life was the strength of his character, not the supposed actions of otherworldly forces. Accordingly, the different orders had committed themselves to developing the minds and bodies of their knights in keeping with ideals of human excellence that were particular to each individual order.

During his years as a supplicant in the Order, Zahariel had absorbed his masters' prejudices in such matters, and had made them his own. He had no particular axe to grind with men like Narel, but he had little time for their beliefs. He did not believe in life after death or journeys into the underworld.

The great beasts of Caliban were extraordinary creatures, but he did not believe they were supernatural in origin. The Watchers in the Dark were a myth, and he did not believe in guardian spirits keeping benign watch on humanity from the shadows.

In their place, he believed in the powers of human wisdom. The actions of men like Lion El'Jonson and Luther, and their campaign against the great beasts, had convinced him that humanity was free to choose its own destiny. The human mind could make sense of the world and of the cosmos and, given a fair and equal choice, most men would choose to help their fellows.

Zahariel reasoned that men were intrinsically good, and, granted the opportunity, they would choose the best and brightest path from among the roads on offer. No man would ever willingly perform an evil act unless forced to it by circumstance.

Perhaps a man could be provoked to evil by hunger, fear or ignorance, but no one would willingly choose to act maliciously when presented with another, viable option.

No one would willingly have the darkness when they could have light.

Putting to one side his disquiet at the curiously bleak nature of Narel's farewell and his ruminations on the nature of man, he concentrated his mind on the quest before him.

At that instant, he was more mindful of Narel's directions than he was of any wider issues of fate or destiny. The woodsman had told him to head eastward along the trail in search of a clearing and a lightning blasted tree. Zahariel followed those directions, using the methods his masters had taught him to clarify his mind and turn his full mental resources to the task ahead. He urged his horse to quicken its pace down the trail.

Spurring his mount on, he rode towards his future.

ZAHARIEL FOUND THE lightning blasted tree easily enough, the path leading him directly to its dead mass. Beyond the tree, a forest of mossy trunks spread out like a march of weathered menhirs. Darkness and shadows haunted the forest, and Zahariel began to understand a measure of the local superstitions.

The Northwilds had long been considered a forsaken place, too close to the mountain lairs of many beasts, too thin of soil to be tilled for much reward, and the forest was too dense to move through in safety. More than that, it had acquired a reputation for unexplained phenomena, strange lights in the forest, disappearances where people lost in the woods for days would return home decades older than when their loved ones had last seen them.

Yes, the Northwilds region was a place of mystery, but as Zahariel steeled himself for venturing into its depths, he felt the first stirrings of fear. Though he had claimed not to be afraid, he realised that his fear had been submerged beneath a layer of contempt for the beast and anger at the death of Brother Amadis.

How easy it was to scoff at the superstitions of the rustics dwelling in Endriago when surrounded by your fellows and the comforting shield of illumination. How easy it was to have that complacency and certainty stripped away by darkness and isolation.

Swallowing his fear, Zahariel urged his mount onwards, sensing that it too felt fear in this place. The trees were gnarled and old, older than any others he had seen, and apparently infected with some creeping sickness that caused them to weep a viscous sap that scented the air with a rank, bitter odour like spoiled fruit mash.

The trees passed by him as he rode into the shadowy depths of the Northwilds, and Zahariel felt a breath whisper past him like the last exhalation of a dying man. The ground under his horse's hooves was spongy and noxious, toadstools and flaring weeds tangling the roots of the forest.

Zahariel rode deeper and deeper into the forest, feeling the emptiness of the place in the depths of his soul, an aching void that chilled him from the very centre of his heart to the height of his reason.

Suddenly, Zahariel felt utterly alone, and a crushing sense of isolation enveloped him.

More than simply the absence of people, this was a loneliness of the soul, an utter absence of any contact or connection with the world around him. In the face of this horrid feeling, Zahariel almost cried out at his insignificance.

How arrogant of him to believe that he was at the centre of the spiral. How conceited to believe that he could ever make a difference to the way the world turned.

His eyes filled with tears as the horse bore him onwards, the beast oblivious to the long, dark night of the soul he endured upon its back.

'I am not nothing,' he whispered to the darkness. 'I am Zahariel of the Order.'

The darkness swallowed his words with a mocking silence, the words snatched from his throat as if by an unseen wind before they could breach the bubble of stagnant emptiness around him.

'I am Zahariel of the Order!' he yelled against the darkness.

Again his words were stolen from him, but his violent exclamation had, for a brief moment, turned the darkness assailing his soul away. Again he shouted, briefly recognising the danger of shouting while on the hunt for a dangerous predator, but more afraid of what might happen should this soul-deep numbness claim him.

His ride through the trees continued as he repeated his name over and over again. With every metre his horse bore him, he could sense an unseen malice and elemental power seeping from the ground, as though some barely suppressed source of malignant energy lurked deep, deep beneath the surface of Caliban. Like trickles of water that leaked from the caked mud of an animal's dam, was there something that lay far beneath the surface of the world that exerted some dread influence on the life above?

No sooner had he formed the thought than he realised that he was not alone.

A gentle pull on the reins halted his destrier, and Zahariel took a long, cold breath of frigid air as he sensed the presence of a number of creatures observing him from the shadows of the trees.

He knows… he senses it…

He could not see them clearly, so completely were they cloaked in the darkness, yet he knew with utter certainty they were there, watching him from the dark.

Watching him from the dark…

He could see them from the corners of his eyes, little more than flitting shadows that vanished as soon as he turned his head to look directly upon them. How many there were, he could not say. He glimpsed at least five, but whether that represented the entire complement was a mystery.

Kill him… he is touched by it…

Whispers flitted between the trees, but Zahariel knew they were not whispers given voice by any human throat, or, truth be told, extant in a realm detectable by any of his five senses. He had the distinct impression of a conversation going on around him, and though the words, if such things had meaning in a discourse held without speech, were unknown to him, he understood their meaning perfectly.

'Who are you?' he shouted, striving to keep his voice steady. 'Stop whispering and show yourselves!'

The shadowy watchers retreated further into the darkness at the sound of his voice, perhaps surprised that he was aware of them or that he had heard their wordless mutterings.

He carries the taint within him. Better to kill him now…

Zahariel's hand slipped towards his sword at the threat, but a ghostly touch upon his thoughts warned him against such hostile action.

You waste your efforts, Zahariel of the Order. You cannot harm us with the weapons of this realm…

The voice echoed within his skull, and Zahariel cried out at the sound, the voice resonating as though the speaker was directly in front of him.

'Who are you?' he cried, regaining control of his senses and casting wild looks around the clearing. He saw nothing of his interlocutors, but spun his horse in a circle, his sword leaping to his hand.

'Show yourselves!' he again demanded. 'I grow weary of these parlour tricks!'

Very well…

No sooner had the words registered in his consciousness than he caught sight of one of the unseen speakers.

A figure stepped from the darkness of the trees. It was no more than a few feet in height, and was swathed from head to foot in a hooded hessian robe that obscured every inch of its flesh. The darkness beneath its hood was more complete than that which surrounded Zahariel, and he had the conviction that were he to see the truth of what lay beneath its cowl, he would be driven irrevocably mad.

Its hands were clasped before it, each sunken in the opposite sleeve. Its posture was servile, though Zahariel detected no servility in its demeanour.

'What are you?' asked Zahariel. 'Are you the Watchers in the Dark?'

That will suffice as an appellation for our purpose.

'Purpose? What purpose?' asked Zahariel.

Communicating with you in a manner you will understand. Humans require labels upon their world to make sense of it.

'Humans?' said Zahariel. 'Such a word implies you are… not human, yes?'

Correct, we are of a species unknown to the majority of your race.

'Then what are you?'

That is unimportant, but what is important is that you leave this place.

'I cannot,' said Zahariel. 'I am sworn to hunt the beast that killed my friend.'

The creature you seek is not here, though it is close.

'You know where it is? Tell me!'

Very well, but you must swear to leave here and never come back. These woods are corrupt and no good can come of humans being here.

'Corrupt? Corrupted by what?'

The diminutive figure shook its head.

No, such things are not for humans to know. Your race already knows too much and seeks to tamper with things that should never be.

'I don't understand,' said Zahariel. 'What are you doing here?'

We are members of, a brotherhood, much like yourself…
a cabal dedicated to thwarting the most ancient evil.

'What evil?' asked Zahariel. 'You mean the great beasts?'

No, they are but a symptom of a greater ill. I will not name this evil, suffice to say it is the bane of your race and will one day consume you.

Zahariel felt a chill steal upon him at the mention of this great evil the creature spoke of, a bone-deep knowledge that it spoke the truth. Its words carried the weight of ages within them, and though such a thing was surely impossible, Zahariel felt that this creature might very well be thousands of years old, if not older.

'This evil. Can it be fought?' he asked.

Of course, all evil can be fought.

'Then let me help you defeat it!' he cried.

The figure shook its head, and Zahariel's spirits fell.

Evil such as this can never be defeated. It can be held at bay for a time, but so long as there are humans, it will exist.

'Then what can I do to help?'

Leave. Go far from this place and never return.

Zahariel nodded, only too eager to be away, but unwilling to leave without discovering more about these… aliens.

'How did you come to be here?'

Again, the figure shook his head, and Zahariel saw two more small figures emerge from the trees, their attire and posture identical to the first.

He asks too many questions!

His race is curious and that will be their downfall. We should kill him.

He had no idea which of the three was speaking, for their voices were multi-layered and swirled around his head like water draining through a sinkhole. Though the speakers were small, and in any physical contest

Zahariel knew he could best them easily, he had no doubt that they possessed powers beyond his understanding and could snuff out his existence as easily as a guttering candle.

'Why should you kill me?' he said. 'What harm have I done you?'

Individually, none, but as a race, your kind threatens to doom the galaxy to eternal suffering.

Zahariel's mind spun with the implications of the creature's words, that humans existed beyond the confines of Caliban and that an entire race of humankind inhabited the stars above. The sensation was exhilarating, and to know that many of the old myths must be true was like the finest wine dancing upon his tongue.

Emboldened by this new knowledge, he held out his sword and said, 'I have already sworn that I would oppose evil to my Order, but I swear I shall do all in my power to stand against the same evil you stand against.'

He sensed the creatures' approbation and knew that they had read the truth beyond his words.

Very well, Zahariel of the Order. We accept your oath. Now it is time for you to go.

Zahariel had a thousand more questions for these watchers, but contented himself with the knowledge he had already gleaned, sheathing his sword and turning his horse, as the Watchers in the Dark melted back into the undergrowth.

As the outline of the watchers blended seamlessly with the darkness, one last question arose in his mind as he recalled something one of the watchers had said.

'Wait!' he cried. 'What did you mean when you said the taint was in me?'

At first, he thought he was to be denied an answer, but in the moment before they faded from view, a voice whispered from the shadows.

Look not to unlock the door that leads to easy power,
Zahariel of the Order. Ride back to the lightning tree and you
will find what you seek.

Then they were gone.

ZAHARIEL RODE FROM the depths of the forest, his spirits
lifting, the leaden weight that hung upon his soul on
the way in, growing less with each kilometre that passed
on the way out. Something terrible had happened in
this part of the forest, something so awful that
guardians from another world had come to Caliban to
watch over it.

Whether the evil they spoke of was still on Caliban or
had left echoes of its malice behind, he didn't know,
and he suspected he was better off in his ignorance. He
recognised that the danger of this part of the forest was
more than just what might threaten his body, but was
something of an order far more dangerous.

He had been made privy to secret knowledge, and if
there was one thing the Order prided itself on, it was
that its members could keep a secret. The things he had
learned and the things he believed would remain
locked in his heart forever, for no earthly means of
interrogation would force him to divulge those secrets.

Zahariel thought back to his conversation with the
Lion atop the tower and how the great warrior had wondered about the existence of Terra or any other
inhabited world. He alone on Caliban knew the answer
to that question, and the singularity of his position
thrilled him.

His journey from the forest's dark heart passed swiftly,
his horse's step light as it picked an easy path through
the tangled weeds and closely packed trees. Even the
shadows that had closed in on him before seemed to be
lifting, as a diffuse glow of warm, afternoon sunshine
broke through the canopies of the forest.

Eventually, the thick underbrush gave way to the beginnings of a hard-packed earth path, and Zahariel smiled as he recognised the track that he had ridden along many hours ago. His horse took the path without need of his command, and he rode through leafy arbours before emerging in the clearing with the blackened, lightning struck tree.

Lost in contemplation, the beast caught Zahariel almost unawares.

The creature sprang at him as if from nowhere.

It had hidden in the shadows behind a stand of twisted and ancient trees near the clearing's edge. At first, as it charged through the foliage towards him, it was as though a monstrously spined rock had come to life.

Zahariel saw a dark, swift shape bearing down on him. The creature was huge and moved with impossible speed. Terrified, his destrier gave a sudden start and reared up in panic. He fought to stay in his saddle, gripping the reins tightly.

A Calibanite lion, and it was nearly on top of him.

Another second and it would tear him apart.

EIGHT

In one frozen, fear extended instant, Zahariel saw a host of the beast's anatomical details as it charged. Its body was wide and powerful, leonine only in the fact that it was a quadruped with a mane of blade-like spines growing from behind its armoured head. Each of its limbs was sheathed in glistening plates of natural armour that had the quality of rock, yet the pliability of flesh. Claws like knives extended from its front paws, and twin fangs, like the mightiest cavalry sabres protruded from its upper jaw.

Zahariel had wondered if the figures of how many people the beast had slain were inflated to better convey its horror, but in one terrible moment, he knew differently.

Only his instincts, honed by long hours in the shooting ranges of Aldurukh, saved his life.

Zahariel lifted the rotary barrelled pistol that the dying Amadis had given him and fired a rippling salvo of shots, sending every bolt towards the centre of the lion's mass as his teachers had taught him.

The bolts struck home, but the lion appeared not to feel the blasts as they hit its thick hide. The rounds from his pistol had explosive cores designed to detonate deep inside a target's body, and had enough stopping power to kill almost anything, even a creature of such startling appearance and shape.

The lion shrugged them off as though it barely felt the impacts.

Roaring in fury, the lion lashed out with a bladed paw as it leapt.

The blow struck Zahariel's destrier, punching through the animal's side with an awful, bone breaking crack. The destrier buckled as the lion eviscerated it, and Zahariel was flung bodily from his saddle, landing in a heap in the mud of the clearing.

Zahariel scrambled to his feet quickly as his horse collapsed, its innards spilling from its ruptured body in a flood of hot viscera. Distracted by such an easy kill, the lion's attention was fixed on Zahariel's dying mount.

Zahariel fired his pistol again, sending another fusillade at the lion as it took a bite of the screaming horse, the swords of its fangs tearing a great slab of meat from the beast's rump. The armoured plates around the lion's body slithered across its body, sparks and chunks of resinous material flying as each bolt struck home without effect.

His gun clicked dry as he emptied the last shots from the magazine, and the lion let out a deafening bellow that was part roar, part howl. Zahariel hurriedly reloaded his weapon, as he backed away from the monster, horrified at the sheer power of it.

The lion prowled around the edge of the clearing, its eyes serpentine and coloured a vivid orange with black slits at their centres. The mane of blades at its neck pulsed with protean motion, each one cutting the air with lethal intent.

Zahariel kept moving, taking sideways steps in opposition to the huge beast. Its throaty growls and the ropes of drool that hung from its opened jaws spoke of its terrible hunger, and he tried not to think of being ripped apart by its fangs.

Though the creature was an aberration, a monster from his worst nightmare, he had the impression that it was glowering at him with dark amusement. Fighting back the onset of fear, Zahariel was reminded of the winged beast he had fought long ago, remembering the spider and fly analogy he had used to describe how the beast had made him feel. This creature displayed the same malicious enjoyment of the hunt, as though he were a meaty morsel to be savoured before being devoured.

His training told him to keep the lion at a distance and use his pistol to full effect, but his knightly code told him to charge the beast and meet it in the glory of close combat.

Keeping his pistol trained on the prowling lion, Zahariel drew his sword as he considered his options. Counting the magazine he had just loaded, he had two clips left for his pistol. There was more ammunition in a pannier hanging from the saddle horn of his thrashing mount, but it was out of reach. Assuming he did not charge into close combat, he had twenty-four shots at hand with which to kill the lion.

Ordinarily, he would have considered twenty-four rounds enough to defeat any foe, or any other creature in the universe, but the great beasts of Caliban were chimerical monsters, combining the worst aspects of several different species of animal into one foul body.

A sticky red liquid stained the front of the lion's body where it had been hit by the bullets, but he did not know whether it was blood or some vile secretion.

Even the chunks blasted from its rock textured hide seemed to have closed over.

Without warning, the lion pounced across the clearing towards him with extraordinary speed. He dived to the side, bringing his sword around in a low arc to deflect the creature's attack. Whirring teeth sliced into the creature's hide and splattered Zahariel with gore.

The lion roared and twisted in mid leap, its heavy hindquarters slamming into Zahariel, pounding him to the ground. He rolled as soon as he hit, keeping his sword extended upwards to avoid being torn apart by his own blade. The lion's spines flared, and its heavy paws tore up the ground where he had fallen.

Zahariel stabbed with his blade, the whirring teeth cutting through the spines at the beast's neck. Drooling fluids sprayed from severed blade spines, spattering his armour with hissing, acidic blood.

The lion spun and snapped at him with its enormous maw. Zahariel hurled himself to the side as powerful jaws slammed closed within centimetres of his torso. He fired as he dodged its attack, putting several bullets into its side. Again, the beast gave no sign of pain or shock, apparently immune to both.

Zahariel's skin was already slick and dripping with sweat, and he could feel a tightness across his shoulders and down the length of his calves. His armour was equipped with mechanisms designed to keep him cool and support his movement, but they were no match for the exertions of his fight against the lion.

His life lay balanced on a knife's edge, and the next few seconds would decide whether or not he lived to see another sunset. The time for caution had passed.

Sweeping his sword in a wide arc to gain a few moments of breathing space from the roaring fury of the lion, Zahariel suddenly leapt forward. Rolling as he hit the ground, he came up with Amadis's pistol blazing, firing another salvo of shots as he ran screaming towards the lion.

For the briefest instant, the lion seemed almost surprised, opening its mouth in a loud bellow of rage. Zahariel and the lion charged towards each other, crossing the no-man's-land between them in moments.

His proximity to the beast made his gorge rise. There was something loathsome, almost leprous about it. It was surrounded by a sickly scent of decay that he was not really sure was a scent at all, as though the creature's inherent vileness was transmitting itself to every object in its vicinity.

Zahariel felt as if the beast's aura of foulness had managed to seep into his pores through his armour. More than ever, its presence felt like a cancer at the heart of the world, a source of vile contagion that must be destroyed.

His hatred gave him strength.

Zahariel was at close range, standing toe-to-claw with the monster. He pumped two more bolt rounds into it at point-blank range in the instant before they met in a melee. Then, as the lion swiped at him with its claws, Zahariel slipped nimbly under their clumsy grasp and thrust hard with his sword towards the creature's wide chest.

The lion bellowed and as its mouth opened. Zahariel fired his pistol into the yawning chasm, angling his shots towards the roof of its mouth.

He thrust again and again, the blade skidding as its whirring teeth cut through the armoured outer layers of the lion's hide. The lion's slamming head hit him a thunderous body blow, and he crashed to the ground, hearing the horrific sound of bones breaking within his body.

Zahariel hit the ground hard, the wind knocked from his lungs as the beast smashed its front limbs down on his chest. Blade-like talons punched through the outer layers of his breastplate, and he screamed as the tips pierced the skin and muscle of his chest.

He could feel the pressure of the lion's weight, its head centimetres from his own and its thick, acrid drool spattering his face. He could barely breathe.

The hand holding his pistol was still free, and he fired several shots into the lion's belly at point-blank range.

He heard an ominous cracking noise as the seals on his armour gave way. The lion stood atop him, knowing he was pinned and powerless, and content to watch him suffer a slow, agonising death as it crushed the life out of him.

Zahariel felt as though there was an iron band around his chest, stopping him from breathing. The lion's claws lifted him from the ground towards its mouth as it prepared to bite him in two. The great maw opened, and the wafting gust of corruption that blew from its impossibly wide gullet was the foulest thing Zahariel could imagine.

The long tusks of its upper jaw extended from its mouth, each one like an organic sword blade, hauling him towards his doom. He struggled uselessly in its grip, the talons of its paw wedged in his breastplate holding him stuck fast. He screamed in anger and fear, feeling his hatred of the beast coalesce in a bright ball of furious energy at his core. He spat into the creature's mouth as the fangs descended upon him.

He closed his eyes as the fangs bit down, and felt an outpouring of his hatred explode from his body in a glittering halo of light.

Everything stopped.

Though his eyes were closed, he could see the shimmering outline of the lion, its every bone and internal organ laid bare to his sight as though lit from within by some strange pellucid sun. He could see the blood pumping around its body, the pulse of its heart and the foul energy that had brought it into existence.

The tableau was in motion, but glacially slow motion. Each beat of the lion's heart was a dull, thudding boom, like the arc of an ancient pendulum. Its fangs still descended upon him, but their movement was so infinitesimally slow that it took him a moment to even realise they were moving.

Every bone and muscle in Zahariel's body ached. His chest was on fire, and he could feel an aching cold seep into his bones as this new and unknown power flowed through him. He looked down at his flesh, seeing the veins and bones beneath his skin.

As he had suspected, the beast had fractured several of his ribs. He could see the splintered ends grinding together beneath the transparency of his breastplate.

He lifted his arm towards the beast, his hand passing through the ghostly outline of its translucent flesh as though it were no more substantial than smoke. He smiled dreamily as he saw that he still held Brother Amadis's pistol, its mechanisms and internal workings laid bare to his newfound sight.

He pressed his pistol against the monster's heart, within the ghostly outline of the beast's body

He opened his eyes and pulled the trigger.

An awful snap of reality reasserted itself, as the beast died in a spectacular fashion.

Zahariel's hand was buried in its flesh, his armoured vambrace penetrating its chest as though it had been implanted there. Its jaw snapped closed on his shoulder guard, the blades of its fangs punching through the plate armour and burying themselves in his body.

No sooner had its jaws closed than the lion's chest expanded with internal detonations.

Fire built behind its eyes and portions of its flanks exploded outwards as ammunition blasted out from inside the monster's body.

Its underbelly exploded in a wash of steaming entrails and it collapsed to the ground, bearing Zahariel down with it.

He groaned in pain, the weight of the beast incredible, and the pain in his shoulder like a furnace of torn muscle and blood. Every muscle ached, and he could feel a burning pain all the way down his ribcage.

Zahariel squeezed his eyes shut and bit down on his bottom lip as he pushed against the lion's corpse, rolling it onto its side. Breath heaved in his lungs, and he cried out as his broken ribs ground against one another.

The pain in his shoulder was extraordinary, the lion's fangs were still embedded in his flesh and armour. Taking a deep breath, he dropped his pistol and placed his hands on either side of the lion's huge head. Its eyes were lifeless, yet its fearsome visage still had a monstrous power. Though he knew it was unquestionably dead, he half-expected the jaw to open once more and finish what it had started.

Faster was better than slower, and he screamed in agony as he wrenched the monster's head backwards. The sharp fangs slid from his body, coated in his blood and, free of its toothy embrace, he slid backwards from its corpse.

Blood streamed from the puncture wounds in his shoulders, and he spent the next few minutes removing the armour plates and tending to the grisly injuries. He cleaned his wounds as best he could with supplies taken from the saddle bags of his broken and gored steed, and applied heavy, wadded bandages to his body.

Curiously, the pain appeared to have diminished, but he knew that was simply shock. Soon enough, it would return with interest. When he had done as much as he could for his poor, battered frame, he sank to his knees in exhaustion and finally allowed himself to think about how he had defeated the beast.

What strange power had allowed him to see the beast as he had? Had it been some after effect of his journey into the dark forest, some unknown energy that the Watchers had imparted to him?

Or was it something darker?

The Watchers had said that the taint was already in him.

Was this the manifestation of that taint?

Whatever it was, he could not explain it, and its utterly unknown quality terrified him more than the ferocity of the lion had. Whatever the cause of this strange, powerful eructation, he swore to keep it to himself. In Caliban's ancient times, people had been burned alive for less, and he had no wish to end his days on a flaming pyre.

Swaying unsteadily, Zahariel got to his feet and gathered up his sword and pistol. It was customary for a supplicant to take some portion of his quest-creature as a trophy, but the explosions within the lion's stomach had reduced much of it to gory fragments.

Searching among the grisly debris, Zahariel knew there was but one trophy he could take back to Endriago and then Aldurukh. Taking his sword, he set to work on removing the lion's head from its body, the saw-toothed blade making short work of the job now that the strange, moving plates of chitinous armour were immobile.

At last the lion's head came free from its body, and Zahariel turned towards the path that the woodsman had shown him what seemed like a lifetime ago.

Though dizzy from pain and blood loss, he was smiling as he set off in the direction of Endriago, dragging the heavy, fanged head behind him.

He wondered at what reaction his return would receive from Lord Domiel and Narel. He bore no grudge towards either man for doubting him and thinking the monster would kill him, he was simply happy to have proven them wrong. He had achieved all the aims of his quest. He had killed the beast, freeing the people of Endriago from their fear of it. At the same time, he had tested himself to his limits.

He had proved his ability. He had proved his commitment to the Order's creed of excellence, and he had proved that he was worthy to be a knight.

But in the end, what mattered most was that he was alive.

Looking back at the beast's head, he felt a deep and abiding sense of triumph. He had passed through his ordeal. He had succeeded in his hunt.

For the first time in his life, Zahariel felt he was truly worthy of the high standards he had set himself. He would never become complacent, not in the matter of proving his worth. He was made for the quest, whether it was given that name or not. There would always be another monster to slay, another battle to fight, another war to be win.

To the last heartbeat of his existence, he would never give up, he would never allow himself to falter. For the moment though, for this moment, he felt he had earned the right to a single instant of pride in his accomplishment.

Zahariel turned away from the clearing and began the long walk back to Endriago.

NINE

At Endriago, Lord Domiel gifted him a new destrier to replace the one he had lost to the lion. Having spent a week of much needed rest at the settlement in order to give his ribs and shoulder enough time to begin healing, Zahariel had eagerly begun his journey home as soon as the joyously happy citizens had let him and he was able to move without agonising pain flaring in his ribs.

Given the fact that he was repeating an earlier journey, albeit from the opposite direction, he knew which paths to take, and he managed to complete his journey to the Order's fortress monastery much more quickly than he would have expected. Thirty-eight days after leaving Endriago, he could already see the towers of Aldurukh in the distance. By the thirty-ninth day, he was at the gates.

The last part of the journey would always seem the most significant to him. As he came closer to the fortress, a sense of joyous expectation rose within him, as he thought about what it would be like to see Nemiel and the rest of his friends again.

Granted, he still had to face the Order's examiners and have his achievement verified, but with the lion's head, he expected no problem. Zahariel anticipated his homecoming warmly, expecting a heartfelt welcome from his friends, all the more so because almost everyone he knew had thought he would most likely die on the quest.

Naturally, he could not comprehend fully what that meant. Life seemed wonderful to him. It was made all the sweeter because of the relative hardships of his recent ordeal. He had faced one of the worst beasts Caliban could produce and he had survived. He wanted to celebrate that feeling with his friends.

He could not know how sorrowfully they had spent the weeks since he had left Aldurukh. His friends had thought him dead. They had grieved for him.

In their minds they had all but buried him.

The fact that he had survived despite all the fears for his safety would lend Zahariel an extra glow of heroism in the eyes of many of his contemporaries, especially those who had been supplicants with him in the Order.

At the time of his return to Aldurukh, though, he did not realise these things.

'WE ALL THOUGHT you were dead,' said Attias eagerly.

The younger lad held a box containing Zahariel's few meagre personal possessions, trailing excitedly after him as he carried his bedroll down the corridor. 'Everyone did. They all thought the beast must have killed you. There was even talk of having a funeral ceremony for you. That would've been funny, wouldn't it? Imagine if you rode back, only to find out we'd already carved your name on one of the memorial tablets in the catacombs.'

It was late afternoon on the first day after his return to Aldurukh. A few hours earlier, Zahariel had entered through the great gates of the fortress to be met by cheering and the stamping of feet. Apparently, word of his impending arrival had already come down from the lookouts, for when the gates opened it seemed as if the entire population of Aldurukh was waiting to greet him.

As Zahariel rode into the courtyard, he saw knights, supplicants and seneschals all rejoicing at his safe return. The noise of their welcome had been deafening. It was a moment he would always keep with him, the end of his first great adventure, a moment of profound homecoming, when he finally felt accepted as an equal among the ranks of the Order.

Nemiel had been waiting for him, when he arrived. He was the first to greet Zahariel, grabbing him in a great bear hug. Nemiel had talked to him, his mouth working at a frantic pace, but his words were lost to the sound of the crowd.

Afterwards, once the excitement had quietened down and Zahariel had reported to the gate keeper as was expected, he was given a time at which he should present himself to the Order's examiners. In the meantime, he had been ordered to move out of the supplicants' barracks. Half a dozen sleeping rooms were reserved in a little-visited corner of the fortress for those who had completed their quests, but had not yet been officially raised to the status of knights.

'So, this is it,' said Zahariel as he pushed open the door to his new room and looked inside. The room was empty. In keeping with the Order's monastic traditions, it was little more than a spartan cell. There was a cot in the corner for him to sleep on, but other than that there were no furnishings, not even a chair.

'I don't suppose they expect you to be here long,' jabbered Attias beside him.

Zahariel smiled indulgently, knowing that Master Ramiel was pleased with the boy's progress.

'You're so lucky,' Attias muttered. The boy said the words quietly, almost whispering.

'Lucky?' said Zahariel. He indicated the room around them. 'I take it you're going blind or haven't you noticed our fine surroundings? You've seen my new room, Attias, and yet, you call me lucky?'

'I wasn't talking about the room,' replied Attias.

Growing tired of holding the box, Attias lowered it to the cell's floor. 'I mean, you got to hunt one of the great beasts. You got to finish your quest of knighthood. I'm happy for you, really I am. You deserve it. You'll be Sar Zahariel. You'll fight wars and battles with the best of the Order's knights, alongside heroes like the Lion and Sar Luther. You'll make Master Ramiel proud. You'll be a knight.'

'And so will you, little one,' said Zahariel. 'I know it seems a long time away, but it won't be long before you are given your own quest. A couple of years, that's all it is. Follow your lessons, practise assiduously, and it will be here almost before you know it.'

'But that's just it,' Attias shook his head. 'By the time I'm old enough, things will have changed. The Order's campaign against the great beasts will be over by then. There won't be any left. And, without the great beasts, there won't be any more quests. There won't be any way to become a knight. You've done something I'll never be able to, Zahariel. You've hunted one of the great beasts. I'll never get that chance.'

As he spoke, Attias wore an expression of wistful sadness that was almost heart-breaking on the face of one so young. Attias saw a world in which there was no longer any way for a man to ascend to knighthood.

Instinctively, Zahariel rejected that bleak vision. He was an optimist and an idealist to the core of his soul.

When he looked at the Order's campaign against the beasts, he lauded its achievements. He was sure the future could only hold the things that Luther and the Lion had promised the people of Caliban before they began their campaign. When he looked to the future he saw peace and prosperity on the horizon. He saw an end to fear. He saw an end to suffering and want. He saw a better tomorrow.

When Zahariel looked to the future, he always saw the best of all possible worlds.

It was his curse.

'You are looking at these things too darkly, my friend,' said Zahariel. He smiled at the boy to reassure him. 'I know every day people talk about the campaign nearly being over, but I suspect it may well last for a good while longer. Certainly, if the monster I fought is any kind of guide, I doubt the great beasts are about to give up and die. They will fight tooth-and-nail to survive, just as they always have. So, I wouldn't worry too much, Attias. You've still got time to kill your beast, and you've got plenty of time left to become a knight.'

There was a slit window at the other end of the room, looking out across the treetops of the forest. Zahariel found his eyes drawn to it.

As had so often happened in the past, he briefly wondered at the dual nature of their world. From a distance, the forests were beautiful in a grim and forbidding way. Yet, inside those same picturesque woodlands, lived creatures that were the stuff of human nightmares, creatures like the one he had killed.

Zahariel loved Caliban, but he was not blind to it horrors. At times, it seemed as though they lived on a planet that was both hell and paradise simultaneously. Yet, the bond he felt towards his home and its forests was stronger and more powerful than almost anything else in his life. He loved his world unconditionally, whatever its flaws.

'Do you know why people sometimes call this fortress the Rock?' he asked suddenly. The view from the window, and the sight of the forests so far below them, had inspired him. He wanted to share his insight with Attias, to coax the boy from his sorrows.

'It is because the name of the fortress is Aldurukh,' answered Attias. 'It means "Rock of Eternity" in one of the old dialects. Master Ramiel said that it was originally the name of the mountain we are standing on. Then, when the Order's founders decided to build a fortress monastery at this site, they chose to use the name of the mountain for the fortress as well.'

'That's one reason,' Zahariel said, 'but there's another as well. Think about the name, Aldurukh, The Rock of Eternity. The Order has other fortress monasteries, but this was the first. It is our spiritual home and the seat of all our endeavours. So, the founders gave it a name that mattered, a name that summed up exactly what they were trying to build here. This place is our rock, Attias. It is our foundation stone. As long as it endures, then some part of our ideals will always be alive. You understand what I am trying to tell you?'

'I think so,' nodded Attias, his face screwed in an expression of concentration. 'You are saying that even after the beasts are gone, the Order will still be here, and there will still be knights.'

'Exactly,' Zahariel agreed. 'So, you see, there is no reason for you to look so sad. If it puts your mind at ease, look at it this way. It is our duty to protect people from the creatures that live in the forests. Even once the beasts are gone, that duty will not change. This is Caliban. There will always be monsters here.'

* * *

Master Ramiel was one of the first to congratulate him on becoming a knight. His former tutor clearly wanted to say more, but he was swallowed up by the throng of knights closing in from all sides to welcome Zahariel to the Order.

In contrast to the solemnity of the ceremony to induct him to the Order many years ago, his ascension to knighthood was marked by sudden pandemonium. It was a great moment in any man's life to ascend to knighthood; a moment that each of the men present had known and shared.

They swept forward en masse to accept the latest newcomer to their ranks. Beneath the hooded surplices, Zahariel saw friendly and joyful faces.

Before he knew what was happening, he was grabbed by a number of the closest men to him. Confused, Zahariel felt them hoist him off his feet. Suddenly, through the action of a dozen knights in unison, Zahariel's body was tossed into the air. He rose to above the level of their shoulders, before falling back to be caught in the hands of the same men who had thrown him.

He heard people laughing as they threw him up into the air again. His body tumbling in mid-air, Zahariel saw skewed kaleidoscope images of the faces of the men around him. They were all laughing. He knew some of them personally, but many were men who had only ever been stern and distant figures in his life.

He saw the Lion, Luther, Lord Cypher and Master Ramiel, all of them were either smiling or laughing.

Of all the sights he would see in his life, that one image would stay with him as the strangest and most improbable.

'It is a tradition,' Luther said to him, laughing as they shared a goblet of wine later, 'the springboard, I mean.

It is something we do for all the new men. Oh, but your face, that was the best part.'

They were in the main dining hall at Aldurukh. Much to Zahariel's relief, his fellow knights had reverted to more prosaic methods of marking his initiation once they had finished throwing him back-and-forth into the air like a rag doll. A feast had been held in his honour, in which numerous celebratory toasts and words of congratulation had come his way.

Knights he had only ever seen before from afar had solemnly clasped his arm and called him their brother. Zahariel did not know whether it was because they respected his achievement in killing the Beast of Endriago, or simply that they treated all new knights in a similar fashion. Either way, he had found the reaction to his ascension to knighthood almost overwhelming.

It was a moving experience, made all the more memorable by the company he was keeping. Once the meal was over and the gathering had begun to mingle and separate into smaller groups, Luther had made a special effort to seek him out.

Evidently, he thought it important that Zahariel should properly enjoy the celebrations.

'Yes, your face,' said Luther, still laughing.

Sar Luther had a good humour to him that immediately put Zahariel at ease. 'Really, it's a shame you couldn't see it for yourself. At first, when you were grabbed, you looked like you thought they were going to kill you. Then, when you realised what was really going on, I swear you looked even more frightened. At one stage, I thought you were about to piss your robes. Probably a good thing you didn't though, considering you were in mid-air at the time.'

'It was just... it caught me by surprise,' said Zahariel. 'I didn't think–'

'What? That we'd have a sense of humour?' chuckled Luther.

He put a hand to his eyes as though wiping away tears of laughter. 'No, well, people don't. That's what makes it so funny. By the way, you know I wasn't joking when I called it a tradition. Granted, it's not the kind you'd hear tell about from your masters or from Lord Cypher. But in many ways, the business of throwing the new initiate into the air like that is as much a tradition as anything else we've put you through over the years. We call it the "invisible springboard". Think of it as an antidote to the dour seriousness of the initiation ceremony. It's how we welcome you to the family.'

'The family?'

'The Order,' explained Luther. 'Do you remember what Lord Cypher said during your first initiation ceremony? We are brothers, every one of us, and brothers don't spend all their time sitting around looking po-faced or bemoaning the hardships of the world. Sometimes, we need to blow off steam. We laugh, we joke, we play pranks on each other. We do the things real brothers do. Look around this room, Zahariel. Any man in here would be willing to die for you, and they'd expect you to be willing to do the same for them. Caliban is a dangerous place, and any of us could be called upon to make the ultimate sacrifice for his brothers. That doesn't mean we can't all laugh together at times. It helps to keep us sane. We all like a joke.'

'Even him?' Zahariel asked, glancing over at Lion El'Jonson standing head-and-shoulders above the other knights around him. There was a brooding sense of aloofness about the Lion that seemed more pronounced when he was seen from a distance. Zahariel remembered the conversation he had passed with the Lion atop the fortress tower, and the sense of isolation

was curiously more palpable when the Lion was surrounded by people.

'No, you have me there,' Luther said. 'My brother is a
man alone. It has always been that way with him. It is
not that he lacks a sense of humour. If anything, the
reverse is true. You must remember that he is as much a
genius as he is a great warrior. His mind is a subtle and
complex instrument, and his humour is shaped by the
same brilliance he exhibits in everything else he does.
When my brother makes jokes, no one understands
them. He tends to pitch them too high for us rough-
house types. They go over our heads.'

A look of sadness briefly passed across Luther's face as
he gazed at the Lion. Spotting it, Zahariel felt as if he had
inadvertently intruded into a private sorrow. It made
him more acutely aware of the strength of the bond
between the Lion and Luther, an emotional attachment
that reminded him of his bond with Nemiel.

It was clear that Luther was a remarkable man, perhaps
more so even than most people gave him credit for. He
possessed phenomenal talent in a number of fields, not
least as a leader, a warrior and a huntsman. With the
exception of Lion El'Jonson, Luther had completed
quests against more great beasts than any man in Caliban's history.

In any other era, Luther would probably have been
acclaimed as the greatest hero of his age. He was a tire-
less champion of the people of Caliban, marked out as
much by his inner qualities of humour and cool
thoughtfulness in times of crisis as he was by the valour
of his deeds. It had been Luther's tragedy to be born in
the same era as a man against whom all his endeavours
would be judged and forever found wanting in comparison. From the day he had encountered Jonson in the
forest and decided to bring him to civilisation, Luther
had sounded the death-knell of his own legend.

From that point on, he had been condemned to live in the Lion's shadow.

To Zahariel's mind, it spoke even more highly of Luther that his affection for the Lion seemed genuine and unforced. Many a man in his situation might have been tempted to succumb to jealousy and begun to resent Jonson's achievements. Not Luther, he was not of that ilk.

With true brotherly devotion, he had turned all his energies to ensuring that the Lion's schemes met with every success. Luther was as much responsible for the campaign against the great beasts as Jonson, but as the campaign drew to a close it was not Luther who was receiving all the plaudits, but Jonson.

Zahariel could sense no bitterness in the man, for Luther had evidently accepted that his role in history was to be the bridesmaid to his brother's triumphs.

'My brother is a gifted man,' said Luther, his eyes still on the Lion. 'I suspect there has never been any other man like him. Certainly, no one alive today can match the range of his accomplishments. Did you know he is an excellent mimic?'

'The Lion? No, I didn't know that.'

'He can imitate the sound of any animal on Caliban, from the hunting cry of a raptor to the mating call of a serynx. He also has a wonderful singing voice. He knows all the old songs, the folk melodies of Caliban. If you heard him sing *Forests of My Fathers* it would bring tears to your eyes, I promise you. As far as I know he has never tried to create original musical works of his own, but you can be sure if he did the results would be inspiring. My brother excels at whatever he turns his hands to, that is his tragedy.'

'His tragedy?' asked Zahariel, wrong-footed for a moment. 'How is it a tragedy to be good at everything?'

'Perhaps tragedy is too strong a word for it,' Luther shrugged as he turned back towards Zahariel, 'but you must remember that my brother is unique. He never speaks of his origins; they are as much a source of mystery to him as they are to everyone else. One might almost think of him as some god or demi-god fallen to earth, rather than a man born of woman like the rest of us. My brother is set apart through no fault of his own. His intelligence is so dazzling, so extraordinary, there are times when even I cannot follow his line of reasoning, and I have known him for years, long enough to grow accustomed to his thought processes.

'Think how boring it must be for him,' continued Luther. 'Don't misunderstand me: my brother loves Caliban and he loves the Order. But sometimes it must feel to him like he is a giant in a land of pygmies, both physically and mentally. Lord Cypher says that intellectual stimulation is based on the free discourse of ideas between equals, but my brother has no equals, not on Caliban. Here, in the Order, we give him an outlet for his energies. We give him camaraderie and a sense of purpose. We give him our devotion. We would follow him unto death, but these things are not enough in a man's life. Even surrounded by friends and followers on all sides, my brother is still lonely. There is no one on Caliban like him. He is the loneliest man in the world.'

'I never thought of it that way before,' said Zahariel.

'You probably shouldn't think of it again,' said Luther with a shake of his head. He raised the wine goblet in his hand and sniffed at it in mock appraisal. 'Listen to me, it is a celebration and somehow I manage to make it mournful. I shall have to have words with the Order's master vintner about the wines he serves at these functions. This one certainly inclines men to pensiveness where they should be jolly. To compound its flaws, it also leaves behind a vinegary aftertaste. And to think, when I came over here to talk to you, my only intention was to apologise for playing the devil.'

'Playing the devil?'

'When you first joined the Order and you were originally initiated,' said Luther. 'It is part of the ritual. You are asked questions by three different interrogators. One of the interrogators is given the task of trying to undermine and belittle the candidate for knighthood. He is expected to find fault with anything the candidate may decide to say or do. The negative interrogator is called "the devil". It's all symbolic of course, based on some old superstition. Lord Cypher could probably tell you more about it. I just wanted you to know that there was nothing personal in the fact that I played the devil at your ceremony. It is a ritual role, that's all. It is chosen by lots, so it was sheer chance I happened to be called upon to do it. I never had any doubts about your abilities. I suspect you will go on to be one of our best and brightest.'

Luther extended a hand to clasp Zahariel's forearm just below the elbow and Zahariel did likewise. It was a traditional gesture of friendship on Caliban.

'I congratulate you, Sar Zahariel,' he said, gazing over Zahariel's shoulder at the knights around them. 'I suppose I should take a stroll around the room. There are several other knights I need to see.'

Luther turned away, only to glance back at Zahariel before he went.

'Oh, and Zahariel, if you ever need advice you know where to come. Feel free to call on me at any time. If you have a problem I will always listen.'

NEMIEL HAD ALREADY spoken to Zahariel that night, as had Master Ramiel. Nemiel seemed thrilled that his cousin had finally become one of the Order's knights.

Having no great head for alcohol, Zahariel had sipped sparingly at his wine, but Nemiel had indulged his thirst more liberally.

Apparently, while Zahariel had hunted the Beast of Endriago, Nemiel had requested a beast hunt of his own. As if to prove that their competitive games were as alive as ever, Nemiel had returned to Aldurukh barely a week before Zahariel.

He was slurring his words by the time they were able to have a proper conversation, his friend holding forth with grandiose visions of both their futures.

'You've made your mark already, cousin,' said Nemiel, breathing out wine fumes as he swayed unsteadily on his feet, 'we both have. We've proved we've got what it takes. This is only the beginning. One day, we'll rise as high in the Order as it's possible to go. We'll be like the Lion and Luther, you and me. We are brothers in all of this, and we will re-make our world together.'

Master Ramiel had been more circumspect. As ever, Zahariel found it difficult to read his master's face. After Nemiel had staggered away to slump into a nearby chair and fall asleep, Ramiel had come to offer further congratulations to his former student.

'Sar Zahariel,' his master said. 'It has a pleasing ring to it. Remember, though, it is when a man has been made a knight that the hard work begins. Until this point, you were only a boy who wanted to be a knight and a man. Now, you will learn just how heavy both those burdens can be.'

Ramiel said nothing more and excused himself, leaving Zahariel to ponder the meaning of his words.

Zahariel wondered what his mentor had meant, recognising a sense of restlessness within him, something different from any subtle disquiet his master's words had caused him.

Having devoted so many of his energies for so long towards becoming a knight, he felt a rumbling sense of discontent, a feeling of being incomplete.

He had achieved the ambition of his boyhood.

What new ambition would he find to guide his life?

LATER IN THE evening, Zahariel found himself in conversation with Lord Cypher, the old man similarly in his cups and waxing lyrical on the subject of the various ranks and positions within the Order.

What had begun as a conversation on the solemn vows he would go on to swear as a knight had evolved, largely by the artifice of Lord Cypher, into a discussion of the upper hierarchy of the Order and his position within it.

'Of course, that is why some think Ramiel will be made the new Lord Cypher when Jonson ascends to become Grand Master.'

'I thought it was only rumour,' said Zahariel, 'about the Lion being made Grand Master, I mean. I didn't think it had been confirmed?'

'Eh?' said Lord Cypher staring blankly at him in confusion. Eventually, after a pause of a few seconds, understanding dawned on his face. 'Ah, I may have been too loose with my secrets, really, an unforgivable mistake for a man in my position.'

Lord Cypher sighed. 'I must be getting older than I thought. Still, there's no making a young man forget something once he's heard it. Yes, you're right. It hasn't been confirmed, but the decision has been made, we just haven't announced it yet. Jonson will be the new Grand Master and Luther will be his second-in-command. As for me, I shall be retiring from my duties in a couple of days. Then, it will be down to Jonson to choose my successor. Really, I have no idea who he'll pick, but Master Ramiel would be a good candidate, don't you think?'

'Very much so,' nodded Zahariel. 'I think he would make a fine Lord Cypher.'

'Yes, he would. That opinion is for your ears only, Zahariel, as is everything else I have just said. Don't compound the dual faults of an old man's memory and a slip of the tongue by telling everyone about it. It would only embarrass me, and make the Order's hierarchy think they should have got rid of me a long time ago. Can I rely on your good intentions in this?'

'Absolutely. You have my word that I will never repeat this conversation to anyone.'

'Excellent,' said Lord Cypher. 'I am glad to see you understand the value of discretion.'

He gazed around for long seconds, his failing eyes taking in the scene of knights enjoying wine and conversation with each other. Then, without warning, the Lord Cypher turned away to leave the gathering.

Unaccountably, Zahariel was put in mind of an old bear shuffling into the forest to die.

'The Order is in good hands,' said Lord Cypher, offering the words as a parting shot over his shoulder as he moved away. 'Between men like Jonson, Luther, Master Ramiel, and even youngsters like you, I am confident it will continue to thrive in the decades ahead. I doubt I will live to see it, but I am content all the same. It is time for one generation to give way to the next, as is the way of things. I have no fear for the future.'

IT WAS THE last time Zahariel would ever speak to the man who had been Lord Cypher at the time he joined the Order. For that matter, it was the last time he would ever see him.

In a few days' time, a quest would be declared against another beast in the Northwilds in the vicinity of a settlement named Bradin. Having retired from his duties, the ex-Lord Cypher would petition the Order's hierarchy to be allowed to take on the quest. They would accede to his request and the old man would ride quietly from Aldurukh early one morning while most of the fortress was still sleeping.

He would never be seen again.

Some would claim the beast he was hunting had killed him; others would say he had more likely been brought down by a pack of raptors before reaching the Northwilds.

The truth would never be known, but in the wake of his disappearance a place of honour would be set aside for him in the catacombs beneath Aldurukh. It was a small space, a rocky shelf no more than a third of a metre wide and half a metre tall, large enough to hold an urn full of ashes or some of the old man's bones if his body were ever found.

His name would also be carved into the rock by the Order's stonemasons.

This was the shape of days to come. Zahariel could not know what would happen in the future, any more than he could know he would never see the Lord Cypher, or rather, this particular Lord Cypher again.

Another individual would wear that title in the Order, and his true character would always be a mystery.

It was all a matter of the future.

For the moment, as the knights of the Order drank and celebrated together, the only thing left to complete Zahariel's ascension to knighthood was to have his status confirmed by the Lion.

'IT HAS BEEN a momentous night for both of us,' said Lion El'Jonson. 'You have become a knight, and I have learned I am about to become its new Grand Master.'

'Our Grand Master?' asked Zahariel. Mindful of the promise he had made to Lord Cypher earlier, and shocked that Jonson would even consider mentioning such a thing to him when the news was not yet common currency, Zahariel was lost for words. 'I… ah… congratulations.'

'Don't act so surprised, Zahariel,' said Jonson.

His tone was neither chiding nor unkind as he steered Zahariel away from the gathered knights towards a secluded corner of the great hall. Firelight and shadows played across the great warrior's face, and Zahariel realised with a start that he doubted whether he had ever seen the Lion in daylight or without the refuge of shadows close by.

The revelries were dying down as the wine did its work, and as the Lion had approached him, Zahariel knew his part in the festivities was almost concluded.

'Let's not pretend you don't know it already,' said the Lion. 'I couldn't help but catch some of your conversation with Lord Cypher earlier. I wasn't trying to eavesdrop, but my senses are sharp, especially my hearing, almost preternaturally so. I heard Lord Cypher's slip of the tongue. I know that you know I am to be made Grand Master.'

'I am sorry,' said Zahariel, bowing his head. 'My finding out about it was entirely accidental. I assure you, I won't repeat it to any–'

'It's all right, Zahariel,' said Jonson, holding a hand up to silence him. 'I trust your discretion and I realise you were in no way at fault. Besides which, it is already the worst-kept secret on Caliban. People tend to forget how good my hearing is. I have heard my impending promotion discussed by at least three dozen different people in the last few days, all when they think I am out of earshot.'

'Then may I offer you my congratulations, my lord,' said Zahariel.

'You may,' smiled the Lion, 'and they are gratefully accepted, though in practical terms my new role will make little difference to my life.'

'You are Grand Master of the Order,' said Zahariel. 'That must feel… important.'

'Oh I'll grant you I'm proud to lead you all, but such was my role beforehand, though I did not have the title for it. How about you? Do you feel any different now that you are a knight?'

'Of course.'

'How so?'

For a moment, Zahariel was flustered, not quite knowing how he felt. 'Honoured, proud of my achievements, accepted.'

'And all of these are good things,' nodded the Lion, 'but you are just the same, Zahariel. You are still the same person you were before you killed the lion. You have crossed a line, but it does not change who you are. Don't forget that. A man may be dressed up in all manner of fancy titles, but he must not let it change him or else ego, pride and ambition will be his undoing. No matter what grand title is bestowed upon you, to thine own self be true, Zahariel. Do you understand?'

'I think so, my lord,' said Zahariel.

'I hope that you do,' said the Lion. 'It is an easy thing to forget, for all of us.'

The Lion then leaned conspiratorially close and said, 'Did you know we two now share a brotherhood shared by no others on Caliban?'

'We do?' said Zahariel, surprised and flattered. 'What brotherhood?'

'We are the only warriors ever to kill a Calibanite lion. All others who tried are dead. One day you must tell me how you killed it.'

Zahariel felt a justifiable swell of pride and fraternity as the import of his killing the beast sank in. The tale of how Lord Jonson had slain a Calibanite lion was well known and was commemorated upon one of the windows of the Circle Chamber, but until now, it had not occurred to him that he had survived an encounter with so unique a beast.

'I am honoured to share that brotherhood, my lord,' said Zahariel, bowing his head.

'It is one that will only ever comprise of you and I, Zahariel,' said the Lion. 'There are no others of their kind on Caliban. The great beasts are almost extinct and there will be no others like them on our world ever again. Part of me thinks I should be sad about that, after all, extinction is such a final solution don't you think?'

'They are beasts that exist only to kill, why should we not exterminate them? They would do the same to us were it not for the knightly orders.'

'True, but do they do it because they are evil, or because it is the way they were made?'

Zahariel thought back to the beasts he had fought and said, 'I do not know if they were evil as such, but each time I have faced one. I have seen something in its eyes, some, I don't know… desire to kill that is more than simply animal hunger. Something in the beasts is… wrong.'

'Then you are perceptive, Zahariel,' said the Lion. 'There *is* something wrong with the beasts. I don't know what it is, but they are not just some other race of beasts like horses, foxes or humans, they are aberrations, twisted mistakes wrought from some early form that has not yet had the good grace to die out on its own. Can you imagine what it must be like to be so singular a creature? To go through life knowing, even on some animal, instinctual level that you are alone and that there will never be more of you. Think how maddening that must be. The beasts were not just driven by hunger, they were insane, driven to madness by their very uniqueness. Trust me, Zahariel, we are doing them a favour by destroying them all.'

Zahariel nodded and sipped his wine, too caught up with the Lion's words to dare to interrupt him. A strange melancholy had crept into his leader's words, as though he was recalling a distant memory that flitted just beyond the reach of recall.

Then, suddenly, it was gone, as though the Lion realised he had spoken unguardedly.

'Of course, there will be some who are upset that you killed the last of the lions,' said Jonson. 'Luther, for one.'

'Sar Luther? How so?'

Lord Jonson laughed. 'He always wanted to kill a lion. Now he'll never get the chance.'

As PARTIES WENT, it had been a fine one.

Zahariel had enjoyed the company of the other knights. He had enjoyed the feeling that he could look at these men as his peers, and with it came a feeling of inclusion, of acceptance. Following his talk with Lion El'Jonson, Zahariel had returned to his fellow knights, where the talk had turned to the war against the Knights of Lupus.

All agreed that the war was in its final stages and that the final destruction of the rebellious order would be complete in the very near future.

He had enjoyed good food and wine, and he had enjoyed the expression in Master Ramiel's eyes, the one that said he had made his teacher proud. Most of all, he had enjoyed the moment, for he knew that such triumphs were rare in a man's life.

They must be handled with care, and then put away as memories for the future.

TEN

'WAR IS A terrible beauty,' the knightly poet philosopher Aureas wrote in the pages of his *Meditations*. 'It is breathtaking and horrifying in equal measure. Once a man has seen its face, the memory of it never leaves him. War gouges a mark into the soul.'

Zahariel had heard those words often in the course of his training.

They were among the favourites of his former mentor, Master Ramiel. The old man had liked to quote them regularly, reciting the same few pithy sentences on a daily basis as he attempted to turn ranks of supplicants from fresh-faced boys into knights.

They had been as much part of his teachings as firing practice and extra sword drills.

Among those who had come to knighthood under Ramiel's tutelage, it was said they went armed with an appreciation of fine words alongside the Order's more usual weapons of sword and pistol.

Still, as often as he had heard the words, Zahariel never truly understood them, not until the final days of the war against the Knights of Lupus.

His first impression as he emerged from the forest, riding his destrier, on the night of the final assault was that the sky was alive with fire. Earlier in the day, he had supervised the gangs of woodsmen cutting timbers for siege engines in the forests on the lower slopes of the mountain.

His duties complete, he returned to camp at nightfall expecting things to be quiet.

Instead, he found his fellow knights of the Order about to attack the enemy fortress.

Ahead, in the distance, the fortress monastery of the Knights of Lupus sat on a brooding crag at the summit of the mountain, a towering line of grey walls and warriors. Surrounded on all sides by the concentric circles of the Order's siege lines, the fortress was a masterpiece of military architecture, but Zahariel's eyes were drawn to the extraordinary spectacle unfolding in the air above the two armies as they fired their artillery at each other across no-man's-land.

The air was thick with flames of a dozen shapes, colours and patterns. Zahariel saw the short-lived green and orange flare trails left by tracer rounds, the streaming red haloes of burning incendiaries in flight and the smoky yellow fireballs of cannon bursts.

A bright tapestry of fire illuminated the sky, and Zahariel had never before seen its like.

He found it equally appalling and spectacular at the same time.

'A terrible beauty,' he whispered, the words of Aureas returning to him as he stared in wonderment at the startling sky. The colours were so exquisite it was easy to forget the fact that they portended danger. The same projectiles that burned through the heavens with such beauty would bring agony and death to some unfortunate soul when they reached their target.

War, it seemed, was full of contradictions.

Later, he would learn that there was nothing unusual in the sights he saw in the sky that night, but this was his first siege and he knew no better. Pitched battles were so rare on Caliban that his training had largely concentrated on close combat rather than questions of siege craft.

Since the coming of the Lion, the knights of Caliban rarely made war against each other, at least not in any major or systematic way. Normally, any conflict undertaken to resolve some issue of affront or insult would take one of the traditional forms of ritual combat.

A conflict of the kind he could see before him, where two knightly orders made ready to bring the best part of their entire strength to bear in a single battle, happened hardly once in a generation.

'You there!' called a voice from behind.

Zahariel turned to see one of the Order's siege masters marching furiously towards him, his expression thunderous beneath his hood. 'The assault is about to begin. Why aren't you in position? Give me your name, sar!'

'My apologies, master,' said Zahariel, bowing from the saddle. 'I am Sar Zahariel. I have just returned from the lower slopes. I was detailed to–'

'Zahariel?' the master cut him off. 'The killer of the Lion of Endriago?'

'Yes, master.'

'So, it is not cowardice that kept you back. I see that now. Whose sword-line are you attached to?'

'I am with Sar Hadariel's men, master, stationed on the western approaches.'

'They have been moved,' said the master. He pointed impatiently to the siege lines to Zahariel's right. 'They are positioned for the assault on the south wall. You'll find them over there somewhere. Leave your destrier with the ostlers on the way, and hurry up, boy. The war won't wait on you.'

'I understand,' Zahariel said, dismounting. 'Thank you, master.'

'You want to thank me, do your part in the battle,' growled the siege master as he turned away. 'You can expect a hard time of it. We've been camped out here too long already, which means the Lupus bastards have had plenty of time to prepare to repel our assault.'

He paused to hawk up a glob of spit, before looking towards the enemy fortress with what seemed like an expression of grudging respect.

'If you think you can see fire now, just wait until you're charging those walls.'

IF ANYTHING, THE bombardment seemed to grow more ferocious as Zahariel hurried through the siege lines on foot. The enemy guns did not have the range to hit the Order's emplacements directly, but their shells fell close enough to shower the forward positions with debris.

As Zahariel neared the front lines, he heard a series of sharp, high-pitched whines as shrapnel ricocheted from the plates encasing his body. The armour did its job, deflecting harm and keeping the meat and bone of him safe, but he was relieved when he finally saw Sar Hadariel's tattered war banner fluttering from the maze of trenches around him.

He jumped down into the trench. Armoured warriors surrounded him in the semi-darkness, the black of their armour shimmering with reflected fire.

'You made it then, brother?' said Nemiel, the first to greet him as he landed.

The speaking grille of Nemiel's helmet distorted the words, but Zahariel would have known his cousin's voice anywhere. 'I was beginning to wonder whether you had thought better of it and decided to go home.'

'And leave you all the glory?' said Zahariel. 'You should know me better than that, brother.'

'I know you better than you think,' said Nemiel.

His cousin's face was hidden within his helmet, but from the tone of his voice, Zahariel knew he was smiling. 'Certainly, I know you enough to realise you probably rushed breathlessly over here from the moment you heard the bombardment begin. You can't fool me, glory doesn't come into it with you. It's all about duty.'

Nemiel jerked a thumb towards the front of the trench and indicated for Zahariel to follow him. 'Well, come on then, brother, let's see what your high ideals have got you into.'

The remaining eight men of the sword-line were already standing beside the front trench wall, looking out into the open ground between the siege lines and the enemy fortress. As Zahariel approached, the flash of nearby cannon bursts illuminated them at irregular intervals.

Each man was armed and armoured in identical fashion to Zahariel, carrying a pistol equipped with explosive rounds and a tooth-bladed sword. They wore black plate armour and hooded surplices marked with the Order's identifying emblem of a sword with its blade pointed downwards.

It was traditional for the knights of the Order to keep their white surplices spotless, but Zahariel was surprised to see that every other man in the trench was daubed in mud from head-to-toe.

'You are too clean, brother,' Sar Hadariel said, turning from his place at the trench wall to glance at him.

'Didn't anyone tell you? The Lion has issued instructions that we should blacken our surplices so we will not present as much of a target for the enemy gunners when the assault begins.'

'I am sorry, sar,' Zahariel replied. 'I didn't know.'

'No harm, lad,' shrugged Hadariel. 'You know now. I'd be quick to rectify it if I was you. The word won't be long in coming. When it does, you don't want to be the only man wearing white in the middle of a night assault.'

Sar Hadariel turned to gaze back towards the enemy fortress, and Zahariel hurried to follow his advice. Releasing the belt that held the loose surplice in place, he lifted it over his head and stooped to soak the garment in the watery mud at the bottom of the trench.

'I always said you were an original thinker,' remarked Nemiel as Zahariel rose and put the surplice back on. 'The rest of us just left them on and spent ten minutes smearing handfuls of mud over ourselves. You come along, take the surplice off and achieve the same effect in fifteen seconds. Of course, I'm not sure what it says about your talent for lateral thinking that it finds its fullest expression in solving the problem of getting yourself dirty.'

'You're just jealous you didn't think of it,' Zahariel shot back. 'If you had, I'm sure you'd acclaim it as the greatest development in warfare since they started breeding destriers.'

'Well, naturally, if *I* did it then it really would be clever,' Nemiel said. 'The difference is that when I come up with a good idea it's through foresight and deep thinking. When you do it, it's usually through plain luck.'

They laughed, though Zahariel suspected it was more a reaction to the tension they both felt than any particular humour in Nemiel's words.

It was a familiar game, one the two of them had played since childhood, a game of one-upmanship that they turned to automatically as they waited out the nervous minutes until the assault began in earnest.

It was the kind of game played only by brothers.

'THEY'RE MOVING THE siege engines forward,' said Nemiel, observing the assault's early stages. 'It won't be long now. Soon, we'll get the signal. Then, we'll be right in the middle of it.'

As though in reaction to Nemiel's words, the enemy guns seemed to redouble their efforts, unleashing yet more fire into the sky. As the noise of the barrage grew to deafening proportions, Zahariel realised that Nemiel was right, the assault was beginning to move forward.

Ahead, in the no-man's-land between the Order's siege-lines and the walls of the fortress, he saw three anikols make their slow, incremental way towards the enemy.

Named for a native Calibanite animal that relied on its shell-like armour to keep it safe from predators, each anikol was a wheeled mantlet covered in an overlapping patchwork of metal plates designed to protect the men inside it from enemy projectiles. Powered by nothing more than the muscles of the dozen men who sheltered within it, the anikol was a necessarily slow and unwieldy siege weapon.

Its only advantage lay in its ability to soak up enemy firepower, allowing its crew to get close enough to lay explosive charges to breach the walls of the fortress. At least, such was the theory.

As Zahariel watched their advance, he saw a flaming missile arc through the air from the fortress battlements and crash through the lead anikol's armour. In a fiery instant the siege-engine disappeared in a powerful explosion.

'A lucky shot,' said Nemiel, dragging his eyes from Zahariel's scabbard. 'They must have hit it at a spot where the armour was weak. They'll never manage to hit the other two in the same way. One of the anikols will get through. Then, it will be our turn. The main thrust of the attack will be against the south wall of the fortress. Once the anikols have created a breach, we'll be the first wave as we take advantage of it.'

'All our eggs in one basket,' said Zahariel.

'Far from it,' said Nemiel with a shake of the head. 'At the same time, diversionary attacks will be launched against each of the north, east and west walls to divide the forces of the knights of Lupus and draw off their reserves, but that's not the cunning part.'

'What's the cunning part?'

'To further confuse the enemy, the diversionary attacks are each going to have a different character from the main assault. The attack on the east wall is to be made using siege-towers, while the west wall assault will involve scaling ladders and grappling hooks.'

'Clever,' said Zahariel. 'They won't know which is the main attack.'

'It gets better,' replied Nemiel. 'Guess who'll be leading the assault on the gates of the north wall?'

'Who?'

'The Lion,' said Nemiel.

'Seriously?'

'Seriously.'

As they watched the remaining anikols move slowly forward, Zahariel said, 'I can't believe the Lion will be heading the attack on the north gates. It's only a diversion. You'd expect him to lead the main attack.'

'I think that's the idea,' answered Nemiel. 'When the Knights of Lupus see the Lion at their north wall, they'll assume it's the focus of our efforts. They'll concentrate their troops there, allowing the real main assault an easier time of it.'

'Still, it's a terrible risk,' said Zahariel, shaking his head in concern. 'Without the Lion, the campaign against the great beasts would never have happened. And, he stands at least two heads taller than anyone else on Caliban. Even if enemy snipers don't pick him out, there's the chance the north assault will be overwhelmed for lack of numbers. I don't know if the Order could stand losing the Lion. I don't know if Caliban could.'

'Apparently, the same points were made at the strategy meeting when the Lion put forward his plan,' whispered Nemiel, leaning forward in a conspiratorial manner, though he had to shout to be heard over the continuing barrage. 'They say Sar Luther was particularly opposed to it. Jonson asked him to lead the main assault, but initially Luther refused. He said he hadn't fought side-by-side with him for all these years only to let the Lion go alone into the midst of a dangerous undertaking. He said his place was where it had always been, right by the Lion's side, until death claimed them both. "If you die, Lion, then I die with you." That's what Luther said.'

'Now I know you're making it up,' interrupted Zahariel. 'How could you know what Sar Luther said? You weren't there. You're just spinning a tale and embroidering it too freely. This is all just camp gossip.'

'Camp gossip, yes,' agreed Nemiel, 'but from a reliable source. I heard it from Varael. You know him? He was one of Master Ramiel's students, but a year older than us. He heard it from Yeltus, who heard it from one of the seneschals, who knows someone who was in the command tent when it happened.

They say Jonson and Luther had a furious row, but eventually Luther acceded to the Lion's wishes.'

'I almost wish he hadn't,' said Zahariel. 'Don't get me wrong, Luther is a great man, but when I heard we would be assaulting the fortress, I hoped to fight under the Lion's banner. He inspires all those around him, and I can't imagine a greater honour than fighting alongside him. I had hoped it would be today.'

'There's always tomorrow, cousin,' said Nemiel. 'We're knights of Caliban now, and the war against the great beasts is not over yet, never mind the war against the Knights of Lupus. There's every chance you'll fight at Lord Jonson's side sooner rather than later.'

In no-man's-land, the anikols' crews had abandoned their siege engines. Having placed their charges and set the fuses, they broke from cover and ran towards their own lines.

The enemy on the battlements opened fire when crewmen were in the open, and Zahariel saw at least half of the men fall before they reached the safety of the Order's trenches. All the while, he crouched in his trench, waiting for the inevitable explosion.

When it came, the blast was spectacular.

The two anikols parked against the fortress walls disappeared in plumes of rising flames as twin explosions rocked the ground underneath him and briefly drowned out the noise of the bombardment. By the time the smoke and dust cleared, Zahariel could see that the anikols had completed their mission.

The outer wall of the enemy fortress was cracked and fire-blackened in two places. In one area it had held firm, but the other the wall had collapsed, creating a breach.

'Arm up,' yelled Sar Hadariel to the men in the trench around him. 'I want safeties off and swords bared. No quarter to the enemy. This is not a tourney or judicial combat. This is war. We take the fortress or we die. They are our only options.'

'This is it, cousin,' said Nemiel. 'Here's your chance to use that fancy sword of yours.'

Zahariel nodded, ignoring the thinly cloaked barb of jealousy in his cousin's tone at the mention of his sword. His hand drifted instinctively to the weapon. The hilt and grip were plain and unassuming, bare metal and leather wound with a bronze pommel, but the blade... the blade was something special.

At Lord Jonson's behest, the Order's artificers had taken one of the sabre-like fangs of the lion that Zahariel had slain and fashioned it into a sword for him. Its sheen was a pearlescent white, like a tusk, and its edge was lethally sharp, able to part metal or timber at a single stroke. As long as Zahariel's forearm, it was shorter than a normal sword, but its added potency more than made up for his reduced reach.

The Lion had presented him with the sword before they had set off for the fortress of the Knights of Lupus, and Zahariel had felt the connection of the brotherhood the Order's Grand Master had spoken of as he had drawn the blade.

Luther and his fellow knights had congratulated him, but Zahariel had seen Nemiel's jealous eyes linger on the blade as it threw back the sunlight on its smoothed face.

Zahariel heard the sound of a serynx horn, calling across the battlefield in a long, mournful tone, and drew his sword to the admiring glances of his fellow knights.

'There's the signal!' shouted Hadariel. 'Attack! Attack! Forward! For the Lion! For Luther! For the honour of the Order!'

Already, dozens of figures could be seen emerging from the trenches around them. Zahariel heard Hadariel's battle cry taken up by hundreds of voices as more knights rose from their trenches and began to charge towards the fortress.

Zahariel recognised the sound of his own voice among the din, even as he leapt from the trench to join the charge.

'You wanted to make history,' shouted Nemiel beside him, 'now's our chance!'

With that, Nemiel took up the cry as it resounded through no-man's-land.

'For the Lion! For Luther! For the Order!'

Together, they charged into the breach.

Afterwards, in the annals of the Order, the chroniclers would record it as a decisive moment in the history of Caliban. The defeat of the Knights of Lupus would be characterised as a victory made in the name of human progress.

Lion El'Jonson's leadership would be praised, as would Luther's bravery in leading the main assault. The chroniclers would write fulsomely of the white surplices of the Order's knights, of how they gleamed in the moonlight as their owners charged in daredevil fashion towards the enemy defences.

The reality was, of course, somewhat different.

It was his first taste of war, of mass conflict, of the life-or-death struggle between two opposing armies, and Zahariel was afraid. It was not so much that he feared death. Life on Caliban was hard. It bred fatalism into its sons. From childhood he had been taught that his life was a finite resource that could be snatched from him at any moment. By the age of eight, he had faced death directly at least a dozen times. In the Order, once he had completed his first year's training as a supplicant, he had been expected to practise with real blades and live ammunition.

As part of that same training he had stalked many of the predators that lurked in the forests, including cave-bears, swordtooths, deathwings and raptors. Finally, to prove himself worthy, he had undergone the ultimate test of his prowess, hunting one of the feared Caliban-ite lions.

He had confronted the creature and he had slain it, earning his knighthood.

War, though, was different from all these triumphs.

When a man hunted an animal, whatever its status, the hunt took the form of an extended duel, a contest of strength, skill and cunning between man and beast. In the course of a hunt, Zahariel would grow to know his adversary intimately. In contrast, war was an imper-sonal affair.

As he charged towards the enemy fortress beside his fellow knights, Zahariel realised that he could be struck dead on the battlefield without ever knowing the iden-tity of his killer.

He might die and never see his enemy's face.

It was strange, he supposed, but somehow it *did* make a difference.

He had always assumed that he would die facing his killer, whether it was a great beast, some lesser animal, or even another knight. The prospect of a death in the midst of battle, brought down at range by some anony-mous foe, seemed almost terrifying.

Unnerved, Zahariel briefly felt icy fingers clutching at his heart.

He did not allow it to get the better of him. He was a son of Caliban. He was a knight of the Order. He was a man, and men feel fear, but he refused to surrender to it. His training as a knight included mental exercises intended to help steel his mind in times of crisis. He turned to them now.

He reminded himself of the sayings of the *Verbatim*, the tome from which flowed all the Order's teachings. He reminded himself of Master Ramiel. He thought of the old man's unblinking gaze, the eyes that seemed to drill into his soul. He thought of how disappointed the old man would be if he heard that Zahariel had failed in his duty.

Sometimes, it occurred to Zahariel, it is the height of bravery in a man's life, simply to be able to put one foot in front of the other and continue in one direction even when every fibre of his being is saying he should turn and the run the other way.

Even as Zahariel ran towards the breach in the fortress wall, he saw bright descending flares as flaming projectiles roared to earth to land among the mass of charging knights. He heard screams, the shrill cries of wounded and dying men rising above the tumult. He saw knights caught in the blast of incendiaries, their bodies wreathed in flame and arms flailing uselessly around them as they stumbled past his field of vision to their deaths.

According to the artificers, each suit was once capable of being sealed against its environment, but such days were now gone. A close enough strike from an incendiary and a knight was all but guaranteed a horrific death as the heat from the fire leaked through his armour.

Scores of knights were dying.

Dozens more screamed in pain as they were wounded.

The assault was faltering.

ELEVEN

THE RUBBLE- AND body-strewn slopes of the breach were thick with fire and fury. The curtain of smoke twitched with the passage of bullets, and Zahariel heard the awful sound of their impacts on the knights' steel plates. The air was filled with buzzing and whining as projectiles whizzed past him.

Zahariel's tutors had schooled him on the different sounds bullets made as they passed and how to tell how close they were, but in the roaring hell of fire, smoke and noise in the breach, he couldn't recall any of those lessons.

He scrambled over heaps of twisted rubble, broken slabs of masonry brought down by the explosions that had blasted the walls and piles of loose spoil that had been used as infill. Here and there, he saw the mangled body of one of his enemies, knights in shattered armour who lay broken and dead.

A shot ricocheted from his shoulder guard, sending him lurching off balance, but he quickly recovered from the impact and pushed on. Nemiel was beside him, scrambling up the slope of the breach with frantic energy, desperate to be the first to the top. Geysers of dirt were punched upwards by bullets, and coiling spirals flitted through the air as hails of missiles sawed from above.

Zahariel could see nothing of their enemies beyond smudged silhouettes and flaring muzzle flashes. Scores of knights were dead, but many more were still alive, wading through the weight of fire, and climbing the steep slope of rock and debris to get to grips with the Knights of Lupus.

The fear of death in this hellish ruin was great, but so too was the fear that his first battle as a Knight of the Order might also be his last. He had endured so much and fought so hard to reach this point that he did not want this inglorious, smoke-filled valley of rubble to be the site of his first and final charge.

Zahariel pushed on, the climb awkward due to his sword, but he was loath to climb to the top of the slope and meet an enemy without a blade in his hand. The ground shifted under his feet and he scrambled for purchase as he heard a hard *thunk* above him, as of timber on stone.

He looked up, seeing the shadow of something bouncing down through the smoke. Its sound was heavy and wooden, and he instantly knew what it was.

'Get down!' he yelled. 'Everyone get down! A mine!'

'No!' cried another voice, a more persuasive one. 'Keep going!'

Zahariel turned to see Sar Luther standing in the centre of the breach, bullets and flames whipping around him as though afraid to touch him. Sar Luther's arm was extended, and Zahariel saw that he held his pistol aimed up into the smoke.

Luther's pistol barked and the barrel of explosives vanished in a blinding white sheet of fire and noise high above them. The noise was incredible, and a cascade of shattered rocks tumbled down upon the knights of the Order.

Sar Luther looked down on Zahariel. 'Up! Everyone get moving up! Now!'

Zahariel leapt to his feet as though the words were hardwired to his nervous system, and began climbing into the fire as though a pack of Calibanite lions were hot on his heels. The rest of his sword line and a dozen others followed suit, the power of Luther's words driving them onwards.

He saw Nemiel up ahead, and pushed himself harder, not caring about the danger or the fear. The storm of shells from above intensified and he felt a number of stinging impacts on his armour, but none serious enough to stop him. Zahariel glanced behind him to see how many of the knights still climbed.

The red edges of the banner of the Order were frayed and scorched, its fabric ripped with tattered bullet holes, but the banner still flew, and the warriors around it climbed on in the face of almost certain death and pain thanks to its presence.

Zahariel took pride in watching the banner fly above the noble knights of the Order, and returned his attention to the climb ahead of him.

He pushed on, following Sar Luther as he forged upwards, passing every other warrior in the breach with unimaginable courage and speed. Luther's steps seemed to flow over the rubble, his every footfall helped, his every step as sure as though he walked on a parade ground and not some terrifyingly dangerous breach.

The knights around Luther followed his shining example and followed him. Zahariel went after him into the smoke and felt the slope beneath his feet growing less steep as he climbed. Shapes resolved from the smoke, and he heard a blood-curdling war cry as the Knights of Lupus charged with their distinctive battle howl upon their lips.

Fearsome warriors clad in wolf pelts and bedecked with fangs, the Knights of Lupus may not have been numerous, but each one of them was a great warrior, a fighter trained in the ways of combat and the pursuit of knowledge.

Zahariel ducked a swinging axe blade and thrust with his sword, the blade punching through his attacker's armour as if through wetted parchment. The man screamed foully and crumpled, blood jetting from his midriff. He wrenched the sword clear and drew the pistol he had been given by Brother Amadis.

All around him was chaos, knights of the Order and the Knights of Lupus caught up in a swirling melee of hacking, roaring chainblades and booming pistols. Zahariel shot and cut and hacked his way through the midst of the hardest fighting, pushing through the screaming throng to reach Sar Luther.

Nemiel bludgeoned his way through the fighting, using brute force and adrenaline to defeat his foes rather than finesse. Even as the knights of the Order began to overwhelm the defenders of the breach, Zahariel wondered how the other assaults were faring.

Had the Lion already carried the north wall?

Could the siege towers already have overwhelmed the defenders of the east wall, or might the troops with grappling hooks and ladders be over the west wall even now? With the Lion's meticulous planning, anything was possible.

The battle might already be won.

A sword crashed against his breastplate, the roaring teeth biting deep into the metal, before sliding clear and ripping upwards into the front of his helm. Zahariel jerked backwards, the teeth of the sword ripping out of the front of his helmet without taking his face with them.

Horrified at his lack of focus, Zahariel swung his sword desperately before him, buying precious seconds to pull his helm from his head and regain his bearings. A knight in grey plate armour, whose face was obscured by a silver helmet worked in the shape of a snarling wolf, danced back from his blows.

Zahariel shook his head clear of the shock of the blow as his opponent came at him again. The chain blade swung in a looping arc for his neck, but he stepped to meet the blow with his sword raised in a classic block. Even as he performed the move, he knew it was a mistake, his opponent luring him into the easy block just to wrong foot him. The enemy knight's blade seemed to twist in mid-air, the blade arcing for his unprotected neck. Zahariel threw himself back, the blade passing within a finger breadth of opening his throat.

He crashed onto his rump as the knight stepped in for the kill. Zahariel rolled away from the killing blow, swinging his blade out in a low arc. The edge of his blade sliced clean through the knight's legs at mid-shin level, and the man toppled like a felled tree.

Zahariel rose to his feet as the knight screamed in agony, the stumps of his legs pumping blood into the dust. Zahariel put a pair of bullets through the man's helmet to spare him further agonies and took a second to reorient himself with the battle.

Knights streamed over the breach and pushed out onto the walls, slaughtering all in their path. While protected behind their ramparts, the fact that the Knights of Lupus were few had mattered little, but with the Order within the walls of the fortress, numbers meant everything.

Everything Zahariel had read of sieges had told him that they were almost always long, drawn out affairs, battles that moved at a slow pace until a tipping point was reached and the battle ended in one brief and bloody frenzy.

This, Zahariel recognised, was the tipping point of this battle. No matter the success or failure of the diversionary attacks, the Order's forces had broken open the fortress and nothing could stop them from achieving victory.

The Knights of Lupus, however, had clearly not read the same military manuals and were determined to fight to the last and prolong their death agonies.

'Zahariel!' shouted a voice from below, and he looked through the smoke to see Sar Luther within the fortress's courtyard, beckoning him onwards. 'If you're quite finished.'

Zahariel set off once more, crossing the threshold of the breach and making his way down the inner face of the breach in short jumps down the screed of rubble. Knights were massing, and with the wall head clear, it was time to sweep through the fortress and eliminate the last of the defenders.

'Form into sword lines, we're going to move through the inner gates towards the keep,' ordered Luther. 'It's sure to get messy, so stay alert! This is the end for the Knights of Lupus, so they're going to fight like cornered raptors. Keep watching the flanks for an ambush and keep pushing forward! Now let's go!'

Zahariel found Nemiel in the crush of bodies of the Order's knights and smiled to see his cousin alive and well.

'You made it!' he said.

'First across the breach,' cried Nemiel, 'before even Sar Luther! I'll get my own banner for this.'

'Trust you to think of glory,' said Zahariel, forming up with the survivors of Sar Hadariel's sword line.

'Well someone's got to,' shot back Nemiel. 'Can't all be about duty can it?'

Only three other knights had survived to make it this far, and Zahariel was thankful that Attias and Eliath had not yet been elevated to knighthood and had been spared the horror of the breach. Sar Hadariel nodded as though in approval when Zahariel and Nemiel formed up with him.

'Good work in staying alive, brothers,' said the hoary veteran. 'Now let's get this finished.'

The great banner that had climbed the breach finally reached them, its fabric even more damaged in the fighting, yet strangely undiminished, as though the scars earned in its passage across the walls imparted some even greater gravitas to it. Zahariel had never fought beneath a banner, but the idea of fighting with the noble banner of the Order flying overhead gave him a sense of fierce pride that he had not felt before.

The banner wasn't just a flag or identifying marker, it was a symbol of everything the Order stood for: courage, honour, nobility and justice. To bear such a symbol was a great honour, but to fight beneath it was something special, something Zahariel understood was of supreme significance.

'Right!' shouted Luther, pointing at the captured outer walls. 'Be ready, we go soon!'

Zahariel followed Luther's gesture and saw that the Order's siege masters had turned the cannons, which had previously been killing their fellows, upon the inner walls to face the gates of the inner keep.

Luther's hand swept down and the cannons fired in a rippling series of staccato explosions. The rampart was obscured in stinking clouds of smoke, and the air was filled with screaming iron and fire.

Fire and smoke erupted from the inner gateways, and huge chunks of rock and timber were hurled skywards.

'Go!' shouted Luther, and the knights of the Order set off once more.

An armoured tide of bodies charged towards the shattered ruin of the inner walls, smoke wreathing the destruction wrought by the captured cannons. More gunfire spat from the inner walls, but it seemed as though the majority of the enemy guns had been mounted on the outer walls, for the fire was sporadic and uncoordinated.

Some knights fell, but after the nightmare charge towards and up the breach, Zahariel felt as though this charge was almost easy. The noise was still incredible: pounding feet, cheering knights, booms of cannon fire and the snap and crack of pistol fire. Rubble crashed, and the cries of the wounded mingled, until all Zahariel could hear was one long, continuous roar of battle, a sound he would forever think of as the music of war.

Drifting smoke from the smashed walls enveloped them, and once again, Zahariel found he was charging in muffled isolation. The sulphurous taste of the gun-smoke caught in the back of his mouth, and his eyes streamed acrid tears.

Fires burned ahead, and he saw that the gates of the inner wall had been more comprehensively destroyed than he could have imagined. Nothing remained of the timbers, simply a ragged hole in the wall with splintered remains sagging from pulverised iron hinges.

'For the Lion and the Order!' shouted Luther as he leapt the heaps of rubble that had fallen from the torn edges of the gateway.

Zahariel and Nemiel followed, vaulting tumbled debris and burning timber as they charged through the shattered gateways. Beyond the smashed walls, the fortress's inner precincts were so unlike anything he had ever seen before that Zahariel had trouble reconciling what he saw with anything resembling military architecture.

Rows upon rows of cages were arranged around the tall, turreted fastness of the inner keep, each one large enough to hold an entire sword line's steeds.

A complex series of rails, chains and gears were laid on the ground of the courtyard, running between the cages towards a raised platform before the gates of the keep.

Some of the cages were occupied, most were not, but it was what the cages held that repulsed Zahariel beyond words. Though his vision was blurred with smoke-born tears, he could see that many of the cages held a multitude of grotesque beasts: winged reptiles similar to the one he had first fought, chimerical monsters of tentacle and claw, howling monstrosities with multiple heads, spines and frilled crests.

A menagerie of beasts filled the courtyard, each one a unique specimen of its kind, kept alive for who knew what reason. The beasts thrashed at the bars of their cages, screaming, howling, roaring and bellowing at the noise of battle.

Perhaps a hundred or so warriors in grey armour, wearing the familiar wolf pelt cloaks of the Knights of Lupus, stood in a long battle line before the walls of the keep, swords and pistols bared. Lord Sartana stood upon the raised platform at the centre of the battle line, his helmet carried by a knight beside him.

The charge of the Order's knights slowed at the sight of such a collection of beasts, horrified beyond words that anyone, let alone an order of knights would dare, or desire, to keep such a monstrous collection of abominable creatures.

Lord Sartana spoke, and it seemed to Zahariel that the sounds of battle diminished, though whether it was the drama of the moment or that the overall level of noise was lowering, he wasn't sure.

'Warriors of the Order,' said Sartana, 'these are our lands and this is our fortress. You are not welcome here.

You were never welcome here. What might once have preserved our world is at an end.'

The Master of the Knights of Lupus reached for a long iron lever attached to a complex series of gears and counterweights that ran through the floor of the platform and connected with the rails and chains that ran throughout the courtyard.

'For that you will die,' finished Sartana, hauling on the lever.

Even before the lever had completed its journey, Zahariel knew what would happen.

With a squeal of metal, gears meshed, slave levers slid from locks and the gates to the beasts' cages opened.

FREE AT LAST, THE beasts roared from their imprisonment with furious bellows of rage, their varied limbs powering them into the open with prodigious strength. Who could know how long they had been caged, but whether that had any bearing on their ferocity would forever be unknown.

Zahariel found himself in a life or death struggle with a monstrous, bear-like creature with a thick coat of spines and a head of wicked horns and snapping jaws. Nemiel fought beside him, along with the remnants of Sar Hadariel's sword line.

A dozen more beasts slammed into the Knights of the Order, tossing bodies into the air with the horror of their charge. The courtyard echoed to the sounds of battle, but this was no battle of honour, fought with blades and pistols in the manner deemed appropriate by centuries of tradition and custom. This was brutal, bloody and desperate combat fought for no noble ideal, but simply for survival. Though the beasts were greatly outnumbered, they cared not for the fact that they would eventually be destroyed. The chance had come to strike back at humans, and whether they were the ones that had imprisoned them mattered not at all.

The bear creature roared and slammed one massive fist into Sar Hadariel's breastplate, sending him flying through the air, his armour torn from his body like paper. Nemiel darted in and slashed his sword across the beast's midsection, no doubt hoping for an eviscerating stroke.

The beast's spines robbed the blow of its strength, and his cousin's sword did little but cut through a number of the spines. Pistol bullets dug wet craters in its chest, but like all the beasts Zahariel had fought, it appeared to care little for pain.

Zahariel edged around the beast's flank as it turned its piggy eyes on Nemiel.

It swiped with another massive paw, but his cousin was quicker than Sar Hadariel and rolled beneath the blow, firing his pistol as he went. Zahariel leapt forward and swung his sword two-handed at the back of the beast's legs, making his best guess at where its hamstrings might be.

His sword easily parted the beast's armoured spines and sliced deep into the meat of its leg. The monster howled and dropped to one knee, black blood jetting from the wound on the back of its leg. It threw back its head and howled in pain, waving its powerfully muscled arms as it fought for balance.

'Now!' shouted Zahariel, dodging further around the beast and stabbing his sword into its ribs. His sword sank hilt-deep into the monster, and as it shuddered in pain, the weapon was torn from his hand.

Its talons slashed for him, catching him a glancing blow, and hurling him back against the bars of its cage. Pistols boomed, and swords cut the beast. Slowly but surely, Zahariel's brothers were winning the fight with the monster.

Its leg cut and useless, the knights could easily keep out of reach of the beast, evading its blows, and firing shot after shot into its body and head. Its roars grew feeble, and at last it pitched forward with a final roar, great gouts of blood erupting from its fanged maw.

Zahariel moved away from the cage and took stock of the battles raging around the courtyard. Dozens of knights were down, torn apart or bludgeoned to death by the beasts, half a dozen of which still fought. The sounds of battle echoed from the walls, and Zahariel could hear triumphant war shouts of the Order coming from all around him, drifting from all the compass points, telling him that the battle was won. Whether the assault on the south wall had been the main thrust or not, it seemed as though the attacks on every face of the fortress had been successful.

Zahariel ran to retrieve his sword from the beast he and his fellow sword brothers had slain, the blade buried deep in its chest. He braced his foot against the beast's flank and slowly slid the sword from its prison of flesh.

'That was a tough one, eh, cousin?' said Nemiel, planting his foot on the beast's body.

'Indeed,' replied Zahariel, wiping the blade on the creature's rough fur.

'Why do you suppose they were keeping them here?'

'I have no idea,' said Zahariel, 'though it explains why they didn't want us to move into the Northwilds.'

'How so?'

'This fortress would have been a staging post for any warriors venturing into the deep woods,' said Zahariel. 'They couldn't very well have let other knights in *and* kept these beasts here.'

'You think that's why Lord Sartana wanted nothing to do with Lord Jonson's quest to destroy the great beasts?'

'Probably, though I can't imagine why you'd ever want to keep beasts.'

'No, nor I,' said Nemiel, 'but come on, there're more to kill before we can move on.'

Zahariel nodded and turned back to the battles being fought around them.

TWELVE

HALF A DOZEN beasts still fought, though many were clearly on their last legs, the Order's knights darting in with long spears and pistols to administer the coup de grace to twisted freaks of mutant evolution. The Knights of Lupus had retreated within their keep, content to leave the beasts to do their work for them, and Zahariel felt a twist of hatred for the knights who had fallen so far from the ideals of honour and virtue that they would stoop to such a base tactic.

However, not all the beasts were struggling against the tide of knights. In the centre of the courtyard, a monstrous lizard-like creature at least three metres long and half again as wide stampeded through the knights like an unstoppable juggernaut. Its huge head was filled with grotesque, warped fangs that prevented its mouth from closing, and its eyes were horrific, distended orbs of milky blue that wept filmy mucus.

Its limbs were bulging with muscle, and its long tail was scabbed with growths, and ended in vicious spines that were covered in the blood of fallen knights.

Warriors with spears surrounded it, but its hide
appeared to be proof against such weapons, the steel
tips bouncing from its thick skin. Sar Luther fought to
get close enough to reach its underbelly, but despite its
massive size, the beast was agile and able to use its low
centre of gravity to face any threat with unnatural swiftness.

'Think we can lend a hand?' asked Nemiel, hefting
his sword over his shoulder.

'I think we have to,' said Zahariel.. 'We can't get any
further until it's dead.'

Zahariel turned to the rest of their sword line and
pointed to one of the warriors. 'Go check on Sar
Hadariel, make sure he's alive. The rest of you, with me.'

As one knight went to check on their leader, Zahariel
led the rest towards the rampaging beast. As he
watched, a knight rashly attempted to get beneath its
snapping, twisted fangs to stab at its throat and was
snatched up and bitten clean in two.

The beast swallowed one half with a quick gulp and
tossed away the knight's lower body. Zahariel was horrified by the casual swiftness of the knight's death, and
his grip on his sword tightened.

Another knight fell, bludgeoned from his feet by the
monster's tail, and yet another was crushed beneath a
stomping foot. More knights rushed over to fight the
last beast, but Zahariel could see they were throwing
lives away in fighting this monster, for surely nothing
born of Caliban could defeat such a terrible creature.

No sooner had he formed the thought than he saw
the Lion lead a host of bloodied knights into the central ring courtyard of the keep.

The Lion had been a magnificent warrior, resplendent in his armour and glorious in his martial bearing,
but the times Zahariel had seen him, he had been at
peace.

Never before had he seen the Grand Master of the Order roused to war.

Zahariel had always known the Lion was taller than any other warrior of Caliban, such was the first thing anyone noticed about him, but to see him now, sword bloodied, hair unbound and the light of combat in his eyes, he realised that the Lion was larger than any man could ever, or would ever, be. His immensity was not just physical, but in his presence and sheer weight in the world.

No man, no matter how mighty, could match the terrible glory of the Lion.

With the fires of war at his back, the Lion was the most wonderful and terrible thing Zahariel had ever seen.

The Lion led his warriors towards the beast without pause, and his warriors followed without a moment's hesitation or apparent fear. As if sensing that a worthy enemy had finally presented itself, the beast turned its horrific, lopsided head towards the Grand Master of the Order.

As it did so, Sar Luther snatched a long pole-arm from one of his warriors and dived forward, rolling beneath its snapping jaws and thrusting with the spear.

At the same time, the Lion leapt towards the beast, his sword slashing for one of its eyes. The beast's head snapped to the side, deflecting the Lion's blow as Luther's spear thrust plunged into the soft flesh of its throat.

The beast screeched with a nerve shredding shrillness that stunned every knight in the courtyard. The knights dropped to their knees and clutched their hands to their helmets as the agonising scream penetrated their skulls with its force. Even Luther, wedged beneath the beast, was laid low by the shrieking vibrations, though he kept one hand on his spear. Blood poured from the beast's neck, arterially powerful, drenching the Lion's second-in-command in gore.

Zahariel felt trickles of blood run from his ears as the beast's cry ripped through the matter of his brain. His vision blurred and tears of agony squeezed from his eyes, but he fought to keep them open, for he was seeing something extraordinary.

Though the knights of the Order writhed in agony at the beast's scream, the Lion seemed unmoved. Perhaps his senses were more refined than those of his warriors, or perhaps his heightened resilience allowed him to resist its effects, but whatever the cause, it was clear that he remained unaffected.

The Lion leapt upon the beast's back, using the unnatural growths scattered around its body as hand and foot holds. The monster thrashed in pain, dragging Luther around beneath it as he held onto the spear haft for his very life.

Even as he wept in agony, Zahariel realised that watching his two brothers slay the beast was an honour. The Lion finally hauled himself atop the beast, and Zahariel saw a flash of silver steel as he raised his sword, point downwards, and thrust it into the beast's skull.

None but the Lion could possibly have had the strength for such a feat.

The blade slammed down into the beast, the quillons of the Lion's blade slamming into the reptilian surface of the beast's hide. The monster's struggles ceased abruptly, and the ear-splitting shriek that had so incapacitated the knights was cut off.

The beast reared up onto its hind legs with a sudden spasm, and the Lion was flung from his perch on its back. The spear haft was torn from Luther's hand, and he scrambled back from the creature, his armour glistening with blood.

The sudden silence that followed the beast's demise was strange and unnerving, the sudden absence of sound like the sudden and unexpected end of a storm that blows itself out in one apocalyptic thunderclap.

The knights began to pick themselves up from the bloody stones of the courtyard, incredulous at the scale of the battle they had just witnessed. The beast's body heaved with one last reflexive breath and then was silent.

Lion El'Jonson came into view from behind the beast and the knights began to cheer at the sight of their heroic leader.

'Jonson! Jonson! Jonson!'

As Zahariel watched the Lion receive their plaudits, Luther dragged himself to his feet from the lake of the beast's spilled blood. Somewhere in the fighting, Luther had lost his helmet, and his face was the one portion of his flesh untainted by bloodstains.

The cheers for the Lion went on undiminished, and Zahariel saw a fleeting look of jealousy flash across Luther's face. It was gone so quickly, Zahariel wasn't even sure he had seen it, but the power of the emotion he had seen on Luther's face was unmistakable.

The Lion raised his hands for silence, and the cheers of the knights died in an instant.

'Brothers!' he cried, pointing to the keep at the centre of the courtyard. 'This isn't over yet. The walls are carried, but the Knights of Lupus are not yet defeated. They lurk within their keep and must be dug out with fire and steel.'

The Grand Master of the Order swung his arms wide, indicating the slaughterhouse the courtyard had become, the dead knights and the defeated beasts.

'Any man who stoops to allow such beasts do his work is not worthy of life,' said the Lion. 'The Knights of Lupus have forfeited their right to mercy and are to

be granted no clemency. We will break into their keep
and leave none alive!'

THE INSIDE OF the keep was eerily deserted, its halls hung
with musty cobwebs and an air of desolation that
Zahariel found depressing. He and Nemiel advanced
down a narrow corridor of dressed stone and tapestries,
their way illuminated by guttering lamps that hung from
bronze fixtures.

The emptiness spoke of years of neglect, where the
dust of abandonment had gathered and the passage of
time had settled upon the keep. The sounds of fighting
elsewhere in the keep could be heard distantly, but wherever the battle was being fought, it was far from here.

'Where is everyone?' asked Nemiel. 'I thought this
place would be crawling with warriors.'

'I guess they must be elsewhere,' said Zahariel. 'It's a big
keep after all.'

Lion El'Jonson had smashed open the gates to the
keep with one mighty blow from his sword, and the
knights of the Order had poured in, spreading through
the fortress in small groups to hunt down the last of their
enemies.

Zahariel and Nemiel had taken the stairs to the upper
levels, hoping to find some enemy warriors to vent their
anger upon, but instead finding only empty halls,
deserted chambers and echoing vaults that had long
been shuttered and forgotten.

'Wait,' hissed Zahariel, holding his hand up for silence,
'do you hear that?'

Nemiel cocked his head and nodded, hearing the same
clatter of footfalls and scraping of furniture that Zahariel
did. The young men looked at one another and made
their way towards the wide set of double doors from
which the sounds emanated, taking up positions on
either side of the door.

The sounds of movement came again, and Nemiel held up his hand with three fingers extended. Zahariel nodded and counted down with his cousin as he curled one finger into his palm, then two and finally his third.

Nemiel spun around and planted his boot squarely on the junction of the two doors, splintering the lock and bursting them open.

Zahariel sprinted through the door, his sword and pistol extended before him, a ferocious war cry on his lips. He swung his pistol left and right, searching for targets, while keeping his sword tight to his body.

The enormous chamber within was vaulted, and edged from floor to ceiling in leather-bound books. Row upon row of books stretched into the distance, and wide tables at the end of each row were strewn with parchments and scrolls.

Vast quantities of information and literature were stored here, a library easily ten times the size of that held within Aldurukh. How long must it have taken to amass such a treasure trove of wisdom?

Zahariel had not believed there was such an amount of knowledge in existence, let alone that it all might be contained within the walls of this keep. Rows of square columns supported the arched roof, and Zahariel guessed that the chamber ran the length and breadth of the keep.

The chamber's sole occupant, as far as Zahariel could see, was a lone man in white robes with grey hair and a drooping silver moustache. Zahariel recognised the man as Lord Sartana, the leader of the Knights of Lupus, who had been goaded to war by Lion El'Jonson in the Circle Chamber, what seemed like a lifetime ago.

Lord Sartana looked up from his labours, the assembled pile of books on a table before an ornate wooden throne draped with wolf pelts.

'So they send beardless boys for me,' said Sartana. 'How old are you? Fourteen, perhaps?'

'I am fifteen,' said Zahariel.

'No respect for tradition, that's what's wrong with your Order, boy,' said Sartana. 'Not a fashionable opinion, I know. Not now, not when everyone is busy celebrating your damn crusade to clear the great beasts from the forest.'

'With your death it will be over,' said Zahariel, emboldened by the defeat he heard in Lord Sartana's voice. 'All that remains is the Northwilds.'

Lord Sartana shook his head. 'It'll all end in tears, mark my words. We haven't even begun to pay for your foolishness yet. That price is still to be collected, and when it is, many will wish that you had never embarked on that course: too many thorns along the road, too many pitfalls and hidden traps.'

'What are you talking about?' asked Nemiel. 'The Lion's quest is the noblest of ideals.'

'It is?' asked Sartana, settling into the throne of wolf pelts. 'Do you want to know where your Lion went wrong?'

'The Lion is not wrong,' said Nemiel with a growl of hostility.

Sartana smiled, amused at the threats of a teenage boy. 'Your first mistake was that you lost respect for tradition. Civilisation is like a shield, designed to keep us safe from the wilderness, while tradition is the shield boss at its centre. Or, to put it another way, tradition is the glue that holds our society together. It gives shape to our lives. It lets everyone know their place. It's vital. Without tradition, soon you are no better than animals.'

'We keep to our traditions,' said Zahariel. 'The Lord Cypher ensures our traditions are upheld. It is you who have forgotten them... consorting with beasts.'

'I think you will find that it was the Order that broke step with the other brotherhoods of knights,' said Sartana, 'when they started allowing commoners to enter their ranks. Imagine… recruiting knights from among the lowborn. Egalitarian claptrap, if you ask me. But that's not the worst you've done. No, the worst element of all this is the Lion's quest to kill off the great beasts. That's the real danger. That's the part we'll all end up regretting.'

'You're wrong,' said Zahariel. 'It's the most glorious thing that's happened on Caliban in the last century! Our people have lived in fear of the great beasts for thousands of years. Now, finally, we are removing their scourge forever. We are making the forests safe. We are changing our world for the better.'

'Spoken like a true believer, boy,' snorted Sartana in derision. 'I see your masters have filled your head with propaganda. Oh, I don't disagree that it sounds like a grand and worthwhile aim to clear the beasts from the forests. Too often, though, reality does not run in accord with our ambitions. We try to achieve one thing, only to find to our horror that we have achieved something quite different.'

'What do you mean?' demanded Nemiel as they edged closer to Sartana.

'Let us assume for a moment that your campaign is successful. Let's say you manage to kill all the beasts. After all, you've got off to a good start. Jonson and the rest have been at it for nearly ten years. Most of the beasts, if not all, must be dead. So, say you kill all the beasts. What then, boy? What will you do, then?'

'I… we'll make things better,' said Zahariel, floundering for a moment to frame his reply to Sartana's question. He had long taken it for granted that the Order's campaign was a noble enterprise, perhaps the greatest in Caliban's history, but he found it difficult to put all the things he felt about it into words once Sartana called him to account.

'We'll clear new lands for settlement, and for agriculture,' he said. 'We'll be able to produce more food.'

'The commoners will do those things, you mean,' said Sartana, 'but what of your kind, boy? What of the knightly orders? What will we do? You see the problem?'

'No, I don't. How can there be a problem when we've made our world a better place?'

'I am surrounded by blind men,' snapped Sartana. 'I am an old man, yet I still seem able to look farther than any of the young men around me. Very well, if you can't see the problem, let me explain it to you. First, though, a simple question. Why are there knightly orders on Caliban? What function do we perform?'

'Our function? We protect the people,' said Nemiel.

'Precisely. At least one of you has sense. And, what do we protect them from?'

'The great beasts, of course,' said Zahariel. Abruptly, he saw where Sartana's line of reasoning was heading. 'Oh.'

'Yes, the great beasts,' smiled Sartana. 'I can see the first glimmerings of understanding written on your face. For millennia, the Knights of Caliban have followed one sacred duty. We have kept our people safe from the great beasts. It is the way our lives have always been. It is the reason for our existence. It has been our war, a war fought in the forests of this planet for five thousand years. This is the way of things, boy. This is tradition, but not for much longer. Soon, thanks to the Order and Lion El'Jonson, the beasts will be no more. What then for the knights of Caliban?'

Lord Sartana fell silent for several moments, allowing time for his words to sink in with Zahariel and Nemiel before he spoke again.

'We are warriors, boy. It is in our blood. It is in our culture. We are a proud and fearless breed. It has always been that way, ever since the first days of our ancestors. Conflict gives meaning to our existence. We hunt, we quest and we fight, and not just because the people of Caliban need our protection. We do these things because we must. Without them, there is emptiness at the heart of our lives, a void that cannot be filled no matter how hard we try. We do not do well with peace. We bridle at the lack of activity. It makes us feel restless and uneasy. We need to feel danger. We need our battles, the ebb-and-flow of warfare and the thrill of the life-or-death struggle. Without these things, we feel incomplete.'

'That is a pessimistic outlook,' said Zahariel.

'No, it is a realistic outlook,' said Sartana. 'We need our beasts, boy. Why do you think my order was capturing them? We were trying to keep the race of beasts alive! There, I have said it. Perhaps it shocks you, but look honestly into your heart and you will see that we need our monsters because they help to define us. As long as there are beasts on Caliban, we are heroes, but if there are no more beasts, we are nothing. No, less than nothing.'

'You were keeping the beasts alive?' asked Zahariel, horrified beyond belief.

'Of course,' said Sartana. 'Without the beasts, our war is over. What will become of us then? What of our future? What will be of the warrior when there is no more war? There lies the greatest danger, boy. Boredom will create unrest, and unrest can turn to anger. Without a war to keep us busy, we are likely to create one of our own devising. We will fall on each other like a pack of raptors. I will not live to see this, but I look to the future and I see only darkness. I see kinstrife and civil war. I see brother turning against brother. I see blood;

all for the lack of having better ways to channel our anger, all for lack of the beasts. That is the future your Order is creating for us, though admittedly, your zealot of a leader was moved by the best of intentions.'

Both Zahariel and Nemiel had closed to within a sword length of Lord Sartana, and the leader of the Knights of Lupus smiled indulgently at them both.

'No doubt you have orders to kill me.'

Zahariel nodded. 'We do.'

'I may be old, but I think it will take more than two boys to defeat me.'

'We'll see,' said Nemiel.

'No,' said Sartana, drawing a long-bladed hunting knife. 'We won't.'

Zahariel aimed his pistol at Lord Sartana's face, but the old man did not have violence towards them on his mind. Swiftly, the leader of the Knights of Lupus reversed the knife and rammed it into his body, the blade angled upwards to pierce his heart.

Zahariel dropped his weapons, rushing forward to catch Lord Sartana's body as he slumped from his throne.

He lowered the dying knight to the cold stone floor of the great library as blood flooded from the grievous wound.

'You know the expression about darkness, don't you?' hissed Sartana. 'That the road into darkness is paved with men's good intentions.'

'I've heard it, yes,' said Zahariel.

'Perhaps someone should have mentioned it to the Lion,' said Sartana with the last of his strength. 'Good intentions or not, Lion El'Jonson will end up destroying Caliban. Of that I have no doubt.'

'WHAT WILL BECOME of us?' Lord Sartana had said, his face grim and foreboding. 'What will be of the warrior when there is no more war?'

At the time, Zahariel had paid no great attention to the dying man's words, so caught up was he in the excitement and terror of the day.

Sartana's words might have been troubling, even unsettling, but it was not hard to dismiss them. Lord Sartana was old, tired, his features ravaged by age and weariness. It was easy enough to think of his warning as the unhinged ramblings of a mind already well across the border to madness.

It was easy enough to dismiss his words and they should have been no less easy to forget. Days and weeks passed following the destruction of the Knights of Lupus, and they returned once more to Zahariel to haunt him.

He would think of them often, and oft times he would marvel at their prescience.

In his darkest moments, Zahariel would sometimes wonder if their meeting that day had represented a missed opportunity. Perhaps he could have passed their message on to the Lion, or he could have been more aware of the force of emotion in Luther.

Zahariel might have understood that brotherhood was no guarantee of harmony; that no matter the closeness of the bonds between men, violence and betrayal were always possible.

A great many years had yet to pass before he would think of those words frequently.

He would wonder whether he could have changed the future.

By then, of course, it was far too late.

BOOK THREE

IMPERIUM

THIRTEEN

WITH THE DEATH of Lord Sartana, the Knights of Lupus ceased to exist. Their last knights were hunted down in the gloomy, abandoned corridors of their shattered keep and slain. No mercy was offered and none expected, for the defeated knights knew that there was no going back from what they had done.

The banners of the Order flew from the tallest towers of the fortress, and the fires of battle reflected from the gold and crimson woven into their ragged fabrics. Swords banged on shields, and the Ravenwing cavalry rode whooping circuits around the broken walls of the mountain fortress.

Cheers and honours were exchanged by the warriors of the Order, and a momentous sense of history stole over each man as the realisation of the closeness of their objective sank in. With the Knights of Lupus destroyed, the Northwilds were open to the Order, and the very last of the beasts could be hunted to extinction.

Zahariel watched as the fortress of the Knights of Lupus crumbled, its walls and keep pulverised by the massed cannons of the Order. No honour was to be accorded the fallen enemy knights, their corpses and effects gathered in the main keep and put to the torch.

The Lion had marched into the great library to find Zahariel and Nemiel with Lord Sartana's body, and he had congratulated them both before turning his attention to the great volumes collected within the massive chamber.

After a cursory glance through several of the tomes gathered by Lord Sartana, the Lion had ordered them to rejoin their sword line, and had busied himself with further exploration of his defeated foe's collection. Entire wagon trains carried the books and scrolls back to Aldurukh and further study.

Zahariel turned from the burning fortress, saddened to see such a mighty edifice cast down, and wondering if all battles ended with this strange mix of emotions. He had survived and acquitted himself with honour, fought bravely and helped in the final victory. He had seen history take shape, and had witnessed the death of their greatest enemy, yet still there was a nagging sense of things undone and of opportunities missed.

Sar Hadariel was alive and would live to fight another day as had many of his sword line. The butcher's bill was steep, but not so steep as to render the victory sour, and already the loss of so many friends and comrades was being overshadowed by the glories won.

In the weeks of marching back to Aldurukh, the infamy of the Knights of Lupus would be magnified tenfold, their villainies growing from deliberate capture of beasts to vile experiments and corruption of the soul. By the time the Order's warriors had returned home, their enemies had been turned into the vilest monsters, corrupt and beyond redemption. It had been a good and necessary war, the knights agreed, a war that had achieved great things, and had brought the freedom of all Caliban that much closer.

Yet amid the celebrations and honours bestowed, Zahariel could not forget the moment in the Circle Chamber when Lion El'Jonson had goaded Lord Sartana to war, the moment that war had been thrust upon them.

Yes, the Order's campaign was on the verge of ultimate glory, but had its integrity been tainted at the last?

Had blood been shed in this battle for less than noble ideals?

Zahariel worried about such things on the ride back, unable to articulate his feelings even to those closest to him. He watched his brothers celebrate their great victory, and a shadow fell upon his heart as he watched the Lion revel in the honours heaped upon him for this latest victory.

Only one other in the Order appeared to bear such misgivings, and Zahariel would often catch Luther riding alongside his brother, and catch a hint of that same shadow in his smile and a chip of ice in the corner of his eye.

If Luther sensed Zahariel's scrutiny, he made no mention of it, but the journey back to Aldurukh was melancholy for him, his achievements during the battle overshadowed by the Lion's feats of arms.

Zahariel and Nemiel's defeat of the beast in the courtyard brought them both honours, and each was rewarded with scrolls upon their armour to commemorate the deed. Nemiel had been overjoyed, and Zahariel had been pleased, but each time he thought back to the fight, he wondered why the strange powers that had manifested in the forests of Endriago had not reappeared.

Perhaps it was as he had suspected… that it had been his proximity to the dark heart of the wood, or the Watchers that had awakened some latent ability within him that now lay dormant. Or perhaps he had imagined it all and his mind had conjured some elaborate fantasy in the wake of his terrible struggle to explain how he had defeated the great beast.

Whatever the reason, he was glad that what had happened seemed now to be a distant memory, becoming less tangible with every passing day. He vividly remembered the beast's death, but the specifics of that day, before he had fought it, were becoming hazier in his mind, as though a grey mist had descended upon his memory.

LIFE WENT ON much as before with the knights of the Order, and Zahariel's unease began to unwind, as Lord Sartana's dying warning seemed increasingly like the groundless mutterings of a frustrated foe. Hunts were organised, and each day knights would ride into the forests to clear out the last pockets of beasts.

Each day brought fewer and fewer beast trophies, and it seemed as though the completion of the Lion's grand vision had finally been achieved.

The Lion ventured into the forests only rarely these days, spending most of his time locked in the tallest towers of Aldurukh with the books taken from the fortress of the Knights of Lupus.

Eliath and Attias both fought and defeated their own beasts and ascended to the rank of knight, a day that brought much celebration to the halls of the Order. All four boys fought together in Sar Hadariel's sword line, venturing out into the forests time and time again to fight the planet's predators and, hopefully, encounter one of the few remaining beasts.

Ravenwing scouts brought word that each section of the Northwilds had been cleared of beasts, and Zahariel had scoured their missives for word of the dark forests around Endriago for any sign of the malaise that had engulfed him during his hunt for the great lion, but whatever he had encountered in the depths of the forest appeared to have vanished.

Perhaps it had never existed and, try as he might, he could conjure no solid recollection of the words spoken to him in the forest, nor any cogent memory of those who had spoken them.

The world of Caliban still turned, life went on as before, and the knights of the Order moved closer to ultimate domination, until the angels arrived.

LIGHT DAPPLED THE leaves of the high branches and spread a glittering shadowplay on the ground before the horses as the group of riders made their way along the paths of the forest. The air was fragrant, rich with the promise of balmy days and peace.

Zahariel held the reins loosely in his hands, letting the black horse set its own pace, and relaxed back into his saddle. The forests were no longer places of fear and horror to the knights of the Order, they were magical places of light and adventure. Fresh paths were being cut through them, revealing landscapes of unearthly beauty and natural majesty that had previously been denied to the populace of Caliban, thanks to the presence of the beasts.

Now, with the defeat of the lurking monsters in the darkness, their world was theirs for the taking. Beside him, Nemiel removed his helm and ran a hand through his hair, and Zahariel smiled at his cousin, glad to have him with him on this momentous ride.

Sar Luther had sent for them that morning, summoning them to the stablemaster's to select the finest mounts to ride on this, the last of the beast hunts. The Lion had been animated, eager to be on the last hunt, to see its completion, as though a fierce imperative burned in his breast that even he did not understand.

The opening portions of the ride had been made in relaxed, comfortable silence, each warrior content to enjoy the beauty of their world, now that it was theirs to call their own. The Lion and Luther led them as they had rode unerringly northwards, skirting settlements that were pushing further out from Aldurukh, now that the beasts had been exterminated.

The new Lord Cypher followed a discreet distance behind them, the role filled by a fresh, nameless warrior. Contrary to most people's expectations, Master Ramiel had not been selected to take the previous Lord Cypher's position, though who had was, of course, a mystery.

A number of new knights and even a number of supplicants brought up the rear, so that the procession was truly a representative slice of the Order's members.

'A strange group to lead into the wilds, don't you think?' asked Nemiel.

'I suppose,' replied Zahariel. 'Perhaps the Lion wants this last hunt attended by men from all ranks of the Order, not just the senior members.'

'You think we're senior members?'

'No,' said Zahariel, 'I think we're up and coming youngsters who will soon make our mark on the Order.'

'You have already done that, young Zahariel,' said the Lion from the front of the column. 'Remember, my hearing is very acute. You are here because of the brotherhood we share.'

'Yes, my lord,' said Zahariel, following the Lion as he rode into a wide clearing before a great cliff of glittering white stone that reared up on their left. Tumbling waterfalls plunged from its top in a cascade, to foam in a wide pool of churning water. Vibrant greenery stretched in all directions, and Zahariel felt peace spread through him, unaware of how empty his soul had become until it was filled.

'Yes, this is the place,' said the Lion from the front of their procession.

The Lion turned his horse, the mightiest beast ever bred by the horsemasters of Caliban, and addressed his warriors as they rode into the clearing before the waterfall.

'You are all here because, as Zahariel rightly supposes, I desired all ranks of the Order to celebrate the conclusion of our mighty endeavour.'

Zahariel tried and failed to quell the blush reflex he felt reddening his face at this singling out for praise.

'Caliban is ours,' repeated the Lion, and Zahariel joined with the others in cheering the Grand Master of the Order's pronouncement.

'We have fought and bled for ten years, brothers, and each of us has seen friends and companions fall along the way,' continued Jonson, 'but we stand on the threshold of our greatest triumph. Everything we have fought for is within our grasp. We have made no mistakes and it is ours. This is our triumph.'

The Lion spread his arms and said, 'A golden age beckons us, my brothers. I have seen it in my dreams, a golden time of new and wondrous things. We stand on the very brink of that age and...'

Zahariel glanced at Nemiel at the uncharacteristic pause in the Lion's speech. Their leader looked off to their left, towards the forest, and Zahariel was seized by fear that they had been ambushed, though what manner of foe would dare ambush a warrior as fearsome as the Lion?

His first suspicion was that the last beast had somehow managed to sneak up on them, or that some rogue survivors of the Knights of Lupus had survived the destruction of their order to come seeking revenge.

But as his hand leapt to his sword hilt, Zahariel saw no such threat.

Instead, he saw a great bird perched on a stout branch of a tree, its feathers golden and shimmering in the afternoon sunlight.

A Calibanite eagle, its plumage vivid and perfect in this setting, regarded the warriors with regal grace, apparently unafraid of the gathering of humans. Such eagles were rare creatures, not dangerous, but regarded as birds of omen by the superstitious of Caliban.

The warriors of the group looked from the eagle to the Lion, unsure what to make of the bird's sudden appearance.

Zahariel felt a shiver travel down his spine as the bird continued to watch them with its strange eyes. He glanced over towards the Lion, seeing an expression that spoke of fearful anticipation, a look of foreknowledge and hope that it had not been misinterpreted.

'I know this,' said the Lion, his voice barely more than a whisper.

As the Lion spoke, a strange wind blew, a hot and urgent ripple of air with an acrid aftertaste, like the tang that hung in the vicinity of the armourer's forge.

Zahariel looked up, seeing something huge and dark roar overhead, a massive winged shape with glowing blue coals at its rear. Another passed overhead, and he cried out as the heat from their passing washed over him.

The knights circled their mounts, and Zahariel drew his sword as the mighty flying beasts roared overhead once more.

'What are they?' shouted Zahariel over the din of the roars that filled the clearing.

'I don't know,' cried Nemiel. 'Great beasts!'

'How can that be? They are all dead!'

'Apparently not,' said Nemiel.

Zahariel glanced over at the Lion once more, seeking some sign that what was happening had been expected, but their leader simply sat in his saddle looking up at the behemoths as they flew over them.

Luther was shouting something at the Lion, but his words were lost in the screaming roar as one of the giant flying beasts blotted out the sun and hovered above them. Its terrible howls filled Zahariel's senses and the hot, bitter tang of its odour was almost unbearable. A powerful downdraught scattered leaves, and bent the branches of the trees with its force.

The eagle took to the air and soared over the great pool at the base of the waterfall, the misting water catching on its wings as it flew, making them shine like beaten gold.

Zahariel followed the mighty bird's course and looked up, shielding his eyes from the baleful blue glow on the hovering beast's belly, as a horrific squealing, like metal on metal, built from above.

'Put your weapons away!' shouted Luther as he rode through their number. 'Sheath your swords by the order of the Lion.'

Zahariel tore his gaze from the shrieking, stinking beast above them, incredulous that they should put themselves at such a monstrous disadvantage.

'Sar Luther,' he yelled over the noise and wind. 'You would leave us unarmed?'

'Do it!' shouted Luther. 'Now!'

Though it violated everything he had been taught, the power of Luther's voice was enough to make him cease his questions and slide his sword home in its scabbard.

'Whatever happens,' shouted Luther, through the whirling hurricane that surrounded them, 'do nothing until the Lion acts! Understood?'

Zahariel nodded reluctantly as he heard what sounded like distant shouts from above.

Then amid the noise and confusion, he saw shapes resolving from the howling winds and noise.

Dark shapes, armoured and descending on wings of fire.

Beside him, Luther shielded his eyes and said, 'And the Angels of Darkness descended on pinions of fire and light… the great and terrible dark angels.'

Zahariel recognised the words, having heard the fables of ancient times when the heroic dark angels, mysterious avengers of righteousness had first fought the beasts of Caliban in the earliest ages of the world.

His heart leapt as the first of the fiery angels landed, his armoured bulk enormous, the detail of his form obscured by the smoke of his landing. Others landed beside him, until ten hulking giants stood before the Lion's group. Zahariel was immediately struck by the similarity between the giants and the armour of the Order.

As the first of the giants took a step forward, he was struck by the similarity in size between him and the Lion. Though the Lion was taller even than this giant, there was a similarity in scale and proportion that was unmistakable.

The fearsome downdraught of air from the great flying beast dissipated the smoke of the giants' arrival, and with its cargo apparently delivered, it moved off. The clearing was suddenly silent but for the crash of water in the pool behind them.

Though there was a fearsome martial power to each of these giants, Zahariel also saw a real sense of awe, a feeling that they had found something precious, with a value they had not previously dared believe.

The giant reached up to his helmet, and Zahariel saw that he was armed with a sword and pistol similar in appearance to his own, though of an order of magnitude larger than those employed by the Order.

A twist of a catch brought a hiss of escaping air, and the giant lifted clear his helmet to reveal a startling face of human proportions, though his features were more widely spaced and gigantic than most men's.

The face was handsome, and an uncertain smile began to develop as the giant looked upon Lion El'Jonson. Curiously, Zahariel felt no fear, his apprehensions fleeing his body at the sight of the giant's face.

'Who are you?' asked the Lion.

'I am Midris,' said the giant, his voice impossibly deep and resonant. He turned to his fellow giants and said, 'We are warriors of the First Legion.'

'The First Legion?' asked Luther. 'Whose First Legion?'

Midris turned to Luther and said, 'The First Legion of the Emperor, Master of Mankind and ruler of Terra.'

FOURTEEN

'IT'S THE MACHINES,' Nemiel said from his position on the battlements. 'That's what I find most impressive. What did you say they called them again?'

'Crawlers,' replied Zahariel.

'Right, crawlers,' nodded Nemiel. 'They cut down the trees, pull out the stumps, and level the land afterwards, and all three tasks are completed by just one machine, controlled by a single rider.'

'Operators,' corrected Zahariel. 'The men who work the machines are called operators or drivers, not riders.'

'Operators, then,' shrugged Nemiel. 'I ask you, have you ever seen anything like it?'

Looking at the scene below them, Zahariel shared Nemiel's sense of amazement. The two of them stood on the battlements at Aldurukh, gazing down at the forest. Except, there was no longer very much forest left, at least not directly in their line of sight.

As far as the eye could see, across the entire parcel of land below the northern slopes of the mountain, the ancient woodlands were disappearing.

From their vantage point, it was difficult to pick out much detail, but the scale of the operation unfolding below them was awe-inspiring.

'If you ask me,' said Nemiel, without waiting for an answer, 'they look like insects, impossibly large insects, I'll admit, but insects, all the same.'

Watching the machines at work, Zahariel agreed that there was something in what his cousin said. The restless activity below the mountain did put him in mind of the regimented movements of an insect colony, an image undiminished by the fact that the fortress battlements were high enough above the scene to make the people below them look like ants.

'Can you imagine how long it would take to do that much work without the machines?' asked Nemiel. 'Or how many men and horses you'd need to clear that much land? I'll say this about the Imperials, they don't do things by halves. It's not just their warriors who are giants, their machines are as well.'

Zahariel nodded his head absently in reply, his attention still riveted on the activities of the crawlers.

The last few weeks had set them all reeling.

By any standard, it had been the most remarkable period in the entire history of Caliban. Nearly six months had passed since Zahariel had become a knight. The campaign against the great beasts was over, the Knights of Lupus were dead and Lion El'Jonson had ascended to the position of Grand Master of the Order, with Luther as his second-in-command.

All these events, however, were as nothing compared to the coming of the Imperium.

The news had spread across Caliban like wildfire, within hours of the first sightings of Imperial flying ships in the sky. Soon, it had become known that a group of giants in black armour had come to Caliban proclaiming themselves as envoys of the Emperor of Terra.

They were called the First Legion, and they had been sent as messengers.

Zahariel well remembered the moment the Imperials had come to Caliban.

'We are your brothers,' the warrior who had introduced himself as Midris had said, as he and his fellows bent their knees and bowed their heads in front of the Lion. 'We are emissaries of the Imperium of Man, come to re-unite all the lost children of humanity, now that Old Night is ended. We have come to restore your birthright. We have come to bring you the Emperor's wisdom.'

Not all the Terrans were giants. In the aftermath of their arrival, it had become clear that the giants – or Astartes, as they were called in the Terran language – had come to Caliban as the pathfinders of a larger expedition. Once it was apparent that the people of Caliban were inclined to welcome them with open arms, more normally proportioned human beings had followed in the giants' wake, like the operators responsible for the crawlers, along with historians, interpreters and those skilled in the arts of diplomacy.

Whether giants or normal men, the Terrans were united in one thing: they all spoke glowingly of their Emperor.

'I wonder what he's like?' said Zahariel, apropos of nothing.

'Who?'

'The Emperor,' said Zahariel, feeling a thrill of anticipation run through him. 'They say he created the Astartes, and that he can read minds and perform miracles. They say he is the greatest man who ever lived. They say he is thousands of years old. They say he is immortal. What does a man like that look like?'

Earlier that morning, Imperial envoys had announced that their Emperor intended to visit Caliban. He was nearby, they said, no more than three weeks' travel time away. With the agreement of the Order's supreme council, it had been decided that a landing site would be cleared for the Emperor's arrival in the forests below Aldurukh.

The crawlers the Imperials had brought with them had been put to work, and the ever-expanding clearing below was destined to become the place where the Emperor would first set foot on Caliban.

Zahariel was not alone in looking forward to the prospect of seeing the Terran Emperor in the flesh, his imminent arrival sparking most of the discussions that had taken place in knightly circles since the giant warriors had arrived. Few could credit the tales the giants told of their leader. If their stories were to be believed, the Emperor was the absolute embodiment of human perfection.

'I'd imagine he'll be at least ten metres tall,' said Nemiel sardonically, 'perhaps even twenty, if his followers are anything to go by. He'll breathe fire and his eyes will be able to shoot out deadly rays like the beasts of legend. Perhaps he'll have two heads, one like that of a man and one like that of a goat. How should I know what he looks like? I'm as much in the dark as you are.'

'Be careful,' warned Zahariel, 'the Terran giants don't like it when you speak of their leader like that. You'll offend them.'

Like most Calibanites, Zahariel found it breathtaking that the Imperials not only had such extraordinary technology at their fingertips, but also that they seemed to take it so much for granted. Even the things his people held in common with the Terrans only served to underline the breadth of the gap between them.

The knights of Caliban were armed and armoured in the same style as the Astartes, but the motorised blades, pistols and power armour the Terrans were equipped with were demonstrably better and more effective in every aspect than the versions used on Caliban.

Zahariel found the difference most visible when he compared the merits of his armour to that worn by the Astartes. Even beyond the gulf in physical stature, Astartes power armour was superior in every possible way. Zahariel's armour protected him from blows and impacts, whether from the claws of predators or the swords of men. He could even close his helm to filter out smoke or other hazards to breathing like the deadly pollen of Caliban's sweetroot flower.

In comparison, Astartes armour offered a much higher level of protection. It gave its wearer the ability to see in absolute darkness. It allowed him to survive extremes of heat and cold that would otherwise be unthinkable. It included its own separate air supply. Equipped with this technology, the warriors of the Astartes could survive and fight in any environment, no matter how hostile.

While such things seemed commonplace to the Terrans, among the people of Caliban they were regarded as little short of miraculous, even more so when it came to the wonders of Imperial medicine.

A few days after the Imperials had arrived, one of the Order's supplicants had suffered an accident in training. A boy named Moniel had been practising walking the spiral with a live blade when he had slipped, inadvertently cutting into his knee with his sword as he fell.

The Order's apothecaries had successfully managed to stem the flow of blood, saving Moniel's life, but they could do nothing to save his leg. In order to prevent the flesh from turning gangrenous, the apothecaries had been forced to amputate the wounded limb.

It went without saying that anyone missing a leg could no longer hope to become a knight. Ordinarily, Moniel would have been returned to the care of his family in the settlement of his birth.

In this instance, however, the Imperials had inter-
vened to ensure a happier ending.

Upon hearing of Moniel's injury, a Terran apothecary
had overseen his treatment, a treatment which, in this
case, involved using esoteric methods to cause a new
leg to re-grow from the stump where the old leg had
been amputated.

NATURALLY, THE IMPERIALS did not call the world Caliban.

The Imperials had no way of knowing what name the
people before them had given to their world. Nor could
they know of Caliban's culture. They had learned of the
knightly orders, and it had been a source of surprise
and delight to both cultures that the hierarchical structure of the knightly orders was very much like the
structure of the Legions of the Astartes.

These were strange days, interesting times.

THE BATTLE HALLS of Aldurukh resounded daily to the
clash of arms, supplicants and knights put through gruelling training rituals overseen by the Astartes. Giants
in black armour marched the length and breadth of the
halls every day, working with the Masters of the Order
to gauge the level of martial prowess and character of
every member of the knightly brotherhood.

Zahariel had fought three bouts already today, his
skin bathed in sweat and his muscles burning with
fatigue. He and Nemiel had passed everything the
Astartes had put them through, pushed to the limits of
their endurance.

'I thought the training for the Order was hard,'
gasped Nemiel.

Zahariel nodded, hanging his head in exhaustion. 'If
this is what it takes to be an Astartes, then I'm not sure
I'm up to it.'

'Really?' asked Nemiel, hauling himself erect and performing a few mock stretches. 'I think I'm about ready for another few laps. Care to join me?'

'All right,' said Zahariel, climbing to his feet.

Though a great many of the Orders warriors had filled the Battle Halls, Zahariel could not help but notice that it was only the younger knights and supplicants who took part in the Astartes trials. He and Nemiel were among the oldest present, and he wondered what bearing this had on the trials.

Day by day, the number of boys taking part in the trials had dwindled, as only the strongest and most dedicated were allowed to pass to the next stage. What the end result of these trials would be had been kept secret, but many believed they were competing for a place within the ranks of the Astartes.

Zahariel pulled at his hamstrings, and stretched the muscles of his calves and thighs before shaking off the lethargy of the morning's training.

'Ready?' he said, calling Nemiel's bluff.

His cousin wasn't about to give him the satisfaction, and he nodded, wiping sweat damp hair from his face.

'Let's go,' said Nemiel, setting off at a comfortable pace. 'Ten laps.'

Zahariel followed him, quickly catching up and settling into the pace set by his cousin. His limbs were tired and he had pushed his body to the extreme edge of its endurance, but this contest with his cousin had been going on for as long as he could remember and not even exhaustion would let him pass up the opportunity to compete against Nemiel.

They completed the first circuit of the Battle Hall without too much trouble, but by the end of the fourth, both boys were tiring, and their breathing had become ragged. In the centre of the hall, fresh bouts had begun under the watchful eye of the Astartes, and Zahariel noticed that their race had attracted the attention of a giant in a suit of armour more heavily ornamented than that of his brothers.

'Tired yet?' gasped Zahariel.

'Not at all,' wheezed Nemiel as they began their fifth lap.

Zahariel fought to control his breathing and ignore the pain building in his chest as he concentrated on maintaining his pace. He forced the despair at the idea of losing from his mind as irrelevant. He would not be second to Nemiel, and he would not be the first to break under the pressure of pain.

The *Verbatim* said that pain was an illusion of the senses, while despair was an illusion of the mind. Both were obstacles to overcome, and as he drew on his deepest reserves of strength, he felt a curious lightness to his flesh, as though his limbs were borne up by a wellspring of energy that he had not known he possessed.

By the seventh lap, Zahariel had begun to pull ahead of Nemiel, his newfound energy allowing him to put on a spurt of speed that broke their stalemate. He heard Nemiel's laboured breathing behind him, and that empowered him further.

The gap between them grew wider, and Zahariel was buoyed up with the elation of victory as he cruised through the eighth and ninth laps. A second wind filled his limbs with energy, even as it seemed to sap his cousin's will.

As he began the last lap, he saw Nemiel's swaying back ahead of him and knew he could administer a final sting to his cousin's pride by lapping him. Zahariel pushed harder and faster, digging deep into the last reserves of his determination, eating up the gap between them.

His cousin threw a panicked glance over his shoulder, and Zahariel wanted to laugh at the anguish he saw there. Nemiel was beaten, and that knowledge robbed him of whatever strength he had left.

Zahariel surged past his cousin and reached the finish line a full ten metres before his cousin. With the race run, he dropped to his knees, sucking in a great lungful of stale air and clutching at his burning thighs. Nemiel crossed the line with an unsteady gait, and Zahariel cried, 'It's over, cousin! Rest.'

Nemiel shook his head and passed on, and while part of Zahariel despaired at his cousin's foolish pride, another part of him admired his persistence and determination to finish what he had begun.

Though he had not an ounce of strength left, Zahariel forced himself to stand and work through a series of stretches. Not to do so would result in his muscles cramping, and who knew when the Astartes would throw the next test at them.

He had just finished his first set when Nemiel lurched over the line with a strangled gasp and collapsed beside him, his chest heaving and sweat pouring from him in sheets.

'You took your time,' said Zahariel, an unaccustomed edge of spite in his voice.

Nemiel shook his head, unable, for the moment, to reply.

Zahariel offered his cousin his hand and said, 'Come on, you need to stretch.'

His cousin waved his hand away, gasping for air and keeping his eyes squeezed shut. Zahariel knelt down and began massaging his cousin's legs, working out the knots of tension in his muscles with hard sweeps of his fingertips.

'That hurts!' cried Nemiel.

'It'll hurt more if I don't do it,' pointed out Zahariel.

Nemiel bit his lip as Zahariel carried on with his ministrations, his breathing gradually becoming more even as his body began to recover from the exertions of the race. At last, Nemiel was able to sit up, and Zahariel began working the tension from his shoulders.

Zahariel said nothing, seeing the wounded pride in his cousin's face and regretting the need to pile added humiliation upon him by lapping him. But Nemiel was old enough to deal with the blow to his pride. The pair of them had done the same all the years they had known each other.

Zahariel turned as he heard heavy footsteps behind him and saw the Astartes in the ornate armour.

'You run a fast race, boy,' said the warrior. 'What is your name?'

'Zahariel, my lord.'

'Stand when you address me,' commanded the warrior.

Zahariel stood and stared up into the face of the Astartes. His features were weathered and worn, though his eyes still spoke of youth. His armour was adorned with all manner of symbols that Zahariel did not recognise, and he carried a golden staff topped with a device that resembled a horned skull.

'How did you win that race?'

'I… I just ran faster,' said Zahariel.

'Yes,' said the warrior, 'but where did the strength come from?'

'I don't know, I just dug deep I suppose.'

'Perhaps,' said the warrior, 'though I suspect you do not know where you dug into. Come with me, Zahariel, I have questions for you.'

Zahariel spared a glance back at Nemiel, who shrugged without interest.

'Hurry, boy!' snapped the warrior. 'Or do your masters not teach alacrity?'

'Sorry, my lord, but where are we going?'

'And stop calling me "my lord", it irritates me.'

'Then what should I call you?' asked Zahariel.

'Call me Brother Librarian Israfael.'

'Then where are we going, Brother Israfael?'

'We are going elsewhere,' said Israfael, 'and there, *I* shall ask the questions.'

ELSEWHERE TURNED OUT to be one of the meditation cells where supplicants were sent to think upon whatever wrongdoing they had been deemed to have committed by the masters of the Order. Each cell was a place of contemplation, with a single window where the penitent supplicant could look out over Caliban's forests and think on what he had done.

'Have I done something wrong?' asked Zahariel as he followed Israfael into the cell.

'Why do you think that? Have you?'

'No,' said Zahariel. 'At least I don't think so.'

Israfael indicated that Zahariel should sit on the stool in the centre of the cell, and moved to the window, blocking out the meagre light with the bulk of his armoured body.

'Tell me, Zahariel,' began Israfael, 'in your short life, have you been able to do… strange things?'

'Strange things?' asked Zahariel. 'I don't understand.'

'Then let me give you an example,' said Israfael. 'Have objects around you moved without you having touched them? Have you seen things in dreams that have later come to pass? Or have you seen things that you cannot explain?'

Zahariel thought back to his encounter with the Beast of Endriago and his vow to keep the strangeness of its defeat to himself. The people of ancient Caliban had once burned people in possession of such powers, and he could imagine the Astartes being no less strict with such things.

'No, Brother Israfael,' he said, 'nothing like that.'

Israfael laughed. 'You are lying, boy. I can see it as plain as day without any need for warp-sight. I ask again, have you encountered any such strange things? And before you answer, remember that I will know if you lie, and you will forfeit any chance of progressing further with these trials if I decide you are less than truthful.'

Zahariel looked into Israfael's eyes, and knew that the Astartes was utterly serious. Israfael could have Zahariel thrown from the trials, with a single word, but he wanted to win through and prove he was worthy more than anything.

'Yes,' he said, 'I have.'

'Good,' said Israfael. 'I knew I sensed power in you. Go on, when was this?'

'It was when I fought the Beast of Endriago. It just happened. I don't know what it was, I swear,' said Zahariel, the words coming out in a confessional rush.

Israfael raised a hand. 'Calm down, boy. Just tell me what happened.'

'I… I'm not sure,' he said. 'The beast had me, it was going to kill me, and I felt something… I don't know… my hatred for the beast rise up in me.'

'Then what happened?'

'It was as if… as if time had slowed, and I could see things that I couldn't before.'

'Things like what?'

'I could see *inside* the beast,' said Zahariel. 'I could see its heart and skeleton. I could reach inside it, as if it was some kind of ghost.'

'Terrorsight,' said Israfael, 'very rare.'

'You know of this? What is it?'

'It is a form of scrying,' said Israfael. 'The psyker uses his power to look beyond the realms of the physical and shifts part of his flesh into the warp. It is very powerful, but very dangerous. You are lucky to be alive.'

'Is this power evil?' asked Zahariel.

'Evil? Why would you ask such a question?'

'People have been burned in our history for having such powers.'

Israfael grunted in sympathy. 'It was the same on Terra long ago. Anyone who was different was persecuted and feared, though the people who did so knew not what they were afraid of. But, to answer your question, boy, no, your power is not evil, any more than a sword is evil. It is simply a tool that can be used for good or evil depending on who swings it and why.'

'Will it exclude me from the trials?'

'No, Zahariel,' said Israfael. 'If anything, it makes you more likely to be chosen.'

'Chosen?' asked Zahariel. 'Is that what they are for, to choose who will become an Astartes?'

'Partly,' admitted Israfael, 'but it is also to see if the human strain on Caliban is pure enough to warrant its inclusion as a world that our Legion can recruit from over the coming years.'

'And is it?' asked Zahariel, not really understanding Israfael's words, but eager to learn more of the Legion and its ways.

'So far, yes,' said Israfael, 'which is good as it would be a hard thing for the primarch to have to abandon his world.'

'Primarch?' said Zahariel. 'What is a primarch?'

Israfael smiled indulgently at Zahariel and said, 'Of course, the word will have no meaning for you will it? Your Lord Jonson is what we know as a primarch, one of the superhuman warriors created by the Emperor to form the genetic blueprint for the Astartes. The First Legion was created from his gene structure and we are, in a sense, his sons. I know that much of this will make no sense to you now, but it shall in time.'

'You mean there are others like the Lion?' asked Zahariel, incredulous that there could be other beings as sublime as Lion El'Jonson.

'Indeed,' said Israfael, 'nineteen others.'

'And where are they?' asked Zahariel.

'Ah,' said Israfael, 'therein hangs a tale.'

ISRAFAEL THEN TOLD Zahariel the most amazing tale he had ever heard: a tale of a world torn apart by war, and of the incredible man who had united it under his eagle-and lightning-stamped banner. Israfael spoke of a time, thousands of years ago, when mankind had spread from the cradle of its birth to the furthest corners of the galaxy. A golden age of exploration and expansion had dawned, and thousands upon thousands of worlds had been claimed by the race of man.

But it had all come to a screaming, bloody end in a time of war, blood and horror.

'Some called it the Age of Strife,' said the Astartes, 'but I prefer the term Old Night. It has a more poetic edge to it.'

What had caused this monumental fall from grace, Israfael did not say, but he went on to tell of an empire broken, reduced to scrabbling fragments of civilisation clinging to the edge of existence by its fingernails, scattered outposts of humanity strewn throughout the galaxy like forgotten islands in a dark and hostile ocean.

Caliban, he explained was one such outpost, a world colonised in the golden age and severed from the tree of humanity by the fall of Old Night.

For thousands of years, the race of man had teetered on the brink of extinction, some worlds destroying themselves in feral barbarity, others falling prey to the myriad, hostile alien life forms that populated the galaxy alongside humanity. Others prospered, becoming independent worlds of progress and light, beacons in the darkness to light the way for future generations of men to find them once more.

Then, as the darkness of Old Night began to lift, the Emperor began to formulate his plan to weave the lost strands of humanity back into the grand tapestry of the Imperium. Israfael spoke not of the Emperor's origins, save to say that he had arisen long ago in the shadow of a war torn land of brutal savagery, and had walked among humanity for longer than any man could know.

The Emperor had fought countless wars on the ravaged surface of Terra, finally conquering it with the aid of the first genetically engineered super-soldiers. They were crude things, to be sure, but they were the first proto-Astartes, which, now that Terra was his, had gone on to develop into more sophisticated creations.

All of which had inexorably led to the development of the primarchs.

The primarchs, explained Israfael, were to be twenty warriors of legend. Heroes and leaders, they would be the generals who would lead the Emperor's vast armies in his grand scheme of conquest. Each one would be a mighty being, imbued with a portion of the Emperor's genius, charisma and force of personality. Each would bestride battlefields like a god unleashed, inspiring men to heights of valour undreamt of, and campaigning across the stars to ultimate victory.

As Israfael told this portion of the story, Zahariel knew without doubt that Lion El'Jonson was such a being.

Israfael's tale took on a more sombre tone as he went on to talk of every forge on Terra churning out weapons, war machines and materiel to supply the Emperor's armies, even as the primarchs matured, deep within the Emperor's secret laboratories.

But disaster struck before the Great Crusade, as many were already dubbing this grand adventure, could even be launched.

Zahariel felt his anger rise as he heard of a nefarious subterfuge that had seen the infant primarchs stolen from Terra and cast across the stars. Some had thought this would spell the end of the Emperor's grand vision, but he had pressed on, resolute in the face of setbacks that would have crushed the spirits of a lesser man.

And so the Great Crusade had launched, pacifying the planets nearest to Terra in a whirlwind campaign that saw the Astartes blooded in wars beyond their homeworld. Having secured alliance with the priests of Mars and completed the conquest of the solar system, the Emperor turned his gaze into the great abyss of the galaxy.

As the last vestiges of the storms that had kept his armies at bay for so long finally abated, he aimed his starships into the void, and began the greatest endeavour undertaken in the history of humanity: the conquest of the galaxy.

Zahariel thrilled to tales of conquest and battle, and his heart leapt as Israfael spoke of how the Emperor had soon been reunited with one of his lost primarchs. Horus, as he was known, had grown to manhood on the bleak, ashen world of Cthonia and gladly took up command of the Legion of warriors that had been created from his genetic structure.

Named the Luna Wolves, Horus and his Legion had fought alongside the Emperor for many years, conquering world after world, spreading further and further from Terra as the Great Crusade moved ever onwards.

That brought Israfael's tale to Caliban.

'We were all set to despatch a scout force to Caliban when we received word from the Emperor that the entire strength of our Legion was to divert to this world, and that he would follow as soon as he was able.'

'Why?' asked Zahariel. 'Was it because of the Lion?'

'So it would seem,' said Israfael, 'though how the Emperor knew of his presence here is a mystery to me.'

'Will it be soon?' breathed Zahariel, unable to contain his excitement at the prospect of a man as mighty as the Emperor coming to Caliban. 'Will the Emperor be here soon?'

'Soon enough,' said Israfael.

FIFTEEN

THE DAYS THAT followed were amongst the most tumultuous in the history of Caliban, seeing many changes wrought to the surface and to the people in an uncommonly short time period. Alongside the Astartes came all manner of men and women from Terra and other worlds with exotic sounding names.

A great many of them were non-military – civilians, administrators, scribes, notaries and taletellers. They spread far and wide in an apparently random swell of exploration, telling of the glory of Terra and the nobility of the Emperor's mighty endeavour. Around hearth-fires and in newly constructed townships, they told versions of the tale related to Zahariel by Brother-Librarian Israfael.

The glory of the Imperium and the Emperor became the most oft-told stories of Caliban, supplanting more ancient myths and tales in the space it took to tell them.

Yet others came to the surface of Caliban, hooded figures of metal and flesh that were known simply as the Mechanicum. These mysterious figures guarded the technology of the Imperium and undertook frequent surveys of the planet from roaring flying machines.

Much was learned in these days beyond the histories lost to the people of Caliban over the thousands of years they had been separated from Terra. Technology and the advances of science, long absent from Caliban, were shared freely, and the people embraced such things with a vigour heretofore unseen on this grim and deathly world.

Freed from the tyranny of the beasts, the people of Caliban had the leisure to devote their attentions to the betterment of their society, utilising the technology brought by the Imperium to clear vast tracts of land for agriculture, open rich seams in the mountains to produce stronger metals, build more efficient manufacturing facilities and lift them from the dark age in which they had been living to a more enlightened age of illumination.

A great many of the new arrivals on Caliban were military personnel, and it was here that the first sources of friction were to emerge.

The Astartes had been welcomed by the general populace of Caliban as the ultimate embodiment of the knightly orders that already ruled their lives, and by the knights as inspirational figures of legend.

As much as the knights had welcomed the fact that the organisational makeup of the Astartes had closely matched that of the knightly orders, they were soon to find that there were more differences than similarities.

Where the knightly orders revelled in their differences and often resorted to combat to settle their feuds, the Legions were united in purpose and will. Such division could not be tolerated, and at the behest of the

Lion and the Astartes, the individual knightly orders were disbanded and brought under the control of the First Legion.

Of course, such a drastic move did not happen overnight, and could not pass without dissenting voices, but when the Lion spoke in favour of the union of knights and the glory that would be theirs for the taking in the service of the Emperor, most such voices were stilled, most, but not all.

More objections were raised when members of the other military arms of the Imperium descended to the surface of Caliban, the soldiers of the Imperial Army. The Astartes trials had already identified the likely candidates for selection to that august body, but the vast majority of the planet's population would still be able to serve the Emperor in the army.

Where before military service had been an avenue open only to the nobility of Caliban until the inception of the Order, Imperial recruiters spread throughout the planet's population, offering a chance to journey from Caliban and fight in the Emperor's armies on a thousand different worlds. They offered a chance to travel, to see strange new worlds and to become part of history.

Tens of thousands flocked to join the Imperial Army, and the knights of Caliban grumbled that if the peasants were allowed to fight then where lay the nobility of combat? War was surely a noble endeavour, one fought between men of equal standing, and if the lowborn were given the chance to fight, what horrors might be enacted in such mass warfare?

When the aexactors of the Army had achieved their quota of recruits, thousands of camps were set up throughout Caliban where discipline masters and drill sergeants began training the adult population of Caliban in the ways of the Imperium's war.

Within an unimaginably short time, the surface of Caliban was transformed from a world of sprawling wildernesses and castles to one of martial industry that rang to the beat of factory hammers and the tramp of booted feet as its populace geared itself up for war.

It was a time of great wonders and hope, a time of change, but no time of change comes without pain.

ZAHARIEL AND NEMIEL walked the length of the outer walls of Aldurukh, their strides long and their shoulders held erect. Both walked a little taller than they had before, their confident bearing more proud than it had been the day previously.

Their armour was freshly polished, the black plates gleaming and reflective, and they had cleaned and polished their weapons as though their lives depended on it. No part of their attire, from their leather boots to the white surplices worn over their armour had been neglected, and both boys cut a fine figure as they made their circuit of the walls.

'Interesting times, eh?' said Nemiel, looking down on a troop of newly invested soldiers as they marched across the vast plateau created by the Mechanicum's crawlers in preparation for the Emperor's arrival. Scores of groups drilled, marched or practised assaults in the glare of the noonday sun, and many more trained within the walls of the fortress, something that would have been unthinkable a month ago.

Zahariel nodded. 'Didn't you say that was supposed to be a curse?'

'It was, but what else would you call these days?'

'Wondrous,' said Zahariel. 'Uplifting, exciting.'

'Oh, I won't deny that, cousin,' said Nemiel, 'but aren't you just a little unsettled by how quickly it's all happening?'

'No,' said Zahariel, gesturing over the expanse of cleared land before the fortress. 'I mean, look at what's happening here. We've been reunited with Terra, something we've all dreamt of for... well, I don't know how long, but as long as we've been able to tell tales of it. Everything we've wanted has come to pass and you're questioning it?'

'Not questioning it,' said Nemiel, holding up his hands. 'Just... I don't know... expressing caution. That's only sensible, isn't it?'

'I suppose so,' allowed Zahariel, crossing his arms and leaning over the tall parapets. Pillars of smoke scored the distant horizon, and he knew that vast tracts of land had been cleared for the raising of giant factory complexes and worker settlements.

He had ridden out to one of those complexes a few days ago and had been shocked by the scale of industry the Mechanicum had unleashed: great scars ripped in the sides of the mountains and thousands of acres of forestland torn down to make way for construction.

Like it or not, the surface of Caliban would never be the same again.

'Yes,' said Zahariel at last, 'it is happening very quickly, I'll grant you, but it's all for the greater good. As part of the Imperium, we have a duty to provide what bounty our world has to the Great Crusade.'

'Indeed we do,' agreed Nemiel, joining him at the wall, 'but it's a shame it has to be like this, isn't it?'

Zahariel nodded as Nemiel pointed at the boxy structures dotted around the outskirts of the fortress: barracks, weapons stores, mess halls and vehicle parks. Ugly grey boxes on tracks were parked there, vehicles that were called Chimeras by the Imperials. They were noisy and uncomfortable to ride in, and they churned the ground they crossed to ruined mud.

There was no nobility to them, and even their very name struck a chord of unease in Zahariel after so long fearing such beasts in the dark forests of Caliban.

'You can't tell me you're happy about sharing Aldurukh with any old peasant? The new Lord Cypher's about to bust a gut at the thought.'

'I'll admit that it feels strange, but I truly believe it's for the better. Come on, aren't you glad that we've been selected for the final Astartes trials?'

Nemiel flashed a smile, and his cousin's old arrogance resurfaced. 'Of course, didn't I tell you we'd be in there?'

'Yes, you did, cousin,' smiled Zahariel. 'Once again you were right.'

'It's a habit,' said Nemiel.

'Don't get used to it,' warned Zahariel. 'I have a feeling we'll be wrong more than right the more we learn of the Imperium.'

'How so?'

'Just the other day, I said to Brother Israfael that the Emperor was like a god. I thought he was going to have a seizure.'

'Really?'

Zahariel nodded and said, 'Aye, he clamped his hands on my shoulders and told me never to say such a thing again. He told me that it's part of their mission to put an end to such mystical nonsense, gods and daemons and the like.'

'They don't believe in things like that?'

'No,' said Zahariel emphatically, 'they don't, and they don't like others who do.'

'That sounds a bit close-minded.'

'I suppose,' admitted Zahariel, 'but what if they're right?'

Nemiel turned from the wall and said, 'Maybe they are, maybe they aren't, but it strikes me that one should always have an open mind when it comes to the unknown.'

'Since when did you become cautious?' asked Zahariel. 'You're normally the first one to leap without looking.'

Nemiel laughed. 'I know, I must be getting wise in my old age.'

'You're fifteen, the same as me.'

'Then I suppose I've been listening more, recently.'

Zahariel's eyes narrowed. 'Listening to whom?'

'People in the Order,' said Nemiel. 'Senior people.'

'And what are these senior people saying?' asked Zahariel.

'Best you hear for yourself,' said Nemiel, the earnestness in his eyes surprising Zahariel, who had only ever known his cousin to be flippant.

'What do you mean?'

'There is a gathering tonight,' said Nemiel, 'a gathering I think you ought to be part of.'

'Where?'

'Meet me at the Cloister Gate of the Circle Chamber at last bells and I'll show you.'

'This sounds secretive,' said Zahariel. 'It sounds like trouble.'

'Promise me you'll come.'

Zahariel took his time in answering, but the look in his cousin's eyes made the decision for him.

Zahariel said, 'Very well, I'll come.'

'Excellent,' said Nemiel, his relief obvious. 'You won't regret it.'

THE ECHO OF last bell had barely faded when Zahariel found himself before the Cloister Gate, the lamp wicks turned down and the seneschals who swept the passageways absent for now. Though he couldn't say why, Zahariel had chosen to avoid being seen by anyone, understanding without anything having been said that secrecy was the watchword for this journey.

He couldn't deny there was an illicit thrill at the idea of this clandestine meeting, a sense of rebellion that appealed to his youthful spirit. The Cloister Gate was closed, and Zahariel checked to left and right to see if he was being observed, before padding across the corridor and flattening himself against the warm wood of the door.

He tested the handle, not surprised to find it unlocked, and gently pushed down on the black iron, pressing his back against the door to open it. The door creaked, and he winced at the sound, slipping through and closing it as soon as a wide enough gap had opened.

Zahariel pressed himself against the wood and turned to the centre of the chamber.

Little light filled the Circle Chamber, only a few candles burning low upon iron candelabras around the raised plinth's circumference. The stained glass of the tall windows glittered in the flickering light, and the eyes of the painted heroes seemed to stare down at him in accusation at his trespass.

He silently asked their forgiveness as he ventured into the chamber, casting his gaze left and right as he searched for any sign of Nemiel. Shadows cloaked much of the chamber in darkness, the fitful light of the candles unable to reach much past the first few rows of stone benches.

'Nemiel?' he whispered, freezing in place as the acoustics of the chamber carried his voice to its furthest reaches.

He called his cousin's name once more, but again, no answer was forthcoming from the darkness. Zahariel shook his head at his foolishness for agreeing to this meeting. Whatever game Nemiel was playing would have to be played without him.

He turned away from the stone benches and started as he saw Nemiel standing at the centre of the raised plinth.

'There you are,' said Nemiel with a smile.

Nemiel stood with the hood of his surplice raised, his features hidden in a wreath of dancing shadows. But for his voice and posture, it would have been impossible to tell who had spoken. Nemiel carried a hooded lantern which cast a warm light around the lowest level of the chamber.

Zahariel quelled his annoyance at his cousin's theatrics and said, 'Very well, I'm here, now what is it you want to show me?'

Nemiel beckoned him to climb up to the central plinth of the Circle Chamber, and Zahariel chewed his bottom lip. To climb the stairs would be to go along with whatever Nemiel had planned, and he sensed that a threshold would be crossed that might only be one way.

'Come on,' urged Nemiel, 'you can't keep the gathering waiting.'

Zahariel nodded and climbed the worn stone steps that led to the plinth where only the masters of the Order were permitted to walk. He felt curiously light-headed as he climbed up and took his first step onto the smooth marble of the plinth.

Level with his cousin, Zahariel saw why he had not seen him when he had first entered the Circle Chamber.

Nemiel stood beside a stone staircase that wound downwards in a spiral through the centre of the Circle Chamber. Clearly, his cousin had climbed from whatever chamber lay below this one, though Zahariel had not known of the existence of these stairs or any secret place beneath.

'Put your hood up,' said Nemiel.

Zahariel complied with his cousin's request and said, 'Where are we going?'

'Below the Circle Chamber,' said Nemiel, 'to the Inner Circle.'

THE INTERIOR OF the stairwell was dark, only a fitful light from Nemiel's lantern illuminating their descent into the depths. Nemiel led the way and Zahariel followed, his trepidation growing with every downward step.

'Tell me where we are going,' he said.

'You'll soon see,' replied Nemiel without turning. 'We're almost there.'

'And where's that?'

'Be patient, cousin,' said Nemiel, and Zahariel cursed his cousin's obtuse answers.

Knowing he would get nothing more from Nemiel, he kept his counsel as they continued, and he counted over a thousand steps before they finally reached the bottom.

The stairway opened up into a brick-walled chamber with a low, vaulted roof, which was bare of all ornamentation. Like the chamber above, it was circular, the stairway piercing the centre of its roof. A number of oil lamps hung from the ceiling at each of the compass points, and beneath each lamp stood a hooded figure in a white surplice.

The figures stood motionless, their features hidden in the shadows of their hoods, and their arms folded across their chests. Zahariel could not help but notice that each one carried a ceremonial dagger, identical to the kind used in the Order's initiation ceremonies.

The surplices the figures wore were bereft of insignia, and Zahariel looked to his cousin for some indication of what was going on.

'This is your cousin?' asked one of the figures.

'It is,' confirmed Nemiel. 'I've spoken to him and I believe he shares our… concerns.'

'Good,' said a second figure. 'There will be consequences if he does not.'

Zahariel felt his anger rise and said, 'I didn't come here to be threatened.'

'I was not talking about consequences for you, boy,' said the second figure.

Zahariel shrugged and said, 'Why am I here? What is this?'

'This,' said the first man, 'is a gathering of the Inner Circle. We are here to talk about the future of our world. Nemiel tells us that you enjoy the special favour of the Lion, and if that is so, you might be an important ally to us.'

'Special favour?' said Zahariel. 'We have spoken a few times, but we have no great closeness, not like the Lion and Luther.'

'Yet you both rode with him when the angels came,' said the third figure, 'and you will march alongside him as part of his honour guard when the Emperor arrives.'

'What?' gasped Zahariel. That was news to him.

'It will be announced tomorrow,' said the first figure. 'You see now why we had your cousin bring you here?'

'Not really,' confessed Zahariel, 'but say what you have to say and I will listen.'

'It is not enough that you listen. Before we go any further, we should be sure we are all agreed on our course of action. Once we are committed, there is no going back.'

'Going back from what?' asked Zahariel.

'From stopping the Imperium taking Caliban from us!' snapped the third man, and Zahariel saw hints of a hawkish face and prominent chin beneath the man's hood.

'Taking Caliban from us?' said Zahariel. 'I don't understand.'

'We have to stop them,' said the second figure. 'If we do not, they will destroy us. All our dreams, our traditions, our culture will be torn down and replaced with lies.'

'We are not the only ones who see these things,' said the third man. 'Do you know, I reprimanded a wall sentry today for being lax in his duties, and he talked back to me? I have never known the like of it. He said we didn't need to guard the walls anymore, because the Imperium was coming to protect us.'

'It was the same in my order before we were disbanded,' growled the second man, and Zahariel realised that these were men of different knightly brotherhoods, not just from the Order. 'The supplicants would not listen to their masters, too eager to submit to the Astartes trials. It is as if the entire world has gone mad and forgotten our past.'

'But they are showing us the future,' protested Zahariel.

'Which only goes to prove the cleverness of our enemies,' said the first man. 'Imagine if they had been more honest about their intentions and made clear from the first that they intended to invade us. All Caliban would have risen up in arms, but instead, they were more subtle, claiming that they came to help us. They say they are our lost brothers, and we welcome them with open arms. It is a cunning stratagem. By the time the majority of our people realise what has really been going on, it will be too late to change things. The oppressor's boot will already be at our throat and we will have helped put it there.'

'True, but remember it also demonstrates their weakness,' said the third man. 'Keep that fact in mind. If they were confident they could conquer us easily, there would be no need for this subterfuge. No, our enemy is not as all-powerful as they would have us believe. To hell with their flying machines and their First Legion, we are the knights of Caliban. We destroyed the great beasts. We can drive these damn interlopers away.'

Zahariel could not believe what he was hearing. Hadn't these knights heard of the Emperor's Great Crusade? Knowing of the glory and honour that could be won, why *wouldn't* anyone want to join it?

'This is madness!' said Zahariel. 'How can you even think of making war against the Imperium? Their weapons are far superior and the walls of the fortress monasteries will be smashed down in a day.'

'Then we will retreat to the forests,' roared the third man. 'From there we can launch lightning attacks and disappear back into the woods before the enemy can counter-attack successfully. Remember the words of the *Verbatim*. "The warrior should choose the ground on which he will fight with an eye to strengthening his own efforts and unbalancing the best efforts of his enemy".'

'We all know the *Verbatim*,' replied the first man. 'The point I was trying to make is that we cannot win this battle on our own. We need to rally the whole of Caliban against the invader. Only then can we hope to win this war.'

'We need to create an event that will let the people see the true face of our enemy,' said the second man. 'We need to get them to look past all the surface smiles and mealy-mouthed words, to the evil hidden within.'

'My thoughts exactly,' the first agreed, 'and we must do it quickly, before our enemy can strengthen their hold on our world any further. I am sure, given long enough, the enemy will inevitably show its true colours to the people of Caliban. But time is not on our side. We may need to speed events along.'

'What in the name of the Lion are you suggesting?' demanded Zahariel.

'I am saying it would help our cause if the enemy committed an act of terror so vile it would immediately turn every right-thinking soul on Caliban against them.'

'Then you will be waiting a long time,' snapped Zahariel. 'The Imperium would never do something like that. You are wasting your breath and my time with this talk.'

'You misunderstand me, boy,' said the man. 'I am saying that we should stage the act on their behalf and make sure they are blamed for it.'

There was silence as the others digested his words.

'You want to create an atrocity and blame it on the Imperium?' said Zahariel. 'Nemiel? You can't possibly agree with this!'

'What choice do we have, cousin?' responded Nemiel, though Zahariel could see that he was unconvinced by the words spoken in this secret conclave, and was as shocked as he was.

'The Imperium is not to be trusted,' said the first man. 'We know they are plotting to enslave us and take our world for themselves. They are not men of honour. Therefore, I say we can only fight them by using their sly, underhand methods against them. We must fight fire with fire. It is the only way we will defeat them.'

'You are talking about killing our own people,' said Zahariel.

'No, I am talking about saving them. Do you think it is better we do nothing? Especially when, by our inaction, we may be condemning future generations of Caliban's children to slavery. Granted, the course I propose will result in a few hundred, perhaps even a few thousand deaths, but in the long term we will be

saving many more millions of lives. More impor-
tantly, we would be preserving our planet, our
traditions, and the way of life gifted to us by of our
forefathers. I ask you, is that not worth a few deaths?'

'Those who die will be seen as martyrs,' said the third
man. 'By the sacrifice of their lives we would be ensuring our planet's freedom.'

'Yes, that is a good way to put it,' agreed the first,
'martyrs. They die so that Caliban can be free. I know
our views are not popular, Zahariel, but this will make
them more palatable, so that when the time comes our
people will fall into step behind us. This act will show
our enemy in the worst possible light and incite hatred
against them.'

Zahariel looked at the four men in disbelief, amazed
they thought he might join with them in this madness.
Of the four hooded men surrounding him, one had
not yet voiced any opinion, and Zahariel turned to this
figure.

'What of you, brother?' he asked the fourth man.
'You have listened to this insanity and you have chosen to remain silent. It is not acceptable for you to stay
quiet at such times. I must ask your opinion, brother.
In fact, I demand it.'

'I understand,' said the fourth man after a short
pause. 'Very well, if you want my opinions, here they
are. I agree with almost everything that has been said.
I agree we must take action against our enemy. Also,
given the strength of the forces arrayed against us, we
must suspend the rules of honour. This is a war we
cannot afford to lose, therefore we must dispense with
scruples and commit acts we would normally find dishonourable.'

'Well spoken, brother,' nodded the first man, 'but
there is something else? You indicated you agreed with
almost everything we said. With what do you disagree?'

'Merely on a matter of tactics,' said the fourth man. 'You talked of staging an act of atrocity, creating an incident so terrible it will turn our people against the Imperium, but I would argue for a more straightforward attack.'

The atmosphere in the chamber seemed to Zahariel to become thicker and darker, as though the light fled from what was being discussed.

'With a single act, we can deal a crippling blow to enemy morale,' said the fourth man. 'Perhaps, if we are truly fortunate, we might even win our war in one fell swoop.'

'This act you speak of?' the first man asked. 'What is it?'

'It is obvious, really,' the fourth man said. 'It is one of the first tactical lessons in the *Verbatim*. "To kill a serpent, you cut off its head".'

Zahariel realised the truth a moment before the others. 'You can't mean…?'

'Precisely,' answered the fourth man. 'We must kill the Emperor.'

THE WORDS ECHOED in Zahariel's skull, but he could not quite believe that he had heard them. Yet, as he looked from one hooded figure to the next, he could find nothing to indicate that these men were anything but serious. He felt his gorge rise at such base treachery and wanted nothing more than to get as far away from this place as possible.

He turned from the gathered figures without a word and began to climb the stairs back through the darkness to the Circle Chamber above. From below, he heard raised voices and urgent imprecations, but he ignored them and carried on upwards.

Zahariel's anger burned like a hot coal in his breast. How could these men have thought he would join them in their mad scheme? And Nemiel… had his cousin lost his reason?

He heard hurried footsteps on the stairs behind him, and turned to face the climber below him, sliding his hand towards the hilt of the knife at his belt. If these conspirators meant to do him harm, they would find him waiting with his blade bared.

A light built from below and shadows climbed ahead of his pursuer.

Zahariel drew his knife and braced himself to fight.

The light drew closer and he let out a breath as he saw that Nemiel climbed from below, the hooded lantern held before him.

'Whoa, cousin!' said Nemiel, seeing the knife blade gleaming in the darkness.

'Nemiel,' said Zahariel, lowering the knife.

'Well that was… intense,' said Nemiel. 'Don't you think that was intense?'

'That's one word for it,' said Zahariel, resuming his climb as he sheathed his blade. 'Treachery is another.'

'Treachery?' said Nemiel. 'I think you're making too much of this. It's just some diehards venting some steam. They're not really going to *do* anything.'

'Then why did they get you to bring me here?'

'To gauge your response I suppose,' said Nemiel. 'Listen, you must have heard the talk that's doing the rounds now that the knightly orders have been disbanded. Folk aren't happy with it, and they need to grumble. Any time there's change, people like to grouse about it and fantasise about what they'd do.'

'They were talking about killing the Emperor!'

'Oh come on,' laughed Nemiel, 'how many times when we were in training did we say that we hated Master Ramiel and hoped that a beast would eat him?'

'That's different.'

'How so?'

'We were children, Nemiel. They are grown warriors. It's not the same thing at all.'

'Maybe it is different, but they're not really going to try to kill the Emperor, it would be suicide. You've seen how tough the Astartes are, so imagine how much tougher the Emperor is. If the Emperor is as magnificent as the Astartes say, then he's got nothing to worry about.'

'That's not the point, Nemiel, and you know it,' said Zahariel as he continued to climb.

'Then what *is* the point, cousin?'

'If this is just talk, fine, I will forget you brought me here and that I heard treason plotted within the walls of our fortress, but if it's not, I will make sure the Lion knows of it.'

'You would renounce me to the Lion?' asked Nemiel, hurt.

'Unless you can convince the men below to cease this talk,' said Zahariel. 'It's dangerous and could get people killed.'

'It's just talk,' promised Nemiel.

'Then it stops now,' said Zahariel, turning to face his cousin. 'You understand me?'

'Yes, Zahariel, I understand,' said Nemiel, his head cast down. 'I'll speak to them.'

'Then we'll say no more of this.'

'Right,' agreed Nemiel. 'We'll say no more of it. I promise.'

SIXTEEN

IT BEGAN WITH a day like no other.

In all the history of Caliban, in the annals of the knightly orders, in the folktales of the common people, there would never be another day like it.

There would be other momentous days, it was true. There would be darker days ahead as part of an era of death and destruction, but this day was different. This was a day of joy. It was a day of happiness and excitement, a day of hope.

It was the day the Emperor descended from the heavens.

It would become known as the beginning of the time of angels.

At this moment, though, that name was unknown.

Giants, Astartes, First Legion, all these names would be used to refer to the newcomers, but as the day of the Emperor's descent dawned, the people of Caliban resorted to a name with mythic resonance.

They called them Terrans once more.

It was a good name, for it spoke of humanity's lost birthright and the origin of the first settlers who had come to Caliban. For two hundred generations, ever since the fall of Old Night, stories of ancient Terra had been told around the hearth-fires of Caliban. Now, those stories were real. They had been given visceral form in the armoured shapes of giants.

The moment of discovery, the moment when the Astartes made first contact with the people of Caliban, was already being mythologised. A vast tree of myth would sprout from the tiny seed of real experience. There would be different stories and competing legends. All too soon, the truth of how it actually happened would be forgotten.

But Zahariel knew he would never forget the truth of that day, for he had been in the deep forest with Lion El'Jonson and Luther when it had occurred.

That Luther had been the first to call them angels was true, for the Astartes had descended on pinions of fiery wings. It was a phrase uttered in the heat of the moment, provoked by wonder and amazement, but Jonson had remembered his words and kept them close to his heart.

Zahariel and the others in the riding party were already being pushed to obscurity, the story needing grander players than them to tell such lofty histories. In time, his name and deeds would be lost, and though his part in the story would soon be pushed aside in the countless retellings, he was not saddened, for he knew that the story was what mattered, not the players who stalked in its background.

In any event, the truth of the tale hardly mattered.

The people of Caliban wanted stories. They needed them. So much was changing in so short a period that they felt the need to be anchored back to reality. Zahariel knew that stories helped them to make sense of their lives.

Of course, there would be dozens of different stories all claiming to be the truth, but in some ways that made his exclusion easier. With so many versions of what had happened that day, each person could pick the one that suited them best. Some would be ribald, others reverential, some full of adventure and others more prosaic.

All would agree on one matter, however.

The name of this tale would remain the same. From the far northern mountains to the great oceans of the south, no matter the variation within the narrative, it would always be known by the same title.

It would be known as the Descent of Angels.

Following the arrival of the angels, wonders and miracles had been shared by those who had come from the stars. But greater even than those was news that the creator of the angels, the Emperor, would descend in all his glory.

In the wake of his arrival, nothing on Caliban would ever be the same.

ZAHARIEL WATCHED THE tens of thousands of people as they filled the mighty arena, cleared before the walls of the Order's fortress monastery. He had never seen such an assemblage of people in one place, and the presence of so many gathered in joy was like a roaring pressure in his head. Come to think of it, he had never seen such a vast open space before, the vistas of Caliban being primarily unbroken swathes of forest, but the machines of the Mechanicum had been thorough in their destructive creativity.

The enormous metal behemoths had rolled across the landscape, slicing down trees and stripping away their branches. Those same machines then swept across the land they had cleared once more, this time uprooting tree stumps and levelling the ground until the whole area was as smooth as the flat of a blade. The tree logs left over from the process were deposited in immense stacks by the side of the newly created clearing to be used as lumber, while the roots and branches were reduced to wood chip to be burned in massive bonfires.

It had been almost apocalyptic, the smoke, the red glow of the fires and the great metal machines so large as to be monstrous. Looking at them, Zahariel was put in mind of the great beasts of Caliban, though those monsters had been hunted to extinction.

Zahariel could hardly believe the good fortune that saw him here on this day of days, for the entire strength of the Order was gathered here, as well as senior knights from those knightly orders that had been gathered together under the banner of the Astartes.

He recalled the words of the hooded men in the room beneath the Circle Chamber and shivered, despite the heat of the day. He had not seen Nemiel this morning, and he was glad, for he was still angry that his cousin had dragged him to that dangerous conclave of rancorous malcontents.

To see such martial power gathered in one place was humbling, for though the knights of Caliban were strong and proud, they were as striplings compared to the might of the Astartes.

Towering giants, the Astartes were golems of men, though to call them men seemed a gross disservice, so removed were they from any common humanity. They soared above Zahariel, their armour burnished black and gleaming, and their voices so gruff and deep that it seemed wholly unnatural that they issue from human mouths.

Even without their armour, they were enormous, more so, for while encased in plate, Zahariel could almost believe that the majority of their bulk was artificial. Seeing them without their armour, such doubts were removed.

Midris had been the first of the Astartes to be seen without his armour, his body massive and lumpen, his flesh packed with too much muscle and hard bone as to be almost without shape or definition. Robed in a simple cream body-sheath, Midris had arms and legs like the great trees of the Northwilds, and the muscles of his shoulders rose to either side of his cranium without apparent recourse to a neck.

One Astartes was impressive enough, but over a thousand of them filled the great space, surrounding it like great black statues, and hundreds more ringed the great amphitheatre at the centre of the plain that had been bulldozed flat by the Mechanicum.

Today was the day the Emperor would descend to Caliban, and Zahariel could barely contain his excitement. Nemiel would be jealous of Zahariel's inclusion in the Lion's honour guard, but such was the lot of their friendship and rivalry.

His armour was polished to a reflective sheen, its ancient technologies hardly the equal of the Astartes' mighty armour. But on this day of days, such differences hardly mattered.

The angle of the ground and the press of bodies around him as he marched through the crowd prevented him from seeing the Lion, but Zahariel knew the Grand Master of the Order was ahead of him without being able to lay eyes upon him.

Cheers and adoring faces pointed the way to the Lion as surely as an illuminated sign, and though it was unusual for their taciturn leader to walk amongst the common folk of Caliban, Luther had suggested it as a means of ensuring that the Emperor knew he was a man of the people, that he was loved by all.

An excited hubbub filled the air, for who would not want to see a being of such magnificence that he could command the likes of the Astartes and inspire such devotion in them? A being with the vision, drive and power to set out on the reconquest of the galaxy was surely to be revered, and perhaps even feared, for what singular purpose of violence must surely lie at his heart?

The thought had risen in Zahariel's mind unbidden, and he recalled again of the secret meeting last night. His expression turned grim as he thought of the sentiments espoused there, but he satisfied himself with knowing that he had forestalled the seditious talk of the warriors gathered in the deep vaults of the fortress monastery with his threat of exposure to the Lion.

Seeing his gleaming armour, the crowds parted before him, and he nodded in appreciation at the respect accorded to his status as a knight of the Order. The sense of fevered anticipation among the people of the crowd was palpable, and their excitement passed to him so easily that it was like an electric charge running around his body. All here gathered knew they were witnesses to history, the passage of which only rarely allowed the ordinary man the chance to witness its unfolding.

At last he reached the outer circle of knights surrounding the Lion, and Zahariel felt his pulse increase as he stepped towards his fellows. Though much younger than most of them, they parted respectfully before him, allowing him to pass into the clear space between the outer and inner circles.

The senior masters of the Order gathered like suppliants around the Lion, their bearing regal and majestic, but still as children compared to the mighty warrior at their centre.

Zahariel had no doubt that Lion El'Jonson was the single most gifted and remarkable human being who had ever lived. Each time he looked at the Lion he felt exactly the same sensation, a sheer mass of presence that seemed to press inside his skull by some mystical osmosis to create a feeling of wellbeing and trust.

More than that, he felt something else entirely…

Awe, he felt awe.

The Lion was a truly imposing physical specimen. A giant, standing at a little under three metres tall, it was impossible to escape the suspicion that he had been cut from a broader canvas than the majority of men. His body was perfectly proportioned and entirely in scale with his height. He was powerfully built, lithe yet muscular.

Given that the people of Caliban had black hair for the most part, the Lion's most arresting feature at first sight was the russet golden shade of his hair. The combined effect of his physical characteristics paled into inconsequence, however, in comparison with his more intangible qualities.

Jonson exuded a raw majesty, an unspoken aura of such magnetic authority that it was clear from the very first instance why Sar Luther had chosen to give him the name 'Lion'. There was no other name that could ever have possibly fitted him.

He was the Lion. No word could have better described him.

As Zahariel approached, the Lion turned to him and gave a brief nod of his head, an unspoken acknowledgment of the brotherhood they shared.

Zahariel greeted his companions, knights who in years past had been distant, unreachable figures of authority and might. Now they were his brothers, by virtue and by valour. His past life of insignificance was over. His new life as a member of the Order had begun in blood and would no doubt end the same way.

'At last we are assembled. We can go,' said Lord Cypher, a note of impatience audible in his powerful tones.

'There's no rush,' said the Lion, his voice deeply musical and filled with sonorous tones that seemed to seep beneath a listener's skin and thrill the nerve endings below. 'My... the Emperor is not yet arrived.'

'Nevertheless we should be ready,' said Lord Cypher. 'The proper traditions and protocols must be followed as always. Now more than ever in these times of change.'

Zahariel smiled at the fresh tones of this new Lord Cypher and caught an amused glance from the tall, powerful warrior who stood next to the Lion.

Sar Luther had been Jonson's boon companion and closest brother in all things since the day he had discovered the feral wildman in the forest. A great man, Luther was still dwarfed by the Lion's stature, but his broad shoulders and open face were those of a man who bore no ill-feelings to his mightier brother.

'Ready?' asked Luther. 'I have a feeling this might be an interesting day.'

'Interesting...' said Zahariel. 'Let's hope not too interesting.'

'What do you mean?' asked Luther.

'Nothing,' replied Zahariel. 'Just making conversation.'

Luther looked askance at him, sensing there was more to his comment than he was letting on, but content to allow him his secrets.

'Come,' said Lord Cypher, 'it is time.'

Zahariel looked into the sky, seeing a dim glow building behind the clouds. An excited ripple spread through the crowd as heads turned to the skies. Only the Astartes encircling the mighty arena kept their gaze resolutely fixed on the crowd, and Zahariel had the distinct impression that they were looking for someone or something.

Even on a planet that had welcomed the coming of the Astartes and the Emperor, these warriors never relaxed their guard and never flinched from their duty, and Zahariel was filled with admiration for the great warriors from beyond the stars.

His musings were interrupted as the Lion set off towards the amphitheatre at the centre of the cleared space, a twin line of knights holding open a path through the cheering crowds. Zahariel almost missed step with the warriors around him, but recovered well enough for no one to notice his momentary hesitation.

Faces surrounded him, the people of Caliban wild and ecstatic to have been reunited with their ancestral brothers, the root race of their culture, and brightly coloured banners flew above their heads. They had lived in fear of the beasts for too long, and of the wars between the knightly orders and the countless other dangers that could part a man from his life, but now they had something to look forward to. An age of peace and prosperity beckoned, for what could the technology and resources of the Imperium not achieve?

With such tools available and such men to wield them, what undreamt of glories might be attained?

His mind filled with such heady thoughts that Zahariel almost missed the sudden vertiginous sense of cold purpose that slithered down his spine.

Dread suddenly seized him, for no reason that he could explain, until he saw the face that stood apart from the expressions of hope and wonder in the crowd.

The man stood out by virtue of the seriousness etched into his face, the intent written in every line and crease of his skin. His eyes were fixed on the marching honour guard, and even amid a sea of cheering faces, Zahariel could pick out the man's face as he kept pace with them towards the arena.

There was something familiar to the cast of his features, but the memory of how he knew them eluded

Zahariel until a shadow fell across the man's face and he recognised the hawkish nose and prominent chin.

The question of how the man was able to move through the crowd with such ease was answered when Zahariel caught a glint of armour beneath a plain woollen cloak, and suddenly he knew where he had seen the man before.

He remembered the vaulted room beneath the Circle Chamber, the lanterns at the compass points and a hooded confraternity of flagitious discussion. Hooded surplices had been worn, but enough light had lit the interior of one hood to illuminate a face… a face that moved with sinister purpose towards the great podium where the Lion and the Emperor would meet face to face.

Thoughts tumbled through his mind like a body in a torrential river that bounced from the rocks as it was carried towards a roaring waterfall.

Fear rose in him as he realised that his words to Nemiel had clearly not been as convincing as he had thought, that the warriors gathered in the depths of the fortress had not been as swayed by his threats of exposure as he had supposed.

He turned to issue a warning, but the words were stillborn in his throat as he realised that he and Nemiel would be implicated in whatever mischief this man had in mind. Who would believe that their presence had been innocent, that he had been lured with promises of open discussion on the future of Caliban?

Zahariel felt a suffocating fear rise in his gullet and a hot rush of nausea settle in his belly as he realised with utter certainty that something terrible was soon to happen. Caught twixt guilt and fear, he made a bold decision and broke step with his brothers.

Surprised gasps greeted his departure from the honour guard, and he felt Lord Cypher's angry glare on his back as he marched with grim purpose towards the line of knights holding back the crowds.

Each warrior wore an enclosing helmet and hooded surplice, but Zahariel could feel their surprise and shock in their sudden stiffening of pose. They parted before him, not knowing what else to do, and Zahariel scanned the faces and heads of the crowd as he pushed his way deeper through the mass of bodies.

For a terrible moment, he thought his quarry had evaded him, but caught the purposeful glide of the man's head, moving against the direction of the crowd's adoration.

Zahariel made his way forwards, one hand pushing people out of his way, the other gripping his sword hilt. A rush of emotions flooded him, a potent mix of fear and betrayal.

Didn't this traitor realise the magnitude of what he planned? Didn't he see the ultimate folly of his course?

As the distance closed, it seemed as though his target became aware of him. A hurried glance over his shoulder and their eyes met over the bobbing, smiling faces of the crowd. A light built in the heavens and heads were turned upwards in joy and rapture, but Zahariel had no time for such sights, his attention fixed on the man before him.

Though he moved with purpose, his posture was stooped, as though he bore some great weight, and his pace was slower, much slower, than Zahariel's.

Aware of his discovery, the man pushed harder in an attempt to evade Zahariel, but as the crowed surged in response to the building light in the heavens, his passage was impeded to the point where forward movement was next to impossible.

Zahariel saw his chance and pushed through the press of bodies, sparing no thought to the damage he was doing as he cleared a path with fists and shoulders.

Angry voices berated him, but he ignored them, too intent on his prey.

The man tried to force a path through the crowd, but alerted to the presence of troublemakers in their midst, the people gelled before him, becoming an impenetrable barrier of angry faces and raised voices.

Zahariel reached out and grabbed a handful of the man's cloak, turning him around and pulling him off balance. The light above him built, bathing everything in a golden glow, and it seemed as though a great, searing spotlight was trained upon them.

'Get away from me!' howled the man, his cloak pulled aside to reveal the shimmering glow of light upon his breastplate. As Zahariel feared, the man was a knight of the Order.

'I won't let you do this!' said Zahariel, sending a thunderous left hook into the man's face. He fell back, but the press of the crowd prevented him from falling.

'You don't understand,' said the man, struggling in Zahariel's grip. The crowd pulled away from them and Zahariel pushed closer to the man, pressed chest to chest with his adversary as they grappled. 'It has to be this way!'

The man was broader and taller than Zahariel, older and more experienced, but his discovery had robbed him of conviction. He tried to turn away from Zahariel, tearing the cloak from his shoulders as he did so. Zahariel saw that the man carried a canvas satchel across his back that clearly bore some considerable weight.

Hampered by his burden, the knight could not fight as effectively as Zahariel, despite the clear difference in age and experience. Zahariel threw another

punch at the man's face, breaking his nose and sending a squirt of blood in a high arc.

More cries of alarm circled them, and Zahariel
followed his punch by hooking his leg behind that of
his opponent and slamming a shoulder into his
chest.

The stricken knight fell, dragging Zahariel with him
as they crashed to the ground, clawing and punching
at one another. The satchel tore at the sudden movement of the heavy weight within, and six discs of
bare, matt-finished metal clattered onto the ground.

They were simple in appearance, each no more
than 30 centimetres across, a few centimetres thick,
and equipped with a rubberised grip on one face.
Though he did not know what they were called, he
had learned enough in his time with the instructors
of the Imperium to know that the pictographic symbols on their faces denoted explosives.

Zahariel's elbow hammered the knight's jaw as they
hit the ground and he followed up the blow with a
cracking right cross to the cheek.

'It's over!' he yelled. 'It was just talk! You were to
stay your hand!'

His opponent could not reply, his face a wreckage
of blood and broken bone, illuminated by the golden
glow from the heavens. Even through the damage, his
eyes widened in amazement, wet with tears.

Despite himself, Zahariel turned his head to see
what might provoke such wonder in one so
wounded, and his mouth fell open and slack as he
saw a great floating city descending from the heavens.

Like a mountainous spire shorn from the side of
some basalt landmass, the city was studded with light
and colour, its dimensions enormous beyond imagining. A great, eagle-winged prow of gold marked one
end of the floating city, and towering battlements like

the highest towers of the mightiest citadel flared like gnarled stalagmites from the other.

His opponent struggled weakly beneath him, but their fight was forgotten as the crowd turned its full attention on the mighty vessel above them and the flock of smaller airships that surrounded it as it descended in fire and light.

Mighty winds whipped around the surface of the planet, whatever means the great spire utilised to stay aloft generating a terrifying, exhilarating downdraught of force.

Shadows played over him and he looked up to see the broad outline of a giant standing over him, its bulk massive and threatening.

Astartes...

Though no outward change had been manifested in the appearance of the Astartes warrior, Zahariel suddenly felt an overwhelming terror engulf him at the sheer physical threat.

Where before the Astartes had been benign giants, albeit with the clear potential for great violence, this potential was now unbound. A gauntlet seized his throat and yanked him from his opponent. His feet dangled and his throat ceased to draw air as the pressure on his neck increased.

The power in the Astartes was immense, and Zahariel knew that with a tiny fraction of movement, his neck could be snapped like kindling.

Through greying vision, Zahariel saw yet more of the Astartes warriors as they unceremoniously scooped up his fallen opponent.

'What do you have, Midris?' asked one of the newly arrived giants.

The warrior looked straight into his eyes and Zahariel felt the fury of the warrior's hatred burning through the red lenses of his helmet as consciousness faded to blackness.

'Traitors,' spat Midris.

SEVENTEEN

WHEN ZAHARIEL AWOKE, it was to find himself in a gleaming cell of bare metal walls illuminated with a soft, off-white glow that had no obvious source. He lay on a metal shelf set into the wall, and as he took a breath, he winced at the painful constriction in his throat. He remembered the Astartes Midris holding him at arm's length like a piece of refuse and the feeling of anger that had radiated from the warrior like a physical blow.

He remembered the word *traitor* spat in his face, and he sat up quickly as he remembered the scuffle of bodies and the attempt on the Emperor's life. Had the other conspirators also been present at the Descent of Angels? Had their vile plan succeeded?

Cold fear settled in his gut and he clutched at his throat as he fought for breath. Though he could not see it, he felt sure that his neck must be blackened with bruising from the pressure Midris had applied.

His legs dangled from the metal shelf and if this was a bed in a cell, then it was clearly designed for someone far larger than him. Looking around, he saw nothing to give any indication as to where the light was coming from or where there might be an exit. The walls were bare and smooth, gleaming and unblemished.

'Hello,' he rasped, the effort of speaking painful, rendering his shout little more than a wheezing gasp. 'Is there anybody out there?'

He received no answer, and slid from the metal bed to the floor. He had been stripped of his armour and wore a simple penitent's robe. Did this mean he had been judged guilty already?

Zahariel made a slow circuit of the room, the cell, and attempted to find an exit or some means of communicating with his gaolers. He found nothing obvious, and banged his fists against the walls, but heard little difference in the tonal quality that might indicate the existence of a door.

Eventually, by pressing his face to the cold wall opposite the shelf and looking along its length, he discovered a pair of vertical seams on the wall suggesting a door, though one without any clear means of opening.

He was no longer on Caliban, that much was certain. Was this one of the ships upon which the First Legion could travel between the stars? The walls hummed with a low resonance, and he could hear what sounded like a faint drumbeat that might have been the slow rhythm of the vessel's mighty heart. Despite his current predicament, he had to admit that he was a little excited to have left the surface of the world of his birth.

He returned to the bed, frustrated at his inability to communicate with the outside world and protest his innocence. He had *stopped* the traitor from committing his act of atrocity, couldn't they see that?

With nothing to distract his mind, his imagination conjured up all manner of dark possibilities.

Perhaps the Emperor was dead and his Astartes had wreaked terrible retribution on Caliban, razing its towns and fortresses with their great weapons.

Perhaps the knights of the Order were even now being held in cells like this, implements of torture used to extract confessions of guilt. As ludicrous as the idea of Astartes becoming torturers seemed, he could not shake the impression of hot brands, knives and all manner of terrible punishments that might be employed.

With nothing else to do, he lay back on the bed, but no sooner had he laid his head down than he felt a whisper of air shimmer across him. Zahariel looked up in time to see two Astartes enter the cell through the strange door. Both wore plain, unadorned black armour, and they hauled him from the bed without ceremony and dragged him from the cell.

Outside, Brother Israfael was waiting for him, together with another Astartes warrior in white armour, who wore an enlarged gauntlet on his right arm. They dragged him down the corridor, constructed of the same bare metal as his cell, though without the brightness of light that had woken him.

'Please!' he cried. 'What are you doing? Where are you taking me?'

'Be silent!' said one of the Astartes who carried him, and he recognised the voice as belonging to Midris, the warrior who had hauled him from the struggling saboteur.

'Please, Brother-Librarian Israfael, what's going on?'

'It would serve you best to remain silent, Zahariel,' said Israfael as they turned a corner and dragged him towards an arched opening that led into a darkened chamber. Passing through the portal, Zahariel felt the temperature drop. He smelled a rank odour and saw his breath misting the air before him.

The only light came from the corridor he had been carried along, but as a door shut behind them, even that was taken away, and he was plunged into darkness. Armoured gauntlets hauled him upright, leaving him alone and blind in the darkness.

'What's happening?' he asked. 'Why won't you tell me what's going on?'

'Quiet,' said a voice he didn't recognise.

He jumped in surprise at the sound, for he was as blind as if his eyes had been plucked from their sockets. He heard footsteps circling him, but how many people were here was a mystery. He knew Israfael, Midris and the warrior in the white armour were here, as well as the other Astartes who had carried him, but were there others in the darkness too?

'Zahariel,' said Israfael from the darkness. 'That is your name, yes?'

'You know it is! Please, tell me what's happened.'

'Nothing,' said Israfael. 'Nothing has happened. The plot failed and the conspirator is being interrogated. We will soon uncover those who sought to do us harm and deal with them.'

'I had nothing to do with it,' said Zahariel, wrapping his arms around his in fear. 'I stopped him.'

'That is the only reason you are not strapped to an excruciator table, having your secrets wrung from your flesh,' snapped Midris. 'Tell us everything and leave nothing out or it will go badly for you. Start with how you knew what Brother Ulient was planning.'

'Brother Ulient? Is that his name? I didn't know him.'

'Then why did you pursue him in the crowd?' asked Midris.

'I saw his face in the crowd and… he looked, I don't know, out of place.'

'Out of place?' asked Israfael. 'Is that all? One face in thousands and you saw it?'

'I felt something was wrong,' said Zahariel. 'I just knew there was something wrong in the crowd and he ran when I challenged him.'

'You see,' said Midris, 'he lies. We must use pain to render his confession meaningful.'

'Confession?' cried Zahariel. 'No! I'm trying to tell you what happened!'

'Lies!' spat Midris. 'You were in on the plot from the beginning, admit it! You knew exactly what Ulient was planning and you panicked. You are a traitor *and* a coward!'

'I'm no coward!' snapped Zahariel.

'But you do not deny being a traitor?'

'Of course I do,' said Zahariel. 'You are twisting my words!'

'Spoken like a true traitor,' said Midris. 'Why are we even bothering with this one?'

'Because whether he is a traitor or not, he will know the identities of the other plotters,' said Israfael. 'One way or another he will tell us.'

'Please! Brother Israfael,' said Zahariel. 'You know I am no traitor, tell them!'

The voices continued to circle him in the darkness, each one darting in like an unseen assailant to wound him with their accusations. As each barb came in, Zahariel felt his anger growing. If they were to kill him for some imagined treachery, then he would not give them the satisfaction of seeing him broken.

'I have done nothing wrong,' he said. 'I am a knight of the Order.'

'You are nothing!' roared Midris. 'You are a mortal who has dared to consort with the enemies of the Imperium. No fate is too harsh for one such as you.'

'I stopped him, didn't I?' said Zahariel. 'Or are you too stupid to see that?'

A hand shot out of the darkness to seize his throat, and though he could not see it, he gasped in pain as the gauntlet threatened to crush his already battered windpipe.

'I will kill you if you speak out of turn again,' said Midris.

'Put him down, Midris,' said Israfael's voice. 'I will look into him.'

Zahariel was dropped to the metal floor of the dark chamber and fell in a wheezing heap as he felt the presence of another warrior come near. He heard heavy footfalls and shivered as the temperature around him dropped even further.

'Brother Israfael?' he said hesitantly.

'Yes, Zahariel, it is I,' said Israfael, and Zahariel felt a bare hand settle on the top of his head, the digits massive and tingling with a strange internal motion.

He gasped as he felt a jolt of power snap through his body, as though a surge of adrenaline had washed through him. He fought against the sensation as he felt himself becoming drowsy and compliant. His defiance of this interrogation began to fade and he struggled to hold onto the feeling as he felt his memories being sifted through by some unknown presence within his mind.

Zahariel tasted metal, though his mouth was clamped shut in pain. His skull filled with bright light as whatever power Israfael was using seared its way through him.

He screamed, as white hot fingers brushed the inside of his skull, and he reached for the same power that had defeated the Beast of Endriago.

'Get out of my head!' he screamed, and felt the touch within him retreat at the force of his imperative. Blinking afterimages flared in his mind and he saw a glittering silver web of light form behind his eyes, the outlines of armoured warriors, their bodies limned with light in the same way as he had seen the beast.

Zahariel twisted his head and saw that the chamber was circular and an almost exact mirror of the structure of the Circle Chamber on Caliban. The edges of every surface trailed a nimbus of glittering light, like shimmering dust blown by unseen winds, and he saw the Astartes around him as clearly as though they were illuminated by spotlights.

'I see you,' he said.

He could see the warriors looking at each other in puzzlement, relishing their sense of unease at his burgeoning power. The glittering silver outlines of the Astartes faded and Zahariel had a fleeting impression of immense power pressing at the edges of his mind.

'Careful, Zahariel,' said a soothing, sourceless voice, one that eased the pain searing along his every nerve ending. 'You are unschooled in such matters and it does not do to tap so recklessly into such power. Not even the most powerful of our breed can know the dangers of such things.'

Though he heard the words clearly, Zahariel knew they existed only for him; that Israfael, Midris and the others could not hear them. By what means they were transmitted into his head, he did not know, but he suspected it was the unknown power that had helped him to defeat the beast, one that the unknown speaker was also clearly imbued with.

No sooner had the voice soothed him than it vanished, and Zahariel gasped as Israfael said, 'I can find what I need to know in your head without your consent, but what will be left of you afterwards will be less than you were, if anything remains at all. It would be better for you if you were to tell us everything you know willingly.'

The touch was withdrawn, and Zahariel let out a strangled moan as he collapsed to the metal decking of the floor.

'Very well,' he said. 'I'll tell you everything.'

ZAHARIEL PUSHED HIMSELF to his feet and stood proudly before his accusers, determined to show no fear before their interrogation. He had faced the Lion, Luther and Lord Cypher in his ordeal of initiation to the Order and he would face this with the same determination.

The silver light that outlined everything began to fade and he told his tale in the dark.

He told them of the clandestine meeting between the conspirators in the chamber beneath the great meeting hall of Aldurukh, though Zahariel left out the part played by his cousin, knowing that to even mention Nemiel's name would be to damn him in the eyes of the Astartes. Nemiel's mistake had been naivety, as had his own, and he hoped these warriors would see that.

Better to be thought young and foolish than treacherous.

He spoke of the four hooded conspirators and how he had recognised the man in the crowd from the brief hint of his features that he had seen beneath his hood that night.

Zahariel then told them of the sensation of unease and cold purpose that he had sensed while walking alongside the Lion as part of his honour guard to meet the Emperor.

This time they did not question his recognition of Brother Ulient, though he could feel Brother Israfael's interest once again piqued by his strange power to sense his presence and purpose.

They questioned him over and over on his story and each time he told them the same version of events. He could feel the presence of Brother Israfael lurking in the back of his head, his mind-touch filtering everything he said for lies or obfuscation. If Israfael sensed his vagueness in how he came to the room beneath the Circle Chamber he gave no sign of it, and Zahariel had a sudden feeling that Israfael did not *want* to delve too closely into that part of his story.

Zahariel had a sudden intuitive sense that Israfael wanted him to be exonerated, so that he might yet become one of the Astartes, so that he might further train him in the use of his powers. The thought made him bold and his tale surged with confidence.

Once again, he finished his tale with his tackling of Brother Ulient, and he sensed the hostility in the darkened chamber, which had once been terrifying in its intensity, diminish and change to a growing feeling of admiration.

At last, Israfael's mind-touch withdrew and he felt a pressure he hadn't been aware of lift from the lid of his skull.

A light began to build and this time it was from an external source. Glowing globes set into the walls of the chamber began to fill with light, and Zahariel shielded his eyes from the rising brightness as he saw his interrogators standing around him.

'You have courage, boy,' said Midris, all his earlier choler vanished. 'If what you say is true, then we owe you a great debt.'

'It is true,' said Zahariel, wishing to be gracious, but still smarting from his harsh treatment at the hands of the warrior. 'Just ask Brother Israfael.'

Israfael laughed and Zahariel felt a pleasurable vindication as the Librarian said, 'He's right, Midris. I sensed no lie in his words.'

'You're sure?'

'Have I ever been wrong?'

'No, but there's always a first time.'

'He is not wrong,' said a voice from behind Zahariel. He turned to see a tall figure, resplendent in a mighty suit of gleaming armour silhouetted in the doorway. The voice was the one he had heard in his head before he had begun his tale, its tones mellifluous and as deep as an ocean trench. Zahariel tried to see past the glare of the light behind the figure, but his eyes were still adjusting from the total blackness to the light, and he could make out little, other than the golden halo of light behind the armoured warrior.

Around him, the Astartes dropped to their knees, heads bowed against the figure's magnificence, and much as Zahariel struggled to see the new arrival's features, he knew that he was not worthy to do so.

'Do not kneel,' said the figure, seeming to carry the light with him as he entered the circular chamber. 'Stand.'

The Astartes rose to their feet, but Zahariel remained rooted to the spot, his eyes locked on a portion of the floor. The light spread over the deck, rippling like golden water as it radiated from the armoured warrior.

'It seems I owe you a debt, young Zahariel,' said the golden figure, 'and for that I thank you. In time you will forget this, but while your memories are still your own, I wished to thank you for what you did.'

Zahariel tried to answer, but found his mouth welded shut, his tongue lifeless on his palate. No power in the galaxy could have forced him to look up into the warrior's face, and like the certainty that had gripped him as he looked into the darkness beneath the Watcher in the Dark's hood, Zahariel knew that were he to look up, he would be driven just as mad.

He tried again to form words, but each time they formed in his mind they were snatched away like leaves in a hurricane. Zahariel could not speak, yet he knew that the wondrous figure knew his thoughts as surely as if they had been his own.

He felt the warrior's presence like a vast weight pressing in on his mind, an immense strength and power that was only kept from snuffing out his existence because it was held in check by a will stronger than the rock of Caliban.

The power he sensed growing in his own mind, and that which he had brushed in Israfael's mind, were like candles in a storm next to this warrior's ability. Zahariel felt as though he was being smothered beneath an enfolding blanket, and the sensation was far from unpleasant.

'He has a touch of power,' said the warrior, and Zahariel felt his spirit soar at such notice, even as he feared the import of his earlier words.

'He does, my lord,' said Israfael. 'He is a prime candidate for the Librarius.'

'He is indeed,' agreed the warrior. 'See to it, but be sure he remembers nothing of this. No suspicion of any dissent must exist within the Legion. We must be united or we are lost.'

'It will be done, my lord,' assured Israfael.

THOUGH THE LION was over half a kilometre away, Zahariel felt as if he could reach out and touch him. The senior members of the Order occupied the great podium where the Emperor had stood the previous week. Thousands of knights filled the parade ground, resplendent in polished suits of armour and proudly standing to attention.

The day had dawned bright and full of promise, the sky crisp and blue, the sun beaming and yellow. Names had been called, rosters taken and identities confirmed by hooded adepts in red with genetic testing apparatus.

Each of those called to attend this great gathering had been individually selected, chosen from the best of the best of Caliban's martial caste of warriors.

Zahariel rubbed shoulders with knights whose courage had been proven beyond doubt, whose stamina, endurance and strength were the envy of those who had failed the Astartes tests. No other warriors on Caliban were as fearsome nor had the potential of those gathered here, and Zahariel felt justifiable pride in his achievements.

Events had passed in a blur since the Emperor's great speech to the masses of Caliban and, try as he might, Zahariel found he could remember little of that moment: a fleeting vision of a warrior in gold, words that stirred his heart, and a sense of belonging that was stronger than anything he had ever known.

Ever since that day he had known, just known, that something big was coming, and when word had come from Luther that the Astartes had made their final selection for advanced training and genhancement to their ranks, Aldurukh had almost erupted in a riot as boys had raced to find out if they had been chosen.

Zahariel's heart had been in his mouth as he perused the lists doing the rounds of the fortress monastery, though some nagging insistence in his mind had told him that he had nothing to worry about.

Sure enough, his name had been on the list, as had Nemiel's, Attias's and Eliath's.

He had sought out his cousin, but it had taken him the better part of two days to find him.

Nemiel had been quiet and Zahariel could not understand his cousin's reticence at the good news of their choosing. Once again, their brotherly rivalry had spurred them on to great things. As the day had gone on, Nemiel had relaxed around him, though Zahariel could think of no reason why his cousin should have been so anxious.

He had put it down to nervousness over the Astartes selection and forgotten the matter, for more important considerations had quickly overtaken any lingering worries over his cousin's behaviour.

It had been announced that those chosen by the Astartes were to gather on the great parade ground before Aldurukh to hear the Lion speak and tell them of their destiny as warriors of the Emperor.

Only those chosen by the Astartes were to attend, and a palpable ripple of frenzied excitement flashed around the fortress in the space it took to give voice to the notion of what the Grand Master of the Order might say.

Zahariel and Nemiel had marched onto the parade ground with the others who had passed the Astartes trials, the pride and martial bearing of everyone around them filling them with a sense of brotherhood that far exceeded anything he had felt as part of the Order.

Though thousands filled the parade ground, Zahariel knew that this represented the elite of every knightly order of Caliban. Hundreds of thousands of knights had been tested, but only these few thousand had met the unimaginably rigorous standards of the Astartes.

The sense of anticipation as the knights had awaited the coming of the Lion was almost unbearable. The majority were younger than Zahariel, he and Nemiel representing the upper age group of those chosen, and he wondered what about the transformation into an Astartes mandated such a young age for their members.

Then the Lion and Luther walked onto the stage, flanked by Lord Cypher and a robed cabal of Astartes in black armour, clad in the ceremonial, bone-white surplices of the Order.

To see these great warriors adopting the habits of the Order was gratifying indeed, and Zahariel turned in

excitement to his cousin, embracing him in a spontaneous gesture of brotherly affection. All the hurt and
jealous feelings between them seemed so absurd in the
face of the new brotherhood they were about to join.

Even standing beside the Astartes, the Lion looked
enormous, towering over the armoured warriors and
dwarfing them all with his presence. A great amplifica-
tion system had been set up to carry the Lion's words
to every corner of the parade ground, but the Lion
needed no such apparatus, for his voice was tuned into
the hearts and minds of every warrior gathered before
him.

'Brothers,' began the Lion, forced to pause as the
swelling cheers of the young knights threatened to
drown out his words. 'We stand on the brink of a new
age for Caliban. Where once we stood on our little
rock and thought that our world was only as far as the
horizon, we now know that it stretches far beyond
such petty visions. The galaxy opens out before us and
it is a dark and forbidding place, but we are warriors of
the Emperor and it behoves us to take his light into the
darkness to reclaim our birthright.

'Once, a lifetime ago it seems, I declared a great crusade to clear the forests of Caliban of the beasts, and
that was a worthy aim. I see now that I was merely
emulating a greater man's dream, that of my father, the
Emperor!'

A roaring cheer once again drowned out the Lion's
words, for where all of Caliban had been speaking of
the Emperor as his father, it was the first time he had
given voice to such a sentiment.

The Lion raised his hands to quell the rising emotions and continued. 'We are part of something larger
now, part of a brotherhood that encompasses more
than just our planet, one that encompasses the entire

race of man throughout the galaxy. The Emperor's crusade is still in its infancy and hundreds, thousands, of worlds remain to be liberated and brought back into the realm of the Imperium.

'You have all been chosen to become part of the greatest warrior order the galaxy has ever seen. You will be stronger, faster and more deadly than ever before. You will fight in wars beyond counting and you will kill the enemies of mankind on worlds far distant from our beloved home of Caliban. But we will do these things willingly, for we are men of honour and courage, men who know what it is to have a duty that transcends personal concerns. Each of you was once a knight, a warrior and a hero, but now you are far more than that. From this day forth you will forget your past life. From this day forth you are a warrior of the Legion. Nothing else is of consequence. The Legion is all that matters.'

Zahariel gripped his sword hilt as the power of the Lion's oratory washed through him, almost unable to contain his elation at the thought of taking the Emperor's war to the farthest corners of the galaxy and being part of this brotherhood that stood at the brink of no less a task than the liberation of humanity's birthright.

'We are the First Legion,' said the Lion, 'the honoured, the Sons of the Lion, and we will not be marching to war without a name that strikes terror into the hearts of our enemies. As our legends spoke of the great heroes who held back the monsters of our distant past, so too shall we hold back the enemies of the Imperium as we set off into the great void to fight in the name of the Emperor.

'We shall be the Dark Angels!'

BOOK FOUR

CRUSADE

EIGHTEEN

THEY HAD MADE him a giant.

Long after he thought he was accustomed to the transformation, Zahariel found that aspects of his altered physiology still had the power to amaze him. It was always the little things that did it. He would become aware of some small detail – he would notice the span of his hand, feel the ripple of psychic energy in his body, or he would hear the rhythm of enhanced blood beating in his chest – and he would be reminded all over again of how much he had changed.

Once, he had been human. He had been a man, born of woman. Like all men, he had been constrained by physical limitations he took for granted. His muscles had been weak, his bones brittle, and his senses dull. He had expected his life to last him a matter of fifty or sixty years at most, in all likelihood not even that.

On Caliban, there were so many dangers. Even the merest cut could become infected and prove to be a fatal wound. He had been only human, and to be human is to be slave to death by a thousand insignificant means.

The Imperium had changed everything. On the day he had been initiated into the Order as a knight, his rebirth had been an entirely symbolic process. With the arrival of the Imperium, it had become literal and real.

He had been made into a new man. His mind and body had both been altered, transformed into something more than human. Through the application of Imperial science and the marvels of gene-seed, he had been re-cast and re-created in a more warlike mould.

Brother Israfael had inducted him into the Legion's Librarius, where he had learned of the warp, the hazards and the power that could be wielded by those skilled in such things. He learned that he was such a man, gifted with powers beyond the normal ken of humans, and that he was duty bound to use his powers in service of the Emperor.

He had taken his first steps along a road that could lead to incredible power, but his first forays into such things were small and nowhere near as amazing as his encounter with the Beast of Endriago.

As much as his newfound abilities would forever mark him out as special amongst the Legion, he was first and foremost a warrior and it was in the crucible of combat that he would earn his renown.

He was no longer an ordinary man, nor was he simply an extraordinary warrior.

The Imperium had made him so much more.

They had made him for war. He had become a god of battle, a member of the Astartes.

He was a Space Marine, a Dark Angel.

He served in the Great Crusade.

He knew he was a small cog in a grander design, a walk-on part in the great drama of human history, but such notions did not trouble him, for the Imperium was a noble undertaking, a dream of a better universe, and he was part of the martial arm that gave it substance.

It was an optimistic time, a period of fine ideals. It was an age of discovery, and he was a part of it.

The early days were great days.

Afterwards, he would look back on them as the happiest of his life. He had a purpose. He had a mission. He was an instrument of the Emperor's will, preparing to wage wars for the betterment of humanity.

Nor was he alone in these struggles. He did not do these things on his own. Throughout his transformation from man to superhuman, Nemiel was there beside him. The taletellers selected to accompany them from Caliban spoke of destiny, and Zahariel could only agree, for it seemed that he and Nemiel were fated to stand shoulder to shoulder throughout life's travails.

From their earliest days on Caliban, their lives had always been linked, brothers even before they became angels. If anything, the process of becoming Astartes had only served to strengthen the bond between them. At times, it was as though one complete soul, split by accident of birth, was incarnated into two separate bodies.

He and Nemiel continued to complement each other perfectly like pieces of the same puzzle; Zahariel, despite everything, still the idealist and Nemiel the impressionable pragmatist.

Of the night beneath the Circle Chamber, neither spoke, understanding that to pick at that old wound would be to open a box of recrimination that could never be closed. It remained an unspoken barb in their friendship, always there between them, though Zahariel's recollections of that night were hazy at best and faded with every passing day.

They were part of the first generation of Astartes to be recruited from Caliban. More tellingly, they were among the first to wear the Legion's new winged sword insignia at their shoulder, the first to call themselves 'Dark Angels'.

Afterwards, this would set them apart from their peers. The older members of the Legion were all men from Terra who could remember a time before the Emperor's First Legion had borne the name 'Dark Angels', while those that came after Zahariel and Nemiel's generation had never known anything different.

For the moment though, a golden age lay ahead.

Their days were brightened by the prospect of fighting at the side of the Lion and Luther. They did their work as newly elevated angels well, assigned to serve in the Twenty-Second Chapter under the leadership of Chapter Master Hadariel. They served their Legion and the Imperium to the limit of their abilities.

Caliban was in the past, and though they loved their homeworld and hoped to see it again one day, it was a distant dream. Their present, and their life in the Great Crusade, was all that truly mattered.

Their first campaign was a time of great excitement, for this would be their chance to take the light of the Great Crusade to the wider galaxy, their first chance to prove their devotion and loyalty to the Emperor.

Dark Angels from the Twenty-Second Chapter were to rendezvous with the 4th Imperial Expedition Fleet, currently at high anchor around a world catalogued as Four Three in the annals of the Crusade's record keepers.

To the planet's inhabitants, an advanced human culture that had managed to survive the long isolation of Old Night with much of their technology and society intact, their world had a different name.

They called it Sarosh.

'So this is it?' said Nemiel. 'This is the reason we've crossed ten star systems? It doesn't look like much.'

'You should know by now that it doesn't matter what a world looks like,' Zahariel told him. 'Do you remember training on Helicon IV? I seem to recall you weren't too impressed with those worlds either until the shooting started.'

'That was different,' shrugged Nemiel. 'At least then there was the chance we'd see action. They were new worlds. Have you read the briefing files? They expect us to wait for months, twiddling our thumbs while some bureaucrat decides whether or not to declare the planet compliant. We're Dark Angels, Zahariel, not guard dogs. We were made for better than this.'

They stood by a view-portal on the observation deck of the strike-cruiser, *Wrath of Caliban*. Through it, Zahariel could see the planet Sarosh, its size magnified by the enhancement technology cunningly concealed in the transparent substance of the portal window.

While Nemiel seemed to regard the blue ball of a world with ill-disguised disdain, its beauty struck Zahariel at once. He saw an expanse of turquoise seas, the broad landmasses of the planet's continents presently hidden beneath a shifting layer of variegated cloud.

Set against the black backdrop of space and surrounded by distant shimmering stars, it could almost have been a round polished gemstone lying on a velvet backcloth amid a scattering of tiny jewels. He had only seen a few worlds from orbit in his time with the

Crusade, but Sarosh was certainly one of the most striking.

'I read the briefings,' he said. 'According to the reports, extensive areas of the planet are covered in woodland. I like the sound of that. It'll be good to be in the forest again, to visit a world that brings back memories of Caliban.'

'To do that it would have to be full of murderous predators, not to mention lethal plants and fungi,' snorted Nemiel. 'We've hardly been away for long enough for you to start getting nostalgic about Caliban. But you weren't listening to what I've been saying about our mission. The point I've been making is that there's no glory in it. They may call the 4th an expedition fleet, but really it's little better than a secondary deployment group. This is what they send in once the fighting is done and they need someone to see to the cleanup. They don't think we're ready yet.'

'I heard you,' said Zahariel, 'and I understand your point, but I see it differently. Don't take me wrong, I'd like nothing better than orders telling us we are about to be dropped into the middle of a firefight. You said it yourself. We're Dark Angels. We are made for war. But duty comes first, and, right now, it is our duty to watch over the planet of Sarosh as it is brought to compliance.'

'Duty,' said Nemiel rolling his eyes in sarcasm. 'It seems to me we've had this conversation before, about seven million times at the last count. All right, I concede the point. You're right and I'm wrong. I'll admit to anything, just so long as you don't launch into another long speech about duty. You could bore a man to death on almost any topic under the sun. I heard you delivering some supposedly stirring words to your squad yesterday. I pitied them.'

'It's called oratory,' Zahariel smiled, recognising a familiar argument. 'Don't you remember what it says in the *Verbatim*? "The arts of the warrior include not only the techniques of combat, nor simply the understanding of strategy and tactics, but also the study of every skill that may have bearing on the leadership of men in times of crisis."'

'I remember it,' said Nemiel, his face growing suddenly stern. 'But you need to remember we are no longer in the Order. All that is behind us. The old ways are dead. I'm serious. They died the day the Emperor came to Caliban and we learned of the Lion's true nature. From that moment on, we became Dark Angels and we put the past behind us.'

'Excuse me, honoured masters?' a voice interrupted before Zahariel could reply. 'I hope you will forgive the intrusion.'

Turning with Nemiel, Zahariel saw a seneschal standing behind them. The man wore a grey tabard over a black bodyglove, the tabard marked with the livery of the Dark Angels Legion. The seneschal dropped to one knee on the deck floor, his head bowed in respect.

'Chapter Master Hadariel sends his regards,' said the man, once Nemiel had given him the sign to speak. 'He reminds you that the transfer of command will take place onboard the flagship *Invincible Reason* in two hours' time. He emphasised that your presence is required at the ceremony, and that he expects you will comport yourselves in the best traditions of the Legion.'

'Our thanks to the Chapter Master,' said Nemiel. 'Assure him we will be there at the transfer, properly dressed as befits the ceremony. We understand the importance of paying full respects to our brother Legion.'

The seneschal stood, bowed once more, and withdrew. As the servant walked away, Nemiel turned to Zahariel with the ghost of a smile playing across his features.

'It seems the Chapter Master is anxious lest we embarrass him,' he said, quietly so the seneschal would not hear it.

'I wouldn't take it personally,' answered Zahariel. 'It is difficult for him. He is a great warrior, but he is not true Astartes. Even after all these years it must be hard to reconcile that fact, especially when we meet our brothers.'

'True,' said Nemiel as he made a sour face. 'We can only hope that the White Scars appreciate his efforts.'

Zahariel raised his hand in quiet admonition. 'Careful. Remember, our honour is at stake. If you say anything to offend them, it will reflect badly on Hadariel, our Chapter, and the Legion.'

Nemiel shook his head. 'You worry too much. I've no intention of offending anyone, especially not the White Scars. They are our brothers and I have nothing but respect for them. Anyway, they had the right idea in leaving this planet and heading out to find real action. If I have cause for annoyance, it's that someone chose us to take up their duties as guard dogs in their stead.'

CHAPTER MASTER HADARIEL had briefed his senior officers around the wide table of the strategium onboard the *Wrath of Caliban* nearly three weeks earlier.

'We have received new orders,' he had said. 'We are to split our strength. A portion of the Legion is to continue on to Pheonis, while the rest will go ahead to relieve the White Scars at a planet called Sarosh.'

'So, an emergency call for aid, then?' asked Damas.

Always inclined to open his mouth before he thought things through, Company Master Damas was the first to speak. 'Our brother Astartes have bitten off more than they can chew, eh?'

'No,' said Hadariel, his face, like a mask, betraying no sign of emotion. 'From all accounts, the situation at Sarosh is peaceful. It is more a matter of the re-disposition of forces. We are being sent to Sarosh to enable the White Scars to be moved on to duties elsewhere in the galaxy.'

It was Nemiel who gave voice to the question forming in the others' minds. 'Forgive me, Chapter Master, but it sounds like you are saying the White Scars are judged more important to the Crusade than the Dark Angels, that we're being shunted sideways to a quiet posting just so the Great Khan's followers will be free to find a real war.'

True to form, Damas jumped to conclusions. 'The Lion would never agree to this!'

Hadariel slapped his open hand down on the table, the noise like a gunshot. 'Silence! You speak out of turn, Master Damas. You show yourself too full of choler. One more outburst and I will relieve you of duty. Perhaps a few days' meditation would restore the balance of your humours.'

'My apologies, Chapter Master,' said Damas, bowing his head. 'I was in error.'

'Indeed you were, and, what of you, Brother Nemiel?'

The Chapter Master's eyes turned like a laser. 'I would have thought you would know better. If I want your opinion on any subject, particularly as regards the interpretation of orders, I will ask for it. Is that understood?'

'Perfectly, Chapter Master,' bowed Nemiel in a more grudging fashion.

'Good,' nodded Hadariel. 'As Damas says, you were both in error, probably more so than you realise. Our orders are from the Lion and Luther, and if our leaders tell us we can serve them best by travelling to Sarosh, we do not argue.'

'THIS IS A weighty duty,' said Shang Khan, the ranking leader among the White Scars. 'There is no glory in it and no Astartes would gladly seek out this task. It is an onerous chore thrust upon us. There is no battle to be won here. Or, at least, not any battle of the kind we were made for. And, without battle, we lack all purpose. We are bereft. We are incomplete.'

Shang Khan stood facing the Lion on the observation deck of the battlecruiser *Invincible Reason*, flagship of the 4th Imperial Expedition Fleet. Luther and a White Scar named Kurgis stood on either side of them as witnesses to the ceremony, while Astartes from both Legions, as well as a delegation of senior officers and dignitaries from various arms of the fleet, watched the exchange from a respectful distance.

Zahariel watched with Nemiel as the solemn ceremony of welcome played out the last of its rites and their Legion accepted the task of maintaining law and order on Sarosh.

'Such is the way with duty,' continued Shang Khan. 'It weighs down on our shoulders, but we feel its weight more keenly in our souls. Brother, do you accept this burden?'

The White Scar held out an ornate brass cylinder with a scroll rolled inside it.

'I accept it,' replied the Lion. He held out his hand and took the cylinder. 'By my life and by the lives of my men, I swear to do honour in this matter by my Legion and the Emperor. Let these words be witnessed.'

'They are witnessed,' said Zahariel and his White Scar counterpart in unison.

'It is good,' nodded Shang Khan.

The White Scar crossed his arms across his chest in the sign of the aquila, saluting Zahariel and his Chapter Master. 'You are well-met, Lion El'Jonson of the Dark Angels. On behalf of the White Scars Legion, I bid you welcome you to Sarosh.'

THEY CALLED IT a ceremony, but it hardly merited the title.

To mark the transfer of command of the 4th Imperial Expedition Fleet from the White Scars to the Dark Angels, a scroll was passed from hand to hand and an oath was made. If anything, meagre as they were, the trappings of ceremony attached to the event outweighed the substance of the transfer itself.

The 4th was one of the smaller expedition fleets of the Great Crusade, incorporating seven vessels in total: the flagship *Invincible Reason*, the troopships *Noble Sinew* and *Bold Conveyor*, the frigates *Intrepid* and *Dauntless*, the destroyer *Arbalest*, and the White Scars strike cruiser *Swift Horseman*, soon to be replaced by the Dark Angels' ship, *Wrath of Caliban*.

The handover of control between the two Legions had been carried out with due respect and reverence, but in reality the fact that there was an Astartes contingent present at all was something of an anomaly. Strictly speaking, the 4th was still a second-line fleet. Lacking the firepower, training or resources to mount a full-scale military campaign against a hostile world, its job was to oversee the transition to compliance among worlds that had already shown they were friendly to the Imperium's aims.

With Sarosh, however, there had been problems.

Initial contact with the planet had been made nearly a year earlier, and, on the surface, its people were friendly. They had welcomed the Imperium with open arms, loudly proclaiming their willingness to accept the Imperial Truth. Yet, in the twelve months since, little or no progress had been made in bringing the planet to compliance.

There had been no violence, and no outright acts of resistance, but each of the procedures embarked upon by Imperial envoys to effect compliance had so far ended in abject failure. Each time a new initiative was launched, the Saroshi government promised to do everything in their power to ensure it would be a success. And, each time, the promised support had failed to materialise.

The government would make fulsome apologies. They would make excuses, citing misunderstandings caused by the differences in customs and language as the reason behind the impasse. They would blame the intransigence of their own bureaucracy, claiming five thousand years of stable ordered society had left them with a bureaucratic system that was both enormously top-heavy and remarkably complex.

Certainly, there seemed to be some truth in their claims. Experienced Imperial envoys, who had overseen the compliance of many worlds in their time, would shake their heads in despair whenever the vexing question of the Saroshi bureaucracy was raised.

The problem was that the bureaucrats of Sarosh were part-timers. The planet's laws allowed its citizens to set aside a generous part of their tax burden by agreeing to spend a proportion of their time working as bureaucrats.

Accordingly, the latest planetary census, compiled at three-monthly intervals on Sarosh, indicated that twenty-five per cent of the adult population held some form of bureaucratic position, with the remainder comprising those who had failed to pass the planet's exacting Examination of Basic Bureaucratic Proficiency.

Based on the same census data, that meant there were currently more than one hundred and eighty million bureaucrats working on Sarosh.

With so many bureaucrats taking part in the process, Imperial envoys had found it almost impossible to get things done. It did not matter whether the planet's government agreed to a measure; for it to be put into practice it still had to navigate the apparently endless levels of local bureaucracy, including various pardoners, petitioners, notaries, exemptors, signatories, exegetists, resolutionists, codifiers, prescriptors and agens proxy.

Worse, the system had grown so complicated in the course of the last five millennia, it was often the case that even the bureaucrats had no idea how to make it work. By common opinion among most of those charged with ensuring Sarosh was brought to compliance, in the last twelve months they had achieved almost nothing in the way of real progress. The planet was still as far from true compliance as it had been on the day it was first discovered.

The *Swift Horseman* had lain at high anchor above the planet through the entire process, as the fleet's envoys struggled to make sense of Sarosh's bureaucratic labyrinth. It was a hangover from the planet's initial discovery, left behind in the hope that the presence of the Astartes might focus the minds of the Saroshi leaders and encourage them to complete the process of compliance quickly.

Instead, for twelve months, the White Scars had found they had to endure an extended period of enforced idleness.

It had not sat well with them. The fleet's senior commanders had grown to dread the weekly strategic briefings when Shang Khan would demand to know how much longer he and his men were to be expected to sit in space doing nothing. The White Scars leader seemed to reserve special contempt for Lord Governor-Elect Harlad Furst, the man assigned to oversee the Sarosh territories in the name of the Emperor once they were compliant.

'If these people are compliant, then certify that compliance so we can leave this place!' Shang Khan was heard to roar at the governor-elect on more than one occasion. 'If they are not compliant, tell me and we will go to war to show them their folly! You may choose it either way, just so long as you make a damn decision!'

In truth, Lord Furst and his functionaries had not made the decision. In a bureaucratic masterstroke, they had continually put off reaching any final judgement, utilising every excuse at their disposal in an attempt to delay the matter indefinitely, in precisely the kind of manoeuvring that often caused the Astartes to look with such disfavour on the growing non-military element accompanying the Crusade.

In such a way, twelve months had passed unproductively while the White Scars had grown ever more frustrated until at last, a signal was sent to Lion El'Jonson requesting that he and his Dark Angels be assigned to stand watch over Sarosh for an interval of two months to allow the White Scars to be moved on to other duties.

Meanwhile, a message was received by Lord Governor-Elect Furst pointedly reminding him that the 4th Imperial Expedition Fleet was needed elsewhere and could not be expected to stay in orbit around Sarosh forever.

The message instructed Furst that he had been granted a period of grace. He had two months to decide the question of the planet's compliance one way or another. If he failed to resolve the matter in that time he would be stripped of his governorship and it would fall to Lion El'Jonson to decide the fate of Sarosh as he saw fit.

* * *

LATER, ONCE THE ceremony was over, it came time for the inevitable social formalities. The Astartes and the assorted dignitaries began to mingle and talk, as attendants in fleet livery circulated amongst them bearing silver trays overburdened with wine and food.

Always uncomfortable in such gatherings, Zahariel did his best to merge with the background. Before long, he was standing beside the wide vista of a panoramic view-portal, staring out at Sarosh slowly turning in the void, much as he had been a few hours earlier when he had stood with Nemiel on the *Wrath of Caliban*.

Perhaps it spoke volumes of the peculiarities of the Dark Angels mindset, but at that moment he was struck most by how much larger the observation deck on the *Invincible Reason* was compared to the one on the *Wrath of Caliban*.

Influenced in part by the monastic traditions of the Order, the Dark Angels tended to a spartan austerity in their ways. Every centimetre of space on a Dark Angels vessel was at a premium. From the fire control room overseeing operation of the ship's main batteries, to the practice cages where the Astartes honed their skills, everything served a warlike purpose.

In contrast, the interior of this ship put Zahariel more in mind of a nobleman's palace than it did a warship. He supposed there was an argument to be made that a ship should be decorated in keeping with the scope and wondrousness of the Imperium. Yet, to his eyes, to have layers of ornamentation choking almost every inner surface of the ship seemed overly elaborate, even ostentatious on a vessel made for war.

Naturally, the Dark Angels' ships had their own share of decoration in an understated style, but the doors, walls and ceilings of the *Invincible Reason* were cluttered with gilded excesses. If a room was a conversation between the architect who built it and the people who made use of it, this observation deck was currently shouting in a dozen competing and raucous voices.

The deck was vast, with an immense vaulted ceiling reminiscent of the great ruined cathedrals of ancient Caliban. One entire wall was dominated by the viewportal that Zahariel was standing beside. More than sixty metres tall, the portal was composed of a number of tall arched panels like stained glass windows in some pagan house of worship.

It was not so much the view-portal itself, but what it represented. The observation deck might be decorated in a manner in keeping with the Imperium's message, with frescos depicting some of its finest victories as well as mural portraits of every captain who had commanded the ship in her two hundred year history, but equally it resembled many of the places of idolatry that the people of Caliban had brought to ruin in the planet's earliest age.

'It looks like a joygirl's house of business,' said a gruff voice behind him, offering a different perspective.

Zahariel's enhanced sense of hearing had warned him of the approach of a brother Astartes. He turned and saw Kurgis facing him, two goblets of wine held dwarfed like thimbles in the White Scar's hands.

'I'm sorry? I don't follow you, brother.'

'This place,' Kurgis inclined his head, indicating the grand sweep of the observation deck around them. 'I was saying I think the same of it as you do, brother. There is too much glitter about it, too much that is golden. It is like the joygirl palaces in the cities of the Palatine, not a ship for warriors.'

'Am I so transparent?' asked Zahariel. 'How could you know what I was thinking? Are you one of your Legion's Librarians?'

'No,' said Kurgis. 'I'm no psyker. Some men are gifted when it comes to hiding their thoughts from others; you could watch their faces for a thousand years and you'd never know what they were thinking. Not you. I saw the sour look you gave this place as you glanced around. From that, I could guess what was in your mind.'

'It was an accurate guess,' conceded Zahariel.

'It helped that I could recognise the emotion. My thoughts were identical to yours on seeing this place. But enough of this, I have brought you a drink. When brothers meet, it is good they share wine and make a drinking oath.'

Kurgis offered him one of the goblets, lifting the other up in a toast.

'To the Dark Angels,' said Kurgis, 'and to the Primarch Lion El'Jonson!'

'To the White Scars,' answered Zahariel, holding up his own goblet, 'and to the Primarch Jaghatai Khan!'

They drained the goblets, and once he had finished his drink, Kurgis threw the goblet against a wall. The sound of the sharp crack as the metal cup shattered was greeted with a start by some of the dignitaries standing nearby.

'It is tradition,' explained the White Scar. 'For the words of a drinking oath to have value, you must break the cup so no one else can swear an oath on it.'

He nodded in approval as Zahariel followed his example, shattering his goblet against the same wall.

'You are well-met, brother. I wanted to talk to you, because we owe you our thanks.'

'Thanks?' said Zahariel. 'How so?'

Kurgis indicated some of the other White Scars around the room. 'You have set us free, you and your brothers. I am only sorry that such noble warriors must take up our former position, keeping lonely watch over this miserable dung heap of a world.'

'We were happy to accept the assignment with good grace,' said Zahariel. 'It is a matter of duty.'

'Yes, it is duty,' said Kurgis, lifting a questioning eyebrow, an expression that emphasised the network of thin honour scars criss-crossing his cheeks. 'But you are being diplomatic, brother. I know it. I am sure dissenting voices were raised when you received your orders. The Dark Angels are too brave and resolute a Legion to accept such a command quietly. As Shang Khan said, it is a weighty duty and a hard one for Astartes to bear. We are warriors, all of us, the Emperor's finest. We should be roaming the galaxy, making war on our enemies. Instead, we find ourselves forced to act as guard dogs.'

He stopped speaking abruptly, and stared at Zahariel closely.

'What is it?' the White Scar asked. 'You are smiling. I have said something funny?'

Zahariel shook his head. 'Not funny, no, it's just that your words reminded me of something a friend said earlier. He also said we were being treated like guard dogs.'

'He did? He is an intelligent man, this friend of yours.'

Kurgis turned to look back at the wider room around them. 'You have brought a great many warriors with you, I understand? I only ask because I was surprised to see that your squads were led by your Chapter Master.'

'We are led by the Lion and Luther,' said Zahariel.

'I know, but your line officer is Sar Hadariel is it not?'

Following the direction of the other man's gaze, Zahariel looked towards where Chapter Master Hadariel stood talking to Shang Kahn and some officers of the fleet.

Shang and the warriors of his bodyguard were much taller than the Dark Angels Chapter Master, towering over him almost as much as Hadariel towered in his power armour over the ordinary human beings around him.

Zahariel noticed that Hadariel was gesturing with his hands as he spoke, making large movements as though in an attempt to demonstrate that he was not intimidated by the White Scars' physical presence. It was a scene Zahariel had observed many times before, and he was not sure Hadariel was even aware he was doing it.

Not for the first time, he felt a surge of sympathy for his Chapter Master. In the time before the Emperor came to Caliban, Hadariel had been considered one of the most able battle knights in the Order. Zahariel remembered serving under him when they had made the final assault on the fortress of the Knights of Lupus.

It had been a good victory, an important one in the history of Caliban, but the coming of the Imperium had been a mixed blessing for Hadariel. He had been chosen to join the Dark Angels Legion by the Astartes, but in common with a large proportion of that initial intake, he had been too old to benefit from the implantation of gene-seed.

In its place, Hadariel and others like him, including Luther, had undergone an extensive series of surgical and chemical procedures designed to raise their strength, stamina and reflexes to superhuman levels. They were taller, stronger and quicker than normal men, but for all that they were not Astartes. They never could be.

'It must be hard to be a man like Hadariel,' said Kurgis.

'Yes,' agreed Zahariel. 'My commander is an exemplary warrior. Despite not possessing the gifts of a true Astartes he has climbed far in the Legion.'

'The Lion favours him from the old days?'

Zahariel shook his head. 'The Lion does not play favourites. Hadariel became a Chapter Master purely on merit. If there is an element of sorrow to the situation it is that Hadariel has never seemed suited to the office.'

'What do you mean?'

Zahariel wasn't sure how much to say, for Kurgis was of a different Legion to his own and the Dark Angels valued their privacy, yet he sensed that the White Scar was a warrior he could trust. 'In the years since his elevation, the mantle of leadership has sat poorly on Hadariel's shoulders. He clashes repeatedly with his officers and fellow Chapter Masters, and has a tendency to take issue with every imagined slight, as if he's convinced he is being subtly snubbed and insulted by all those around him.'

'I suspect it boils down to the fact that Hadariel had never received gene-seed.'

'Perhaps,' agreed Zahariel. 'Or perhaps his rise up the ranks has been fuelled as much by a desire to prove himself as by his devotion to the Imperial ideal.'

Zahariel did not add that rumour had it that the Lion had spoken with him sternly on the matter of his fractiousness. No matter his successes, it appeared that Hadariel could not escape his inner conviction that he was being looked down upon because he was not full Astartes.

'It has always been Chapter Master Hadariel's way to take the lead whenever our Chapter is sent to a new theatre of operations,' said Zahariel. 'He likes to be able to see things for himself.'

'A wise practice,' nodded Kurgis.

Kurgis glanced back towards the view of Sarosh through the portal, holding his gaze on the planet for long seconds as though weighing the words he was about to say.

'Don't trust them,' said the White Scar.

'Who?'

'The people of Sarosh,' Kurgis replied. He faced more fully towards the view-portal and indicated the planet. 'You haven't met them yet, brother, so I thought I should warn you. Don't trust them, and don't turn your back on them.'

'I thought they were peaceful? According to the briefings, they have been welcoming from the first.'

'They have been,' agreed Kurgis, 'but still, I would not trust them, not if you have sense, brother. And, don't trust the briefings. Lord Governor-Elect Furst and his cronies have too much influence on what is written within them.'

He turned momentarily to grimace towards a silver-haired, medal-festooned dignitary holding court among a sea of sycophants off to the side of the deck.

'That is the lord governor-elect?' asked Zahariel.

'In his day he was a great general,' shrugged Kurgis, 'or so they say. It happens sometimes. A man is made chieftain and, soon all that is important to him is his status. He becomes deaf to any voice that doesn't try to soothe and cosset him. Before long, he only listens to those who tell him what he wants to hear.'

'And that is what is happening on Sarosh?'

'Without a doubt,' said Kurgis, pursing his lips in frustration. 'If Furst had any sense he'd ask himself why the Saroshi are stalling. If they truly wish to be part of the Imperium, as they claim, you'd think they would be ready to move the very stars to satisfy our requirements. Instead, there are always more delays, more intransigence. Don't misunderstand me, they are unfailingly polite, the Saroshi. Whenever a new problem arises with the compliance process, they throw their hands in the air and wail like women mourning an elder's death. To listen to them you'd think it was all accidents and bad luck. That is why I say don't trust them. Either they are intentionally putting off compliance, or they are the unluckiest people in the galaxy. And, I don't know about you, brother, but I don't believe in luck, neither good nor bad.'

'I agree,' said Zahariel. He scanned the crowd of figures spread throughout the observation deck for unfamiliar uniforms. 'I don't see any Saroshi at this gathering.'

'You'll see them tomorrow,' Kurgis told him. 'A celebration is planned. The Saroshi intend to welcome your arrival on their world exactly as they welcomed our arrival a year ago. There will be a feast, entertainments and the like, both here on the *Invincible Reason* and down below on Sarosh. I am sure it will be… convivial. No doubt the Saroshi leaders will make many great promises. You will hear them tell you that compliance is just around the corner. They will say they are working night and day to achieve the tasks the Imperium has set them. They will talk fulsomely of their newfound devotion to the Imperial cause, of how happy they are that you have come to rescue them from their ignorance. Do not believe it, brother. I have always held that the true worth of a man is demonstrated by his actions, not his words. So far, by that mark, the Saroshi appear to possess no worth at all.'

'You suspect their motives, then?' asked Zahariel. 'Do you think the Saroshi are delaying compliance for a reason?'

'I don't know. There is a saying on my homeworld, "If a man follows wolf tracks, it is likely he will find a wolf." But I cannot offer you any proof of my suspicions, brother. I simply thought I should warn you in the spirit of comradeship. Be wary of these people. Do not trust them. Soon enough, the White Scars will be gone from this place. Shang Khan has already ordered preparations to be made for us to get underway and head to our new duties. The *Swift Horseman* is to leave this system in four hours.'

Kurgis smiled, though there was no humour to it.

'After that, you are on your own.'

NINETEEN

'WHAT ARE THEY like, your angels?' Dusan asked her, his
face hidden beneath an unblinking golden mask. 'To
hear their taletellers, the Dark Angels are fierce and
warlike giants. They walk astride the stars and rain
down destruction. Have they come to destroy us?
Should we fear them?'

'There is nothing for you to fear,' replied Rhianna
Sorel, inwardly cursing the Calibanite tale-spinners
and their excesses. She almost frowned, but she
reminded herself that Dusan could see her face even if
she could not see his.

'Yes, the Dark Angels make war on the Emperor's
enemies, but that does not include the people of
Sarosh. You are part of the Imperium. You are our
brothers.'

'That is reassuring,' said Dusan. He turned and gestured to the city with a sweep of his arm. 'We have
taken such pains to prepare for their arrival, to greet
them. It would be a tragedy if they had come here to

331

destroy all this. The city is beautiful, is it not? Is it worthy of your image-maker?'

'It is more than worthy,' she said, holding up the pict-recorder she wore on a strap across her shoulder. 'With your permission, I'd like to take some picts before the light changes. They'll give me some reference to work from later when I am composing.'

'As you wish.'

They stood on a balcony overlooking the city of Shaloul, planetary capital of Sarosh. It had been nearly twelve months since Rhianna had come to Sarosh, but in that time she had rarely been allowed to journey to the planet's surface. Despite the amicable attitude of the local people and the apparent benevolence of their culture, officially this world was not yet compliant. It was clear that the Imperial commanders were loath to let civilians down to the planet any more than they had to, though Rhianna suspected that the leaders of the Astartes had played at least some role in blocking civilian requests for access. She had no idea if the situation was the same in every fleet of the Crusade, but the Astartes with the 4th seemed to resent any attempt to record native societies in their pre-Imperial states.

Rhianna was a composer. She had been told that the folk songs of Sarosh were characterised by haunting melodies incorporating the sounds of several traditional types of musical instrument that were unique to this world, but all her information came second-hand from conversations with Imperial Army troopers who had visited the planet more regularly than she had.

So far, she had heard nothing of Sarosh's music herself. She had some idea in mind of a symphony combining Saroshi folk melodies with the bombastic musical forms that were currently the height of fashion in the Imperium. Until she heard the melodies, however, she had no way of knowing whether the idea was viable.

For the moment, she satisfied herself by taking picts of the city in search of inspiration.

Dusan was right. It *was* beautiful.

The sun was setting, and in response to the imminent fall of night the city began to show itself in its most alluring aspect as the glow-globes were lit. Unlike other cities, Shaloul did not possess any form of communal street-lighting system. Instead, by order of the city fathers, the inhabitants were furnished with three floating glow-globes each, to light their way whenever they left their houses.

Man, woman or child, every citizen of Shaloul was accompanied by the bright hovering globes when they went outside. The effect from Rhianna's vantage on the balcony, as thousands of people walked to the city's eateries and drinking places, or simply stepped out for an evening stroll, was astonishing.

The entire city appeared to be alive with distant, bobbing points of floating light like a gently eddying sea of earthbound stars. It was extraordinary, but it was only one of the city's diverse wonders.

In contrast to many of the other settlements she had seen, whether on Terra or elsewhere in the galaxy, Shaloul was not crowded. It was a city of open horizons.

Nor was it dirty. From the first instant she laid eyes on it, it was plain that Shaloul was a city designed for ease of living. It was a place of wide boulevards and broad public spaces, of parks and greenery, of inspiring monuments and grand palaces.

Rhianna was accustomed to hive-cities, to the press and squalor of hab-life, to every dwelling being built in uncomfortably close proximity to its neighbours. Shaloul couldn't have been more different.

It seemed a kinder, more contented place than any she had known before.

The Saroshi claimed their society had not known war for more than a thousand years, and certainly the architecture of their cities indicated nothing to disprove their claims. No walls enclosed the city's perimeter and she had seen no obvious defences or fortifications.

On the few brief occasions when she had been given permission to visit the city, Rhianna had experienced none of the vague unease and nebulous sense of menace she usually felt when she explored the streets of an unknown city for the first time.

The streets of Sarosh felt safe and secure.

Perhaps it was the harmonious, well-ordered nature of Saroshi society that caused the Astartes to look with suspicion on any attempts to record it. To all intents and purposes, the city of Shaloul appeared to be a perfect place to live. So did the rest of Sarosh, for that matter. Perhaps the Astartes feared the comparisons that would inevitably be made between the past and the present, once the Imperium was granted its wish and the planet was made compliant.

It occurred to her that these were curious thoughts. She was as much a servant of the Imperium as the Astartes, yet she found herself almost doubting her mission. These people appeared perfectly happy with their lives. What right did they have to change them?

It was the city, she told herself. The place was bewitching. It wasn't just the floating lights and the architecture. It was everything about it. The walls on either side of the balcony they were standing on were covered in a climbing plant with lustrous green-black leaves and brilliant purple flowers. It produced a heady scent, an intoxicating musk that mixed with the night air and seemed to have a calming, restive quality. It was easy to think of this world as paradise.

'You are content?' Dusan asked her.

'Content?'

He pointed to the pict-recorder in her hands.

'You have stopped operating your machine. You have all that you need?'

'I have,' she said, 'but this machine records more than images. It can also record sound. I had hoped to hear some examples of your music.'

'My music?'

It was impossible to see Dusan's face beneath the mask, but the questioning note in his voice was obvious, as was his unfamiliarity with the grammatical forms of Gothic. 'This is a metaphor, perhaps? I am not a musician.'

'I meant the music of your culture,' explained Rhianna. 'I have been told it is exquisite. I was hoping to hear some.'

'There will be musicians at the festival tonight,' said Dusan. 'In celebration of the Dark Angels' arrival, our leaders have decreed a planet-wide holiday. I am sure you will hear music worthy of recording once we join the celebrations. Does this news please you?'

'Yes, it pleases me,' answered Rhianna.

She had noticed there tended to be a stilted quality to conversations with the Saroshi as they grappled with the nuances of a newly learned language. On some worlds visited by the Crusade there had been an adverse reaction among the local inhabitants when they were told that the Imperium expected them to learn Gothic and use it in all government business.

On Sarosh, though, they had warmly embraced the official Imperial language. Rhianna had already seen a few street signs on Shaloul written in Gothic, and she had been told that some of the great works of Saroshi literature were in the process of being translated.

It was another sign of the goodwill the local people had shown to the Imperium from the arrival of the first Imperial ships in orbit around their planet. Again, it brought home to her just how ridiculous the current situation was. Despite the warmth with which Saroshi society had greeted the Imperium, their planet had so far been denied the certification of compliance.

She had heard much muttering on fleet ships about Sarosh's bureaucracy, but it seemed to her that Imperial bureaucracy was every bit as invidious. Time and again, the Saroshi had shown they were a friendly and peaceful people, eager to take up their place in the broader brotherhood of humanity.

How could anyone find reasons to distrust them?

DON'T TRUST THEM, Kurgis had told him. After less than a day spent in orbit around the planet of Sarosh, Zahariel felt there was every indication that the White Scar had given him good advice about its people.

He did not have any evidence to confirm it. It was more a gut feeling, a presentiment born of his awakening psychic potential.

If Zahariel had been called upon to give his opinion of the Saroshi, he could have cited precious little in the way of precedent to explain his distrust. Ordinarily he was inclined to be trusting. He was an honourable man, and it was one of his flaws that he occasionally fell into the trap of believing that everyone else was as honourable as he was.

Nemiel was the one with the suspicious mind, forever questioning the motives of those around him. Zahariel took individuals as he found them. He had a soldier's innate dislike of hypocrisy and double-talk. Yet, with nothing to support his reaction, he found he distrusted the Saroshi from the moment he met them.

Perhaps it was the masks that did it.

It was the cultural norm for all adults and children on Sarosh to continually wear masks. Excepting their most intimate and private moments, the Saroshi went masked at all times, not just in public, but in their homes as well. Zahariel had heard tell of many surprising customs among the peoples of re-discovered worlds, but the Saroshi practice of mask-wearing was easily the most remarkable he had encountered.

The masks were rigid and made of gold. Covering the wearer's face entirely, but not the ears or the rest of the head, each mask was shaped to show the same handsome and stylised facial features, identical for both men and women. They reminded Zahariel of the ceramic death-masks created in some cultures, cast from the faces of the recently deceased.

He had always found such death-masks to have a sense of emptiness about them. They recorded the dimensions and features of the face in question, but after death they were unable to record the true nature of their subject. There was something vital missing, a lack of expression and detail that reduced the death-mask almost to the level of caricature.

It was the same with the masks of Sarosh. Zahariel was sure that a poet would probably find some manner of poetic metaphor in the fact that the Saroshi confronted life from behind a mask, but he saw only a culture accustomed to keeping things hidden.

Zahariel was no poet, but he understood that the face was an essential tool of human communication; it revealed its owner's thoughts and moods by a thousand minute signs. In communicating with the Saroshi, however, the Imperium was denied this source of information, and was forced to make do with blank, permanently smiling façades.

No wonder there had been such difficulty in bringing their world to compliance.

Then, there was the question of criminal justice on Sarosh or, rather, the lack of it.

Again, Kurgis had brought the matter to his attention.

'They have no prisons,' the White Scar had said to him during their meeting after the exchange of commands. 'One of the surveyors noticed it as she was checking over the aerial picts of Shaloul. She checked through the maps of every other settlement on Sarosh and found the same thing: no prisons, nor anywhere else where prisoners could be kept.'

'Not every culture imprisons its criminals,' said Zahariel.

'True,' nodded Kurgis. 'We didn't on Chogoris. In the old days, before the Imperium came, we followed plains law. It was a harsh code, in keeping with the landscape. A man who committed a crime might be punished by being stoned to death. Or we might hamstring him, or leave him to die in the wilderness without water, food or weapons. If he had murdered another man, he might be enslaved and forced to serve the dead man's family for a number of years until he had worked off the blood-debt. But the Saroshi consider themselves a civilised culture. In my experience, civilised men don't like their justice kept so simple. They like to complicate things.'

'Did anyone ask the Saroshi for an explanation?'

'According to the Saroshi, crime is rare on their world. When a crime is committed, they punish the criminal by making him work more hours in their bureaucratic service.'

'Even the murderers?' frowned Zahariel. 'That sounds unlikely.'

'There's something else. As part of the process of compliance, the calculus logi with the fleet asked to see the census data from Sarosh for the last decade. I have no head for figures, brother, but something I heard when the logi reported back to the fleet strategium has stayed with me. Based on the planet's birth-rate and the number of deaths recorded in the census, it is estimated the population on Sarosh should be much bigger than the figure the Saroshi have reported back to us. When asked about this, the Saroshi government claimed the census data must be in error.'

'What kind of figure are we talking about?' Zahariel asked him.

'Eight per cent,' Kurgis told him. 'Put that way it doesn't sound much, I know, but if the calculations are right, it means more than seventy million people have disappeared on Sarosh in the course of the last ten years.'

It was a wonderful night. As Rhianna walked the streets and passages of the city of Shaloul she marvelled at the extraordinary sights she saw all around her. The festival Dusan had spoken of earlier was in full swing. The streets were crowded with masked revellers, the roadways made vibrant with colour as legions of lithe dancers swayed rhythmically along in outlandish costumes, trailing swooping kites and long paper streamers behind them.

She saw jugglers and painted clowns, contortionists and sleight-of-handers, mummers and mimics, tumblers and acrobats. She saw giants on stilts, sword-devourers and men breathing fire, and, above it all, she heard the music.

Strange sounds drifted to her from across the carnival throng. The songs of Sarosh were beautiful, yet perplexing. They switched mood constantly, alternating between complex patterns of harmony and discord, expressing conflicting emotions of sorrow and joy without warning.

She heard musical notes and key changes she never even knew existed, as though some special quality of the music had broadened the range of her hearing.

Underlying it all, almost hidden, were the most startling rhythmic variations she had heard in her life.

Listening to the sounds of Sarosh, Rhianna understood for the first time just how perfect and splendid music could be. She had trained her entire life as a composer, but nothing she had written could compare to the astonishing sounds she heard echoing through these streets. It was an experience as heady in its own way as the perfume of the flowers had been on the balcony.

Dusan was beside her, his hand at her elbow, leading her through the crowds. Earlier in the day, when Rhianna had made landfall, they were told that the Saroshi authorities had assigned them each a guide to ensure they would not get lost. She supposed Dusan was intended to serve as her minder as much as anything else, following forever close at hand to keep her out of trouble.

Initially, when they met, she had asked him what he did for a living. He had told her he was an exegetist. As she understood it, he was a professional explainer. Due to the scale of bureaucracy on Sarosh, it was not uncommon for even relatively trivial matters of governance to become fiendishly complicated as dozens of bureaucrats had their say on the issue, each with a different interpretation of the planet's statutes.

These situations sometimes escalated to long-running disputes lasting up to twenty years or more, long after all those involved in it had forgotten the question that had initially triggered the impasse.

In such occurrences, an exegetist was hired to research the causes of the dispute and explain it to the contesting parties to ensure they fully understood it.

It was a curious system, but whatever the byzantine complexity of local custom, Rhianna had suffered far less convivial escorts in the past. In the initial months of the Imperial presence, on the few occasions she had been granted permission to explore Sarosh, she had been accompanied by a half-squad of Imperial Army troopers stalking her steps like bored and ill-tempered shadows.

It had been embarrassing, not to mention difficult to establish a rapport with the local people when a fireteam of heavily armed men lurked just over your shoulder.

Thankfully, in recent months, at the urging of Lord Governor-Elect Furst, the fleet had adopted a more enlightened approach. The planet of Sarosh might not be officially one hundred per cent compliant, but it had been decided it was safe enough to permit Imperial personnel to walk about on their own without requiring a full military escort.

At the same time, in the hope of building bridges between the locals and the Imperials, Army and fleet commanders had begun to allow more of their men to visit Sarosh on shore leave.

'This way,' said Dusan.

At some point in the night, he had begun to steer her through the streets as though he had a specific destination in mind. His grip on her elbow had grown tighter, but she found she hardly noticed. Drunk on the music and the scent of purple flowers, she let him lead.

'Where are we going?' she asked him, dimly perceiving that her words sounded slurred.

'There is a place where they make better music,' he said from behind his mask. 'It is just a little further.'

He began to walk faster, his hold on her arm forcing her to hurry her pace to keep up with him. Looking around, Rhianna became suddenly aware that they had left the main boulevards behind for a series of twisting, narrow alleyways.

It was dark. The glow-globes that had once floated above their heads had abandoned them, staying behind at some distant corner. They were alone in the night, the only light coming from the silver sickle of the moon high overhead.

Despite the darkness, Dusan did not miss a step. He seemed to know exactly where they were heading.

'Dusan? I don't like this.' She found it harder to speak. Her tongue felt numb. 'I want you to take me back.'

He did not answer. No longer in the humour to explain anything, he dragged her through the alleyways as a creeping paralysis spread through her limbs. She realised he had poisoned her somehow. The air was heavy with the scent of flowers.

Flowers. Perhaps that was how he did it. She was staggering, barely able to keep her feet, even less able to fight him.

'Dusan…' Her words sounded distant and hollow. 'Why?'

'I am sorry. It is the only way. The Melachim have decreed you are an unclean people. Your liar angels must not be allowed to pollute us. You will be our weapon against them and there will be pain, I am afraid. It seems cruel, I know, but be assured you serve a higher purpose.'

They turned a corner into a courtyard. Ahead, Rhianna could see a handcart of the kind used to sell bottled drinks to the carnival revellers. Two figures stood by the side of it, wearing baggy multi-coloured costumes covered in dangling knots and ribbons.

Seeing them, Dusan released his hold, allowing Rhianna's body to fall unceremoniously onto the cobbled surface of the courtyard. She heard him snap out orders in his native tongue, and then she saw the two figures advance towards her.

There was something wrong in the way they moved. Whoever had made their costumes had tried to cover it, but Rhianna could see it clearly. They walked with an odd sideways gait, their knees and ankles flexing at peculiar angles.

Their mannerisms put her in mind of the movements of reptiles.

There was something unnatural about them. The closer they came, the more she became convinced they were inhuman. Paralysed, she could only watch as they drew nearer and looked down upon her. As the two strange, clownish figures bent forward to lift her between them, Rhianna saw the mask on one of them slip for a moment.

She saw his true face.

Despite her paralysis, she screamed.

TWENTY

'NOT TO SEEM dismissive of what is potentially a terrible human tragedy,' said Nemiel, 'but do you remember you told me there was a chance that seventy million people had gone missing on Sarosh?'

'Yes.'

'Well, I think I know what happened to them. From the look of it, I'd say their leader ate them.'

He made the comment by private encrypted channel, vox to vox, so no one else could listen in on the conversation. For his own part, Zahariel was glad he was wearing his helmet. If not, the notables and functionaries crowding the deck might have seen his sudden smile.

Their exchange took place on the embarkation deck. A visiting delegation of government officials from Sarosh had come aboard the *Invincible Reason* via shuttle, and the Lion had insisted they be greeted with all due ceremony. Zahariel had been chosen to lead the honour guard for the Saroshi delegation, alongside

Nemiel and a selection of men from the first squads of their respective companies.

It was a serious business, at least as far as the commander of the Legion was concerned.

Zahariel had never felt entirely at home at such high state occasions, but his devotion to duty meant he had accepted the task without argument. Still, it would have been easier to treat it with solemnity if it was not for his cousin's voice in his ear, secretly denigrating the guests and deflating their pretensions.

'I mean, look at him,' said Nemiel, unheard by anyone but Zahariel. 'He's nearly as big as an Astartes, and that's just his gut! If you ask me, these people should start calling him the lord wide exalter.'

It was true, the lord high exalter – to give him his proper title – was fat, almost stupendously so. Zahariel estimated him at a little under two metres in height, but the enormous girth of his belly was so pronounced that it made him look more like a ball with arms and legs than a man.

His stature seemed doubly unusual because every other Saroshi that Zahariel had seen to date tended to be slim and lithe in build. Whatever his misgivings about their habit of going masked, Zahariel had to admit that they were a graceful people.

Barring the extravagance of their golden masks, the Saroshi leaned towards simplicity in their garments, men and women wearing little more than sandals and a robe wrapped loosely around their bodies, held in place with metal clasps at the shoulder and a belt at the waist. From what he had learned, they cultivated the same simplicity in their daily lives, leading a quiet, peaceful existence that eschewed both war and violence.

According to Imperial surveyors, the only time the Saroshi showed any excess of emotion was during regular festivals of the kind currently being held on the planet's surface to celebrate the Dark Angels joining the Imperial fleet.

During these carnivals, many of the normal rules of social behaviour on Sarosh were suspended, allowing for a temporary licentiousness, which had been a source of unexpected pleasure to those Army and fleet personnel granted shore leave to attend the festivities.

As an Astartes, he was above such concerns, but Zahariel understood there was widespread disappointment among some of the fleet's officers that duty had forced them to be present during the ceremony to welcome the lord high exalter and his delegation when they would rather have been on Sarosh for the carnival.

Zahariel had ordered the men of the honour guard to form up in two lines facing each other, leaving a broad avenue between them for the lord high exalter and his entourage to pass down. The Lion had offered to send one of the Dark Angels' Stormbirds to pick up the Saroshi party, but the high exalter had insisted on using his own shuttle, an ancient conveyance with over-sized engines that struggled to lift its mass from planetary gravity and had only now passed through the rippling integrity field that prevented the internal atmosphere from bleeding out into space.

Zahariel did not know quite what he had expected the most senior political leader on Sarosh to look like, but the waddling corpulent creature that emerged from the shuttle had never featured in his thoughts. Given that he had grown up in the harsh environment of Caliban, Zahariel had never even seen anyone who could be called fat until he had left his homeworld and visited other human cultures elsewhere in the Imperium.

Shockingly, unlike the rest of his people, the lord high exalter did not wear a mask. His face was exposed, revealing a sweating, florid featured, middle-aged man with a bullfrog neck, who seemed unable to move at anything faster than a slow processional stride.

There was a symbol drawn on his forehead in an indigo-coloured dye: a circle with two unevenly sized upturned wings at its base. In the style of some barbarian potentate, he was flanked on either side by young women bearing baskets of purple flowers, which were strewn in his path to be crushed to scented pulp by his ample tread.

'Visitors aboard!' called out Zahariel, switching his helmet vox to external address as the lord high exalter stepped between the twin ranks of Dark Angels. 'Honour guard, salute!'

As one, the Dark Angels complied in a smooth motion, crossing their arms in front of their chests in the sign of the aquila.

'Angels of the Imperium, we salute you,' said the lord high exalter, waving a bloated hand as he passed. 'Praise the Emperor and all his works. We welcome you to Sarosh.'

'And may I welcome you to the flagship *Invincible Reason*, my lord,' said the Lion, stepping forward to greet him. Behind him stood Luther, looking about as pleased to be at this ceremony as Zahariel felt.

The primarch of the Dark Angels wore his ceremonial armour, his surplice freshly pressed and starched with the symbol of the Dark Angels picked out in crimson thread. 'I am Lion El'Jonson, legion commander of the First Legion, the Dark Angels.'

'Legion commander?' said the lord high exalter, raising a painted eyebrow. 'You are the autarch here, then? These angels serve you?'

'They serve the Emperor,' corrected the Lion, 'but if you meant to ask if I am their leader, then the answer is yes.'

'I am pleased to meet you, master of angels. We have much to discuss. My people are very eager to become... compliant, I believe you call it. Too much time has been wasted already, lost to cultural misapprehension and foolish misunderstandings. Today, we can begin a new page in the relationship between us. Are the other leaders of your fleet present? I had hoped to address them all and make clear how ready we are on Sarosh to take the final steps to becoming full Imperial citizens.'

'I am sure they will be glad to hear it,' said the Lion as he turned to lead the lord high exalter away from the embarkation deck. 'If you will follow me, I have arranged a reception where you can meet the rest of the fleet commanders. You can speak there and enlighten us with your thoughts.'

'"Enlighten?" It means to bring light?' the fat man smiled. 'Yes, that is a good word. There is so much you do not understand about my people. I hope to bring light to you all.'

THE EMBARKATION DECK of a starship was always busy, but the deck on the flagship *Invincible Reason* seemed almost quiet when the Lion, the lord high exalter, his entourage and the other dignitaries had left it.

Once they were gone, the work crews and servitors who constituted the deck's permanent garrison returned to the routine tasks of maintenance that had been interrupted by the arrival of the Saroshi shuttle and the welcoming committee that had greeted it.

Free of the presence of interlopers standing uselessly about and cluttering their working space, the crews made up for lost time in ensuring that all currently unused aircraft were fuelled, ready to go and in good functioning order.

Zahariel remained behind in the embarkation deck, while Nemiel and his warriors had followed the primarch and the Saroshi envoys to where the fate of Sarosh would be decided.

Knowing that he and the rest of the Dark Angels would soon be deploying to the surface of Sarosh, regardless of the outcome of the talks between the Lion and the lord high exalter, Zahariel decided to remain on the embarkation deck to prepare for that deployment.

The deployment to a planet was fraught with danger, and a million and one tasks needed to be overseen before the Astartes would even encounter the enemy, if such was to be the Saroshi's fate. Zahariel was soon lost in the details of his work, prepping his armour and weapons for the drop, and he did not hear the approaching footsteps until their owner addressed him.

'It will be soon,' said a friendly voice behind him.

Zahariel turned to see the powerfully armoured figure of Luther, still resplendent in his ceremonial armour, black and gilded gold. 'The drop to the surface, I mean.'

'I thought so,' replied Zahariel. 'That's why I wanted to get a head start.'

Luther nodded, and Zahariel sensed that his commander wished to say more, but did not yet know how to broach the subject. Luther tapped him on the shoulder and said, 'Let's take a look at that shuttle, eh? The Saroshi one.'

Zahariel looked over to the battered old shuttle, having had little interest in it once it had disgorged its fat cargo.

'It doesn't look like much, does it?' said Luther, walking across the deck.

Zahariel followed the Lion's second-in-command and said, 'Apparently the Mechanicum adepts scanned it on the way in. They said it was of an obsolete design well-known from before the Unification Wars on Terra, so they immediately lost interest.'

'Ah, well they are immune to the romance of history, Zahariel,' said Luther, walking around the battered shuttle with its oversized engines and bulbous front section. 'I mean, it's clearly thousands of years old. It must have taken generations of mechanics to keep it in a working state of repair.'

'Then it should be in a museum,' said Zahariel, as Luther ducked beneath a stubby wing and examined the underside of the conveyance.

'Perhaps,' agreed Luther. 'It's the last functioning relic of an earlier age. It might be the only vehicle on Sarosh still capable of trans-atmospheric travel.'

'So why bother using it?' asked Zahariel. 'Why not accept the Lion's offer of a Stormbird?'

'Who knows?' said Luther, frowning as he saw something puzzling. 'Perhaps the Saroshi kept it running because they knew they would need it in the future.'

'Need it for what?'

Luther emerged from beneath the shuttle on the far side from Zahariel, and he could see that the Legion's second-in-command had gone utterly pale. His face was ashen, and he looked at the shuttle with a strange expression that Zahariel could not read.

'Is everything all right?' asked Zahariel.

'Hmmm?' said Luther, glancing towards the great, arched doors that the Lion and the Saroshi delegation had earlier passed through. 'Oh, yes, Zahariel. Sorry, I was distracted.'

'Are you sure?' asked Zahariel. 'You don't look well, my lord.'

'I'm fine, Zahariel,' said Luther. 'Now come on, return to your battle-brothers, it's not good to be too far from your fellows when you might be about to go into battle. It's bad luck, you know.'

'But I have things to finish here,' protested Zahariel.

'Never mind them,' insisted Luther, leading him from the embarkation deck. 'Go. Be with your company and stay there until I call for you. Do you understand me?'

'Yes, my lord,' said Zahariel, though, in truth, he could not fathom the sudden change in Luther's behaviour.

He left the Legion's second-in-command at the door to the embarkation deck, watching as Luther stared in fascination at the Saroshi shuttle.

'IS IT YOUR custom to pick smaller men for positions of authority?' the lord high exalter asked blithely as he stood with a crowd of dignitaries beside the wide arch of the view-portal on the observation deck. 'I ask this because I notice the man you call Chapter Master is not as tall as the men he commands. Also, there is the fact of these other men, the ones you call the leaders of your fleet.'

The high exalter gestured to the military officers, fleet captains and other Imperial functionaries assembled around them.

'They are also smaller than your angels,' he continued, with an expression that was open and guileless. 'Is it your custom to let only those who were born as giants bear the brunt of the fighting, while the small men act as their officers?'

'It is not a question of custom,' answered the Lion in a diplomatic tone as Chapter Master Hadariel bristled in anger beside him. 'Nor are all of us born as giants. The Dark Angels are members of the Astartes. We are a product of the Emperor's science. We are given physical enhancements to improve our abilities.'

'Ah, so you are changed,' said the high exalter, nodding his head slowly. 'You are vat-grown. Now I understand. But what of you, Sar Hadariel? You stand taller than most men, but you are not as tall as your warriors. Please, why is this?'

'I was unfortunate,' replied the Chapter Master. 'By the time I was chosen, I was too old to be granted gene-seed. In its place, I was given surgery to modify my body and make me a better warrior.'

Nemiel stood at the other end of the observation deck with the rest of his squad, close enough to hear every word of their conversation with his enhanced hearing, wincing at the lord high exalter's line of conversation.

The lord high exalter had no way of knowing how sensitive the Chapter Master was about the fact that he had not been given gene-seed. Inadvertently, the Saroshi leader had managed to broach the one subject most likely to lead to crossed words and some form of diplomatic breach.

It was to Hadariel's credit that he had so far managed to keep any suggestion that he was offended by his visitor's line of questioning from his face. Anxious to defuse any potential outburst from Hadariel, the Lion said, 'May I take it, you have some understanding of such technologies? You used the word "vat-grown". Does your culture have experience of genetic science?'

'Yes, but I am here to discuss more important matters.'

Waving the question away with a dismissive hand, the lord high exalter turned to face the broad expanse of the view-portal behind him. He spread his arms wide, the gesture taking in the blue globe of Sarosh visible through the portal.

'The world is beautiful, is it not? I have never seen it from this angle before. Granted, some of our historic books include picture-images of our world taken from orbit. But before today, the shuttle that brought me here had not flown for nearly a century. Even if I had ordered it to take me into space, the view-portals on the shuttle are no bigger than my hand. If it weren't for the Imperium, I would never have seen the magnificence of the sight I see before me. I thank you for that. To look down on the world I have known, to see its seas and continents laid out before me, it has granted me a new perspective.'

'It is only the beginning, my lord exalter,' said Governor-Elect Furst. Perhaps sensing the tension, he pushed himself forward to stand beside the Lion. 'You can scarcely conceive of the wonders we can bring to your world once it is compliant.'

'Ah, yes. Compliance,' grimaced the fat man. 'An interesting choice of words. It refers to the process of conforming to a demand or proposal. Also, it means to become yielding, flexible, submissive. And if we do not submit, what then? Will you unleash your angels, lord governor-elect? Will you destroy us if we do not comply with your wishes?'

'Well, I…' said Furst, visibly squirming. 'That is to say…'

'It is not the governor-elect's decision to make,' interrupted the Lion, 'it is mine. Your question implies a criticism of our ways, lord exalter. You must understand, the aim of this crusade is to re-unite all the lost fragments of mankind. We come to you as brothers. We have no wish to use force to bring about your compliance, but experience tells us that it is sometimes necessary. Occasionally, whether through ignorance or because they are controlled by an unsuitable regime, the people of a re-discovered world choose to oppose us. It makes no difference. We have come to rescue you. Whether or not you wish to be rescued is hardly material to the outcome.'

'And what of our regime?' asked the lord high exalter.

The Saroshi diplomat turned back from the view-portal to face the Lion and the ranks of Imperial commanders behind him. 'What of the Saroshi government? Have you judged us to be unsuitable?'

'The decision has not yet been made,' said the Lion. 'I must say I am pleased we talk so frankly. I had heard your people have a tendency to be... evasive on these matters.'

'Yes, we were evasive,' said the high exalter, holding the Lion's gaze coolly, 'until we found the time fast approaching when we were called upon to make a choice. I understand the Imperium does not worship any gods. In fact, you forbid it. Is this true?'

'It is,' said the Lion, caught unawares by his guest's sudden change of tack, 'but I do not see its relevance. I was told that you share our view of religion on Sarosh. You have no priesthood or places of worship.'

'In that you are incorrect,' said the lord high exalter. 'Our temples are in the wild places, in the forests and the caves, where the messengers of our gods speak to their chosen representatives, the Ascendim. We are a pious people. Our society is founded on the divine mandate granted to the Ascendim. We have followed their dictates for more than a thousand years, and we have achieved the perfect society.'

'Why am I hearing this now?' snapped the Lion, looking around at the governor-elect and other Imperial dignitaries for answers, only to see that they were as mystified as he was.

He turned back to the Saroshi leader. 'You hid this from us?'

'We did,' agreed the lord exalter. 'We were aided in this by the fact that faith is a private matter among my people. When your first Imperial scouts came to our planet, there was nothing on our world for them to recognise as signs of religion, no grand temples or sacred precincts inside our cities. We keep our holy places hidden away, simply because the Melachim have ordered that it should be so.'

'The Melachim?' echoed the Lion, dumbfounded.

'They are our gods. They speak to the Ascendim, the only ones who can hear their divine voices. They speak to them when they walk in the wilderness, away from civilisation. They tell the Ascendim what is to be done, and their word is relayed to the rest of our society. By such methods is the will of the gods made clear.'

'This is foolishness,' said the Lion, growing angry. 'You are rational people, from a technologically advanced society. You must be able to see this superstition for what it is.'

'You showed your true faces too early,' said the lord high exalter. 'When your scouts revealed themselves to us, they spoke eruditely of how you had thrown down religion and damned it all as childish superstition. From that moment, we knew you were evil. No society can make claim to be righteous if it does not acknowledge the primacy of divine power. Secular truth is false truth. When we heard that your Emperor preaches there are only false gods, we knew his real nature at once. He is a liar daemon, a creature of falsehood, sent by dark powers to lead mankind astray.'

ZAHARIEL MADE HIS way through the corridors of the ship to where the rest of his squad was currently billeted, running through the items he still needed to attend to before returning to the *Wrath of Caliban* and the drop to Sarosh. He had few illusions that they would be making planetfall soon, for Kurgis's warnings that the Saroshi were not to be trusted still rang in his ears.

Even as the thought occurred, he wondered again at the strange expression he had seen on Luther's face as he had come up from underneath the Saroshi shuttle, wondering what the Legion's second had seen that had…

Had what?

Unnerved him?

Zahariel pictured Luther as he had come up, his face pallid and uneasy. What could he have seen that would unsettle a great warrior and hero such as Luther? The more he studied the image in his face, the more he let his mind drift, looking into the eyes of the man whose face was held in his mind's eye.

He saw pain there and sadness, and years of living in the shadow of another.

Zahariel's senses that were, even now, becoming surer and more sensitive, thanks to the training of Brother-Librarian Israfael, tried to make sense of the emotions and feelings coming off the image in his head.

Don't trust them… and don't turn your back on them.

Zahariel halted as a sudden wave of nausea swept through him. As an Astartes, he almost never suffered from any such feelings, his genhanced metabolism compensating for almost every sensation that might trigger such a reaction.

However, this was no physiological reaction, this was a sure and sudden sense of something deeply wrong.

Worse still was the sense that he was not the only one to realise that something was wrong, but that he was the only one who desired to stop it.

THE EMBARKATION DECK was quiet and that, in itself, was unusual.

Zahariel stepped over the threshold of the blast door and scanned for the normal personnel, techs,

Mechanicum adepts and loaders that should be filling the space with life and bustle.

The hiss and creak of the deck and the ever-present thrum that filled a starship were the only sounds, and Zahariel immediately knew that his suspicions had not been groundless.

Something was definitely wrong.

He crossed the embarkation deck towards the Saroshi shuttle and circled it, looking for anything out of place or otherwise unusual. As he had said while talking to Luther, the design was old and practically obsolete, the engines vastly oversized for such a small conveyance.

He ducked beneath one of the wings, crawling on all fours beneath the shuttle, hoping to see what had so unnerved Luther.

The underside of the shuttle stank of engine oil and hydraulic fluids, the plates of metal crudely bolted and welded together with little regard for the quality of workmanship. At first, Zahariel could see nothing unusual, and moved further along the belly of the shuttle.

He ducked his head around a loose plate and...

Zahariel turned back to look at the plate. The hinges holding it were rusted and stiff.

He shook his head as he realised that it was a miracle that this shuttle had even broken atmosphere, let alone expected to return.

As he stared at the open panel he suddenly realised what was wrong with the shuttle, at least partly. This was no orbital shuttle, for there was no heat shielding on the craft's belly, this was a purely atmospheric craft, primarily designed to fly within the bounds of a planet's airspace, which explained the oversized engines, presumably retro-fitted to allow their one craft to reach orbit.

Without heat shielding, anyone who tried to descend to a planet's surface in this craft would not survive the journey. The craft would turn into a flaming comet as the heat of re-entry seared anyone inside to ashes before melting to nothing as it plunged to its death.

The people that had boarded this craft had clearly done so with no intention of ever returning to the surface.

That meant that their mission was one way.

Zahariel crawled from beneath the shuttle, horrified at the idea that they had been boarded by enemies who posed as friends. He looked at the shuttle, seeing it for the vile transport of the enemy it truly was.

'But what could they hope to achieve?' he whispered to himself.

Barely a handful of Saroshi had boarded the *Invincible Reason*, hardly enough to trouble even one Dark Angel, let alone a ship full of them.

So what purpose did this visit serve?

Zahariel circled the shuttle, tapping his fist on the battered fuselage, the softly humming engines and its bulbous front section. As he reached the front of the shuttle, he wondered again at the strange design of the craft, for its nose was surely a poor choice of shape for any craft designed for atmospheric flight.

Though he was no aeronautical engineer, he had learnt enough to know that aircraft depended on lift created by their shape and wings to keep them aloft, and that such a heavy-looking front section made no sense.

Looking more closely at the nose, Zahariel could see that it had been a later addition to the craft's structure, the paint and workmanship different from the rest of the ship. He stood back and looked at the lines of the shuttle's front, seeing now that the entire section had been added over and above where the original nose of the shuttle ended.

Zahariel took hold of one of the access hatches and pulled.

As he had feared, it was welded shut, but he knew that something dreadful was concealed within. He took a deep breath and gripped the release handle, pulling it with all his might.

Metal bent and buckled, and finally came free, the welded joint unable to withstand the strength of one of the Emperor's finest. Zahariel tossed aside the ruined panel and stared into the gap he had torn in the front section.

Inside he saw a mass of thick blocks of dark metal fitted around a circular core about a metre across. Thick struts of the same dark metal protected the central core, and a procession of winking lights circled the device hidden within the secret compartment.

'It's a weapon of some sort,' said a voice behind him, 'an atomic warhead I think.'

Zahariel spun, his fist raised to strike the speaker.

Luther stood before him, his face a mask of anguish and regret.

'An atomic warhead?' asked Zahariel.

'Yes,' said Luther, coming closer and peering into the opened access panel. 'I think the whole shuttle is nothing but one giant missile.'

'You knew of this?' said Zahariel. 'Why didn't you say anything?'

Luther turned away from him, his shoulders slumped as though in defeat. He turned back to Zahariel, who was shocked to see tears in his commander's eyes.

'I almost did, Zahariel,' said Luther. 'I wanted to, but then I thought of what would be mine if I didn't: the Legion, command, Caliban. It would all be mine, and I would no longer have to share it with someone whose shadow obscures everything I do.'

'The Lion?' said Zahariel. 'His deeds are great, but so are yours!'

'Maybe in another age,' said Luther, 'one in which I did not share the same span of time as a man like the Lion. In any other age, the glory of leading Caliban from the darkness would have been mine, but instead it goes to my brother. You have no idea how galling it is to be the greatest man of the age and have that taken from you in an instant.'

Zahariel watched the words flow from Luther in a flood. For a decade and more, these feelings had been contained within a dam of honour and restraint, but the dam was crumbling and Luther's true feelings were spilling out.

'I never realised,' said Zahariel, his hand sliding towards his sword. 'No one did.'

'No, even I did not; not fully,' said Luther, 'not until I saw this shuttle. I wouldn't have to lift a finger. All I'd have to do is walk away, and everything I wanted would be mine.'

'Then why are you back here?'

'I ordered everyone out of the embarkation deck and walked away,' said Luther, one hand covering his eyes as he spoke, 'but I hadn't gone more than a few steps before I knew I couldn't do it.'

'Then you're here to stop it?' asked Zahariel, relieved beyond words.

'I am,' nodded Luther, 'so you can stop reaching for your blade. I realised that it was an honour to serve a warrior as great as the Lion, and that I was the luckiest man alive to be allowed to call him brother.'

Zahariel turned back to the shuttle and the deadly cargo it contained.

'Then how do we stop it?'

'Ah,' said Luther, 'that, I don't know.'

'You GO TOO far,' said the Lion, his hand going to the ceremonial sword at his side.

'No, *you* do,' responded the high exalter. 'You are abominations, all of you,' he snarled, his fat jowls wobbling. 'The only reason I bear your presence is because I have been granted the honour of pronouncing the judgement of my people upon you.

'Your Imperium is the work of evil men,' said the lord high exalter. 'Your words are falsehoods. You are craven and dishonourable, and your angels... your angels are the worst, the product of rutting beasts. You are liar angels. You are loathsome and unclean.'

'Enough!' roared the Lion.

The commander of the Dark Angels Legion was enraged, his hand gripping the pommel of his sword so tightly that his knuckles were white. 'By the Emperor–'

'I spit on your Emperor,' said the fat man, and the gathered Imperials gave a collective intake of breath. 'And I spit on you, Lion El'Jonson!'

The high exalter stretched out his arms, laid three fingers from his right hand on top of the five fingers of his left and touched them to the symbol painted on his forehead.

'You are not men, nor worthy leaders. You are–'

He was not allowed to finish the sentence.

Before the lord high exalter could say another word, the Lion drew his gleaming sword and clove through the fat man's shoulder and down into his ample gut.

ZAHARIEL LOOKED DOWN at the device in the shuttle's front section, as the blinking lights suddenly began to speed up, and a single pulsing red light lit up in the centre of the sphere. The engines of the shuttle coughed to life and a rising whine of ignition built from within.

'Damn,' said Luther.

MELPOMENE

TWENTY-ONE

THE SEQUENCE OF lights was speeding up, and a second red light had winked into life on the sphere at the centre of the device. A rising hum, felt in the bones as well as heard, built from the sphere, penetrating even the screaming roar of the engines as they gathered power.

The heat from the engines and the device was growing, and Zahariel and Luther were forced back from the shuttle as it began to lift from the deck as automatic systems kicked in, responding to some remotely activated signal.

'How do we stop it?' cried Zahariel over the roar of the shuttle's engines.

'I don't know,' shouted Luther, pointing at an inter-ship vox station on the wall of the embarkation deck, 'but we have to warn the Lion!'

Zahariel nodded in understanding as Luther fought to reach the shuttle through the rippling heat haze that surrounded it and the growling wash of superheated air billowing from the engines.

Emergency lights flashed to life and a wailing siren sounded as deck systems registered the massive build up of heat and radiation.

'I can't get near it!' shouted Luther.

Zahariel slammed into the wall of the embarkation deck and pressed the 'all-decks' stud, sending a warning to the entire ship.

'Embarkation deck one reports hostile vessel on board!' he yelled over the screaming din of sirens and the ever-growing roar of the shuttle's engines. Even as he watched, the shuttle lifted from the deck in a blast of heat. Zahariel heard a scream of pain, and Luther staggered away from the… missile… for he could no longer think of it as simply a shuttle.

'Repeat?' said a voice through the vox-station. 'Hostile ship?'

'Yes!' cried Zahariel. 'The Saroshi ship! It's a missile or a bomb of some sort!'

Luther staggered over to him, his armour blistered and scorched by the heat of the enemy weapon's engines. Zahariel looked over to where the missile had lifted off, its nose angling as though homing in on some unseen beacon… some unseen beacon aboard their ship.

Blast doors rumbled open in response to the alarm, and work crews and emergency fire-fighters rushed onto the embarkation deck. Orange jumpsuited techs threw up their arms in response to the intense heat flooding the compartment.

Zahariel felt his skin blistering under the intense heat, and knew that they had seconds at best before the enemy missile's primary thrusters ignited, filling the deck with killing plasma and thrusting its warhead deep into the belly of the ship.

In that instant he realised what he had to do.

He left Luther at the vox station and ran for the control panel further along the wall, ignoring the pain as his hair was burned from his scalp. Already his armour was bubbling as the paint melted, and his steps were becoming leaden and heavy as the heat fused the joints.

He pushed grimly onwards, knowing that he would only get one chance to save the ship and everyone on board.

His steps became slower and his armour heavier, but he fought the pain to reach the wall-mounted deck controls.

He glanced over his shoulder to see the missile fix on a point that would send it deep into the vitals of the ship, right where the Lion was meeting with the lord high exalter.

At last, Zahariel reached the deck controls and smashed his fist through the plexglas panel in front of the emergency controls. Desperately, he gripped the lock-down lever and hauled it shut. The blast doors at the deck's perimeter began to rumble closed, but before they had even reached half way to the floor, Zahariel hammered his fist on the integrity field override stud.

More blaring sirens joined the ones already filling the embarkation deck with noise, but this one was louder and more strident than the others. A booming voice from overhead speakers blared into the deck.

'Warning! Integrity field shutting down! Warning! Integrity field shutting down!'

Zahariel pressed the stud again, holding it down in an attempt to hurry the shut down procedure. Emergency crews ran for the closing blast doors in panic.

'Warning! Integrity field shutting down! Warning! Integrity field shutting down!'

'I know!' shouted Zahariel. 'In the name of the Lion, just shut down!'

As if in response to his words, the fizzing glow surrounding the generators along the edges of the wide entrance bay faded and the rippling haze of the stars steadied.

A howling gale engulfed the embarkation deck as the atmosphere and everything not fixed in place was explosively vented into space.

The sudden rush of air grabbed them like leaves caught on the wind and dragged them towards the opened bay.

ZAHARIEL GRABBED ONTO the railings that ran around the edge of the embarkation deck and held on for dear life as the howling rush of air bellowed towards the open bay. Crates, boxes of tools and gurneys of ammunition careened through the bay, spiralling towards the void of space as it decompressed.

The instant before his feet left the ground, he activated the magnetic soles of his boots, and the weight of his armour slammed to the deck, fixing him in place. Fuel pipes writhed like pinned snakes, and loose cabling waved and sparked in the gale.

The rigged Saroshi shuttle was caught in the rush of air, the power of the decompression gripping it tightly and hurling it from the ship just as its engines fired. Spiralling out of control, the missile corkscrewed wildly as it tumbled away from the ship.

Those techs and emergency personnel who had not yet reached safety were instantly blown into space, their bodies frozen and ruptured. Their screams were swallowed in the roar of escaping air.

Zahariel watched as the Saroshi shuttle spun away from the *Invincible Reason*, and he was suddenly blinded as the warhead secreted within it detonated.

Outside, in the cold unforgiving darkness of space, it seemed as though the battlecruiser had given birth to a miniature sun. In less than a thousandth of a second, a brilliant ball of light appeared at its flank, flared to incandescence, and was gone.

Despite having been designed to withstand hostile bombardment by enemy guns, many of the view-portals on the ship's hull shattered, fragments of toughened glass raining out into the void like glittering diamonds.

The blast wave thundered towards the ship, and only its automated damage control systems prevented further loss of life. Reacting to the abrupt decompression, blast proof panels slammed shut all along the ship's length.

The ship shuddered as though in the grip of a great leviathan of the deep, yet more klaxons and warning lights coming to life in the wake of the explosion. The blast wave rolled over the ship, and Zahariel felt as though every bone in his body was being shaken loose.

At last, the terrible juddering ceased, and he collapsed to the deck, exhausted and groaning at the pain of his burns. He lay there for several minutes, the sirens, flashing lights and shouts of rescue crews sweeping over him without understanding.

'Brother, are you injured?'

Zahariel turned his burned head and smiled as he saw that Luther was still alive.

'I thought you were dead,' said Luther, shouting to be heard over the shrill warning klaxons.

'My armour saved me,' he said.

'It is a good thing you are lucky, Zahariel.'

'What? Lucky? How do you come to that conclusion?' asked Zahariel, his voice slurring as the balms of his armour sought to counteract his fierce pain.

'Look around,' gasped Luther. 'Those Saroshi bastards nearly managed to kill the entire command hierarchy of the fleet, but you stopped them.'

Zahariel could only look at the broken bodies littering the deck and feel rage at the atrocity he saw before him, but as quickly as the emotion surfaced, he suppressed it. The mental conditioning the Astartes went through helped them to control their emotions and make the optimum use of them when they were needed.

Rage had its place in the heat of battle, but this was a moment for a cooler head. He pulled himself to his feet with Luther's help and leaned on the wall, gasping for breath in the frigid air of the restored atmosphere.

Luther adjusted the comms-frequency of the wall vox-station, patching into the *Invincible Reason's* command-net.

'This is Luther of the Dark Angels,' he said. 'Multiple casualties sustained on the embarkation deck! I want medicae teams sent here immediately! Bridge command, are you receiving me?'

'Aye, this is bridge command. Receiving, sir,' said a grainy, static-washed voice. 'We have reports of a hull breach on your level. Instruments record it as under control.'

'That's correct, bridge command,' confirmed Luther. 'The breach was the work of the Saroshi delegation brought onto the ship half-an-hour ago. The Saroshi shuttle on the embarkation deck was... was rigged with an atomic warhead. Any Saroshi forces left on board are to be arrested immediately. Lethal force is authorised.'

Luther spared a look at the destruction around them and whispered to Zahariel, 'As of approximately one minute ago, we are at war with the Saroshi people.'

Another voice cut in over the voice of bridge command and Zahariel instantly recognised it as belonging to the Lion.

'I want a strategium meeting with all commanders and seconds-in-command onboard the *Invincible Reason* in half an hour's time. Is that understood?'

'Understood, my lord,' said Luther, sharing an uncomfortable look with Zahariel.

THE ATTACK ON the *Invincible Reason* was just the beginning.

All across the fleet, and in the cities and lands of Sarosh, the Imperials found they were suddenly attacked by the people they assumed regarded them as heroes. They had come to liberate the Saroshi from their ignorance, to deliver them from Old Night. They had come to bring them the wonders of the Imperium, to show them marvels.

But the inhabitants of Sarosh had rejected the Imperium and everything it stood for. They rejected it with great violence, perpetrating appalling deeds of horror and bloodshed. They carried out dozens of atrocities, unleashing all manner of acts of terror.

More than a thousand Imperial Army and Naval personnel were on shore leave, enjoying the delights of the carnival, when the uprising began.

Some were murdered, but most of those affected were the victims of abduction. They disappeared into the night, gone without trace, leaving no evidence behind of where they had been taken or who had kidnapped them.

The situation was clearer when it came to the fate of the Imperial institutions already present on Sarosh. In the space of twelve months, even with compliance yet to be fully certified, a dozen different organs of government had been transplanted from the fleet onto the planet's surface.

Naturally, Lord Governor-Elect Furst had established a residence in an appropriately palatial building in the administrative district at the heart of the capital city of Shaloul. Similarly, in preparation for the eventual transfer of powers, various offices of liaison had also been established in the vicinity.

At around the same time as the Saroshi shuttle exploded, an angry mob attacked the governor's residence on Sarosh, as well as the nearby Imperial offices. Quickly overwhelming the few Army troopers who had been left on guard duty, the riot's ringleaders dragged the Imperial functionaries out onto the streets and hacked them to death with axes and knives as the crowd bayed for blood.

Their bodies were spat on and dismembered, and then condemned to the fire as the mob set light to the Imperial buildings and cast the evidence of their outrage into the flames.

A few of the Imperials present on Sarosh managed to escape being murdered or abducted. Later, when these survivors told their tales, it would become clear that the entire population of the planet had exploded in a frenzy of bloodletting every bit as sudden and dramatic as the blast that nearly tore through the *Invincible Reason*.

The survivors would talk of a primal savagery that descended on the people of Sarosh without warning. One minute, the Saroshi had been their normal charming selves. The next, they had erupted into shocking, ferocious violence.

Yet, at the same time, there was never the suggestion that this violence was in any way wild or out of control. According to the survivors' accounts, the opposite held true. There was a terrifying calmness in the manner in which the Saroshi went about the killings.

They were highly organised, as though each and every one of the thousands of rebels had earlier agreed on a specific role in the conspiracy, as well as an exact timetable by which all these tasks would take place.

Most frightening of all, and many who believed in the Imperial truth would find this especially troubling, was the almost machine-like perfection of this timetable. There would never be any definite proof of communication between the conspirators on Sarosh and their confederates elsewhere, yet, they appeared able to synchronise their actions to the very second.

Even when some part of their plan failed, their remaining agents seemed capable of adapting to new circumstances quickly, despite having no apparent means of communications with the rest of the rebels.

It was an enigma, though it was hardly the most pressing issue commanding the attention of the Dark Angels.

'MAYDAY! THIS IS *Bold Conveyor*! Our hull is ruptured and we are leaking atmosphere. Request transfer of all available work crews and medicae teams from other ships in the fleet. We need help here!'

'This is *Wrath of Caliban* calling the flagship! We demand an immediate update on the current status of our commanders. Over.'

'*Intrepid* calling! Mutineers have been subdued and the situation is under control.'

'*Arbalest*, this is *Invincible Reason*. Retreat from high anchor position at once and relocate to anchorage beta or you will be fired upon as a hostile vessel. This is your final warning.'

The bridge of the *Invincible Reason* was alive with a confused babble of voices. As Zahariel entered the command area with Luther beside him, he was immediately struck by the tension in the air.

A dozen officers and ratings sat nervously at their stations, issuing terse instructions or holding conversations by inter-ship comms with the other vessels in the fleet. Zahariel recognised controlled desperation in the voices of the men around him.

It was the same sound he expected to hear in the voice of an army commander whenever the situation was fluid and the progress of the battle was uncertain. It was the sound of men holding fast to their duties even when they suspected that war was about to render their duty, even their lives, irrelevant.

It was the sound of warriors on the verge of panic.

That sound ceased as a rating called out, 'Master on the bridge!'

Zahariel looked over to where another door to the bridge had opened and the Lion strode in, his face thunderous, and his sword bared and bloody. Zahariel had never seen the master of the First Legion looking so angry, and he felt a kernel of apprehension stir in his belly at the thought of the war that such a fury might unleash.

Nemiel walked alongside the Lion, his expression similarly furious, as they marched towards an officer in the uniform of a fleet captain, who stood talking to the ship's astropath. Zahariel and Luther made their way painfully over to the conference of senior officers.

The fleet captain turned at the Lion's approach and saluted sharply.

'Captain Stenius,' demanded the Lion without preamble. 'What is the situation? I want an update.'

The captain turned to the blind woman beside him. 'This is Mistress Argenta, the fleet's senior astropath. I am happy to see you, Lord Jonson. I was hoping you would–'

'Now, Captain Stenius,' said the Lion, the tone of warning in his voice unmistakable.

'Of course,' said Stenius as he bowed and turned to the servitor manning a nearby bank of instruments. 'Raise the shutters.'

A click, followed by a distant whirring noise, sounded as the blast shutters protecting the bridge's observation blisters slid back into their recessed bays to reveal the scene out in space.

'We lowered the shutters as a precaution,' said Stenius. 'What with the failed attack on us and the attack on the *Bold Conveyor* I decided it best to take the fleet to general battle stations. Fortunately, the worst of it seems to be over.'

'The attack on the *Bold Conveyor*?' said Luther. 'What attack?'

The Lion turned at the sound of his brother's voice and his eyes narrowed as he took in the wounded state of Zahariel and Luther. He said nothing of their condition, clearly filing it away to ask about later.

Zahariel looked through the observation blister into space, horrified to see bodies floating in the cold of the void. Hundreds drifted slowly past the ship's observation blisters like some grotesque form of parade inspection.

'We've had attempted mutinies on three ships,' said Stenius. 'In each instance, small groups of no more than half a dozen men launched attacks on the bridges of their ships. Mostly, the mutinies were suppressed before they could do any real damage, but on the *Arbalest* the mutineers managed to let off a torpedo salvo. They hit the *Bold Conveyor* and damaged her. The bodies you can see outside are casualties from the *Bold Conveyor*. Once the shooting started, I ordered the fleet to different stations to put more distance between each ship. Some of the bodies from the *Bold Conveyor* must have got caught in the backwash from our engines. That's why they're in orbit around us.'

'How badly was the *Bold Conveyor* damaged?' demanded the Lion.

'Hull rupture,' explained Captain Stenius. 'Most of the dead were Army troopers who were sucked out into the vacuum when the torpedo hit.'

He shrugged. 'It could have been worse. I've sent extra repair crews to the *Bold Conveyor* via shuttle. Early reports indicate that the damage isn't bad enough to threaten her space worthiness, though it's likely to be a few days before she's fully operational again.'

'So the situation in space is under control?'

'For the most part, yes,' answered Stenius, 'but according to Mistress Argenta, that's the least of our worries.'

A CONFERENCE WAS held in the *Invincible Reason's* state-rooms, the senior members of the Dark Angels gathering to hear the words of Mistress Argenta. The Lion and Luther spoke in a huddled corner, their words unheard by anyone, though the intensity of their conversation was plain for all to see.

Brother-Librarian Israfael stood beside a robed member of the Mechanicum, and a number of servitors accompanied them both. The atmosphere was tense, and Zahariel could sense the urgent need in every man gathered here to strike back at the Saroshi.

He and Nemiel sat at the briefing table trying to make sense of the last few hours that had seen brother turn on brother and former allies take arms against them. Initial theories suggested that the mutineers on the Imperial ships had been drugged and rendered open to treacherous suggestion by a concoction distilled from the perfume of the plants that thronged every building and surface of the capital city.

This was a morsel of information to be digested later, for a much greater threat was apparently arising in the dusty hardpan of the deserts in the north of the main continental mass of Sarosh.

The Lion turned away from Luther abruptly, his face a mask of unreadable emotion as he took his seat at the head of the table. Luther took his seat at the table too, and Zahariel could read his features much more easily. Their second-in-command's expression was one of despair and anguish.

'We do not have much time,' snapped the Lion, cutting through the babble of voices around the room. At his tone, every head turned in his direction and every voice was stilled.

'Mistress Argenta,' said the Lion. 'Speak.'

The astropath took a hesitant step forward, as though being near the awesome figure of the primarch was too much for her to bear for any length of time.

'You may have heard the high exalter talk of beings known as the Melachim during his outburst against the Imperium. It is my belief that this is the Saroshi name for a certain breed of xenos creature that dwells in the warp.'

'How are they a danger to us?' asked Nemiel. 'Surely they are confined to the warp.'

'Normally that would be the case,' said the astropath, turning her blind eyes towards Zahariel's cousin, 'but the Astropathic Choir has become aware of a growing build up of psychic energy in the northern deserts, indicative of a major warp rift.'

'And what is causing this?' asked the Lion.

'We do not know.'

'Speculate,' ordered the Lion.

'Perhaps the natives of this planet have some way of focusing the energies of the warp by some means we are not aware of, my lord.'

'For what purpose would they do this?'

'It is said that if one has a host of strong enough will, it is possible to imbue it with the presence of a creature from beyond the gates of the Empyrean.'

'And you think that is what's happening here?'

'If such a thing is even possible,' pointed out Zahariel.

The Lion shot him a venomous look that shocked Zahariel. 'We must assume that it is, for now. The treachery and deviousness of the Saroshi are without bounds. We must trust nothing from this point onwards and assume the worst.'

The Lion turned his attention back to the astropath, and Zahariel felt a wave of relief wash over him at being released from that hostile glare.

'Mistress Argenta,' said the Lion. 'If the Saroshi can indeed summon some xeno beast from the warp, how bad might it get?'

'If they succeed, it could be the worst thing you have ever fought.'

'Why can't we simply bomb the site from orbit?' asked the Lion. 'That would put paid to most threats.'

'Not this one, my lord,' said Argenta. 'The psychic build up is already underway, and any attack that fails to halt that build up will be doomed to failure.'

'Then how do we fight it?'

In response to the Lion's question, Brother-Librarian Israfael stepped forward. 'I may be able to answer that, my lord. Ever since our Legion fought on the bloody fields of Perissus, I have been working to develop a means of fighting such creatures. This was before you joined us, my lord.'

The Lion scowled, and Zahariel was reminded how much their primarch disliked being reminded that the Legion had existed before he had become its master.

'Go on,' ordered the Lion. 'How do we fight this rising power?'

'An electro-psychic pulse,' said Israfael. 'Of course, it is difficult to know precisely how it will interact with the energies being gathered, but I am confident it should disrupt of the ambient psychic field and–'

'Please, more slowly, Israfael,' said the Lion, raising his hand with the palm facing outward to stem Israfael's words. 'I am sure you know what you are talking about, but remember we are warriors. If you want us to understand you, you will need to keep it simple and start from the beginning.'

'More simply, of course,' said Israfael, and Zahariel did not envy him being under the white heat of the primarch's gaze. 'I believe it may be possible to counteract the build up of psychic energy by detonating an electro-psychic pulse weapon in the vicinity.'

'What is this "electro-psychic pulse weapon" you talk of?' asked the Lion.

'It is simply a modified cyclonic warhead,' explained Israfael. 'With the help of the Mechanicum adepts, we can remove the explosive part of the warhead and replace it with an electro-psychic pulse capacitor that will generate a massive blast of energy inimical to creatures composed of immaterial energies. As for destroying the psychic build up, ideally we need to detonate the device as close to the source as possible.'

'I see,' said the Lion. 'What form will the device take? Obviously, it is a bomb, but can you adapt it to be dropped from a shuttle?'

'No,' said Israfael, 'for the pulse of the blast must be directed by one schooled in the psychic arts.'

'In other words, you need to be there when it detonates.'

'I do,' confirmed Israfael, 'along with as many other brothers with psychic potential who can fight.'

The Lion nodded. 'Begin work on adapting such a weapon immediately. How long do you estimate the work will take?'

'A few hours at most,' said Israfael.

'Very well,' said the Lion. 'Begin at once.'

TWENTY-TWO

THE DARK ANGELS of Zahariel's squad gathered around the assault ramp of the Stormbird to listen to Sar Hadariel's final mission briefing before taking the fight to the surface of Sarosh.

The Stormbirds gathered on the portside embarkation deck, ready to be unleashed on the planet below, and the assembled warriors were in a killing mood. The Lion would lead this attack personally, and though Zahariel was still in great pain from the attack on the *Invincible Reason*, his training in the Librarius had selected him for this mission despite his injuries.

Nemiel had been chosen to accompany the Lion's squads, and even in the urgent fervour that gripped every warrior before battle, Zahariel was stung by his cousin's inclusion in the group. Luther was not present, and Zahariel had been surprised by his absence, but had left the matter unremarked, seeing the Lion's hooded expression when Sar Hadariel had mentioned their second-in-command.

'This smacks of great danger,' said Attias, and Zahariel
was glad to hear the familiar voice of his friend. Attias
had made a fine member of the Astartes, and was a valued and trusted battle-brother.

'We always face danger,' said Eliath, quoting some of
the Legion's teachings. Like Attias, Eliath had come
through the training of the Astartes with honour and
was one of the Legion's best heavy weapon troopers.
'We are Astartes. We are Dark Angels. We were not made
to die of old age. Death or glory! Loyalty and honour!'

'Loyalty and honour,' echoed Attias. 'Understand, I
am not questioning the need for danger. I merely ask
whether we should base our strategy in this theatre on
the workings of an experimental device. If the bomb
doesn't work, what then? I'd hate to face an enemy with
Eliath's good looks as our only fallback weapon if it
proves to be a damp squib.'

There was momentary laughter among the assembled
warriors. Even from Eliath, whose squat, hardworn features and heavyset build were the source of some
occasional fun at his expense.

'Better my good looks than your swordsmanship,'
responded Eliath, 'unless you hope the enemy will be
driven to distraction by the whistling sound your blade
makes as it misses them over and over again.'

'We are Dark Angels,' said Hadariel, and the laughter
stopped. 'We are the First Legion, the warriors of the
Emperor. You ask whether we should trust ourselves to
the science of the Mechanicum and the wisdom of our
Brother-Librarian? I ask you, how can we not? Is not
science the Imperium's guiding light? Is it not our
bedrock? Is it not the stone on which the foundations
of our new society have been built? So, yes, we will
trust their science. We will trust our lives to it, just as we
trust ourselves and all humanity to the guidance of the
Emperor, beloved of all.'

'I am sorry, Chapter Master,' said Attias, chastened. 'I meant no offence.'

'You caused none,' said Hadariel. 'You simply asked a question, and there is no harm in that. If ever a time comes when the Dark Angels see reason to avoid questions, we will have lost our souls.'

Zahariel looked across the faces of the men surrounding him as he listened to the Chapter Master's words. Some were men he had known back on Caliban, and the bond that existed between them as brothers and fellow warriors was as strong as ceramite, stronger, in fact, for where ceramite could be cut through with the right kind of weapon, he could never imagine the bond of loyalty he felt for his brother Astartes ever being broken.

'The Chapter Master is right,' said Zahariel, as words he had heard long ago returned to resonate within his skull. 'We Astartes were made to serve mankind. We are Dark Angels and in the practice of war, we follow the teachings of the Lion. He tells us war is a matter of adaptation, and whoever adapts most quickly to changing circumstances and takes advantage of the vagaries of warfare, will be victorious. We have been presented with a powerful weapon with which to defeat our foe and we would be fools not to use it.'

'So we will make use of the device,' said Eliath. 'I hope you will forgive my presumption, Chapter Master, but I have known you for long enough to know when there is a plan forming in your head. The device is only part of what we need. We also need a plan to help us put it into operation. Do you have a plan?'

'I have a plan,' agreed Hadariel.

Zahariel looked into the faces of his brothers and saw an expression of complete determination in each of them as Sar Hadariel outlined their plan of attack.

The Saroshi were doomed, they just didn't know it yet.

IT WAS MIDDAY, and the burning sun had reached its apex.

Among the indigenous folk of Sarosh, it was seen as a quiet time, a part of the day usually spent sleeping in the shade of their dwellings until the worst of the afternoon heat had passed. The planet's newly arrived Imperial forces did not choose to follow the same routines however, least of all the warriors of the Astartes.

Four Stormbirds screamed over the desert, keeping low and fast as they flew towards their objective, a cluster of prefabricated buildings identified from orbit as Mining Station One Zeta Five.

In the lead Stormbird, Zahariel sat against the bucking fuselage of the aircraft as it tore through the air towards battle. All around him, Dark Angels sat clutching their weapons, ready to take a measure of revenge for the attack on their ships and people. The Saroshi had started this war, but the Dark Angels were going to finish it.

'This is the Lion to all assigned units,' said their leader's voice over the vox, and despite the growing aloofness the Legion's master had been displaying recently, Zahariel was still struck by the commanding tone of his voice. 'Mission target is confirmed as Mining Station One Zeta Five. Initiate all mission protocols.'

Zahariel heard a flurry of vox-traffic as the relevant units responded in the affirmative.

The Stormbirds were heavily armoured assault shuttles, designed to ferry a complement of Astartes warriors into the middle of even the most ferocious of firefights.

Each was painted black and marked with the winged sword icon on its hull, in accordance with Legion heraldry.

'We are ready, my lord,' said Hadariel, and Zahariel could hear the relish in his Chapter Master's voice. It was a relish shared by every man in the Stormbird.

Eliath sat across from Zahariel, his broad shoulders and thickset build making a flight seat a cramped proposition for him. His friend was an impressive physical specimen, even for an Astartes, and he saluted as he sensed Zahariel's scrutiny.

'Not long now,' said Eliath. His friend was not wearing his helmet and had to yell to be heard above the roar of the craft's engines. 'Be good to strike back, eh?'

'Aye, that it will,' replied Zahariel.

'How are we going to make the assault, Chapter Master?' asked Attias.

'We will be using jump packs for the descent,' said Hadariel. 'Our orders are to deploy from the shuttle at an altitude of five hundred metres to make a controlled combat drop. We'll land in the area of open scrub north of the station. From there we will advance to clear the station building by building until we rendezvous with the approach of the Lion and his men from the south. Naturally, we can expect the enemy to respond. In fact, we are counting on it.'

Around the compartment, the Astartes listened to his words intently. From his own position, seated at the head of the troop compartment, Zahariel was struck by the almost reverential air with which the men of his company greeted the news.

'Remember, our mission here is to fight through any resistance as quickly as possible and deliver the Brother-Librarian and his cargo,' said Hadariel. 'Once we have deployed from the Stormbirds, the pilots will ascend to a holding pattern ready to pick us up when they are given the order to begin the extraction. I want helmets on and all purity seals engaged. One Zeta Five is to be treated as a toxic environment.'

Zahariel could barely contain his excitement at the prospect of combat. He had been trained to counteract any fear, but as much as the Astartes were defined by fearlessness, they were defined equally by their aptitude for war.

Their bodies had been crafted to superhuman levels so that they would not just defeat the Imperium's enemies, they would annihilate them.

The Astartes expected to face danger in the natural course of their lives; in fact, they welcomed it, as though without a battle to fight they were incomplete.

'Finally, let us be clear on one thing,' said Hadariel. 'This is a mission of destruction, not capture. We are not interested in prisoners, so if there is anyone alive at One Zeta Five we do not stop fighting until they are dead.'

His words were punctuated by a trilling from the Stormbird's inter-vox as a red light began to flash inside the compartment. Hadariel responded with a wolfish grin.

'There's the signal,' he said. 'We are approaching the target. Helmets on and activate your seals. And, good hunting to all of you.'

Zahariel's heart quickened at the prospect of action. 'If we are not fighting within the next five minutes, I shall be disappointed,' he said to Eliath and Attias.

He could feel his senses sharpening as the prospect of the drop came closer.

Eliath nodded in response to his words and gave the Dark Angel battle-cry. 'For the Lion! For Luther! For Caliban!'

'For the Lion! For Luther! For Caliban!' repeated the Astartes, and the combined tenor of their words seemed to shake the metal bulkheads of the compartment. At Hadariel's signal, they rose from their seats and filed towards the assault door at the back of the shuttle, ready for the drop to begin.

The Stormbird began to shake around them as the pilot decreased the shuttle's speed in preparation for the drop. The assault doors opened and the red lights positioned all through the interior of the Stormbird turned green.

A continuous ringing tone sounded over the inter-vox: the signal to jump.

Zahariel was first down the ramp and he felt the air screaming around him, alongside the sudden feeling of weightlessness in the split-second before gravity caught hold of him and he activated his jump pack to compensate. Eliath, Attias, Hadariel and the others were right behind him, exhaust flares spreading from their packs like fiery wings as they descended towards the mining station five hundred metres below.

He missed Nemiel's presence for a moment, but pushed such thoughts from his mind as he saw the dusty hardpan rushing up towards him.

It was time for war, time to let the Dark Angels fly.

As the angels descended, they were not met by anti-aircraft fire from ground-based batteries, or entrenched and heavily armed defenders. Their drop was unopposed, and Zahariel was thankful for such small mercies, remembering far worse training drops where live ammunition had been used to make things more 'interesting'.

They made their landing in the area of open scrub in good order.

Having landed, the Dark Angels fanned out, advancing on the mining station at One Zeta Five in a loose skirmish line, helmets down and weapons at the ready. At first sight, it was as though they had entered a ghost town. The station was eerily quiet, though Zahariel's senses were alert to the growling psychic presence buzzing at the edge of perception.

A ridge of high cliffs rose above the station to the west, but otherwise its perimeter was surrounded by open desert on three sides. In the centre of station, over the minehead, there was the enormous drum of the cable-winch, designed to bring the miners up and down to the angled mineshaft that ran at a forty-five degree angle into the ground, as well as raising the ore they had mined to the surface. In turn, it was surrounded by a ramshackle collection of prefabricated huts, and the barracks used as sleeping quarters for the miners.

Wheeled ore-bins were dotted throughout the station, some overturned with their cargo spilled out. As Zahariel and his men moved from the outskirts of the settlement towards the admin buildings in the immediate vicinity of the minehead, they found all the intervening huts and barracks empty. One Zeta Five seemed to be deserted. The only sound Zahariel could hear was the terse back-and-forth of inter-squad vox. Beyond that, the entire area was silent.

'There's something here,' he heard Hadariel say. 'I can feel it.'

'I agree,' replied Zahariel. 'There should be animal sounds, but all I can hear is silence. There's something here and its frightened away the local fauna.'

Using the same channel, Zahariel heard Hadariel link comms with the squads on the other side of the station.

'Hadariel to the Lion. Any sign of the enemy?'

'Nothing so far,' came the terse reply. 'I can see their leavings, though.'

There was blood on the sand.

In some places it had hit the ground in small scattered droplets, in others it took the form of larger puddles, staining the soil and already starting to stink in the midday heat.

Here and there, Zahariel could see objects scattered around their advance.

Discarded auto-weapons, a las-torch, a broken comms-unit, detonator cord: all left lying in the sand. Zahariel glanced up at the sky, where the Stormbirds turned in wide and endlessly repeating circles, thousands of metres above them.

Zahariel suddenly became aware of a rising and repulsive odour like the slaughterhouse smell of rancid blood mixed with the cloying sickly sweet stench of rotten fruit.

He tried to shout a warning, but it was too late.

The prefabricated metal of the building nearest Attias ruptured as something massively powerful tore through it and leapt to the attack. Zahariel saw a glimpse of scales, vertically pupilled eyes and a fanged mouth opening wide.

The creature spat something in Attias's face and his helmet erupted in hissing smoke as though doused with acid. It leapt upon the stricken warrior, its whip-thin arms wrapping around Attias as it tore at him with razor claws that sliced open its victim's power armour like tinfoil.

It wrapped its forearms around Attias's torso and there was a wet, awful sound as dozens of retractable claws hidden along the creature's limbs emerged from inside muscular sheaths and stabbed through the warrior's armour.

Attias dropped, his blood staining the sand as the monster leapt away, its strangely jointed legs propelling it over the rough terrain at an incredible speed.

Bolter rounds chased it, exploding against the buildings of the mining settlement, but failing to hit their
target.

Zahariel watched as the beast vanished from sight.
There was something wrong in the way it had moved,
its knees and ankles flexing at peculiar angles.

More gunfire erupted from around the compound
and frantic cries came over the vox as more of the Dark
Angel squads came under attack.

Choking back a cry of rage, Zahariel rushed to the
side of his fallen comrade.

Attias's helmet was a smoking ruin, the stench of
scorched metal and skin sickening, even filtered
through the auto-senses of Zahariel's armour. Attias
writhed in agony, and Zahariel fought to tear his helmet free. The helmet's armour clasps had burned
through, and Zahariel had no choice but to wrench the
smouldering armour from his friend's head.

The helmet came free from the armoured gorget and
Attias screamed as the skin of his face came with it,
ropes of flesh drooling like molten rubber from the
remains of his helm.

'Get back!' cried the squad's Apothecary, pushing
Zahariel from his comrade's convulsing body. The
Apothecary went to work, the hissing tubes, needles
and dispensers of his narthecium gauntlet the best
chance of ensuring Attias's survival.

Zahariel stepped away, horrified at the bloody mess
where his friend's face used to be.

Hadariel pulled him away. 'Leave the Apothecary to
his ministrations. We have work to do.'

Eliath stood next to Zahariel and said, 'By the Lion,
I've never seen the like.'

Zahariel nodded in agreement and slapped his hand
on the heavy bolter his friend carried. 'Keep your
weapon ready, brother. These things move fast.'

'What are they?' asked Eliath. 'I thought this was a human world.'

'That was our mistake,' replied Zahariel as more gunfire and vox-chatter cut through the shock of Attias's wounding.

'Hostile contact,' reported another squad sergeant, 'Reptilian beasts. Came out of nowhere. Fast moving, but I think we wounded it. One dead. Moving on.'

'Understood,' said the Lion. 'Message understood. All units continue to the centre of the settlement.'

THE STRANGE REPTILIAN beast attacked twice more, each time emerging from hiding to attack with unnatural speed and ferocity. Each time the monsters attacked, they would draw blood, but no more warriors fell to their ambushes, though many were forced to discard portions of armour as the xeno creatures' acid eructations melted their Mark IV plate.

The Astartes pushed deeper into the settlement, bolters chattering as they methodically advanced in an overlapping formation, one squad moving forward as another covered it.

The attacks grew more frequent as they drew nearer their objective, and as they gained the inner reaches of the settlement, Zahariel saw that the creatures had gathered in a mass of rippling, scaled bodies before the entrance to the mineshaft.

Zahariel felt his gorge rise at the sight of such unnatural creatures, their anatomy twisted so far from the human ideal that he could think of no classification of form to assign them. Each limb was multi-jointed and appeared to move and rotate on a number of different axes. Their bodies were sinuous and rippled with iridescent scales that were translucent and somehow ghostly, as though their bodies were not quite… *real*.

'What are they?' asked Eliath.

'Unclean xenos creatures,' answered Hadariel.

Gunfire sounded from the three open sides of the settlement, and Zahariel saw the Lion emerge from behind a tall structure of rusted sheet metal. Once again, he was struck by his primarch's physicality as he led the warriors of the Dark Angels from the front, his sword raised and the fury of battle in his eyes.

No sooner had Lion El'Jonson appeared than the xenos creatures set up a terrible keening cry, though whether this was in fear or anticipation, Zahariel could not say.

They surged forward in a boiling tide of scales and claws, and the Dark Angels charged to meet them.

Bolters blazed and exploded wetly inside the creatures. Each wounded creature fell to the sand and began dissolving into a pool of glassy, viscous fluid.

The two foes met in a storm of blades and claws. Zahariel was face to face with a screeching creature with an elongated head and rippling, coloured eyes with vertical slits. It hissed and bit at him with such speed that its first attack nearly took his head off.

He leapt back and fired into the creature's belly, the bolt passing through before detonating. Wounded, the creature slashed at him with its claws and spat a gobbet of acid mucus towards him. He swayed aside from the acid, but took the brunt of the monster's claws across his chest.

Zahariel cried out as its claws seemed to pass *through* his armour to slice the meat and muscle of his chest. The pain was intense and cold, and he gasped at the suddenness of it.

In the instant of contact he recalled the soul-numbing chill he had felt in the forests of Endriago just before he had encountered the Watchers in the Dark. This beast was just as unnatural as whatever the

Watchers had been set to guard, and he knew with utter clarity that they were not simply another form of xeno creature, but something infinitely more dangerous.

Zahariel dropped his bolter and drew the sword fashioned from the Lion of Endriago's tooth. The monster came at him again. He swept his sword through the creature's slashing limb, and stepped in to cut upwards into its chest, the keen blade slicing the insubstantial meat of its body like a sopping cloud.

For all their speed and ferocity, the ghost-like monsters could not hope to stand against the relentless stoicism of the Dark Angels, who closed the noose of their warrior circles and slaughtered them without mercy.

Zahariel watched the Lion fight his way through the monsters as though possessed with a killing fury beyond imagining. His sword clove through the creatures, turning half a dozen to wet piles of jelly-like fluid with every blow.

Nemiel fought alongside the Lion, his skill nowhere near the sublime majesty of the primarch, yet no less determined. His cousin was a fine warrior and, beside the Lion, he looked every inch the hero he was.

Within moments of the battle starting, it was over, and the last of the creatures were despatched. Where before the mining settlement had rung to the sounds of bolters and screaming chainswords, silence now fell as the Dark Angels regrouped.

'Secure the site,' said the Lion as the last of the monsters was destroyed. 'I want that Stormbird with Brother-Librarian Israfael's weapon on the ground in two minutes.'

'Where are we going next?' asked Chapter Master Hadariel.

The Lion pointed to the yawning chasm of the mine-shaft that plunged steeply into the flanks of the cliffs.

'Underground,' said the Lion. 'The enemy is beneath us.'

RHIANNA SOREL HAD been afraid on many occasions, but the fear that had gripped her since her abduction from the streets of Shaloul was like nothing she had ever known before.

When the soporific effect of the flowers had worn off, she had found herself bound and blindfolded as she was taken to some unknown destination, carried in a conveyance of some comfort into the searing hot deserts around the city.

Their destination had been a mystery, for her captors said nothing on their journey, but had fed and watered her over her protests. Wherever they were taking her and for whatever purpose, they clearly wanted her alive and healthy when they got there.

Her only method of telling the passage of time was that the heat of the day had diminished and that the night was cool and silent. She could hear footfalls around the vehicle she travelled in and the creak of its wheels, but the only sounds beyond that were the soft cries of the wind over the grainy sand.

Despite herself, she had slept, and upon awakening had been carried from her conveyance by a number of people. She wept as she feared the touch of the crea-tures she had seen wearing the masks during the festival of lights, but her bearers appeared to be human, inasmuch as they sweated and grunted like humans as they bore her onwards.

Her blindfold had slipped and she had caught sight of prefabricated metal structures, like those used to house workers in mining or agricultural settlements. Strange sounds surrounded her, odd shuffling movements that sounded like footsteps, but which had an odd, off-kilter rhythm that made her think of the strange creatures once more.

Her journey had continued underground, the cool, musty air of a cavernous passage unmistakable. A strange metallic taste hovered in the air, and an electric tension crackled in her hair and from the jewellery she still wore.

The metallic reek grew more powerful, the stink of it filling her nostrils, and she gagged on the cloth in her mouth. She had kept her eyes screwed tightly shut as her captors carried her deeper and deeper into the earth, terrified of what she might see if she attempted to discover where they were.

Then followed a series of transfers, as she had been handed reverently from one set of arms to another, until she had been laid against an upright slab of what felt like smooth stone.

She stood with her back to the slab of stone, the sound of a slow and terrible heartbeat booming in the air, as though she were trapped in the ribcage of some enormous beast. Her hands were untied, though they had been secured to the stone slab by some metallic clamps fixed with sliding bolts.

Hands gently cradled her face, and she shuddered at the touch.

She felt her blindfold being removed and blinked in the sudden light.

Before her, she saw a man in a crimson robe with a mask of gold, expressionless and unknowable, on his face.

'Dusan?' she asked, more in hope than in any expectation of being right.

'Yes,' said the masked man. 'It is me you speak with.'

Even in this nightmarish situation it made her want to cry to hear a familiar voice.

'Please,' she cried. 'What are you doing? Let me go, please.'

'No, that cannot be,' said Dusan. 'You are to become the Melachim, a vessel for the ancient ones who dwell behind the veil. You will bring us victory against the unclean ones.'

'What are you talking about? This doesn't make any sense.'

'Not to you,' agreed Dusan. 'You are godless people and this is a godly act.'

'Your god?' said Rhianna. 'Please, let me go. I promise I won't say anything.'

'You lie with your words,' said Dusan neutrally. 'It is the way with your people.'

'No!' shouted Rhianna. 'I promise.'

'It makes no difference now. Most of your people are dead and the rest must soon follow when you host the Melachim. As I said, there will be pain, and for that I am sorry.'

'What are you going to do to me?'

Though she could not see his face, Rhianna had the distinct impression that Dusan was smiling behind the immobile surface of his mask.

'We are going to defile you,' he said, pointing upwards. 'Your impure flesh will be home to one of *our* angels.'

She followed his gaze and wept tears of blood as she saw the angel of the Saroshi.

TWENTY-THREE

THE DARKNESS OF the mineshaft was no obstacle to the Dark Angels, their armour senses easily compensating for the utter blackness beneath the cliffs. Each step took them deeper into the planet's surface and brought retribution for all the deaths suffered at the hands of the Saroshi treachery closer.

Zahariel felt the psychic power beneath the earth as an actinic tang in the roof of his mouth, an unpleasant taste of rancid meat and corruption. He glanced over at Brother-Librarian Israfael and saw that he too suffered the vile reek of the warp.

Israfael's Stormbird had touched down barely moments after the Lion's order had been issued, a team of servitors and Mechanicum adepts helping to deploy the modified cyclonic warhead from the aircraft's interior.

Zahariel had been reminded of the bomb secreted in the Saroshi shuttle when he had first seen the device. It resembled an ovoid cylinder strapped to a hovering gurney with chain link restraints. Numerous wires and copper-plated tubes surrounded the device, and Zahariel could plainly see why it could not have been dropped from the air.

Without any words spoken, they had set off into the depths of the world, the Lion leading the way as the angels began their descent.

The going was easy, and Zahariel wondered what the Saroshi were doing beneath the world. Mistress Argenta had spoken of creatures being dragged from the empyrean and given material form, and though such things sounded like the dark nightmares of madmen and lunatics, the things he had seen on the surface had made him rethink that comforting delusion.

If such things were possible, what other kinds of creature might lurk in the depths of the warp? What manner of powers might yet exist there, of which humanity was not yet aware?

Their path wound deeper and deeper into the ground, and the Dark Angels travelled in silence, each warrior wrapped in a cocoon of his own thoughts. Zahariel kept company with his worries that an irreparable gulf had opened between Luther and the Lion, for the two warriors were normally inseparable, yet here was the Lion going into battle without his brother.

Zahariel had told no one of what Luther had told him in the moments before the Saroshi bomb had activated, and he feared for what the future might hold if that fact came to light. Indeed, it might have already come to the Lion's notice, for little escaped his understanding.

He forced such gloomy thoughts from his mind as the Lion raised his hand to indicate a halt. The Lion sniffed the air and nodded.

'Blood,' he said. 'Lots of it.'

The Dark Angels advanced more cautiously, their bolters held at the ready, fingers on triggers. Soon Zahariel could smell what his primarch had sensed earlier, and he gagged on the powerful scent of old, rotten blood. A dim glow built from ahead, and the passageway widened until it opened into a great archway that led into a cavern thick with a miasma of fine smoke.

Only as Zahariel approached did he realise that the smoke was in fact etheric energies, visible only to Israfael and himself. The rest of the Dark Angels appeared oblivious to the drifting clouds of smoke, the twists and curls of it imbued with agonised suffering and fear. Perhaps the Lion could see it too, for his gaze seemed to follow the drifting trails of pain and anguish traced in the smoke.

The Dark Angels entered the cavern, and the mystery of what had become of Sarosh's missing population was a mystery no more.

The enormous space vanished into the distance left and right, illuminated by glaring strip lights hanging from the cavern's roof. Steel walkways crossed an immense chasm that was filled almost to the brim with dead bodies, millions of dead bodies.

It was impossible to say how many, for the depth of the chasm was beyond sight, but Zahariel remembered Kurgis of the White Scars talking of a figure in the region of seventy million missing people. Could this be the remains of so many?

It seemed inconceivable that so many dead could have been secreted here, but the evidence was right before them.

'Throne alive!' swore the Lion. 'How–'

'The missing people,' said Nemiel. 'Zahariel, so many…'

Zahariel felt his emotions rushing to the surface and quelled them savagely. An Astartes was trained to control his emotions in a combat situation, but the sheer volume and density of the fear emanating from the endless chasm of the dead was overpowering.

'Steady, Zahariel,' said Israfael, appearing at his side. 'Remember your training. These emotions are not yours, so shut them out.'

Zahariel nodded and forced himself to concentrate, whispering the mantras he had been taught by Israfael over the years of his transformation into an Astartes. Gradually, the feeling subsided, only to be replaced with a towering sense of furious righteousness.

'We move out,' said the Lion, heading for the nearest of the gantries crossing the chasm. His footfalls on the metal echoed loudly in the cavern, and the Dark Angels followed their primarch further into the depths.

Zahariel kept his gazed averted from the ocean of corpses, though he could not completely shut out the anguished echoes of their deaths. Whatever came next, whatever death and destruction the Angels of Death visited upon the heads of the Saroshi, it would not be nearly enough.

RHIANNA'S SCREAMS CAME from the heart of her being, for the sight above her was so hideous, so unnatural that it defied any understanding. The entire roof of the cavern was covered with what appeared to be a creature of translucent mucus, its surface gelatinous and festooned with a million unblinking eyes.

It occupied the roof of the chamber like some enormous parasite, hundreds of metres in diameter, and it seemed to shift and ooze so that its boundaries were fluid. Dripping tendrils like writhing tentacles hung down from the body of the vast, amorphous... thing that filled the air with nonsensical hissing, hooting and buzzing sounds.

Stars glistened within its body, distant lights of long dead galaxies swirling in its depths, like morsels devoured in ages past and not yet digested. Her breath came in short, painful gasps as she fought to hold onto her sanity in the face of something so utterly wrong, something that plainly should not be.

'What... what...?' she gasped, unable to force her mind to think of the right words.

'That is the Melachim...' breathed Dusan, his voice full of reverence and love. 'It is the angel from beyond that will defile your flesh and wear it as a cloak to walk amongst us.'

Rhianna wept, and as the trails reached her lips, she knew that she wept blood.

'No, please... don't,' she pleaded. 'You can't.'

Dusan nodded. 'Your vocabulary is incomplete. We can. We will.'

'Please stop,' she said. 'You don't have to do this.'

The Saroshi cocked his head to one side, as though digesting her words and trying to find the meaning.

'Ah,' he said, pointing to the masked figures that surrounded her. 'You have misunderstood. It has already begun.'

ONCE ACROSS THE gantries that spanned the chasm of bodies and into the narrow tunnels that plunged into the deep, Zahariel felt the echoes of the dead begin to fade. They were still there, pressing at the walls of his skull, but he could feel them recede. At first, he was grateful for this, but then he realised that they were simply being drowned out by something stronger and more insistent.

It felt as though a hammer had been taken to his head.

Zahariel dropped to one knee, a blinding spike of pain shooting through his head as if someone had jammed a hot skewer into his ear.

Brother Israfael staggered under the psychic assault, but remained on his feet, the psy-damping mechanism wired into his helmet protecting him from the worst of the pain.

'My lord!' gasped the Librarian. 'It has begun... the xeno creature from the warp. It is attempting to pass fully into our world.'

'You're sure?' asked the Lion.

'I'm sure,' affirmed Israfael. 'Right, Zahariel?'

'It's definitely coming,' said Zahariel through gritted teeth.

'Then we have no time to waste,' said the Lion, turning and picking up the pace.

Zahariel used the cavern walls to pull himself upright, his mental wards no use against the force of the power filling the air around him.

Nemiel reached out to him and said, 'Here, brother, take my hand.'

Zahariel gratefully accepted his cousin's hand. 'Just like old times, eh?'

Nemiel grinned, but Zahariel could sense the awkwardness behind the gesture. He hauled himself to his feet and tried to shake off the dread feeling building in the pit of his stomach.

The Lion was already some distance ahead and Zahariel had to jog as fast as he was able to catch up. Every step was painful, his wounds and burns from the embarkation deck not yet healed, despite his speeding metabolism. Worse than this was the psychic pain that seeped into his very pores, against which his armour offered no protection.

The deeper the Dark Angels ventured into the depths, the more insistent the sound became, and Zahariel hoped that Brother Israfael's device could defeat it. He spared a glance over his shoulder to ensure that the hover gurney and its servitors were keeping pace with the Astartes.

The lobotomised servitors appeared not to feel the soul-deep anguish of this place, and Zahariel envied them. The electro-psychic pulse weapon gleamed in the half-light, and he shivered at the fearsome potential he could feel in the warhead.

From ahead, Zahariel could hear the sounds of voices and a throbbing noise that reverberated through every sense and even those beyond human understanding.

A sickly light, unhealthy and life-draining, filled the chamber ahead, spilling into the tunnel that the Dark Angels descended like a slick. The Lion was first into the cavern, with Nemiel a close second.

Brother Israfael followed the primarch, and the remainder of the Dark Angels swiftly joined their battle-brothers.

A wave of revulsion flowed through Zahariel as he emerged into the cavern, though he was not the source of that emotion. It washed from the robed figures that surrounded an upright slab of dark, veined stone as they chanted and sang a hideous chorus around a screaming woman bound to the slab.

Zahariel followed the howling gaze of the Saroshi's prisoner and felt a crawling, sick horror as he saw the source of the monstrous evil that dwelled in this forgotten, red-lit cavern beneath the world.

Its jelly-like body was like that of some deep ocean trench-dweller, shimmering, apparently fragile, and lit from within by bursts of coloured, electric light. A million eyes stared out from its hideous form, and he could feel its raw hunger as a gnawing ache in his chest. Even as he watched, the outline of the creature was fading, but instead of a sense of triumph, Zahariel knew that it was close to achieving its goal of translation.

Where others, including Zahariel, remained paralysed by the horrific sight of the creature above, the Lion was already in motion. His pistol shot down two of the robed and masked figures as they chanted, and his sword flashed into his hand as he charged.

Seeing their primarch in action spurred the Dark Angels to follow, and with a fearsome war cry they leapt to the attack.

Pistols blazed and swords glittered in the dead light of the monster above, but as each of the masked chanters died, Zahariel sensed a dreadful amusement course through the air.

The masked figures made no attempt at defence, and Zahariel was seized with a sudden conviction as to why, as he looked into the agonised eyes of the woman bound to the upright slab.

Her face was stretched in a soundless scream, her eyes empty and glassy, as though filled with black ink. Dark power floated in her eyes, and as Zahariel looked into her, something inhuman looked back.

Zahariel raised his pistol, but even as the monstrous essence of the creature on the roof of the cave began to pour into its host, something of the woman surfaced for the briefest second, and a moment of connection passed between them, more profound than Zahariel had ever experienced before, or ever would again.

She simply said… *Yes.*

Zahariel nodded and pressed down the trigger.

A TRIO OF bolts erupted from Zahariel's pistol and crossed the space between him and the woman in a heartbeat. They penetrated her skin and muscle, and went on to punch through her ribcage with equal ease.

As the mass-reactive warheads within the shells detected an increase in the local mass, the explosive charges inside detonated.

Zahariel watched as the three shells blasted the woman apart, her ribcage blown out, and her stomach opening like the bloom of a red rose. Her skull ceased to exist, expanding in a confetti of blood and brain fragments.

A terrible, ageless scream of frustration filled the chamber, echoing throughout all the realms of existence simultaneously as a creature older than time was thwarted in its ambitions.

But such a creature was not to be denied its spite.

As the spinning chunks of the woman's flesh flew through the air, a grotesque crackling sound ripped through the chamber and each piece froze, in defiance of gravity and every natural law of man.

The creature on the cave roof had faded to almost nothing, its slithering viscosity a distant memory, and the masked figures were slain to a man, but the hunks of blasted flesh still hung in the air.

'What's going on?' demanded the Lion. 'What did you do, Zahariel?'

'What needed to be done,' he replied, the pain in his body and the ache of sorrow in his heart making him insubordinate.

'Now what?' said Nemiel, staring in revulsion at the floating chunks of raw meat.

'The creature is not yet defeated,' cried Israfael, running towards the modified cyclonic warhead. 'Stand ready to fight, Dark Angels.'

'That thing had better work, Librarian,' warned the Lion.

'It will,' promised Israfael. 'Just give me time!'

No sooner had the Librarian spoken than the woman's flesh hissed and vanished, leaving brightly glowing holes in the air. Horrid light seeped from the holes, multi-coloured and unclean, and Zahariel knew that what lurked on the other side was pure and undiluted evil.

Without warning, a host of tentacles emerged from the light, writhing like striking snakes towards the Dark Angels.

A trio of whipping appendages speared straight for Zahariel.

He slashed at them with his sword, severing them all in one smooth movement. With his other hand, he fired his bolt pistol and sent a salvo of rounds towards the empty space from which the tentacles had appeared.

He heard a shriek, the noise deep and inhuman, like the sound of one of the beasts of Caliban. The familiarity was terrifying.

The battle was hardly a few seconds old and already the enemy was right on top of them. As the Dark Angels moved to form a circle with their primarch, the number of attacking tentacles multiplied with extraordinary rapidity.

Each was two or three times the thickness of a human arm, several metres long, and strong enough to crush the ceramite outer plates of Mark IV Astartes power armour. Some were tipped with talons of bone and curved like the blade of a scythe, while others seemed made for gripping and constricting prey, or were lined with retractable claws.

The tentacles did not appear to be attached to anything, but simply floated in the air, the broad end of each tentacle disappearing into bright nothingness as though they belonged to some manner of disembodied, invisible creature that only needed to show itself in parts.

'It's like fighting ghosts!' shouted Zahariel.

'Aye,' replied Nemiel, slashing his blade through another tentacle. 'But these ghosts can kill!'

As if to prove the point, one of their number was jerked from his feet and dragged through the glowing rent from which the tentacles emerged. A battle-brother nearby reached out to save his comrade and was in turn eviscerated by a taloned claw.

The worst of it was the one-sided nature of the battle. An enemy fully capable of killing them attacked, yet it was difficult for them to respond in kind. Zahariel cut at the tentacles while aiming his bolt pistol at the point where they emerged from the air.

How successful such tactics were, however, he did not know. Did severing a tentacle inflict a mortal wound on the creature it belonged to, or were the tentacles as disposable as human hair?

Eliath's heavy bolter barked a staccato rhythm that punctuated the screaming noise of battle with a booming counterpoint. Where his shells struck, wet liquid, possibly blood, splashed, but no matter how badly the tentacles were mutilated, more always appeared.

Sometimes, Zahariel heard screams from beyond the glowing tears in the air, but it was impossible to know whether they were of pain or some manner of triumphant hunting cry.

Fighting them, Zahariel was reminded of the tales of his childhood, of fairy tale monsters like daemons and devils.

He was fighting invisible monsters. It was not hard to think of these creatures as something beyond the ken of human understanding, creatures from the primordial depths returned to punish man for his hubris.

'Israfael!' bellowed the Lion. 'Whatever you are doing, you had better do it faster!'

'Just a moment longer!' cried the Librarian.

'A moment may be all we have!'

'We will hold the line,' shouted Nemiel, 'until the Great Crusade is ended!'

There was bravado in Nemiel's tone, but Zahariel knew that the Lion was right, they had moments at best. Another two warriors were down and the brutal arithmetic of combat meant that the rest of them would soon follow.

The tentacles were relentless, pressing the Dark Angels with no time to rest or think.

Zahariel saw a tentacle suddenly fly to attack Brother Israfael. He responded with a fast cut from his sword, slicing through the tip of the tentacle and forcing its invisible owner to swiftly withdraw it.

As quickly as one disappeared, however, more tentacles took its place.

Zahariel recalled something he had read about one of the ancient myths of Terra, about a creature called the Hydra, which was capable of growing two new heads to replace each one that was severed.

In the legend, the hero of the story had defeated the monster by applying fire to the cut end of each of its necks to cauterise them before the heads could grow again. Zahariel could only wish that something as commonplace as fire could defeat this dread foe.

'Zahariel!' called Brother Israfael. 'Now!'

He turned at the sound of his name, watching as Brother Israfael mashed the activation stud on the warhead's firing mechanism.

A colossal bass note erupted from the device and a titanic wave of psychic force erupted from the warhead in an ever-expanding halo. The Dark Angels were swatted from their feet by the blast and Zahariel felt the force coalesce in his mind alongside the iron will of Brother Israfael.

Knowing what he had to do, Zahariel focused every ounce of his psyche and took hold of the electro-psychic force, turning it to his own ends, wielding the power as a technician wields a plasma cutter.

He felt the force within him grow and take flight, and he relished the fearful potential that flowed through his veins. Fierce fires blazed in his eyes, and as he stared at the tentacles emerging from the streaks of light in the air, they snapped shut.

More screeches filled the chamber, but Zahariel and Israfael blazed with pure white light, the power of a million suns flowing through them, shaped by their will. As though they were fire-fighters in a hangar blaze, they washed their borrowed power around their comrades, destroying the waving tentacles and sealing shut the tears in reality from which they had emerged.

Within moments, though it felt like an age, the chamber was silent once more, the battle was over, and the angel of the Saroshi had vanished.

Zahariel cried out as the power of the electro-psychic blast faded, and he collapsed as the fuel of his body was spent. He lay still, letting his breathing return to normal after the fury of battle and the exhilarating, yet exhausting, channelling of so much power.

He looked over to Brother Israfael and smiled wearily.

'Is it over?' asked the Lion.

Brother Israfael nodded. 'It's over, my lord.'

THE DARK ANGELS gathered up their dead and made their way back to the surface of Sarosh, winding their way back through the cramped tunnels, over the chasm of the dead and up through the galleries of the mineshaft.

Afternoon had given way to night and the air was cool. The freshness felt good on their bare skin, as helmets were removed, and great draughts of fresh air were sucked down into heaving lungs.

The Stormbirds returned to pick up their charges, and Army units were summoned to secure the tunnels beneath the Mining Station One Zeta Five, though no one expected them to find anything hostile now that the angel of Sarosh was no more.

Zahariel was exhausted beyond words, his entire body aching and battered, though his thoughts were clear and fresh, uncluttered by echoes of sacrifice and the loathsome touch of a creature from beyond the veil.

The Lion had said nothing on their journey to the surface, keeping his own counsel, not even offering words of praise to his warriors.

As they boarded the Stormbirds, Zahariel felt a strange sensation of unease along his spine, and he turned to discover its source.

Lion El'Jonson was looking straight at him.

AFTERMATH

Zahariel watched as the *Invincible Reason* diminished in the viewing portal, the Stormbird streaking through space towards the *Wrath of Caliban* and disgrace.

Barely six hours had passed since the victory at Mining Station One Zeta Five, and events had moved with such rapidity upon their return to the expedition fleet that he could scarcely believe what had happened at all.

No sooner had the warriors of Zahariel's company returned to the *Invincible Reason* than they had been issued with new deployment orders.

A declaration from the Lion announced that the flow of new recruits from Caliban was not proceeding as swiftly as was hoped. Therefore, experienced Astartes were to return to the homeworld with all speed to ensure that the recruitment of new warriors was put back on track.

The Great Crusade was entering a new and vigorous stage, and the Dark Angels needed fresh warriors to take the light of the Imperium onwards.

As to the pacification of Sarosh, the fight had gone out of its inhabitants following the battle beneath Mining Station One Zeta Five, the knowledge of their world's avenging angel's demise travelling the globe in the time it took the news to reach the expedition fleet.

Army units from nearby expedition fleets, as well as a demi-legion of Titans from the Fire Wasps, were en-route to crush any last resistance, and all that remained was to implement full compliance once the last smouldering coals of rebellion had been smothered.

Zahariel studied the deployment order to see who was being sent back to Caliban. He saw that Nemiel was to remain, and had sought out his cousin before the allotted hour for departure.

But Nemiel was nowhere to be found, and Zahariel had done his duty as ordered, reporting to the embarkation deck with the rest of the warriors earmarked to return home.

The sense of crushing dejection was total, and though there was no outward stigma attached to their departure from the fleet, every warrior knew the truth of it in his heart.

The Lion did not want them with him, and that was the greatest hurt of all.

Brother-Librarian Israfael was there, as was Eliath and the wounded Attias, as well as hundreds upon hundreds of other loyal warriors.

Their contribution to the Great Crusade had been so small, so insignificant in the scale of what was to come, that Zahariel doubted the chroniclers would even bother to record the short war on Sarosh.

The Great Crusade would continue, though it would continue without Zahariel.

Worse than that, it would continue without the man sitting furthest away from any other in the Stormbird.

It would continue without Luther.

ABOUT THE AUTHOR

Mitchel Scanlon is a full-time novelist and comics writer. His previous credits for the Black Library include the novel *Fifteen Hours*, the background book *The Loathsome Ratmen*, and the comics series *Tales of Hellbrandt Grimm*. He lives in Derbsyhire, in the UK.